MW01608570

THE FOURNIER DOCTRINE

THE FOURNIER DOCTRINE

James Buckingham

Book Guild Publishing
Sussex, England

First published in Great Britain in 2011 by
The Book Guild Ltd
Pavilion View
19 New Road
Brighton, BN1 1UF

Typesetting in Baskerville by
Keyboard Services, Luton, Bedfordshire

Printed in Great Britain by
CPI Antony Rowe

A catalogue record for this book is available from
The British Library

ISBN 978 1 84624 527 5

For Jill

All the forces in the world are not so powerful as an idea whose time has come.

Victor Hugo

Prologue

July 5th, 1955. Brittany.

Father Fournier climbed into his old, rather tired-looking *charrette*, spurred the waiting horse into motion and set off on his twice weekly drive over the five or so kilometres from his tiny parish of Saint Gregoire into the centre of Rennes. It was Saturday and that meant that the journey would be busier than usual due to the local farm traffic. Market day was always special, he thought. It seemed somehow to liven things up and add a renewed sense of vitality to the town. People would meet, exchange some local gossip and interact in a way that seemed all too lacking in a world where individuals were becoming strangers to each other.

He stopped on the way through the village to pick up an old acquaintance of his. *'Bonjour François, ça va?'*

'Très bien Merci, Pierre,' François replied.

François Marceau ran the village *boulangerie* and always had a few stories to tell. Pierre needed to hurry and so listened to François' one-sided conversation until they were virtually in the centre of the city. Farm carts of all shapes and sizes were converging on the town from the outlying communities and the horses' hooves made an amazing amount of noise as they walked over the cobbled streets. Arriving at the Marché des Lices, François climbed down and with an *'A bientôt'* went about his work as usual. Today was no different from any other. Pierre had made the trip into Rennes almost every week since he had been

1

placed in the parish, but today's prospect was ominous; he had an audience with the Bishop again. He wore his best cassock and biretta and seemed oddly out of place amongst all this bustling commerce.

From the Marché des Lices, Pierre drove his *charrette* down the Rue des Dames and found a convenient place to leave it close to the Cathedral Saint Pierre de Rennes.

Bishop Rousseau, Bishop of Laval was a balding, early middle-aged man of some 40 years of age. His girth left little doubt in the eye of the beholder that his comfortable life as a rural prelate suited him immensely. His rather ruddy complexion and a friendly appearance created the impression, to the casual observer, of a man well able to withstand the social pressures and pastoral duties to which he had grown accustomed over the two years since his enthronement. Bishop Rousseau, in his unflinching loyalty to the Catholic Church was quite a different being. He had risen quite rapidly through the ranks of the Church to his current position by sheer determination alone; his knowledge of the finer points of catholic theology was adequate, but he was by no means an academic. It was he who had summoned Father Fournier.

Father Fournier had been placed in the archdiocese by the archbishop about four years previously. It was thought that his troublesome activities and resultant 'academic' publications could be best subdued and even stifled if, during this time, he had become pre-occupied with the unceasing duties of a local parish priest. This, Father Fournier had managed to do with great care and a noticeable ability to respond to the needs of the parishioners with a conviction derived solely from his own personal beliefs and ideals. It had, however, not limited his questionable 'academic' output.

'Come in, Father. It has been a while since we last met.'

Fournier found these meetings difficult. It wasn't because he felt in any way ill at ease but he preferred to know the reason for his summons before his actual audience. This time, he felt sure that he knew why he had been ordered, yet again, to appear.

Fournier advanced and knelt to kiss the outstretched hand and the rather ostentatious ring.

'Pleased be seated.'

The bishop waited while his secretary left the room and closed the door behind him.

'The archbishop is most displeased. He has informed me that it has come to his attention, yet again, that you have deliberately disobeyed his earlier order not to publish or indirectly assist in the publication of what he recently called, in my presence, "political heresy"! Your continued rebellion against church doctrine and indeed the church's moral authority are causing great embarrassment, particularly to me!'

Fournier thought of a response but remained silent.

'Father Fournier, you will not, I repeat, not make any further statements, submit any writings, documents or messages of this kind to anyone,' Bishop Rousseau continued. 'The archbishop has expressly asked me to convey to you that any future contravention of this final order will result in the most severe consequences.'

'Your Grace, may I be permitted to keep all my writings?'

The bishop, by the wave of his hand and a slight nod of the head both acknowledged and acceded to this request.

Bishop Rousseau held a very mixed opinion of Father Fournier. He admired, even envied the young priest's academic prowess but couldn't accept the continual challenge that Fournier's publications represented to both his and the church's authority.

The archbishop had made it extremely clear that, as Bishop of Laval, Rousseau needed to exercise much greater control over the priests in his diocese and Father Fournier in particular.

'Your latest publication has come now to the attention of the authorities in the Vatican. The Cardinal Secretary has been most displeased at what he considers to be an affront to current Church doctrine.'

'You will therefore desist from writing any further such documents. Do I make myself perfectly clear?'

Father Fournier looked at Bishop Rousseau but remained silent. He had nothing further to say, nothing at all. There were no words that would either benefit his cause or alleviate the disregard in which he was quite obviously held.

'That is all, Father Fournier,' Bishop Rousseau added and the very brief audience was at an end.

Pierre Fournier left the archbishop's palace and walked down the dusty street in deep thought. Pierre knew that his various literary articles and more formal published writings challenged the rules of obedience to the Church and his archbishop but since his student days in Toulouse he had always kept hidden away in his soul a part of him that could not be touched or influenced, even by the brainwashing of four years in a catholic seminary.

He knew, within himself, that for him to be completely at peace it was also obligatory to believe in a greater truth than the simple obedience of religion; that greater truth was in the rights and freedoms of all individuals to live their lives in peace and harmony and for those placed in positions of authority over them, to act solely in the preservation of those interests.

Fournier rounded the corner and into the busy market place. He loved this beautiful old town, especially its fine examples of medieval buildings. He loved the sense of continuity that seemed to come from their great age. He wondered at all the events that these buildings must have witnessed over the years and of all the people that had passed their lives living in them.

He spotted François Marceau busily engaged in an obviously excited conversation with some of the other regular tradesmen and women. Marceau was in his element, Fournier thought with a wry smile.

Fournier slowly walked towards them, surveying the scene. Marceau noticed his friend and turned to Fournier with a smile of recognition.

'You all know Father Fournier; he has had an audience with the bishop this morning.'

Fournier preferred that not everybody in Rennes should know his business, but the damage was done.

'François, I am going to spend some time in the cathedral, shall we meet here at about 2.30 this afternoon?'

Marceau replied that the arrangements would suit him perfectly and so the two friends parted again.

Fournier wandered around the narrow dusty streets for a while before entering the Romanesque cathedral. He needed time to think about his earlier final admonition and to consider how best to continue utilising his literary talents.

The cathedral was empty of people and so Fournier sat in one of the pews and allowed his mind to roam over his many regrets. Two hours passed.

A nearby clock tower reminded him that time had passed quickly and so he left this oasis of quiet and calm and returned to the small courtyard outside the archbishop's palace and his patiently waiting horse.

Once back in the market place he trotted back and forth until his friend appeared. Marceau was soon sitting in the *charrette* and the two men retraced their journey back to Saint Gregoire. One man satisfied with his social day in the big town, the other pre-occupied with his own thoughts.

Fournier dropped Marceau off at the same spot where they had met earlier in the day, waved to a couple of his parishioners and continued on through the little village to its church and the humble building that he had called home for the past four and a half years. He unhooked the *charrette* and led his horse into the stable at the side of his house and made sure that the old animal had plenty of hay and water. He gave it a pat on its flank, closed the stable door and entered the sparsely furnished dwelling.

He would not conform to the archbishop's wishes. He knew that he could not be seen to continue his writings in public, but they couldn't stop him writing in private. One day people would read his thoughts and take action. He had grown up as a child under the German Occupation and all the barbarity that it had brought with it. His own parents had both been rounded up and shot as traitors and this had left a lasting impression on the young teenager. Those dark days that had brought with them the rise of militarism engulfing most of Europe and the uncertain peace that followed might delay this dream, but Pierre knew in his heart that he was in the right and was, for the moment, full of a sense of personal courage and conviction.

Chapter 1

January 5th, 2008. Besançon.

The three men gathered at a table outside a quiet little café on the Rue Mairet to consider their latest assignment. The little café in the centre of the old town was popular with the student population in Besançon, but at that hour of the morning was not busy and was hence a good choice for their discussion. Dubois spoke.

'Are we all agreed about this?'

The three men looked at each other for agreement. All nodded.

'It has to be carried out no later than March 16th. The Ambassador takes up his new appointment in Paris after that date,' Deschamps pointed out.

'Who should we use this time?' Levert asked.

Dubois looked around to make sure that he was not overheard and then leant forward for added privacy.

'Mr Roland will leave his position as French Ambassador and, I am reliably informed, will be publishing his farewell itinerary shortly. This should cover most of his movements up to the time of his departure.'

'This is going to need a lot of inside information; we will need to know his precise movements almost before he does,' said Levert.

'Anyone know why Breton is not here?' Dubois asked, raising his head to look at each of his compatriots.

'He is away for a few days; something to do with the operation last year in Germany. He did contact me to say he couldn't make this meeting,' Levert answered.

They paused in their conversation as a delivery driver pulled up outside the café, deposited several cases of wine onto the cobbled pavement and then drove off.

'This operation will be more expensive than last time. I hope you told them that,' Deschamps remarked. 'It will need to involve all of us if we agree.'

'Don't worry, they want it carried out and money is no object with these people,' Dubois replied. 'I think that this might even require some additional specialist help.'

'All right,' Dubois continued. 'I suggest you both consider your various roles and we will meet here again tomorrow morning at 11.00 am. I have already placed the usual ad in the *Suddeutsche Zeitung.*'

The two men left the café and went their separate ways. Dubois remained a while to consider his own next move. This was definitely a contract for their prime operative in Munich to execute. He would be perfect for this one.

Chapter 2

January 5th, 2008. Munich.

His eyes scanned the careers section in the Saturday morning edition of the *Suddeutsche Zeitung*. It did not take him long to find what he was looking for.

'Experienced cleaner needed for short term assignment. Terms negotiable. Contact PO Box 717 for more details.'

Another contract no doubt, he thought. What will they want this time?

He finished his coffee and left the small apartment on Marienstrasse. He always used a public phone box to return these calls and was always prompt in doing so.

'This is Kessler,' the man said in a quiet voice. 'I have seen your message.'

'We have another assignment for you. It is more complicated than last time,' Dubois began. 'We will provide you with all the usual logistic support and will communicate all of that in the usual manner.'

'Send all the details to the usual address,' Kessler added. 'I will take a look at it and let you know.'

The abrupt conversation was at an end leaving Dubois to duly comply with this request.

A week later Dubois received the call for which he had been waiting. The answer was in the affirmative.

'No, there is no mistake about your target,' Dubois replied, purposely not using any actual names. 'He will be visiting Montreal sometime in the middle of March. Your job is to eliminate him.'

'This will cost a lot more than last time,' Kessler replied. 'The targets are becoming too risky these days. Movements are very closely monitored. This will take a lot more planning. My price will be at least double the normal rate!'

Dubois hesitated for a moment.

'I think that we can agree to that.'

'Twenty-five thousand now and a further twenty-five on completion, plus expenses. I will contact you again when I have received the first payment.'

'Agreed,' Dubois replied and replaced the receiver. This was going to be another expensive mission.

Dubois opened his office safe and withdrew a red folder containing a small notebook. Referring to it for some coded details it contained, he dispatched an appropriate e-mail communication to the other four members of the group. They would know what to do.

Chapter 3

March 17th, 2008. Oxford.

Professor Fullerton picked up a copy of that morning's edition of *The Times* and stared at the headlines.

FRENCH AMBASSADOR FOUND DEAD
The French Ambassador to Canada was found dead in his room at the Queen Elizabeth Hotel in downtown Montreal early yesterday morning. Mr Marc Roland, a career diplomat, had been the French Ambassador to Canada for three years. He was attending a meeting of influential Canadian businessmen in the city and was due to leave for the airport today on his way back to Paris. Mr Roland had recently been appointed as the new French Foreign Minister and this apparent suicide has come as a great setback to the French Government and to the continued implementation of some of its more questionable foreign policies.

It is not clear yet as to the exact sequence of events. There was heightened security for the Ambassador following some recent similar attacks on high profile politicians and influential business leaders in Europe. The police have focused their attention on the activities of certain extremist groups, but there has been no official word yet from the authorities.

He replaced the newspaper on his desk, removed his glasses and stared out of his first-floor window onto the sunlit lawns of Magdalen College. There were the usual groupings of students hurrying to their various classes and a solitary blackbird hopping here and there on the green turf. He could hear the muffled sounds of a distant church bell as it rang out over the city and he subconsciously tried to place which one it could be.

Fullerton spotted the unmistakable profile of Sebastian Thurlow hurrying across the Quad. He opened one of his windows and shouted at him.

'Good morning, Sebastian!'

Thurlow heard his name and stopped to see who was addressing him in such a raucous manner. He looked up and saw Professor Fullerton half leaning out of his study window and waved a response as he continued his strange half-run, half-walk antics.

'That man is quite unable to organise himself and his affairs properly. For a Senior Fellow, he is quite undignified,' Fullerton said to himself.

He moved away from the window a little and sat down again at his large oak desk from where he could still glimpse most of Magdalen Tower opposite.

He picked up the folded newspaper once more and re-read the headlines.

These worldly happenings all seemed so far removed from his peaceful, and some would call idyllic, existence in Oxford.

Fullerton had briefly watched the late night TV news broadcast the previous evening but that preliminary bulletin had not contained much in the way of substantive detail as it was then still a breaking news story.

There were already strong rumours circulating that the official line referring to 'death from natural causes' concealed what might have been a successful assassination attempt.

He wondered about the people who could have been involved in any successful assassination attempt. What was it that drove people to carry out such an act, he wondered? What did they feel would be achieved; what were their aims and why would people become so desperate that they would resort to this kind of violence?

He thought back to stories earlier in the year involving the apparently unexplained deaths of other well-known individuals, particularly the strange case of a prominent German politician who had allegedly committed suicide whilst on holiday in the South of France.

Those cases were still under investigation he seemed to recall. No satisfactory explanation had yet been given for any of these events and it seemed quite apparent that no tangible progress was being made by the responsible authorities.

Snapping back into the present, Fullerton reminded himself that he had a busy day in front of him. A departmental meeting had been scheduled for 10.00 am followed by an interview with his literary agent to promote his latest economics publication.

He had then arranged to meet some other faculty members over lunch and the afternoon was fully booked with postgraduate tutorials.

He put on his jacket and gown and searched his desk for the departmental agenda. He decided that he really had to do something about the state of his desk; it was altogether too cluttered and untidy. He was preparing to leave his rooms when the telephone rang. This always seemed to happen when he was in a hurry and had allowed just enough time to arrive at his next scheduled commitment. Maybe this was Thurlow's excuse.

Fullerton was in half a mind not to answer the wretched thing. There was something about being too available that he disliked.

He however picked up the receiver and was glad that he had done so as he recognised the voice of Marguerite De Saulx de Tavannes, no doubt calling him from Paris.

'Hello, Michael, I hope that I haven't caught you at a bad time.'

13

'Hello, Marguerite. What a lovely surprise. You know that I always enjoy hearing from you, but I do have an important meeting to go to very shortly.'

'OK, Michael, I'll be quick. I received your letter late last week and just wanted to call you to say that your suggestion is a lovely idea. I will write to you next week in more detail. Won't keep you. Bye.'

The conversation was over and she was gone before he had even thought of what to say next. That was Marguerite!

Still, that was something to look forward to next week.

Leaving his rooms for the inevitably boring departmental meeting, Fullerton descended the stairs and walked out into the sunlight. He found that he had an unexpected spring in his step.

Chapter 4

March 18th, 2008. Montreal.

La Croix had received vital information too late yet again. This time it was to do with the circumstances surrounding the 'death' of the French Ambassador to Canada.

He had booked the first flight he could obtain out of Heathrow that flew directly to Montreal. The Air Canada flight was quite punctual and after a short taxi ride he was downtown.

His task this time was to piece together as much information as he could about the Ambassador's last known movements and exact cause of death.

He decided that this could take a couple of days and so found a convenient yet unobtrusive place in which to stay. It was one of those clean but sparsely furnished apartment hotels where businessmen often stayed for short durations when visiting the city and it also afforded a high degree of anonymity.

He soon learned that the Ambassador had only been in Montreal for a few hours, his visit having been planned at the last minute. La Croix knew that his assignment indicated that somebody thought there was a lot more to do with this than a straight case of 'death from natural causes' as had been publicised. He had the benefit of some extremely good, albeit belated, intelligence and knew from reading his notes on the plane that Marc Roland was also being blackmailed.

A search of local newspapers had quickly provided La

Croix with some interesting facts. The Ambassador had planned a quick excursion to Quebec City as part of the same official visit to the Province but this had been cancelled at very short notice. No one had told him why. La Croix knew that those involved in the blackmail attempt must have had regular access to the Ambassador. He needed to cross-check all those present in Montreal with his own intelligence.

Posing as a French newspaper reporter, he was able to obtain the guest list for the meeting at the Queen Elizabeth Hotel. It read like a Who's Who of provincial dignitaries and city bigwigs. A cursory scan of the list did not produce any obvious clues and he decided that a further analysis was a pointless waste time. Whoever was involved was unlikely to have been in their number.

From the published police press statements, Mr Roland had died sometime on the Sunday evening but his body had only been discovered the following morning by one of his aides. Doctors had been called but nothing could be done.

La Croix's job was to find out if the Ambassador had indeed taken his own life and if so, by what means and whether anyone else had been with him.

He walked back over to the hotel and engaged himself in conversation with a couple of the local Quebec media reporters.

'Did you see the Ambassador arrive at the hotel?'

'Yes,' came the reply. 'His car pulled up outside the main entrance to the hotel and he went straight inside.'

La Croix noted that the temperature outside had been a chilly minus 20 °C and nobody was just going to stand around outside.

On arrival at the hotel, Mr Roland had had some fairly private meetings with various dignitaries and close colleagues. Then there was the meeting with a group of

Canadian businessmen and bankers followed by a public banquet also in the hotel.

La Croix confirmed, by talking to hotel staff, that the Ambassador had then gone straight up to his room following the banquet accompanied only by his personal staff. That had been at about 11.00 pm.

La Croix easily obtained a copy of the banquet guest list and scanned it for any possible leads.

He sent the list to his superiors for their further analysis, but didn't expect any significant revelations. This was either a natural death, the official story, or a very well-planned assassination. The time window between the time at which the Ambassador retired for the night and the time the next morning when he was found was quite long and La Croix knew that anyone with the right knowledge and access could have done almost anything during that period, quite unnoticed.

The Ambassador's room had been sealed off by the Montreal police since early on the Monday, ever since his staff had discovered his body.

La Croix decided that he needed to inspect the Ambassador's room before any further time elapsed.

He entered the hotel through the employees' entrance at the rear and descended to the basement complex. Finding some suitable clothing, he grabbed what he knew was a service personnel pass key, conveniently left on top of the night manager's table and for the next hour or so assumed the identity of a liveried room service employee.

Taking the service elevator to the seventh floor he found a deserted service trolley and wheeled it ahead of him as extra cover as he searched for Room 734.

Rounding the bend in the corridor La Croix could see that there was a police guard sitting outside of the room.

He slowly approached the police officer, pushing his trolley as if he was just passing along the corridor to

17

another room. Stopping just past the policeman as if some thought had just come into his head, he spoke to the officer about the unfortunate news and indirectly received confirmation that this indeed had been the Ambassador's room. Looking up and down the corridor, La Croix checked to see that he was alone with the young officer.

A swift trained blow from his right hand and the unsuspecting officer slumped onto the floor. La Croix dragged the unconscious officer back onto his chair and arranged him to look as if he was asleep.

Using the pass key, La Croix entered the room, and turning on the lights, quickly took in the scene.

The room had the appearance of still being occupied by a guest. There were some glasses on the table in front of the sofa, the bed had been left unmade and bath towels were draped over the back of one of the chairs. There was a suitcase still on the luggage rack.

He moved across the room, his experienced eyes looking for anything unusual. He pushed the half-open bathroom door. The mirror facing him had been completely smashed and the whole area surrounding the washbasin and wall was covered with glass splinters and splatters of blood. There was also, to his trained eyes, the tell-tale sign of a small-calibre bullet impact mark on the wall where the mirror had been. This provided him with all the information that he needed.

This had been the work of a professional killer. The Ambassador must have been in the bathroom, possibly using the mirror when he was approached by the killer from behind. La Croix noted that the door to the bathroom seemed to always swing partly closed of its own accord. This would have allowed the assassin to approach without being either heard or seen. One quick shot to the back of the head and the job was done. He thought that the killer could quite easily have adopted a similar method to his own to gain unforced entry. It was all so simple.

The Ambassador's staff had then fabricated the official story to explain his death. No doubt these instructions came directly from Paris.

La Croix moved back over to the entrance, quietly opened the door and glanced both ways down the corridor. Seeing no one except for the still 'sleeping' policeman, he retraced his steps, carefully leaving his trolley where he had found it and returned to the basement of the hotel, this time using the stairwell.

He quickly discarded his hotel uniform, replaced the pass key where he had found it and left the hotel by the rear exit.

He returned to his hotel room and sent an encrypted e-mail back to Paris. It was now early morning in Paris and so La Croix knew that he would have to wait for several hours before receiving any kind of a response.

Now that his superiors in Paris were duly informed of his findings, he decided to relax and enjoy what Montreal had to offer in terms of restaurants and bars. He left his hotel and quickly hailed a passing taxi. Chatting to the driver, he soon obtained all the information he could ever need about the choice of night life. His driver was from a small rural town east of the city and spoke with a very heavy Quebecois accent. After a very interesting conversation, and having completed a mini-tour of the snow-banked downtown area, the taxi driver dropped him off in the old part of the city on the Boulevard Saint Laurent close to the *Vauquelin Vieille France* restaurant.

La Croix hurried from the warmth of the taxi and across the street. The wind was bitterly cold. Once inside, he enjoyed the choice of venue immensely. All the other diners seemed to be French speakers and he had the sensation almost of being back in Paris.

After a light meal he wrapped up and walked a couple of blocks, taking in a couple of bars. One proved to be exclusively for gays. This only made his all too brief visit the more memorable.

He returned to his hotel sometime in the early hours, grateful for the extensive internal walkway system normally frequented by shoppers and office workers. He had not consumed that much alcohol all evening and so was not too the worse for wear. He never did drink much when on this kind of assignment. La Croix looked at his watch and realized that it was now mid morning in Paris. A response should be coming through any moment, he thought.

He lay back on the bed, turned on the TV and switched on his laptop. The local Montreal news channel was still carrying reports relating to the recent event at the Queen Elizabeth hotel but had no further details.

Looking over at his laptop he could see that a message had just been received. He opened the e-mail and saw that it had come from Paris.

'Imperative that exact cause of death is ascertained asap.'

La Croix thought that a bullet to the back of the head was quite exact but knew that they were looking for corroboration of the fact contained in his report.

The following morning he studied the various Montreal papers that had covered the recent events in some detail. Mention was made of the Ambassador's body having been taken to the McGill University Health Centre and so he walked the few blocks from his hotel onto the McGill University Campus and the hospital.

A few discrete enquiries allowed him to ascertain exactly where the ambulance would have taken the Ambassador's body.

Arriving at the department in question La Croix again needed to dress for the part.

He walked along a number of corridors until he spotted some locker rooms obviously used by medical and operating staff. Making sure that he was not being observed, he entered one of the rooms. Emerging a few minutes later, he looked every bit the part of a resident doctor with white coat, a pair of stethoscopes and even a clipboard which had conveniently been left on a nearby desk.

He walked back along the main corridor finally reaching the central admissions desk. He knew that these people would have been notified of any recent arrivals.

'I am missing some forms belonging to a recently admitted patient.'

'What was the name?' came the reply.

'A Mr Mark Roland.'

The young woman checked her computer screen and confirmed the admission. 'Mr Roland has been admitted but we don't seem to have any paperwork here, maybe you should try the main records office. They should be able to assist you.'

La Croix followed her directions and soon found the door he was looking for.

He opened the door gently. The office inside was not busy and only a few individuals were around.

Using his new-found authority as a doctor, he asked to see the Roland file. The records clerk asked him for the date of admission. Initially unable to locate the file, the clerk fortunately also searched the trolleys containing recently returned documents and was proud to present him with what he needed.

Time was of the essence; La Croix walked over to a nearby filing cabinet and used it to support the folder while he surveyed its contents. There were a number of reports from various specialists but he soon found the details he needed.

The patient admission form had been clearly written

21

up by whoever had been the attending physician when the Ambassador's body had arrived at the hospital. *'Gun shot wound to rear cerebral cortex -----. Patient DOA.'* Finding all that he needed, he wasted no time in returning the folder to the trolley, thanking the clerk and leaving the office. It was a simple matter of retracing his steps to dispose of his clinician's coat and stethoscope and to exit the hospital as discreetly as he had arrived.

Back in his hotel room, he sent an appropriate e-mail to Paris with his findings.

His job complete, La Croix checked out of the hotel, took a taxi to the train station and boarded the next train to Ottawa. A flight from Ottawa via Toronto back to London concluded his albeit brief visit to Canada.

Chapter 5

March 26th, 2008. Oxford.

Professor Fullerton continued to stare out of his window at the expanse of lawn that made up the Great Quad and at the geometrically arranged cloisters. The mid-morning sun left a silhouette of the roofs of the college tower and buildings on the grass and the combination of colours and textures of the old stonework seemed at their very best. It reminded him of the many happy hours that had been spent out there with Evelyn.

The clock on the mantelpiece chimed ten times as if to say 'time for lectures.' The weekend newspapers lay in an untidy pile on the sofa, partly read and partly untouched. There was an article in the magazine section dealing with the abortion debate and the position of the Catholic Church on this crucial issue. The Archbishop of Westminster's pronouncement on the subject was completely as expected, even if the exact wording of his interview on the subject did leave room for quite a wide-ranging interpretation of the detail. The Cardinal was expected to make such statements of conformity. Why don't people discuss the really serious issues, he thought to himself.

Hidden away on one of the *Sunday Times* inner pages had been another article debating the issue of increasing globalisation. He had cut this particular article out and it was now staring at him from on top of a pile of papers on the right-hand corner of his desk. This article was well written by one of the *Times'* best-known columnists, following an interview with James Fullerton, principal shareholder and CEO of the Axxon Group and international financier. Axxon, a global, multi-national conglomerate, had its headquarters in Geneva.

Fullerton had not met his twin brother for over thirty years and too much of life had passed since then to envisage any likely reconciliation. Even though Michael and James were identical twins, they shared no other social or professional similarities and, in fact, were as unlike in their nature as two twins could possibly be. The old topic of discussion about nature versus nurture could be disproved or verified on any number of facets of their human identity.

Michael and James had been reasonably close during their teens, attended the same public school and shared a number of school friends in common, but had seen nothing of each other since that time.

He always thought how lucky they had both been to receive the advantages of a formal, structured education.

Time had passed and their interests in the academic side of things had created two totally disparate career paths. James went on to read Law at St John's College, Cambridge, followed by several years of study at Harvard leading to his MBA in 1980. Michael decided to continue with his love of modern languages but in the end gained a scholarship to the Sorbonne in Paris to read Economics. A university career seemed to beckon as Michael came to the end of his undergraduate years of study. There was no other clear career path that appealed to him other than the diplomatic service and so he had accepted a postgraduate position. His life as a student in Paris had been wonderful and he had formed many special relationships with people his own age. One of these had been with Marguerite. He had however married a postgraduate history student when aged only twenty-three and they had adopted a child. His academic career continued with successive fellowships until his appointment to a professorship in Business and Economics at the University of Oxford.

Fullerton closed the window and turned his attention to the photographs on the nearby bookshelf. There was the usual array of family groups. He observed his two children, his grandson, his marriage photograph and the portrait of his wife taken twelve months before her death. He studied each of them for a few moments and many memories came flooding back into his mind. Those were the good old days, he thought as he muttered the words under his breath.

Early retirement seemed like the only option for him after Evelyn had died but now and then he sensed the real desire to be active and feel alive again.

Richard, his adopted and only son was living with his wife and young son in Muswell Hill in north London. He had spent fourteen years in the Army, the last four being with the SAS; he had now settled into a comfortable job with an import/export firm based in the East End. He had always been a somewhat secretive and difficult child.

Louise had just finished drama school and was living in digs with two of her college mates in Hampstead.

His children had no real knowledge of their uncle; they of course knew of his existence but had never tried to make contact or form any kind of relationship with him. Uncle James, for his part, had seemed singularly focused on his potential for advancement in the world of big business and shown an apparent and equal lack of interest.

Fullerton had a home, situated in the pretty Oxfordshire town of Witney, but he had not spent much time there since his wife's death. Being in Oxfordshire though had allowed him relatively easy and frequent contact with both his children and so he felt he had maintained a sense of ongoing family connection. There was, however, remaining that huge gap in his life once filled by Evelyn.

James Fullerton, for his part, had returned from the US to England in early 1981 and had gained a position with the Axxon Group in their London office. This was followed by two successive placements in Frankfurt and New York before his particular talents came to the notice of his superiors and he was appointed CEO of the Axxon Group subsidiary in Paris. This was followed by further promotions; a very lucrative period with an investment bank in Zurich, a hedge fund or two and a move to Geneva. James had never married. Michael always thought that a good marriage and a family would have got in the way of his brother's career.

Fullerton looked at the opened envelope on his desk postmarked 'Paris'. He always enjoyed receiving letters from Marguerite. They had been all too few in recent months. He felt sure that Marguerite had given him some space after the funeral in order to come to terms with his loss.

Fullerton was particularly glad in this instance as Marguerite had warmed to his suggestion that they arrange a holiday together in Rome.

It would be good to get away and spend some time in the company of an old friend, he thought. He hadn't been away at all since Evelyn had died and had buried himself in his academic work and the publication of a new book entitled *Economics as a Force against Government*.

The book had been well received in academic circles but derided by politicians as the writings of 'a typical academic' and 'the misguided ranting of an economic dinosaur'. He was used to the criticism and didn't mind these kinds of comments but what he couldn't abide was the way in which any attempt by anybody to force a debate on the real issues was stifled, ridiculed and generally discredited.

Still, a holiday in Rome with Marguerite would take his mind off such frustrations at least for a while and re-kindle some lovely memories of his last visit there with Evelyn five years ago. He decided that he was quite looking forward to the trip.

Chapter 6

March 26th, 2008. London.

In a conference room at the headquarters of the Secret Intelligence Service (SIS) in central London a select group of operatives, intelligence gatherers and logistics personnel had been gathered together for an important briefing by senior staff. Thirty or so individuals prepared to listen to the latest policy update relating to their new taskforce assignment.

'Ladies and gentlemen, thank you for your attendance this morning, I know that you all have important work to do.'

This opening statement came from Alex Thornton who had been recently appointed by the Joint Intelligence Committee (JIC) to take direct, executive control of this particular taskforce.

'You have all been handed briefing notes relative to your various specialities and so I don't need to waste your time with any opening formalities. The effort involved in compiling the pages in front of each of you should give you an indication as to the priority which is being attached to this group assignment.'

He asked for the lights to be dimmed as he placed a series of transparencies on the overhead projector screen.

'Acquiring intelligence on the ADF, to give it the title by which it is known to governments and various other national intelligence agencies around the world, is the sole focus of this taskforce.'

Those watching noted the full description of the acronym ADF (*L'Agence de la Doctrine de Fournier*) on the first transparency.

'Not a lot is known about this rather exclusive group of highly placed individuals and its particular raison d'être. You will find appropriate case material in your notes and, as you will see when you study it, the intelligence gathering to date has been spasmodic at best.' He added an aside, 'There have always been other more pressing activities for our government to spend both their time and limited budgets on!' then resumed his formal briefing. 'It is known however that the current ideology of the Agency had its very early roots in France in the fifties.'

Everybody stared at the picture of a young French priest on the large screen on the wall.

Thornton turned from his notes and also faced the screen.

'We are in Brittany in France. The year is 1955. A young priest in his late twenties by the name of Pierre Fournier, from an insignificant rural parish in Brittany, had taken the then extraordinary idea of politicising the role of the Catholic Church and committed his thoughts to paper. He had reached the conclusion that the Catholic Church, even after the horrors of World War II and the anticipated post-war return of individual rights and freedoms, was still exercising its power and control over the hearts and minds of the ordinary man in a way that served only its own, total self-interest. He felt that people in power, whether religious or political, had a prime duty to serve the common man. These writings had largely been ignored as the ramblings of an extremist idealist. His friends that knew him from these early years and in the immediate post-war period understood his rationale and, whilst not prepared at that time to provide open support did, however, retain a comprehension of Fournier's thinking which would endure longer than any of them thought possible at the time.'

Thornton paused as he flashed up various newspaper articles and other publications by Fournier from the period.

'The key difference between these writings and those of any other "avant-garde" writer of the time, and there were many, was the connection Fournier made between straight political dialogue and the more effective use of direct "pressure". The Catholic Church at the time had censured Father Fournier in the most forceful way possible, but with little or no support from outside the church, these writings received equally little or no public interest for a further ten or so years.

'Please note the supporting facts and reference material that you'll each find in your briefing notes,' Thornton added.

'It wasn't until the early sixties that Father Fournier's writings once again came under scrutiny. The political upheaval in so many European countries over the previous decade and the almost seismic shift in both the political values and aspirations of politicians and the general population alike had caused some fundamental rethinking of the views held by certain like-minded individuals. These people were no longer just insignificant employees, but strong-willed individuals who'd risen through the ranks of their various professions and were now in positions where they could exert ever increasing levels of control and, more importantly, influence over the minds of others.

'This was about the time that we believe the ADF was formed. The exact extent of the present day membership, its numbers, authority, location or position is impossible to quantify. Indeed, their numbers have been added to in recent years by a certain mix of other, so-called idealists. Academics, lawyers and other like professions have been drawn to lend their like-minded support to the organisation's basic founding tenet. The Agency now involves itself in the very effective lobbying of national governments by the careful targeting and influence of key politicians particularly where those individuals have, to them, become either too unaccountable or just plain corrupt.

'You'll note that I'm now paraphrasing their own dogma,' he interjected thoughtfully amid a few chuckles of some of those appreciating the irony.

Thornton looked up and the room, once again, fell silent.

He continued.

'For this to be implemented to any large degree in the twenty-first century, the range, uses, influence and abilities of the Agency's membership has had to become far more sophisticated.

'The eighties and nineties have seen the influence of this organisation and the focus of its thinking combine into what can only be described as critical mass. The intelligence community has collectively calculated that its membership extends internationally and encompasses all walks of life. In the late nineties, it started to become a real concern to governments that the organisation's influence appeared to be coming increasingly more effective. From the advent of the European Union to the present time, government policy has been, and is being, seriously challenged. There are now increasing instances of it even becoming violent.

'University professors, heads of big business, lawyers and even physicians are known to be committed to its ideals. Leaks from within the organisation itself come now on increasingly few occasions. The Agency has tightened its own security.

'The intelligence community now has good reason to believe that, at its heart, there is some connection with other extremist elements. The ADF, for its part, remains a most powerful lobby and one that, with increased globalisation, is now in a position to be even more effective. These, ladies and gentlemen are the facts. The sole objective of this taskforce is to infiltrate the ADF and find any and all connections with extremists.'

Thornton sat down after concluding his outline commentary.

'This assignment has been given top priority by the JIC; you all have your notes. Now the real work begins.'

Returning to his office on the fourth floor, Thornton picked up the phone and dialled a certain number from memory.

'Thornton here, Sir. I have just given out the official line to the taskforce. It should keep the pressure up for a while and give the appearance that we are actively involved.'

'How's the other matter progressing?' the voice at the other end of the line asked.

'I, in fact, had dinner with our subject last night. Everything went as planned at the restaurant. Nobody suspected a thing,'

'Are we absolutely sure that the desired result will be one hundred per cent accurate?' the voice added.

'These people that I use do not make mistakes. We should hear about the results soon enough,' Thornton replied confidently.

Both Thornton and the person to whom he was speaking knew all too well that no specifics would or could be discussed over even this 'secure' line.

Thornton went on.

'We're also sure that the party involved has not yet seen fit to divulge anything he knows and is unlikely to do so just yet. Our sources inform me that he still needs corroboration of his evidence from Tehran. Steps have been taken to ensure that this will take some considerable time.'

'Fine; let me know as soon as you know anything further.'

Thornton replaced the receiver and mulled over what else, if anything, needed to be done.

Chapter 7

March 30th, 2008. Oxford.

Professor Fullerton had returned to Oxford late the previous evening following an exciting but tiring three-day conference in Vienna. That Sunday morning he again sat in his comfortable wing-backed chair in his rooms in Magdalen College and studied the Sunday papers. He took two newspapers on a Sunday: *The Times* and *The Telegraph*. He subscribed to them as he felt that these illustrious journals would provide him with a good balance of opinion and cover a complete range of current social and political topics.

There was the usual informed analysis by the same usual columnists and critics, but again it all seemed so trivial and meaningless.

Here we are in the twenty-first century,' he thought to himself 'and all I seem to read about are people and articles expounding the apparent virtues of this and that form of democracy. Each one taking the viewpoint that their version is the only one that matters and the only one with substantiated proof of actually working.'

There was a knock at the door.

'Come in,' he called out.

Two of his postgraduate students had been invited to visit their mentor that morning for an informal discussion. Fullerton liked these informal gatherings; he felt that lively conversation could create a more lasting impression in young minds than the far more impersonal general lecture format.

The two students entered into the room – a place that, to them, was to be treated with some degree of awe.

'Good morning,' Fullerton said as the two young men sat down on the sofa.

Fullerton dropped the newspaper, removed his glasses and contemplated the broader picture of society in general.

'Democracy, as we think we know it, is a meaningless name, bandied about by all the so-called Western countries as some kind of Utopian dream model. What do the two of you think?'

'I think that we all have to make our views known and understand what we each believe.'

Fullerton looked up and a wry smile came to his face. Oh, the innocence of youth! he thought.

'Do you not think, gentlemen that the practical reality is that western civilisation is imperceptibly becoming a place where governments of all stripes aren't interested in the views or aspirations of the general population. Governments are in fact quite openly, in many respects, moving inexorably towards a situation where general governance and even the rule of law itself is becoming the preserve of the political elite. A kind of democratic deficiency as someone has aptly put it.'

'The general public can decide to vote for change if they don't agree with the current political ideology,' came the response. 'I think that if people really cared about the important issues enough, they would do something about it.'

'But, do they end up with something any better as a result. Is there really an honest choice out there for any of us?' Fullerton countered.

'We must find a way then of creating that honest choice.'

'I take it that we don't want to see revolution in the streets, but do we retain a real longing for positive change where change is a means to an end, not the end in itself?' Fullerton said, posing yet another question.

'Perhaps you have to define what you mean by change first. Who is it that feels the need for change and what would they then do if they achieved that change?'

'Clever analysis,' Fullerton added. 'Let's look at this from another viewpoint. What can politicians possibly do,' he mused, 'to create a more equitable and coherent society for everybody?'

'Now you are crediting the politicians with the will and the appetite for that change, they only want what is good for them.'

Fullerton smiled and gave a chuckle.

'Too much cynicism for a young man, I think.'

Fullerton continued. 'Modern life is becoming more and more complicated. The pace of life, the immediacy of news in this electronic age and the ever more pressing need, as a direct consequence of all this, for politicians of all stripes to invent, if need be, a new way of dealing with it.'

'Politicians are largely made up of a grouping of self-seeking individuals who have gained notoriety by their extremely well-honed verbal ability to talk indefinitely on any subject without actually saying anything at all. What, in fact can they say! Most of them have never had a real job and they certainly won't be able to survive in the real world. These people rise to real positions of power and make decisions that affect the lives of millions of ordinary people without ever having to suffer the consequences of their inevitably idiotic ideas.'

Fullerton chuckled to himself. This was not a chuckle of amusement, it was one of those chuckles when a person realises the total futility of the conclusion of his analysis.

'Sir, you have written many articles to newspapers and your latest book is extremely thought-provoking.'

'Economics as a Force against Government,' Fullerton said, stating the title of his latest book.

'What did you think of it?' he asked his two devotees.

'It raised the issue of there being a real need for someone or something to act as a counter-balance against the over-powerful state,' came the reply.

'Did you agree or disagree with its central tenet?' Fullerton asked.

'It would require an awful lot of careful organisation to have the desired impact. Maybe we should start our own organisation!'

'That would be a start, wouldn't it?' Fullerton replied. 'Please provide me with a full critique of my latest book then. You are free to agree or disagree with the views expounded in my book as long as your remarks represent your own honest opinions and thoughts.'

'I will expect your work to be submitted no later than two weeks today.'

'Thank you, gentlemen for giving up some of your time on a Sunday.'

The two young men stood up and left Fullerton's rooms and him to his thoughts once more.

Fullerton wondered at the effect that his numerous letters to *The Times* and magazine articles had really had. He had of course also counted the cost. The letters he had received from the university authorities, not to mention the actual vote of censure passed by the university Council only the year previously, stood to remind him that obedience and conformity were the two essential ingredients of the new creed by which everybody was unwittingly now living.

There had of course been many letters of support from all over the world. Some had come from ordinary individuals, some from obvious extremists and crackpots and the occasional, more considered letter from influential members of the business community.

He decided that if he ever had the opportunity to redress the balance in favour of some down-to-earth thinking then he would grab it with both hands.

Enough of this depressing thought he decided. He had a lecture to prepare for some final-year students the following morning. 'Economics in an Age of Political Domination'. He felt no doubt that, this morning at least, his students had acquired a sense of his enthusiasm for the subject, if not totally agreeing with his reasoning.

He grabbed his notes and began again to confront the realities of the world once more with thoughts that would provoke the eager young minds of his students.

Chapter 8

April 16th, 2008. Rome.

Michael Fullerton and Marguerite De Saulx de Tavannes eventually arrived in Rome on a delayed early evening flight from Paris. They had had a lot of time to talk both at the airport and on the flight and much to catch up on. Michael had not seen Marguerite since his wife's funeral almost a year earlier and both of them had been getting on with their lives in the meantime. The conversation had remained for the most part in safe territory with topics ranging from issues of academic interest to what they would do in Rome.

Fullerton retrieved their bags, and they made their way through the airport controls and flagged a taxi to take them into the centre of the city. He liked Rome at this time of year; not too oppressively hot and not too cool. He sat back in the rear of the rather shabby vehicle and watched the passing scenery. Marguerite wound down her window.

'I love the warmth here in Italy,' she remarked, 'but right now I could really do with some of the breeze.'

'I think that I could enjoy Italy at any time of year; there is so much to observe,' Fullerton replied.

They both observed the dusty roads and crumbling buildings, the cypress trees, the local population going about their business, the calm between the hustle and bustle of the day and the increased activity as people ventured out once more to walk, shop or meet friends and frequent any one of numerous local restaurants. It was this apparent show of normal humanity that most appealed to Michael.

He had again made a reservation, at relatively short notice, to stay on the Via Rosa not far from the main railway station. The apartment building was one of those ubiquitous structures that typified the less frequented and rather run-down neighbourhoods in the city. The taxi finally reached the Via Rosa after some impatient and at times, erratic driving on the part of the foreign-looking driver. Welcome to Rome, Fullerton thought to himself.

Fullerton paid the driver and eased himself out of the vehicle. He was hit by a strange mixture of sounds and smells, muffled car horns, the distant whine of mopeds, the almost overpowering smell of spices and cooking food. This was a mainly immigrant quarter and the rubbish-strewn doorways stood testament.

The driver unloaded their suitcases from the boot, placed them on the pavement and without a word of farewell disappeared down the street and round the bend.

'Well, this is it,' Fullerton announced, hoping that Marguerite would spare any comment until they had at least gone inside.

The entrance to the apartment building was a huge but rather battered wooden door which had seen better days. Fullerton thought that this area of town must have been quite prestigious at one time. He surveyed the array of names against the intercom buttons and located the appropriate name. He rang the buzzer twice and then turned to survey the street scene once more. The air was warm but there was enough of a breeze to make him feel comfortable. The door clicked open to the sound of the buzzer and Fullerton led Marguerite into the entrance courtyard. Eight stone steps took them up to the inner entrance door which opened into the hallway. The hallway was clean and tidy and the stairs to the upper floors wound their way round the ornate central lift well. His memory came flooding back; it must be five years he thought to himself since he had stayed here before. The apartment that Fullerton had booked was on the third floor. He decided that they would take the stairs. The ornate grandeur of the lift cage and the faded frescos on the walls now seemed all too familiar.

The concierge was waiting for them at the entrance to the apartment and greeted them with the usually flamboyant outstretched arms and a verbal torrent of Italian.

Fullerton thanked her for her welcome in his limited Italian, introduced Marguerite and informed her that as they were rather tired they would require nothing except a good night's sleep. She showed them to their rooms and then retired to her own quarters.

Coincidentally, he had been given the same suite of rooms as before, which again brought back memories. He placed his case on the bed and went over to the window in order to open the shutters. The street below was still fairly deserted and the noise was the noise of a city, breathing. Distant sounds, the occasional dog bark and again the aromatic smells.

He checked next door to see that Marguerite had everything she needed and after a brief conversation and a 'Bonne Nuit' he returned to his own rooms.

A good night's sleep, he thought, would make all the difference. He had looked forward to this holiday and planned to enjoy every minute.

Fullerton awoke early the next morning to the clatter of bins being emptied into a refuse vehicle disposing of the weekly accumulation of rubbish. He lay back in bed for a while. Then, not being able to go back to sleep, got up, opened the shutters and leaned out of the window to take in the scene.

The sky was clear and so the day promised to be fine; he decided to shower and get dressed. Marguerite had also awoken early and was up and ready when Fullerton knocked on her door. It was a simple decision therefore that they pay the local café a visit.

Seated at a street-side table with a pot of strong coffee in front of them and some 'panini', Fullerton agreed with himself that he was finally on holiday. The two of them had a whole two weeks in which to enjoy themselves, revisit places that had all but disappeared from his memory and generally relax. His notebook would provide the means for planning his daily activities and so he started to jot down some of the activities that he wished to complete.

Marguerite drank some of the strong black coffee and opened up a map of the city.

'I haven't been in Rome, Michael, since I was a schoolgirl in Normandy. We came on a school trip; I remember it all being so exciting, but we were not allowed to go anywhere without the teachers. I remember thinking how handsome the Italian boys were. Can we please visit the Pantheon? I have heard so much about it.'

Fullerton looked up from his notes.

'We can go anywhere you like; this is why we are here.'

As it was a fine spring day, they decided that they would walk over to the Coliseum and then work their way round through the ruins of the old Roman Forum and back into the centre of the city for lunch.

Fullerton found it quite wonderful being in Marguerite's company; it reminded him of two students in Paris all those years ago, madly in love and their whole life ahead of them.

The next days seemed to pass all too quickly but totally enjoyably; they walked and talked, sat and watched the local population going about their everyday business; ate when they felt hungry and took taxis and buses when they felt tired.

Evenings were spent enjoying the Italian wines and the local cuisine even if the pasta was starting to become a little too repetitive. Their visit to the Vatican had proved a real success mainly due to the fact that they got up that morning particularly early in order to be near the front of the queue. The sheer splendour and size of the Basilica and the marvel of seeing the Sistine Chapel was one of the highlights of their trip.

It was nearly at the end of their first week in Rome that Marguerite found the courage to ask Fullerton about his family, particularly Richard who used to visit Marguerite a lot when he was young. Michael and Evelyn Fullerton even arranged for Richard to go to school in France for a couple of years. This had been a particularly great sacrifice on Evelyn's part and Fullerton knew just what it had meant to her.

'How's Richard?' she asked.

'He's just fine; he's still that deep thinker that he always was. He seems to be settled and now that he is married, he seems content.'

'That's good,' Marguerite added. 'He always enjoyed his visits to France when he was young and picked up a second language as if he was born to it.'

'Well, in a way he was, wasn't he?' Fullerton replied.

The conversation moved on to safer ground as they planned the next activity.

They had been in Rome for a full week already and Fullerton was so glad that he and Marguerite had spent this time together.

The registered letter was waiting for him when he returned to the apartment that afternoon. Marguerite was out shopping and was not expected to return until the early evening. The rather innocuous-looking white envelope with a London postmark conveyed no outward indication as to its contents or purpose.

Fullerton placed it on the mantelpiece in his sitting room and went into the bedroom to change out of his dusty clothes. He ran a bath for himself and sank back into the relaxing water and mulled over in his mind all the people that he knew who could possibly need to contact him here in Italy. Who, in fact, in London knew he was even in Italy and Rome not to mention the exact postal address of the apartment?

His impatience to open the letter now got the better of him. He climbed out of the bath, hurriedly dried himself, slipped on his slippers and dressing gown and returned to the sitting room. The envelope, still taking pride of place on the mantelpiece was made from one of those stiff almost card-like papers making it all but impossible to determine the nature of its contents.

Fullerton opened the envelope and removed the single sheet of paper inside. The letter had a vaguely familiar logo in the top right-hand corner.

Mr M. A. Fullerton
Apt 33
14 Via Rosa
Roma
14320
Italy

Dear Mr Fullerton
You are urgently requested to contact the undersigned at your earliest convenience with a view to your immediate travel back to London and the listed address.

Confirmation of the receipt of this letter and your anticipated arrival details in London are requested by phoning the following number: 020 7629 8888.

H. W. Matthews (Harry)
Executive Assistant to the CEO, Brentmark Holdings,
Geneva.

He stared at the words for a few moments. All sorts of
thoughts started to race through his mind. Why had this
man Matthews written to him? Why did he not say anything
further? Why now?

Obviously this had to have something to do with his
brother, but what the exact reason was for the urgent
communication he had no idea.

He placed the letter on the small table at the side of
the ornate sofa and went over to the window, opened the
shutters and stared down onto the street below. Deep in
thought his attention was regained by the sight of Marguerite
walking along the opposite side of the street. She was
carrying several shopping bags and so had obviously been
successful in her excursion.

Fullerton heard her enter the apartment's main door;
he listened to her footsteps as she walked down the tiled
hallway to her room and heard her door open and close
behind her. He sat down on the sofa and picked up the
letter once more and stared at the words as if to obtain
some further meaning from them.

He knocked on Marguerite's door. She opened it and
he asked her to come along the corridor to his room.

'I am going to have to return to London fairly soon
I'm afraid,' he told her. 'I'm so sorry about the last bit
of our holiday, but this matter simply can't wait.'

She was about to ask for an explanation, but he spoke
first.

'I can't tell you anything more about this right now,
Marguerite, but it is something to do with my brother.
What do you want to do about *your* travel arrangements?'

'I'll still go and visit my sister in London as planned,'

Marguerite replied. 'She won't mind if I show up a few days early.'

'All right, I'll contact the airline first thing in the morning and see if we can change our return flights to next Monday. This will still give us another four days here.'

'Let's make the rest of our trip really special then,' Marguerite said. 'We don't know if we will ever come here again.'

Chapter 9

April 28th, 2008. London

The flight touched down at Heathrow just about on time. It was raining and cold after the warmth of Rome. They went through the interminable process of passport control and watching other people's luggage go round and round on one of the many baggage carousels. Finally, their luggage appeared which Fullerton loaded onto a trolley and they made their way to the exit of the Terminal building and out into the open air and the taxi rank.

The skies were overcast and it had just started to rain yet again. A typical grey day in April, Fullerton thought.

They did not have to wait long for a ride and quickly got into the cab and out of the weather which seemed to get worse just as they left the shelter of the waiting area. The cab made its way through the circling airport traffic and down into the exit tunnel.

Fullerton looked at Marguerite and asked, 'Where can I drop you off?'

'At the Hammersmith underground station if you like, it's on your way. I'll stay with my sister in Hampstead for a few days and then return to Paris.'

'I'll call you when I know what all this is about,' Fullerton said.

The taxi left the M4 and continued on into the centre of London and soon reached Hammersmith. Fullerton spoke to the driver and soon they dipped down off the elevated roadway and pulled over close to the underground station.

'Take care, Marguerite, I will call as soon as I can,' Fullerton half shouted after Marguerite as she jumped out, waved and then hurried off through the crowds and into the station entrance.

The taxi continued on its journey, rounded Hyde Park Corner, travelled along Park Lane and was soon at the Dorchester Hotel.

'Is this OK, gov?' the taxi driver half snorted in his cockney accent.

'Yes, this'll do fine,' Fullerton replied. He paid the driver, opened the cab door and collected his case from the front of the taxi.

Fullerton walked the few steps from the kerb into the hotel foyer. He noticed that the foyer was quite busy with numerous people arriving and departing. He placed his suitcase on the ground as he took in the details of his surroundings.

'Can I be of any assistance?' the smartly dressed young woman at reception asked.

'Hmm, yes. I'm looking for a Mr Matthews, I believe that he might be staying in the hotel. Do you know where I can find him?'

'A moment, please,' she replied and gave him a quizzical look as she searched the computer screen in front of her for the name Matthews.

'Mr Matthews can be contacted on the house phone over there, I will put you through if you will pick up the receiver.'

Fullerton's eyes moved in the direction she was pointing and he soon spotted the phone in question. He picked up the receiver and waited while he heard the ringing tone.

'Matthews here,' a voice answered.

'Hello, this is Professor Fullerton, I believe that you are expecting me,' Fullerton replied.

'Mr Fullerton, I'll be right down,' Matthews shouted and the phone line went dead.

Fullerton had never been to the Dorchester before; it was a little outside his price bracket. He paced back and forth, keeping an eye on his case which was still by the reception desk and absorbed the internal architecture of the building. His eyes eventually focused on the hugely ornate central artwork and its elaborate decoration. The lobby was quite busy with people from all walks of life coming and going. Arabian sheiks to smartly dressed business types. It was all hustle and bustle and he felt distinctly under-dressed.

A member of the hotel staff came over to him and said, 'Can we look after your suitcase?'

'Thank you, no,' Fullerton replied, picked up his suitcase, went over to one of the many sofas and sat down.

He observed the comings and goings of people, all busying themselves with their various tasks. A copy of the *Financial Times* was on the table and so Fullerton picked it up and started to scan the various newsworthy articles on the front page. All the usual stories were covered; the state of the economy and the latest political headlines. Which corporations' annual results were due out etc., etc.

He turned to the inside pages and glanced at an article about the Axxon Group. He had barely started to read the first few lines when he was interrupted.

'Mr Fullerton?' a voice quietly questioned from close behind him.

Fullerton swung round to see who had spoken.

'I am Harry Matthews, thank you for coming. Please follow me.'

Fullerton was still wearing his linen shirt and trousers which had served him well whilst on holiday in Rome but which now seemed completely inappropriate.

They walked over to the lifts, entered one and Fullerton observed Matthews indicating the seventh floor. Exiting the lift after it had come almost imperceptibly to a halt, Fullerton followed Matthews down the hallway until they reached a door with 'Audley Suite' on the front.

Matthews opened the door, allowed Fullerton to enter and then closed it behind him.

'Please sit down, Mr Fullerton, can I get you a coffee or perhaps something stronger?'

'A coffee will be fine,' Fullerton replied. He was just about to ask the obvious question as to why he had been summoned in such haste from Rome when a door opened from the bedroom and his brother entered.

James Fullerton was wearing his pyjamas and a dressing gown. He seemed tired and not at all as Michael would have expected him to look.

'Thank you for coming Michael, you're probably wondering why you are here.'

'Yes, I was rather,' Michael replied as the two brothers shook hands. He immediately thought how redundant that response must have sounded.

James asked Matthews to leave them alone for at least forty-five minutes.

'I'll call you, Harry, when we've finished.'

Matthews made his exit and James turned to his brother.

'You're looking well; how are Evelyn and the family?'

'Evelyn died last May in rather unfortunate circumstances, but I'm learning to adjust. That was why I was in Rome.'

'Sorry to hear that, Michael, I didn't know,' James continued. Michael thought his brother sounded like he was addressing one of his numerous board meetings.

'I have asked you to come because I have something to tell you,' James went on. 'I am in London on the pretext of attending a meeting with business associates and politicians. At least that is what the press will be told. I have in fact been to Harley Street for some further tests. The preliminary results were made known to me late last week and that is when I issued instructions for you to be contacted.'

'How did you know where to find me?' Michael enquired.

'Your housekeeper in Oxford informed my staff that you were in Rome and in the company of a Madame De Saulx de Tavannes. It was a simple matter to contact her office at the Sorbonne and obtain the forwarding address that she had left.'

James looked at his brother with a strangely fixed gaze.

'I have cancer. The doctors do not yet know the full picture. I was fit and healthy until about five weeks ago. They tell me that the cancer seems to be particularly aggressive and of unknown origin. It may be treatable but they needed me here to perform some more tests. If it is not treatable, I probably will have about twelve months to live.'

James held up his hand and continued.

'Yes, they can prescribe courses of chemotherapy and all the usual treatments, but the cancer has surprised them by spreading so far so fast. They don't even know what the primary cancer is.'

Michael found himself unable to offer any kind of a response. Just to say 'I'm so sorry' seemed at that precise moment a much too useless a remark.

'They say,' continued James 'that I could be in remission for a period of a few months after this first round of treatment, but that they will know more shortly. The prognosis is not good. Further such treatments may be needed and they have warned me that each time the intervals will be greatly reduced. I am guessing that twelve months is about right.'

'Who have you told so far?'

'Just you,' was the reply. 'Even Harry thinks it is just stress that has caused this latest illness.'

Michael walked over to the window and looked out at the London skyline. Here was his brother, his twin; he was like a stranger and yet there was a strange feeling of a closeness that he couldn't for the moment explain.

'Why have you told me?' Michael asked.

Before James answered that particular question he picked up the phone and looked at his brother.

'Perhaps I could arrange for you to stay in the hotel?' Michael thought for a moment

'Yes that would be of great help, I was thinking of returning directly to Oxfordshire, but of course I will stay.'

James dialled the hotel reception and waited for somebody to answer.

'This is James Fullerton. I need an additional room for one night. It is for a Mr Davidson.'

Michael looked at James as if to question his apparent mistake.

'Thank you very much, could you please arrange for Mr Davidson's key to be brought up to the Audley Suite.' There was a pause followed by 'Thank you' after which James replaced the receiver.

James had returned into the bedroom leaving Michael alone for a moment. He returned with a glass of water and some tablets.

'They won't be very long, please inform the hotel of anything that you require; it has all been taken care of.'

'Did you have a good trip back from Rome? How was the weather during your stay?'

Michael acknowledged that this period of inane conversation was necessary.

'It was fine, James, not too hot and not too cold,' Michael answered. 'Marguerite and I had a really delightful time. I hadn't been to Rome for about five years. It brought back some lovely memories.'

Michael thought about a more suitably appropriate topic of conversation, but was beaten to the punch by the sound of the door bell.

James walked over and opened the door, had a brief word with the hotel clerk and closed the door again.

'Here is your room key, Michael. If there is anything at all you want don't hesitate to contact Harry. He is in room 131, just across the hall.'

'Perhaps you and he could meet later for dinner. He'll meet you in the lobby.'

'That would be very nice. What about yourself?' Michael replied.

'I prefer to eat in my room. I can only eat certain things at the moment and will retire quite early in any case,' James responded. 'Please remember that for the time being you are Mr Davidson should anyone ask. Do not breathe a word of this to anyone and that includes Matthews.'

Walking over to the door with his arm pressed into his brother's back, James opened the door and whispered, 'I have a lot to discuss with you tomorrow. Remember, not a word!'

Michael Fullerton walked back along the hallway towards the lifts with his brain trying madly to take in everything that he had just been told.

Room 116 was an extremely pleasant room. He entered and placed his suitcase on the luggage rack. The room had the same outlook as his brother's but not quite the same advantage in elevation. He sat on the edge of the king-sized bed and picked up the hotel welcome folder and studied its contents for a while.

After unpacking his case, he opened the mini-bar and poured himself a large whisky and water. He did not normally drink in the middle of the afternoon but this news seemed to justify at least one. Slipping off his shoes he realised that he still didn't know precisely why he was in the hotel and why he had been summoned. No doubt all would become clear in due course.

Fullerton enjoyed a relaxing few hours and left his room, allowing himself just enough time to be perfectly punctual for his dinner engagement with Harry Matthews.

'Hello, Michael, that was perfect timing,' Matthews remarked as the two men met in the hotel foyer.

'What do you feel like eating?'

Fullerton indicated that he would be satisfied with any choice of restaurant and left it up to Matthews to make that important decision.

The two men hailed a taxi from the front of the hotel and travelled the relatively short distance to a little known but quite obviously exclusive French restaurant.

'I thought that this place would be a suitable place for a quiet discussion,' Harry added as the taxi drew up outside.

'*Bonsoir Monsieur Matthews*,' the *maître d'hôtel* crisply added as they entered the premises. Michael observed that this must be a familiar haunt of Matthews, given his immediate recognition.

'A nice table for two please, somewhere where we won't be disturbed.'

They were led to an area towards the rear of the restaurant and a table conveniently set in a small alcove.

'*Merci*,' Harry said and the two of them slid into the rather tightly placed seats either side of a square-shaped table.

'Red wine, Michael? I hope you don't mind me calling you Michael? The beef that they serve here is absolutely fabulous.'

'Yes, that sounds fine,' Fullerton replied.

The wine duly arrived, the two men placed their order and finally it was time to have that 'quiet discussion' that Fullerton had been told to expect.

'May I begin?' Matthews asked with a glance in Fullerton's direction. He paused and seemed to be searching for the right tone with which to conduct the conversation.

'As you have seen, your brother is a very tired man, he is working too hard and personally we think that he is very over-stressed. I trust that all this travel has not come as too great an inconvenience for you?'

Fullerton remained silent and just stared at the array of knives and forks in front of him.

'We have expected his health to suffer for some time and now it is upon us. Did you know much about your brother's circumstances?'

Fullerton replied that he knew nothing at all and that this whole visit to London and its reasons had come as a complete surprise to him.

'We did know that you were not particularly close to your brother,' Matthews continued. Fullerton thought that that last remark was a complete understatement and just how little Matthews must know about the relationship between himself and his brother.

'As you know, your brother holds a position of considerable importance and influence within the Axxon Group in particular and also with his many other business interests. We believe that he is considering making some significant changes in the near future.'

Matthews paused and thought of replacing the last phrase but continued.

'Maybe he is thinking of reducing his workload and handing the reins of power over to someone else. There must of course be an orderly transition, this is absolutely imperative,' Matthews added seemingly gaining momentum. 'There has been an awful lot of talk about who will succeed your brother, but I am not privy to the politics of the boardroom. We have increasingly less and less involvement in the Axxon Group itself in any case.'

Fullerton wondered about the particular use of the 'we' in everything that Matthews said and astutely realised that Matthews was on a fishing expedition, no doubt wondering about the future of his own position, but did not dwell on the thought long as Matthews continued.

'I believe that your brother has been quite anxious for you two to meet?'

'It would certainly seem so,' Fullerton answered with a poker-faced expression and volunteering nothing.

'Are you expecting to meet on a regular basis?'

'Mr Matthews, I'm afraid that I am going to be of little help to you this evening. I am quite sure that my brother will provide you with the answers to all your questions if you were to address them to him.'

Matthews surveyed his dinner guest and realised that this nice, cosy dinner engagement was not going to yield the results that he had hoped for. Mr Michael Fullerton was far more astute than he had expected.

The rest of the evening was spent in an interesting social debate about the state of the world, the obvious consequences of the UK government's current foreign policy and Professor Fullerton's academic activities.

Returning to the hotel later that evening, the two men took the lift to the 1st floor where Fullerton almost felt relieved to get out.

'Good night, Michael. We'll probably meet again tomorrow.'

'Thank you for a very pleasant evening,' Fullerton replied and he was left alone to walk down the corridor to his room.

Chapter 10

Fullerton dressed early the following morning and left the hotel on foot. He had decided to take a walk across part of Hyde Park to collect his thoughts and clear his head with some fresh air.

There were not too many people about at that hour and so he was able to concentrate on his own little world without any of the usual distractions. He reached a bench along one of the footpaths and sat down for a while. All the trees were starting to show their early foliage and even the grass was demonstrating signs of new life. The sky was clear and blue; in fact a very pleasant late April morning in central London.

His surroundings seemed to strike a stark contrast with the harsh reality of his day ahead.

Fullerton thought about what he would say to his brother when they met again in an hour and a half's time. He wondered what his brother would be thinking. Just how does one deal with this kind of medical prognosis. He found himself thinking again about his own wife's death and how he had felt in the days and weeks after that event and realised that one never quite gets over any of it. Grief is displaced by anger and that in turn is displaced by some kind of acceptance and understanding.

'Good morning,' a passing stranger addressed to him as he walked on by. Fullerton acknowledged the stranger with a slight nod of his head and wondered whether it would in fact be a good morning or not. No doubt he would soon find out.

Returning to the hotel after about an hour, he felt that the walk and the fresh air had done him some good. He had cleared his mind and although he was always quite fatalistic about the outcome of events, he found himself in an appropriate frame of mind to meet his brother for a second time.

Back in the hotel, Fullerton walked along the corridor leading to the Audley Suite with a strange sense that he would not overly react to anything that was about to be discussed or said. He had not seen his brother forever it seemed and so, in a way, this meeting was going to be with what was to all intents and purpose, a stranger.

Fullerton knocked and waited. The door was opened by the ubiquitous Harry Matthews and Fullerton was ushered in to the room. His brother was already seated on the sofa and seemed in good spirits and so Michael felt somewhat reassured.

'Hello, Michael, do come and sit down,' James said with a welcoming smile. 'Coffee?'

Fullerton nodded and Matthews walked over to the breakfast buffet that was still on the long side table near one of the full-length windows.

'I believe that you had a good evening last night at *La Tulipe d'Or*,' James remarked.

'Yes, it was an extremely pleasant and interesting evening,' Michael replied, glancing at Matthews who was busying himself at the buffet table.

Matthews placed the coffee on the table in front of Michael.

'Please leave us, Harry, if you wouldn't mind.'

Matthews showed some slight annoyance at being asked to leave but concealed his reaction well. Collecting some papers on the table, he made his way to the door and without further comment disappeared, closing the door behind him.

'It's been a long time, Michael, hasn't it? I can't think of where it was we met last. Time just seems to fly by. I don't think that I will be seeing too much more of it,' he added ruefully.

The feeling of strange closeness came over Michael Fullerton once more as he listened to his brother.

'I have some matters that I want to discuss with you that are of a rather personal nature,' James went on, reaching for a briefcase that had been placed at the side of the sofa and within easy reach.

James removed several glossy folders from within the briefcase and searched for one in particular.

'This is a copy of my Last Will and Testament,' James said as he briefly raised the document in the air.

'You have been appointed as my executor and sole beneficiary. It is my earnest wish that you will use your knowledge of business to continue what I have started to create. I have left a legacy for my nephew and niece, which should see them both amply provided for.'

Without waiting for Michael to comment he continued.

'A small part of my estate is still bound up in my corporate holdings in Axxon; that is the company that I am known to be mostly connected with by the public at large. I have been divesting myself of much corporate stock in recent months. You know of my house in Geneva, *Bellerive*, but I also have properties in the South of France and New York. With a number of other corporate involvements, certain Venture Capital interests and cash on hand, you will be the beneficiary of an estate estimated to be worth about £300 million at today's market valuation.'

Michael Fullerton attempted to grasp what he had just heard and picked up the coffee cup, steadied it with both

59

hands and took a sip in order to conceal his reaction to this revelation.

'I won't go through all the rather extensive details with you now; I will arrange for you to meet my London solicitors in due course. They handle most of my legal work and can give you a more detailed briefing. There will also be a need for you to travel to Geneva as well I'm afraid. No doubt this can all be arranged to suit your present commitments.'

James replaced the document into his briefcase and paused for some kind of response from his brother.

Michael Fullerton's command of the English language, which was considered by many academics to be almost legendary, failed him completely.

'I don't know what to say, James,' he found himself whispering.

'Don't say anything then,' James Fullerton replied.

James then changed the subject.

'How are my nephew and niece these days? You must be very proud of them. I was sorry to hear about poor Evelyn's tragic death but it happens to us all eventually. In my case, it may be quite soon.'

'Both Richard and Louise are fine. Richard works for an export company in London and Louise has just finished college.'

Michael gave his brother a rundown on his own professional affairs in Oxford and more about his family's activities and progress. Time seemed to have passed in a flash, during the course of which James had made a quick call to his executive assistant. A few minutes later, the door opened and Harry appeared once again.

'We have finished for now, Harry,' James stated. 'I'm sorry Michael, I think we'll need to meet again this afternoon if that's OK with you,' he added, looking across at Michael.

'Now I have to get ready for my meeting with the Prime Minister. Can't keep Blakemore waiting, can I?'

As Michael Fullerton was returning to his own room he realised that nearly ninety minutes had elapsed since he had first entered his brother's room. He thought about phoning Marguerite as soon as he reached his own room but was reminded of the final command that his brother had issued.

'Do not, I repeat *not* tell anyone at all about what we have just discussed.'

Once back in his own room, Michael Fullerton sat down and tried to absorb what his brother had just told him. He pulled some writing paper out of the desk drawer and started to list the main points of the conversation. It was as if the act of writing these items down would somehow confirm their authenticity. These revelations had all come as a complete shock.

He decided that he needed to leave the claustrophobic atmosphere of hotel rooms behind, at least for a while.

Chapter 11

April 29th, 2008. London.

James Fullerton himself opened the door when Michael returned to his brother's room that same afternoon.

'Come on in, Michael,' James said briskly. The two men sat down next to each other on the L-shaped sofa.

'I don't suppose you know too much about what I do, Michael, these days,' James stated as he reached for the folder that was lying next to him.

'Well, I do see your name in print occasionally,' Michael answered.

'All too often, for my liking,' James retorted. 'These press types seem to want to quote me on every subject imaginable.'

'I have asked you to come back so that I can fill you in on some other activities that I am involved with. There is a lot that you are going to need to know in a very short space of time,' he continued without waiting for any reply. 'There are a number of key individuals that you will need to meet. I'll set everything up. Is that OK with you?'

'Yes, that will be fine, but can I . . . ?' Michael started to say.

'Good, then that is all settled,' James continued. 'You'll have to pack in that sleepy, academic existence you have in Oxford.'

The two men continued to discuss the broad details of James's business empire for an hour or more and Michael found himself losing track of a lot of the names that were mentioned.

Finally James said: 'There is one other matter that I have to discuss, Michael.' He looked intently at his brother. 'I have read a lot of your published papers over the years; you talk about economics very eloquently and professionally but I detect some kind of hidden rationale in all of it.'

Michael looked back at his brother. Here he was having a quite normal conversation with his estranged brother, nearly thirty-five years since they had been at school together. He couldn't remember having anything like this kind of conversation before.

'I do sit and wonder about the effectiveness of our illustrious politicians,' Michael answered. 'They either spend their whole lives working their way up through the political system or get parachuted into some safe seat by being known around. Then, with no experience of the business world at all they're elected to office and made responsible for making decisions that affect the whole population.'

'I didn't realise that you felt so strongly, Michael,' James responded. You must become really frustrated by the motivation and self-interest of the political elite.'

'I try in my own small way to convince people of the logic of economic argument, James, but I have this growing realisation that the ordinary man in the street is effectively powerless to influence the very processes that could result in an improvement,' Michael continued. 'It's all right for you, James; you have obviously made it in spite of the system, not because of it. In any case, I doubt that you care what the ordinary man thinks or might want.'

'How wrong you are, my dear brother!' James retorted. 'You know, we are still very much alike, even now after all these years. I want to talk to you about something that means more to me now than it has for many years. I am not just an insensitive corporate leader, as you would

63

probably put it. I have a number of very close friends with whom I share a much more honest and honourable view of the world than you might think.' James paused as he collected his thoughts. 'Michael, have you ever heard of an organisation that goes by the acronym ADF?'

'Isn't that the society that has based its ideology on the early writings of Father Pierre Fournier?'

'My God!' exclaimed James. 'I had no idea that you had even heard of this organisation, never mind its history. Not many people know of its roots.'

'You don't know me as well as you thought you did, James,' Michael said, somewhat triumphantly.

'I got to know Father Fournier by coincidence when I was in Paris as a student. He was a man in his early fifties then, but still active in his own way and very much listened to by students and people of influence alike. We became close friends. He had that quiet confidence about him that made you listen to what he had to say. He had spent most of his life fighting against what he saw as the political power that the Catholic Church had over the minds of men and was eventually excommunicated for his continually outspoken views. There were many students and even professors that agreed with what he said. I used to visit him a lot; you know what students are like, always searching for the true ideals of our existence. We have kept in touch over the years and I have admired his tenacity in sticking with his beliefs since that time.'

'Well, he is very much alive and well for a man in his eighties,' James continued.

'Yes, he is. How would you come to know that?' Michael replied inquisitively.

'This is what I need to talk to you about, Michael,' James said.

'The ADF is an organisation that bases its activities, as you rightly stated, on the writings of Father Fournier even if those same activities have progressed somewhat over the years to become now an organisation with international connections and an extremely effective lobbying group. Through its network of members, it does extremely important work and has achieved adjustment and sometimes reversal of political policy. I am extremely proud of its achievements.'

James studied his brother for any reaction.

'Recently there have, as you know, been some shocking murders of leading political figures and both the police and intelligence services are progressively reaching the misguided conclusion that the ADF could be involved. Much more importantly, certain governments are using this false connection between the murders and the ADF both to discredit the organisation and to gain a hold over its membership, thereby neutralising its activities and influence. I will not allow this to happen! I will be in touch with you in the next few days and let you know more,' James concluded and looking at his watch realised that this discussion was going to have to be continued at a later date.

'You'll have to excuse me again now, Michael, as I need to leave for the Foreign Office in about fifteen minutes and I will be returning to Geneva tomorrow. Thanks for coming and all the best. Remember, Michael! It is imperative that you say nothing to anybody about what we have just discussed or even that we've met.'

With that, the meeting between the brothers was deemed at an end. Michael took his cue, stood up and walked over to the door. He turned to glance back at his brother, but James already had the telephone in his ear and was flipping through his diary pages no doubt to address the next important issue.

Michael closed the door behind him. He decided that he wouldn't delay his departure from London and so made arrangements to return to Oxford.

Chapter 12

June 12th, 2008. Hong Kong.

Michael Fullerton had been a guest speaker at the annual International Forum for World Economics which was held every year at some suitably exotic location. This year it was in Hong Kong and it brought back memories of his first visit to that unique island when he was in his thirties.

It had been a good opportunity to meet some old acquaintances and to be introduced to others. There had been the usual mixture of government ministers, diplomats and business leaders. His brother was there but their paths had crossed only once.

On that rare occasion Michael and James had had dinner together in James's suite on the Tuesday evening. Michael had duly arrived at his brother's suite to find his brother still looking very tired.

'Come in, Michael. Didn't know that you were going to be here in Hong Kong this week. I was going to call you when I got back to Geneva in any case.'

Michael sat down on the large sofa and watched his brother as he poured them both a large glass of whisky.

'I am not supposed to be drinking alcohol at all right now, but to hell with the doctors for one night at least.'

James came over and sat down slowly next to his brother. He leaned his head back on the back of the sofa.

'I had the results of all those tests that they carried out in Geneva and London just before I flew out here,' he continued. 'They have found traces of heavy metal poisoning. They don't know exactly when this could have entered my body, but they are definitely of the opinion that it was not an accident and that it has, in all likelihood, caused the sudden appearance of cancerous growths in some of my vital organs.'

Michael was absolutely shocked by this revelation.

'You mean that someone has tried to poison you?' he blurted out.

'That's what it looks like.'

'What are the police doing about it?' Michael asked anxiously.

'They have not been involved.'

'Why on earth not, James?'

'Because I do not want this to become public knowledge if and until I know the result of any corrective action that the doctors have prescribed.'

'Who would want to kill you?' Michael asked incredulously.

'Oh, I think that there are a few that I could probably name.'

'A few! My God, James, who are these people and why would they want to kill you?'

'That would take too long to tell you, I'm afraid,' James said with a sigh.

'Anyway, let's have something to eat; well, you have something to eat at least. I ordered a nice buffet and it is waiting in the next room.'

'To hell with food!' Michael almost shouted. 'I don't believe what I am hearing!'

'Well you will soon enough when I get the latest medical assessment,' James replied quietly.

The evening ended as it had begun with the two brothers drinking another large whisky. Michael Fullerton left his brother and wondered if it would be the last time he would see him. They didn't see each other again during the final two days of the conference and Michael didn't make any enquiries. He knew that he would hear any news soon enough.

The return flight from Hong Kong to Heathrow had just taken off and Fullerton settled down for the twelve-hour duration. Business class made the journey a lot more enjoyable and he was able to relax and reflect on his two-week visit.

His travelling companion on the flight back to London was his fellow Oxford don and long-time colleague, Sebastian Thurlow. Thurlow was a senior fellow at Balliol College and had travelled out to Hong Kong after Fullerton.

'I must thank you again, Michael for getting me upgraded to business class,' Thurlow remarked as his glanced away from the finely printed menu that had just been handed to them both.

'Not at all, Sebastian, I just happened to make a certain remark to one of my keenest corporate admirers earlier in the week that I would be returning on the same flight as yourself but that, as you were not on a speaking engagement, we would not be sitting in the same cabin section. "Let me see what I can do," was all that he said and I thought no more of it.'

'That would explain why I was asked for my return flight details by hotel reception,' Thurlow commented with a cognitive gaze. 'What did you think of the week's events, Michael?' he continued. 'I thought that our government chaps were quite inspiring, didn't you?'

Fullerton studied the menu for a few moments before replying.

'You know, Sebastian, I find these days that I am really getting totally fed up with all the rhetoric and grandiose statements that politicians seem to be able to produce virtually on demand.'

He removed his glasses and turned slightly towards his companion.

'Are we really supposed to be that gullible? Does a gathering of the world's supposed economic, financial and business elite really listen to, never mind agree with, what's being said?'

Thurlow leant back in his seat, sipped a little champagne from his glass and then replaced it on his fold-down table.

'I think that everybody knows that much of what is being said is only for public consumption and isn't what any of them really and truly think or believe.'

'Then why do they continue with this charade?' Fullerton snapped. The two men sat in silence for a few moments.

'You know, Sebastian, I really think that world politics and western so-called democratic politics is nothing more than so much window dressing. It's about time that someone or something came along to shake all these smug, self-serving, autocrats off their safe little perches. Democracy is a meaningless name that is over-rated, over-used and completely misrepresented.'

'My word, Michael,' Thurlow ventured, 'I didn't know you were so opinionated, maybe you should stand for election yourself.'

'I would if I thought that I'd get anywhere or even be listened to,' Fullerton answered with some degree of emphasis in his voice.

'You know, Sebastian, there really must be a way in which the average man in the street can ensure that his voice is heard and, together with the voices of millions of others, can achieve tangible results. The politicians aren't listening any more, if they ever were; they are only in it for what they can get out of it and to hell with the rest of us.'

Further conversation was temporarily halted as the flight attendant arrived with the hors d'oeuvres.

After the very acceptable meal and all the debris had been cleared away, Fullerton reached for his thin leather document case that had been placed under the seat in front of him and removed a file containing some recent correspondence that had reached him at his home address in Oxford over the couple of weeks before he had left for the Far East.

Of all the correspondence that Professor Fullerton received on a regular basis and which was quite a sizeable amount, three letters in particular had made a real impression on him.

One was in Marguerite's handwriting; it had contained a couple of pages with the usual humdrum domestic type content and the odd rundown on her academic activities. It ended with a suggestion that he should consider coming over to Paris for a few days. He had read and re-read this note several times but had not yet decided how to formulate a suitable response. He took out his pen and decided that now was as good a time as any to deal with this invitation. Yes, he would like to visit her in Paris very much.

The other two letters had both been invitations from certain illustrious institutions. One from Harvard University in Cambridge, Massachusetts and one from Simon Fraser University in Burnaby, British Columbia. These would both be speaking engagements and Fullerton had been presented with several possible dates in each case. The dates for both were much later in the year and Fullerton had not considered them further in the light of recent developments.

He knew that he could not postpone a response to them indefinitely, but for the moment they could wait.

Finishing his short note to Marguerite and addressing the envelope, he replaced all the envelopes into his document case and decided to try and get some sleep.

He was awoken some hours later from an unusually long sleep by the attentions of the same flight attendant and the imminent prospect of more food.

He felt better for the nap; he didn't usually sleep well on planes. Sebastian was busy reading a book which he replaced in the pocket in front of him as the meal arrived.

'When do we arrive in London?' he asked the flight attendant.

'I believe that we are running about fifteen minutes ahead of schedule and so should be at Heathrow in about two hours' time,' came the answer.

'Are you returning straight to Oxford, Sebastian?' Fullerton asked his travelling companion.

'Yes, I don't like breaking my journey in London. Much rather get home straight away.'

'Well I have to be in London tomorrow evening in any case so I have already decided to stay in town,' Fullerton continued.

The meal over, the two men turned to their own affairs; one to reading, the other to writing.

The plane touched down about ten minutes early at a wet, windswept Heathrow and the process of negotiating the airport facilities began.

Chapter 13

June 14th, 2008. London.

This was the weekend that Michael Fullerton had looked forward to for the past month. These family get-togethers always seemed to pass with so little time in which to say all the things that needed saying and to put right all the things that had been said that should never have been said.

This one had been arranged and finalised before Fullerton had left for Hong Kong. Richard said that he and Michelle would arrange everything and book a nice restaurant in Muswell Hill for the four of them. Louise was only an underground ride away and being a student was only too willing to enjoy a few free meals and listen to all the family gossip.

Fullerton thought about this get-together and hoped that this time it would be an enjoyable occasion. The last one had not been a particular success. Maybe it had come too close after Evelyn's death. That event had ended with Louise becoming very upset and Richard having to leave rather suddenly part way through the weekend. Everyone understood that this was just his way of handling a situation that he couldn't, or wouldn't, deal with head on. His children had in fact both dealt with the loss of their mother in their own way, as he had himself. But there was still a hidden tension in the family that Fullerton had not been able to explain or alleviate. On the surface, everything was sweetness and light, but he had sensed a void developing between him and his children that couldn't just be explained by force of circumstances.

Louise wondered what all the fuss was about but was nevertheless happy to fall in with everyone else's plans

Fullerton only lived in Oxford, which was barely forty-five minutes away by car from London, but family visits and gatherings had become quite rare events of late, each person with their own lives to lead.

Evelyn had been the glue that had held the family together and without her presence they were all in danger of becoming strangers.

Fullerton had arranged to stay in a nearby hotel so as to not waste time travelling back and forth over the weekend and to be conveniently situated for the Friday evening. He had travelled directly from Oxford by train and then taken a taxi from East Finchley to Muswell Hill and his hotel. 'To hell with the expense,' he thought to himself.

His phone rang while he was in the taxi. 'Hi, Michael, it's me,' the voice said. It was Richard calling to check in with everybody.

'I should be at my hotel in a few minutes; I'll meet you all at the restaurant.'

'That's great; Michelle is also on her way. I haven't heard from Louise since last night, but she said she'd be there and would be coming straight from town.'

Richard had chosen a nice little Thai restaurant on the high street in Muswell Hill. It was only a short walk away for Fullerton and he found it with no trouble at all. He arrived a few minutes early and was about to walk along the street a bit to kill a few minutes when he spotted his son walking towards him from the other direction.

'Hi, Richard,' Fullerton said as his son drew near.

'Hi, Michael,' was the response. It was strange but both his children had grown used to calling their parents by their first names.

'Anyone else shown up yet?' Richard asked.

'I don't know, I have only just arrived and haven't looked inside. I was killing time.'

'Is Michelle here yet?'

'Not yet, she will be along shortly,' Richard added without further explanation.

Fullerton had never had much of a conversation with his son. It always seemed limited to a few words here and there, but the two of them had a certain understanding that allowed them to maintain a close relationship in spite of the limited dialogue between them.

Richard disappeared briefly into the restaurant to see if his sister had already arrived, but soon returned to announce that they were the first to arrive. They waited outside in the street so as to be in a position to spot the others when they appeared. The town centre was beginning to get quite a bit busier as other local people appeared, met friends and disappeared into other eating establishments nearby.

Louise came round the corner having taken a bus from the centre of town and greeted her father and brother with the usual 'Hello.'

'We are waiting for Michelle to arrive,' Fullerton informed his daughter.

Let's go in,' Richard said abruptly. 'She can find us all right.'

Inside the restaurant, they were taken to a nice curtained booth as Richard had notified their waiter that there would only be the four of them. They ordered a round of drinks and guessed what Michelle would want.

'How's the job going, Richard?' Fullerton enquired.

'OK, I am away quite a lot right now, Michelle hates it when I am away; but a job is a job,' Richard replied.

'Where do you have to go?' Fullerton questioned.

'All over the place,' was the singularly uninformative

74

answer. Fullerton knew his son and took that answer to mean that he wasn't going to get any more information on that subject.

'I should receive my course marks any day now,' Louise announced cheerfully. Louise was always the cheerful one and saw only the good things in life.

'That's exciting,' Fullerton replied, looking across the table at his daughter. 'How do you think you have done this year?'

'My teachers think that I should be OK for next year going by my practical work, but I'll let you know when I see the results,' Louise answered enthusiastically.

Michelle arrived at that moment and sat down next to her husband.

Fullerton had always secretly adored his daughter-in-law. She was the same age as Richard and had met Richard in a bar in central London about a year before they got married.

'How are things at the University?' she asked.

'The usual academic curriculum takes up less of my time than it used to take. But I have been away quite a lot recently. I only returned from Hong Kong yesterday.'

Fullerton purposely didn't mention anything about meeting his brother James there or indeed their meetings in London earlier in the year.

'And how's my grandson?' he asked.

'He's fine. He would like to see more of his father though,' Michelle responded, looking at her husband.

'Well, I can't help it if I am away a lot; the job would be totally boring without the overseas trips,' Richard snapped back at his wife.

Fullerton studied the two of them and looked for any reaction to this outburst from Louise. There being none except for the predictable raised eyebrows, Fullerton changed the subject.

'How's college treating you, Louise, and how's that friend of yours?'

'Everything's just great at the moment. Lots of final assignments to complete; I have been given some really exciting projects to work on lately.'

Fullerton could always count on his daughter to keep a conversation going when things became difficult.

'Clare, my best friend, had to go and visit her sick mother again at the last minute; she really wanted to come but I think she made the right choice,' Louise added.

'Why don't we order some food; does anyone want another drink before we do?' Fullerton said in an attempt to move things along a bit.

'I had a lovely holiday in Rome in April,' Fullerton said. 'The weather was hot but not too hot and we both enjoyed ourselves.'

'How is Marguerite?' Richard asked. 'I haven't seen her since I stopped living with her.'

'She is just fine. She enjoys her work in Paris at the Sorbonne. We stay in touch.' Fullerton hoped that this answer came over in a suitably matter-of-fact way. He didn't add that Marguerite was always asking after him.

'I see that Uncle James is in the papers a lot recently,' came the shock remark from Richard.

'Yeah, he must be really rich,' Louise said. 'I wouldn't mind some of that money right now. I am just a poor student making ends meet.'

'Ah, you poor old thing,' Richard said derisively. 'You are going to have to get a real job like the rest of us soon.'

Fullerton allowed this friendly banter to continue. His children had always teased each other and Louise, in particular, had had to cope with an older brother.

'Do you hear from Uncle James?' Richard asked.

76

Fullerton had hoped that this subject had come and gone, but he provided his son with an answer nevertheless.

'You know that Uncle James and I have never had much in common. We are different people and our paths just haven't crossed since we were a lot younger.'

The table fell silent for a few moments.

'I'm sure that Uncle James and I will become closer at some stage,' Fullerton remarked. More than that he was not going to say, even though the temptation was immense.

The food arrived fortuitously at that moment and Fullerton allowed the conversation to revert to a discussion over whose dish was the most interesting.

Another round of drinks took care of the interval between the main course and the inevitable dessert. Louise ensured that she was not the only one to eat dessert and induced Michelle to keep her company.

'I wish mum could have been here,' Louise remarked.

'Yes, it would have been nice, wouldn't it?' Fullerton said. 'She would be very proud of all of you.'

The conversation then turned to the state of the economy and the current political climate; this bored Louise and Michelle wasn't too thrilled either.

'The present policies of the British and French Governments right now regarding the Middle East is criminal,' Richard stated to the surprise of his wife.

'My goodness, I didn't know that you were interested in all that, Richard!' she exclaimed.

'Politics is for people that enjoy a sense of power over the rest of us; not for you Richard in your boring import-export job.'

'It pays the bills though, doesn't it!' Richard retorted quietly, looking at his wife.

Louise, always the observant one, saw a different side to her brother in that outburst, as did his father. Fullerton observed his son and wondered at the extent of his success

77

in returning to the more mundane world of a nine to five routine after his military career.

'I'm going to have a coffee-liqueur,' Louise announced. 'I told you that I would make the most of this get-together, didn't I?'

Fullerton laughed. Trust Louise to bring some good, down-to-earth reality back into the conversation and some humour.

The evening ended as it had begun with people now departing at intervals.

Michelle and Richard decided that they would need to relieve their baby-sitter soon and so departed for their short walk home.

This left Fullerton with his daughter who was quite intoxicated by this time.

'I think you should come back to my hotel for the night. I don't want you to travel back to your flat in this state,' Fullerton said firmly.

The bill was settled and the two of them left the restaurant and walked down the high street and back to Fullerton's nearby hotel.

The night porter gave Fullerton a very disapproving look and was in no way convinced when Fullerton informed him that Louise was in fact, his daughter.

Once in the room, Fullerton allowed Louise to crash out on the bed fully clothed. He covered her over with the quilt and adjusted to the prospect that his night would be spent on the inconveniently short sofa.

Chapter 14

Michael Fullerton arrived at the duly appointed time at the offices of Andrews, Thompson & Claybourne.

He introduced himself at reception and had hardly taken a seat before a very smart young lady came up to him.

'Mr Fullerton? I'm Mr Andrews' secretary, would you be so good as to follow me.'

Fullerton stood up and followed her over to the lift. The doors opened at the sixth floor and Fullerton observed the expensive wood panelling and the opulent décor.

He walked down the wide corridor and past several offices before entering a large conference room. The broad, highly polished table must have been a good thirty feet in length and was surrounded by some two dozen or so upholstered chairs. There was a full-length window down one side of the room that Fullerton could see looked out on the internal atrium of the building.

'Please be seated, Mr Fullerton, Mr Andrews will be with you directly.'

'Can I get you a coffee?' she added.

Fullerton nodded and added 'Just black, please.'

Fullerton wondered what kind of corporate and individual clients a firm like Andrews, Thompson & Claybourne must have. Well, he knew the name of at least one of their clients.

The door at the far end of the conference room opened and a tall, lean-looking man entered. He was dressed in a very well tailored, dark blue two-piece suit. His hair was a mixture of grey and white and Fullerton guessed that he must be a man in his early sixties.

'Mr Fullerton, thank you for coming,' Andrews said. 'I am Clayton Andrews and I have represented your brother and his UK business interests for some years. Your brother has left explicit instructions with me about the things that I need to discuss, please be seated. I hope that your brother is feeling better than he was when I met with him a few weeks ago; he looked quite run down.'

'James has always kept himself very busy; he was probably very tired,' Fullerton replied tactfully.

Andrews went on.

'As you probably know, your brother is a very rich and influential man. He has instructed me to review with you the size and complexity of his UK business interests. You might find this comment somewhat redundant, but I am led to believe that he has discussed the broad context with you already. I, for my part, have been asked to go into a lot of the corporate details from my position as one of his legal representatives.'

Andrews opened the file that he had brought with him.

'There are a number of corporate entities controlled either directly or indirectly by your brother's holding company in Switzerland. I can only inform you of those activities that he has transacted within the UK. I am not privy to any of his external activities. Let me deal with the first section,' Andrews said as he turned to the second page of the bound document. You will see that Mr Fullerton's sphere of influence has extended to a number of UK corporations; he has an involvement in some forty companies that are either stand-alone enterprises or subsidiaries of larger, in some cases, foreign owned entities. I can only explain the inter relationship between them and go through each one in turn so that you can better understand the complexity of the total framework.'

80

Andrews droned on as Fullerton pretended to listen. 'Mr Fullerton!' Andrews said loudly. 'I will not bore you with all the remaining details if you would rather read some of the contents of this folder for yourself.'

Fullerton replied that he would indeed like to go through the subject documents in his own time and felt sure that Mr Andrews could leave him alone in the conference room and come back in an hour or so.

Andrews saw the upside of this suggestion and readily agreed to leave Fullerton in possession of the folder in his conference room.

'Please contact my secretary when you have finished reading the remainder of this file and are happy to conclude your visit. I will, of course, try and answer any questions that you might have when I return.'

Fullerton acknowledged what Andrews had just finished saying and asked if the information that was contained in the file was everything that he was required to inform him about.

'Yes, Mr Fullerton, that is all I have been instructed to inform you, I think that it is quite enough, don't you? Unless you have any questions, I will see you again when you have finished. I do have some other rather pressing engagements to attend to if you will excuse me.'

Fullerton felt mildly irritated by the rather superior attitude and tone adopted by this slick London solicitor.

The two men shook hands and Andrews left the conference room. Now that he was on his own, Fullerton spread out the various pages of information and studied each and every detail. There was indeed quite a complex arrangement of corporate shareholding. Fullerton quickly comprehended that most of James's shareholding had been structured for optimum offshore control without incurring much, if any, liability to UK tax. He could see why his brother had amassed such a considerable fortune. All that legal training had indeed been put to good use.

An hour and a half later, Fullerton notified Andrews' secretary that he had finished and waited for Andrews to return.

'Is there anything that you need further explanation about?' Andrews asked him.

'No, I don't think that will be necessary, thank you,' Fullerton replied.

There was definitely something about Clayton Andrews that Fullerton didn't like, but he couldn't quite put his finger on what. Andrews collected the file and motioned to Fullerton to follow him back to the lift. Andrews pressed the button for Reception and without waiting for the doors to open, bid him good day.

Chapter 15

August 5th, 2008. Oxford

Marguerite had invited Michael to visit her in Paris at the beginning of September. Their correspondence was starting to become a regular occurrence, particularly this year and certainly since their trip to Rome. They had corresponded in the past quite infrequently but they had met up on occasion when Evelyn was alive and even made some trips together. Michael and Marguerite had known each other since their student days in Paris and even before Michael met Evelyn, but they had exchanged addresses and remained in reasonably close contact since that time.

Marguerite had not married. Fullerton had never known why this was; it seemed like certain people just never found it possible, found the right person or found themselves in the right situation. She had a tenured position at the Sorbonne and spent the week in Paris at her apartment just up the street from the Place St Michel; very conveniently placed for the courses she lectured in at the University. She apparently had a weekend retreat somewhere in Normandy but Fullerton did not know exactly where.

Fullerton always looked forward to any visits to Paris. It had to be one of his favourite cities and he adored the French 'mode de vie'. There was an almost indiscernible texture to life in France that was all too sadly missing in England and elsewhere.

Fullerton had responded to Marguerite's letter by stating

that he would love to come and would combine the trip to France by trying to trace what had happened to an old friend of his.

The dates were now set and Fullerton focused his attention on the fact that he should really make some train reservations before the week was out.

He had asked Marguerite if she could make some enquiries about Father Pierre Fournier and to let him know when she found out anything. He couldn't tell Marguerite that he already knew that Fournier was still alive, but it was true that he didn't know the current whereabouts of his old friend. He felt confident that Marguerite would be able to track him down.

It had come as quite a surprise when his brother had told him that he knew about Fournier and that the old priest was still alive and in his eighties. It would be nice to meet him again he thought. It seemed to be a year in which he was meeting up with a number of old acquaintances.

As a form of preparation before his trip to France in September, Fullerton decided to do a bit of research into his old friend's writings and its influence in founding this secretive ADF organisation which his brother had mentioned. He felt sure that there would be certain members of the University faculty that could shed some light on this apparent enigma, but he had to be a little vague about why he was interested. He could always invent some remote connection between his theories on world economic reform and the apparent attempt made by earlier academics to justify their particular set of circumstances in times gone by.

Some of Father Fournier's writings had been well publicised in the early fifties and sixties and copies of some of his publications had found their way into the university's library. Fullerton requested the relevant archives and had to wait a couple of days before they had been located and he had been informed.

He went over to the library archive building the following morning.

'I am Professor Fullerton; I believe that you have located some of the documents that I requested.'

He was duly taken to a lower level of the building where a huge number of archived documents were housed. The librarian left him alone to go though two heavy-backed tomes that had quite obviously not seen the light of day for many a year. The tomes dealt mainly with French political reform in the 1950s but he did not take long to come across several articles that had originally come from French newspapers. One rather disturbing article dealt with the notoriety surrounding the apparent excommunication of one Father Pierre Fournier. It had not received that much coverage; no doubt the church authorities saw to that.

He continued his reading and at the end of it had found an extraordinary amount of detail surrounding the life and work of his old friend. He was thankful that some over-zealous researcher had unwittingly saved him a lot of time in his quest for knowledge and background information on Father Fournier. Fullerton never knew, when he had been a student in Paris, just what this honest cleric had been through, starting from his early days as a young local village priest; his struggles during the war and his almost total abandonment by the church during his most creative years.

He replaced the large volumes on their shelf and returned to his own rooms with his detailed notes.

Now he could start to understand why an organisation such as the ADF had grown out of this man's own beliefs. He could also now comprehend why this had struck such a nerve with many people over subsequent decades. The simple philosophy had affected many people who had had similar aspirations to his own brother.

August 5th, 2008. Paris.

The Minister of the Interior left his office at Place Beauvau and was driven the short distance across the city to his brother's residence. Ives Rousseau had not seen his older brother for some months and so this meeting was correctly understood by His Eminence Maurice Cardinal Rousseau to be more than just a polite chat.

'Ives, how nice to see you again after such a long absence,' the archbishop said as he greeted his younger brother.

'Nice to see you too, Maurice,' Ives replied, stooping to kiss the heavy ring on his brother's outstretched hand.

'What important matter has brought you here this morning?' the Cardinal enquired, coming directly to the point.

'Fournier has managed to publish some more of his libellous articles. The French Government will not allow this to continue. I need your assurance that the activities of this wretched old man will be both controlled and suppressed. It can't continue. Do I make myself perfectly clear?'

Maurice Rousseau sat back in his chair and thought for a few moments before providing his brother with a suitable response.

'Ives, I have only last week returned from a visit to Rome. The Cardinal Secretary has already made it abundantly clear that the Holy Father is most upset by these incessant publications. I don't know what more I can do. It has been a thorn in my side for several years now and my health is starting to be affected by all this political pressure.'

'Well then, we both find ourselves in the same predicament,' came the snap reply from the consummate politician.

'I will leave you with that thought, Maurice, but this matter has to be dealt with somehow and preferably sooner rather than later.'

The two brothers stood up, looked at each other, and the meeting was over.

Chapter 16

August 8th, 2008. Oxford, London and Düsseldorf

'Professor Fullerton, we would like you to confirm that you can come up to London tomorrow afternoon for an important meeting; imperative that you attend. Will tell you more when we meet.'

This rather cryptic e-mail from a person named Fletcher in the Foreign Office told Fullerton nothing.

'Am available to suit your schedule, will await your further instructions. What's this all about?' Fullerton replied even more cryptically. He thought it best to reply straight away; something told him that this was going to be important.

'Be at the Radisson SAS Portman Hotel in Portman Square tomorrow afternoon at 1.30. Ask for Mr Fletcher when you arrive.' The response made everything sound so very much like a cloak and dagger operation.

Fullerton took the late morning train from Oxford arriving at Paddington around lunchtime. He grabbed a taxi at the rank and sat back as he was driven through the congested streets. The Radisson was only a short distance away and Fullerton arrived there in good time for his 1.30 pm appointment.

He went straight to the reception desk and inquired if a Mr Fletcher had made himself known to the hotel. He was a little early, but Fletcher had already arrived and left word at the desk that he was expecting a guest.

Fletcher was sitting at the bar with a glass of what

looked like fizzy water in front of him. The bar was effectively deserted at that hour and the two men fixed their gazes on each other in a silent form of mutual recognition.

'Mr Fullerton, is it?' Fletcher said as he got up from his stool.

Fullerton nodded and the two men shook hands.

'Thank you for coming at such short notice. My name is Jason Fletcher, let's sit down over there. Can I get you anything to drink?'

Fullerton shook his head.

'The purpose of this meeting, Mr Fullerton, hmm – can I call you Michael?' Fullerton nodded reluctantly – 'is to acquaint you with some facts concerning your brother.'

Fullerton sat up and stared intently at Fletcher; he hated all this false familiarity.

'You know that I don't see much if anything of my brother,' he said.

'We have known about your trip to Rome and your trip to Hong Kong. In fact, we know quite a lot about you, Michael,' Fletcher replied.

'Who are you and what's with the 'we'?' Fullerton retorted.

'As I have already indicated, I work for the Foreign Office and I can understand that you are undoubtedly wondering what this has to do with you.'

Fullerton stared back at Fletcher.

'Why the Foreign Office?' Fullerton said. 'Yes, why would you people need to meet with me indeed?'

'Suffice it to say that you are of great interest to us,' Fletcher continued. 'We have prepared a short dossier that will, I think, provide you with most of the answers to those questions that I see forming in your head. We do need to maintain the Fullerton involvement.'

Fullerton was completely confused by this last remark.

Fletcher then handed Fullerton a manila folder which contained a number of sheets of paper.

'Please take really good care of this. Read it at your leisure and we will speak again soon. But do remember, your assistance is of great importance to us. You can call me on this number if you have any questions.'

Fletcher handed Fullerton his business card.

'Please keep this meeting to yourself and divulge it to no one; the success of all this depends greatly on your cooperation and involvement. You will understand more, I think, when you have read the contents of the folder. Please destroy all the details when you have fully absorbed the contents.'

The return journey to Oxford seemed to be over in no time at all. Fullerton had read and re-read the information contained in the folder. All the details concerned his brother, his brother's business affairs and recent movements and the urgent need to 'understand the Fullerton involvement'. This last euphemistic phrase left Fullerton completely puzzled.

But what this document was implicitly suggesting and Fletcher's final comments expecting, was for him to cooperate with the Foreign Office and provide any feedback to them about his brother; in effect to spy on James Fullerton. He was reminded of what his brother had said to him that afternoon in April that he had found so vague. It was now slowly starting to make some kind of sense.

My God, was his brother involved in some kind of illegal business activity! Quite apart from all the other genuine corporate responsibilities that had to be dealt with in his position.

None of this matched what he had been told by his brother. It was quite implausible and Fullerton dismissed this thought entirely. But what could James possibly be

90

involved with that would be of such interest to the Foreign Office? A thought occurred to Fullerton that Fletcher had made no mention of the ADF. It required little ingenuity and was quite self-evident that the Foreign Office was trying to find out more about his brother than they could ascertain by other methods. Fullerton placed the pages back in the folder and wondered how on earth he should react.

He needed to contact his brother at once. The train slowed as it entered the station in Oxford and for a while Fullerton could return to his safe, secure existence amongst the dreamy spires.

Once back in his rooms at Magdalen College, he used the private number that his brother had given him and picked up the phone.

'James, is that you?'

'Hello, Michael, how's things?'

'That's what I need to ask you.'

'You mean about my health? Well, the doctors aren't very optimistic at the moment, to put it mildly. They try and put the best spin on things but I don't think that I will have too much longer.'

Michael wondered what to say in reply but listened as his brother spoke again.

'Anyway, tell me why you are calling.'

'I have just returned from a meeting in London with a gentleman by the name of Fletcher. He said that he was with the Foreign Office and seemed to know quite a bit about you.'

There was silence. Then James said, 'Did you say anything to him, Michael?

'No, I remembered what you told me when we last met and so was singularly uninformative. This man Fletcher gave me a whole dossier about you and left me with the distinct impression that I should cooperate with him.'

91

'Good man,' James replied. 'I doubt very much if this Fletcher person is anything to do with the Foreign Office. This smells of the SIS – MI6 to you.'

'He wants me to meet with some of his European colleagues in Germany shortly.'

'Well, they are unlikely to be who they say they are either,' James replied. 'Don't tell them anything about our recent meetings; let them think that we haven't met for over thirty years. That shouldn't be too hard for you. Listen to what they have to say and then call me when you get back, OK?'

'I will play the innocent twin brother and let you know what happens,' Michael said.

Fullerton couldn't help wondering just what he was letting himself in for.

Fletcher's next e-mail did not come as a complete surprise, but Fullerton was itching to know which individuals he was being asked to meet with during the trip to Germany.

Fletcher's communication had simply stated that Fullerton should free up his academic schedule so as to be available to fly to Düsseldorf sometime in the next two or three days if at all possible; to be prepared to stay for at least a full day and that all local arrangements would be taken care of for him.

Fullerton had, as a result of this contact, rescheduled a lot of his university duties and passed a number of key assignments onto other faculty members.

Fullerton dispatched an e-mail back to Fletcher which stated that he had made appropriate flight reservations and would be arriving in Düsseldorf on flight BA 1089 arriving at 11.45 am on Thursday.

August 12th, 2008. Düsseldorf.

The plane from Heathrow arrived at the international airport in Düsseldorf on schedule. The airport was busy with business flights arriving from all over Europe. Fullerton had no idea why he had been asked to travel to Düsseldorf, no doubt this would become clearer as events unfolded.

Fullerton had been told to look out for his contact in the arrivals area. This person would be holding a sign with the name 'Fullerton' printed on it.

The airport terminal building was a very modern construction, all steel and glass which gave the impression of being very futuristic. With only carry-on baggage, Fullerton was soon at the meeting point where passengers merged with the general airport population.

The sign was unmistakable, even when surrounded by a dozen or so other placards all held by people eager to locate their own particular traveller.

The sign itself was held by a very smart-looking young woman in her early thirties. Fullerton went up to her and introduced himself. The young woman in turn introduced herself and stated that she would be driving him to his hotel in the centre of Cologne.

The large, silver coloured Mercedes pulled out of the airport parking facilities and was soon speeding along on the A44. The Mercedes soon glided off the A44 and joined the A3 heading south. The weather was quite warm for that time of year even though it was early summer. The countryside, made up of a mixture of agricultural landscapes and the occasional urban area allowed Fullerton to relax a little and enjoy the scenery. Very little was said after they had exchanged the usual pleasantries about the weather and the recent flight.

Fullerton soon started to see exit signposts announcing that they were approaching the city of Cologne. At exit

'Kreuz Köln Ost' the Mercedes veered off from the main lane and up the incline to the overhead roundabout.

'This is the Deutzer Brücke,' came the remark as the car headed over the Rhine River which flowed majestically through the centre of the new city. 'We are nearly there.'

'We have a room booked in your name at Le Meridien Dom Hotel,' continued the young woman as she placed a call on the car phone. 'Mr Von Beck will be waiting for us outside the hotel and will be eager to meet you.'

Fullerton was struck by this last remark.

After winding down a couple of local streets, the car came to a halt in front of an area obviously known for its shops. Fullerton could see a large open square and the unmistakable side profile of the cathedral.

The young woman got out and walked a few paces to converse with a middle-aged man wearing a dark grey suit. She returned to the car and beckoned Fullerton to get out.

'Welcome to Cologne Mr Fullerton, I do hope that you had a comfortable journey from London,' Von Beck said as the two men shook hands. 'Do follow me; your luggage will be looked after.'

A further few words in German with Von Beck and the young woman returned to the Mercedes and pulled away

'I think that we will have some interesting things to discuss with you, Mr Fullerton. A colleague of mine is waiting for us in the hotel so shall we continue in this direction?'

Le Meridien Dom Hotel was situated adjacent to the cathedral; it was an impressive five-storey building with some quite elaborate stone features. Fullerton followed Von Beck into the hotel foyer where they were greeted by a second, slightly younger man, also wearing what seemed to Fullerton like the obligatory grey suit.

'Please meet my associate, Mr Benoit,' Von Beck said.

Fullerton shook hands and the three men then moved to a small seating area to one side of the foyer.

'I suggest that you check into your room and make yourself comfortable. Shall we meet here in the foyer in twenty minutes?' Von Beck asked, handing Fullerton his room key.

Fullerton took the lift to the third floor and found his room. After a cursory inspection of the facilities, he returned to the foyer of the hotel to find his two acquaintances in conversation by the main entrance.

'Let's go into the bar,' Von Beck said. 'We can have a brief conversation there to start with and then order some lunch.'

'Have you been to Cologne before, Mr Fullerton?' asked Von Beck.

'No, this is one city that I haven't visited before. I hope that I can see something of it before I leave,' Fullerton answered politely.

'I think that I should start by first explaining why you have been asked to come all this way and the reasons why we are here to meet you,' Von Beck continued.

'As we will hopefully be seeing a lot of each other, maybe we should get on first name terms; I am Johannes, he is Jean-Claude and we both know who you are. We are both working for the German Foreign Ministry. Your meeting with Mr Jason Fletcher last week in London will have informed you of our involvement and the reasons why we wished to meet you.'

'Actually, I was told very little at all by Mr Fletcher, but I am sure that you will explain everything,' Fullerton answered rather stiffly. He was reminded of his brother's remarks and that he should play along with things.

'We are currently working very closely with the British Foreign Office and we are going to need your invaluable assistance.'

'Yes, Mr Fletcher did briefly mention the involvement

of the German government but he didn't elaborate,' Fullerton commented.

'Your brother', Von Beck began again, 'has connections with many business organisations both in Europe and overseas. He is a very wealthy individual with much influence.'

Fullerton sat silently and listened.

'We understand that you do not see much of your brother.'

Again Fullerton did not volunteer an answer.

'He lives in Geneva but travels quite extensively around Europe, the United States and the Far East,' Von Beck continued with what was becoming a monologue.

'We have reason to believe that your brother is using his business contacts to conceal some seriously illegal activities.'

Fullerton listened intently to every word that was being spoken and wondered just how far this conversation was going to go and what would be expected of him.

'We cannot divulge the specifics of our investigations, but suffice it to say that anything which you can say will be most helpful to us. We have some questions to put to you and then we will be seeking your complete cooperation.'

This time it was the turn of Benoit to speak. Placing another official-looking dossier on the table in front of Fullerton, he opened it and took out some photographs.

'We would like you to look at these photographs and tell us if you recognise anything or anyone.'

Fullerton looked at the photographs but did not notice anything familiar.

'Gentlemen, I am afraid that you have brought me here on an incorrect premise. I have had no involvement or indeed contact with my brother for over thirty years. We never did see eye to eye on anything. All I know of my brother's business activities can be read in the newspapers.'

Fullerton found that he was starting to enjoy himself.

He knew that these individuals from the German government, if that was who they were, needed him to assist them in some tangible way, but as yet he could not put his finger on the precise role that they obviously had planned out for him.

Von Beck tried a different approach.

'Mr Fullerton ... Michael,' he commenced with a forced smile. Fullerton always distrusted people who smiled too much.

'Your brother could be in very serious trouble with the authorities and we would hope that you will see the expediency of providing us with as much assistance as possible.'

'I will, of course, be only too happy to help you in your enquiries,' Fullerton said. 'Which particular department did you say you both work for in the Foreign Ministry?'

This forward approach caught the two men a little off guard, but Von Beck maintained the pretence by informing Fullerton that they were part of an inter-governmental task force into corporate corruption. Fullerton realised that this all too convenient an answer would be unverifiable.

'We would like you to make contact with your brother; we will leave it up to you as to the reasons for the contact. Once you have done that and established a new relationship with him, we will contact you again with further instructions,' Benoit said.

'Won't my brother be suspicious of this sudden contact out of the blue?'

'I'm sure, Michael, that you are capable of acting the part.'

Fullerton thought of what their reaction would have been if they only knew that he was already acting the part.

'Right now, however, we have some questions that we

would like you to answer to the best of your ability,' Benoit said, turning to some hand-written notes.

Fullerton picked up on the fact that Benoit was now taking the lead in the questioning.

'You have told us that you haven't seen your brother for over thirty years. Did I hear you correctly?' Benoit continued.

'Yes, that is correct,' Fullerton answered.

We have, however, learned that both you and your brother attended the same conference in Hong Kong recently.'

'Yes, I did hear that my brother was supposedly in Hong Kong but our paths never crossed. I was quite busy with my meetings and the two speeches I gave took quite a bit of final re-working.'

Fullerton replied somewhat flippantly, but immediately decided that he should continue by using a more serious tone of voice. He did not want these two 'gentlemen' to benefit from a single word that he said.

'I have no idea what my brother's itinerary was and only have hearsay evidence that we were even there at the same time.'

Fullerton also comprehended the fact that they appeared to know nothing about the April meeting in London.

The lunch order arrived at their table and so the conversation turned to topics such as the local customs in that part of Germany and the places that Fullerton should visit if they had time later in the day.

'We would like to ask you about the people you both knew in your teens,' Benoit continued again.

'That is very easy to answer,' Fullerton retorted. 'We went to different universities after leaving school, had no contact at all during that period and therefore had no friends in common.'

'Did you involve yourself in any political organisations when you were at University?' Benoit questioned.

Now Fullerton could see why he had been brought over

to Germany. This whole process of contact and discussion by Fletcher and now, by these two, was in order to find out anything they could about James's political leanings through him.

'I involved myself in some sports but had no interest in politics,' Fullerton answered. 'I really do think that this whole line of questioning is leading us nowhere, gentlemen. I do not know why you have such an interest in my brother and even less knowledge as to how you think I can be of any help to you. Maybe you should explain now exactly what it is that you want to find out.'

Von Beck looked across at Benoit and seemed to receive a slight nod in return.

'All right, Mr Fullerton, I am going to come to the point. Did you know that your brother is allegedly involved in an organisation known as the ADF?'

Here we had it, Fullerton thought to himself. This is what this whole exercise had been all about. He felt glad now that he had met his brother and knew exactly why he was being asked this question.

'I have no idea what you are talking about,' Fullerton answered incredulously.

The acting was good because both Von Beck and Benoit seemed to believe Fullerton's honest reaction.

'We mentioned earlier', Von Beck continued, 'that we would like you to make contact with your brother again. This organisation that we have just spoken about is involved in some very disturbing activities and your brother is allegedly quite closely involved.'

Benoit added, 'We will continue to be in contact with you and would like to think that you understand the seriousness of this situation.'

'I suggest that we show Mr Fullerton something of this wonderful city now,' Von Beck said. He picked up his mobile phone and placed a call.

'Let's go outside, the car will be brought round in a few minutes.'

Chapter 17

August 13th, 2008. Cologne and Geneva.

Fullerton had already informed his hosts in Cologne that he would be flying back to London via Paris the following morning. He knew that they knew he was friendly with a certain lady by the name of Marguerite De Saulx and so they would not have found this itinerary out of the ordinary.

Fullerton returned to his room in the hotel and contemplated his next move. He decided to go for a short walk and use his mobile phone to call Geneva.

'James Fullerton, please. This is his brother calling.'

'I'm sorry,' came the reply 'but Mr Fullerton is in an important meeting in Milan and can't be reached until later this evening.'

Fullerton decided that he had to play the part of the innocent professor a little while longer until he could reach his brother and discuss what he should do next.

After an interesting tour of the city, courtesy of the German government or whoever it was that paid Von Beck's expenses, and a quite enjoyable evening in a couple of *bierkellers* in the old part of the city, Fullerton and his two hosts returned to the hotel. They did not plan to meet in the morning as Fullerton's flight was an early one. He was thankful for this as it saved him from any further show of pretence.

His brother's voice answered when he called the second time and was most interested to learn of the discussions.

'You had better book a flight to Geneva when you get to the airport in the morning; things are starting to get too involved; besides, I have a plan which will need some careful explanation.'

Fullerton was up early and saw nothing of his two 'friends' as he climbed into a taxi and headed out to the airport. The driver took a different route out of the city from the one that he had been brought in on. The roads were not that busy at that early hour but the driver seemed to know what he was doing and so Fullerton didn't make any conversation. The airport signs then appeared on the autobahn and Fullerton was soon standing inside the departures hall.

'I need to change my return flight from London to Geneva,' Fullerton instructed the Lufthansa employee.

'There is a flight leaving in thirty-five minutes.'

'That'll do fine.'

He waited whilst the various changes were made, collected his new boarding pass and barely had time to text his brother with his flight details before the flight was called and he was on the plane.

August 13th, 2008. Geneva.

James's chauffeur-driven car was waiting for him when he arrived at the airport in Geneva.

'Mr Fullerton is waiting for you at the Crowne Plaza Hotel,' the driver informed him. 'It's not very far.'

The journey was only a few minutes; the car swung onto the Route François-Peyrot and Fullerton was dropped off at the entrance.

James was waiting in the hotel foyer as Michael arrived.

'Michael, thanks for coming to Geneva.'

Michael noticed that his brother was looking considerably

102

more worn out than he remembered from London in April. It was James's eyes that particularly caught Michael's attention. They always say that one can see into a man's soul through his eyes.

The two brothers walked slowly up the stairs and over to one of the small conference rooms just off the mezzanine level.

'I thought that this would do for what we have to discuss,' James explained. Michael could not take his eyes off his brother; he seemed to have aged ten years since they met last. His eyes had a strange yellow pallor which Michael all to clearly recognised as the outward sign of his brother's progressing cancer.

'As you can see, Michael, I am not doing so well. I'm still keeping active but each day seems harder than the last. There is so much more that I need to do and I'm afraid that I will not be there to accomplish it. Now, tell me about your meetings in London and Cologne.'

Michael faithfully related all the events of the last few days and his discussions with Fletcher, Von Beck and Benoit. He left nothing out and gave his brother a complete account of every little detail. He didn't know what his brother was involved in and didn't really care. This was his brother, his twin, and even though they had not seen much of each other over the years, blood was most certainly thicker than water. He found himself, in that instant, feeling an intense mixture of sadness and love for a person who he really knew nothing about.

James listened to what Michael had to relate and then with a sigh, leaned back in his chair.

'This is all to do with the Intelligence Agencies; they are trying to infiltrate the ADF. You remember me telling you about the ADF when we met in London? Well they will stop at nothing to besmirch the good name of the ADF and are fully behind the false insinuations that the

103

ADF is a front for extremist activities that supposedly have been responsible for these recent assassinations. I am sure that none of my associates within this Agency have anything at all to do with these extremist activities. It is crucial that we are not discredited because the work we do is just too important.'

James then paused and looked at his brother. It was a look that would remain with Michael for the rest of his life. It was as if his brother had managed to erase all those intervening years and the two brothers were teenagers again, sharing all their thoughts and dreams.

'Michael, I want you to take my place. Not just carry on where I have left off, but become me. I want you to become James Fullerton. I only have a few more weeks to live and there is important work still to be completed; besides someone has to find the bastards that have poisoned me!'

Michael looked at his brother and for the first time thought he saw the deep humanity that existed underneath the cold ruthless exterior of what he and everyone else thought that James had become.

'You don't know what you are asking,' Michael gasped. 'I cannot become you; we are different people, you and I.'

'Oh, I don't think that we are so different, Michael. You talk about changing the world in your profound academic lectures; you write articles about all the injustice and undemocratic policies of politicians and governments. Well, I am exactly the same except that I am actually doing something about it. I have been lucky in my life inasmuch as I can use my resources, contacts and influence. But this would all be rendered useless and even destructive if it wasn't focused on the right targets. Father Fournier tried in his own small way to change the system that he knew and experienced. Now it is up to us, yes, us to continue with that good work and not allow those who would wish to see our influence snuffed out or discredited to be victorious.'

'If I do become you, then what happens to me? Michael said, beginning to grasp some of the potential logistical nightmares.

'You will have to "die", Michael. I am going to die before much longer; you take my place and I am buried in England as Michael Fullerton.'

'What about my children?' Michael said as he walked over to the table, clasped a glass in his left hand and poured himself a very large whisky. 'That is an appalling thought! I couldn't contemplate putting them through the agony of losing their father. My God, they have only just got over losing their mother! It just can't be done, James! There is nothing that you can say or do to convince me otherwise.'

James paused in thought for a moment.

'Think of all the good you could do; think of how you could continue with what I have been working so hard to achieve. Someone has poisoned me, Michael. I don't know when or even how. The specialists are still trying to calculate these parameters. Their data needs a lot of analysis yet before they can come up with a suitably accurate answer.'

Michael looked at his brother and the look of complete helplessness in his face. All that his brother had achieved, all the wealth that had been accumulated and, most of all, the dedication, were all going to end with his untimely death.

'Michael, I have something further to tell you. All these assassinations that have occurred in recent months. Well, they have been happening as a direct result of knowledge obtained solely from within the ADF organisation. I have been investigating what started out as just coincidences between the time and place of the assassinations and the activity of certain ADF members. I think that I have discovered a direct relationship between the two but haven't yet come up with the final proof of guilt. Some individuals have decided that I have come too close to the truth for their own liking. It is very likely that they are the ones that have arranged to have me poisoned. Michael, you owe it to your brother to bring these bastards to justice and eliminate this extremism. Will you not take up where I have left off for my sake?'

'I need some fresh air, James. I will be back in a short while,' Michael said as he looked at his brother once more.

The air was warm and the slight breeze made the vegetation sway ever so slightly. The sky was clear and he could just see the outlines of the lake in the far distance. The hotel was a popular location for businessmen and there were quite a few taxis coming and going which created a renewed sense of reality.

Michael Fullerton walked across the road to the landscaped gardens opposite and sat down on one of the stone seats. He was alone in the garden and watched the birds flying down onto the grass and then, after a few pecks at some insect or other, up and away again. He realised that he needed time to reach a decision of this magnitude and would not provide his brother with an answer until he had given himself that time.

He went back into the hotel to give his brother his decision.

'James, I cannot give you the answer you want right now; I have to give this whole situation some considerable thought. There is a lot that would need to be considered, not to mention how we would even get away with the whole plan!'

'That's OK, Michael,' James replied. 'I've given you an

awful lot to think about. Take your time, but not too much. I think that I may be on borrowed time already.'

The two brothers looked at each other and they knew that each needed some time to come to terms with the reality of the situation.

'I promise that I will be in touch with you very soon. This has all come as quite a shock,' Michael said.

James's car was waiting to take Michael back to the airport and a flight back home to England.

Michael looked at his brother as they shook hands and parted. This memory was to haunt Michael for a long time to come.

Chapter 18

August 14th, 2008. Oxford.

Fullerton took the train back from London to Oxford and then by bus to Witney. He had informed his housekeeper that he would be arriving back sometime in the late afternoon. He was always glad to get home and it had been a while since he was last there owing to his various commitments in Oxford and elsewhere.

The bus dropped him off in the centre of the town and it was only a walk of a few hundred yards to his neat little barn conversion just beyond the parish church.

He let himself in to the house and disposed of all his travelling items before entering his study to sort through the accumulation of post that had been carefully collected and placed on his desk.

The effect of the discussions that had taken place in Cologne and the latest meeting with his brother in Geneva and before that in London, was now starting to sink in. He found himself looking at his used airline boarding passes to convince himself that he had actually been in Germany and Switzerland at all.

This whole situation was going to take some very serious thought. The ramifications of what had been proposed were of such a magnitude and would impact on so many people that he hardly knew where to begin in digesting the situation in which he now found himself.

All that he held dear would be swept away and it would be as if none of it had ever existed. What made his situation far, far worse was the dawning realisation that nothing could be said and no one told either about his discussions or the permanent nature of the decision he had to make. He had been given a few weeks, possibly less, to arrive at his decision and once made, he knew that there would be no going back. I need a drink he thought to himself. The local pub, The Duke, was one of those typical 'olde worlde' pubs that were found in rural villages, particularly in this part of Oxfordshire. It had a history going back to the fifteenth century but had gained its name in the early eighteenth century following the various military successes of the Duke of Marlborough whose estate at Blenheim, located at nearby Blandford, must have been the talk of the country at the time.

Fullerton walked back into the village and into The Duke. He was greeted by the landlord who saw enough of him to be on terms of passing acquaintance.

'Professor Fullerton isn't it? Nice to see you again,' the landlord remarked. 'What will it be?'

Fullerton asked for a large glass of French red wine and, having paid for it, decided to remain on a stool at the counter.

'How's the university life treating you these days, still knocking 'em dead are we?' the landlord quipped, trying to make some light conversation. Fullerton replied with an equally trivial response and with that, the landlord left him alone to attend to some other customers in the adjoining room at the far end of the bar.

There was a well-stocked fire in the large medieval hearth over against the end wall of the room and Fullerton collected his drink and moved over closer to the brightness and warmth that it was giving off.

His mind was so full of conflicting thoughts and confused ideas that he hardly knew where to begin to sort out the details.

'Hello, Michael, we don't often see you in here.'
Fullerton turned round to see two of his former university
colleagues sitting over by the window.
'I haven't come in that much at all since Evelyn died.
How's retirement suiting you two?'
'We miss the college and all that intellectual stimulation,'
came the tongue in cheek reply.
'A couple of pints and a good chat and we find that
we have sorted out all the worries of the world.'
'You know, I envy you two,' Fullerton remarked. 'You
have your wives to go home to and nothing to disturb
your otherwise ordered retirement.'
'How are the powers that be treating you these days,
Michael? No more stupid, politically correct reprimands?'
'No, I have had to toe the party line, at least for the
present,' Fullerton replied. 'I have other matters that need
some serious thought right now.'
'That sounds ominous. Do tell.'
'How does one measure loyalty,' Fullerton stated. 'I
mean true loyalty.'
'Depends on the context within which that loyalty is
set and has to be measured, surely,' came the astute
response.
'OK, let me try and give you both a clear example of
what I am trying to rationalise.'
'If someone close to you asked you to perform him or
her a big favour and in agreeing to the request you had
to sacrifice other loyalties which you also held very dear,
how would you know what was the right choice to make?'
The three friends sat in silence for a few moments
before one of them spoke.
'I think that the answer to this difficult moral dilemma
is quite a simple one. I don't know the exact details of
the problem that you are wrestling with Michael and don't
need to know really. At the end of the day, the decision

that you make will just feel 'right'. It won't have a rational justification; that's the way we humans respond sometimes.'

Fullerton thought about what his friends had just said and realised that he was being given good advice. When the time came to make the decision and let his brother know, he knew what his answer would have to be.

Chapter 19

September 12th, 2008. Paris.

Fullerton had left his rooms at Magdalen promptly in order to catch the 6.28 am train to St Pancras. There was something about train journeys that appealed to him. Maybe it was the act of sitting back and watching the changing scenery. He wasted no time changing trains and once he had found his seat on the Eurostar he felt that his trip had really begun.

The Kent countryside flew by and in no time at all the train entered the tunnel under the English Channel. Reappearing a matter of minutes later, the rolling landscape of northern France greeted his eyes.

After a journey of only a little over four hours, the Eurostar train pulled into the Gare du Nord just about on schedule.

Fullerton had planned to stay for two nights. This period of time over a weekend, was about as long as he could reasonably expect his colleagues to take over his lectures and cover his other college responsibilities.

Exiting the Gare du Nord, Fullerton climbed into a waiting taxi.

'*Notre Dame, s'il vous plaît.*'

He chose to be dropped off in front of the Notre Dame cathedral. From here it would be a nice walk to his lunch appointment.

He stood and admired the massive façade and twin towers of the huge cathedral. Checking his watch which he had made sure to adjust on the train, he realised that he still had about forty minutes to spare. On an impulse, Fullerton joined the line of jostling tourists that slowly shuffled towards the entrance of the cathedral. He had been to Paris on several occasions since he was here as a student but had not been inside this magnificent edifice for a long time. He stood and marvelled at the medieval grandeur of the intricate stonework and the skill that the medieval craftsmen must have possessed in order to construct such an imposing structure. The whole building served one single purpose: to convince the faithful of the supreme authority of the Church and to remind them that it alone held the power to determine the ultimate fate of the Christian believer.

In this ecclesiastical setting, Fullerton wondered what his afternoon meeting with his old friend Father Fournier would be like. Father Fournier was in his eighties now and Fullerton hoped that he would find his old friend in both good health, good spirits and able to converse about the things that mattered to both of them.

He lit a candle and placed it amongst the hundreds of already burning flames and offered up a silent prayer for his brother of whom he had heard little or nothing for several weeks now.

He detected the faint strains of a piece of music by Gabriel Fauré. Someone somewhere was practising quietly on the organ in preparation for some service or recital. It added to the ambience of his visit. The incessant flashes from innumerable cameras however seemed to spoil his enjoyment of this magnificent medieval edifice. Maybe the intrusion of twentieth-century technology was a kind of invasion of the cathedral's privacy that shouldn't have been allowed. The modern church had however to balance the necessities of income against its equal need for religious purity.

113

He completed his loop round this oasis of calm and left the cathedral after an all too short visit and almost had to fight his way back across the over-crowded square and onto the Petit Pont. From the bridge, he paused and gazed down at the sparkling water and the ubiquitous tourists in one of the Bateaux-Mouches. Crossing the Quai Saint-Michel at the lights, he continued straight on before turning right into the Rue de la Huchette. The aroma hit him within a few paces. This was the Latin Quarter with all its different food smells.

He had arranged to meet Marguerite for lunch at a certain restaurant on the Rue de la Harpe. He strolled along the narrow streets and arrived outside the restaurant just as she approached from the opposite direction. She saw him and smiled.

'That was excellent timing,' Marguerite said as she greeted Fullerton with a kiss on both cheeks.

'I arrived early and so I have just had a look round the cathedral,' Fullerton replied. 'That place never ceases to amaze me.'

Marguerite looked back at Fullerton and said:

'I hope that you will like this place.'

They entered the restaurant; Marguerite spoke to the waiter who obviously knew her quite well. He showed them to a nice table in a delightful little outside courtyard at the rear of the establishment. It contained several tables and there were two small trees planted in enormous wooden wine barrel halves that had been cut for the purpose. They added to the charm and also provided some respite from the sun which shone down onto the stone flags of the courtyard from between the assortment of roofs of the adjacent, tightly packed buildings.

'Not too many people know about this courtyard, I asked for a table out here especially for you. It's really lovely in the summer, but today is also fine.'

'This is an excellent place to meet,' Fullerton remarked. 'It can't be too far from the University from here, can it?'

'No, it is only about a five minute walk through the back streets. I come here a lot with my friends.'

'It doesn't feel that long since we were in Rome together,' Fullerton said. 'Although much seems to have happened in between times.'

'Have you seen anything more of your brother since April?' Marguerite enquired.

'Not really,' Fullerton replied, not wishing to be drawn on that particular subject.

Marguerite picked up on Fullerton's apparent reticence to talk about his brother and so moved the conversation onto safer ground.

'Father Fournier, whom we shall visit this afternoon, is living now in a retirement home just outside the city. It didn't take me too long to track him down. I haven't contacted the home or made any enquiries so we will just have to take it as we find it when we arrive.'

'I thought that we could drive out there after lunch if you would like to do so today. We can then spend the weekend doing other things before you have to travel back on Sunday.'

Fullerton always found Marguerite to be both efficient and businesslike. They were attributes that he found somehow appealing.

'Yes, that sounds just fine to me,' Fullerton replied. 'Do you have a car?'

'No,' Marguerite replied. 'I don't need one in Paris. We can hire a taxi; it isn't all that far to go and a taxi will be the most convenient way for us to get to Crecy.'

'What have you managed to find out?'

'I'll tell you on the way out to Crecy,' Marguerite replied. They enjoyed each other's company for about an hour

115

or so before Marguerite noticed the time and thought that they should perhaps think about making the journey to Crecy.

It was easy enough to find a taxi and Marguerite used her feminine charms to convince the driver that it would be worth his while to drive them both out to Crecy and wait while they met with an old friend.

'You will find the journey to Crecy quite interesting in itself, Michael; it follows the river for a bit before we head east and out of the city.'

The taxi joined the Autoroute de l'Est and took them the remaining forty or so kilometres to the small community of Crecy La Chapelle.

The small Abbaye was not difficult to find, being centrally located.

'*Merci beaucoup.* We will be here for about an hour,' Marguerite informed the driver.

'*De rien,*' came the response and the driver said that he would find something to occupy his time and provided Marguerite with his mobile number. It was agreed that Marguerite would call him when she was ready for him to pick them both up.

They walked down the cobbled side street following a high stone wall until they came to what appeared to be the main entrance to the Abbaye. Fullerton rang the bell at the side of the huge wrought iron gates and waited for somebody to appear. A nun eventually arrived.

'We are old friends of Father Fournier and would very much like to meet with him if it is at all possible,' Marguerite asked.

The Sister ushered them in to the Abbaye grounds closing the heavy wrought-iron gate behind them. They followed her as she walked along the gravelled path-way. Fullerton was struck by the apparent dilapidated state of the buildings which stood in stark contrast to the

116

delightfully maintained lawns and planted borders; they still held a lovely show of colour even for September.

'*S'il vous plaît, attendez ici*,' the nun said as they entered the main entrance hall.

A couple of elderly priests passed them as they waited and nodded their silent welcome.

'So this is where you end up when the church has finished with you', Fullerton remarked softly.

Marguerite gave him a disapproving scowl with her eyes.

Another nun now appeared.

'*S'il vous plaît, venez avec moi!*'

They followed her down the dingy corridor and into a smaller communal sitting area where they were asked to make themselves comfortable. Fullerton was reminded of an ornately tiled Victorian hospital ward. In a way, this is what this place in effect was, he thought.

Michael and Marguerite sat down and surveyed the other occupants of the room as they waited. There were three other people, all quite obviously old, retired priests who relied totally on the church for their care and sustenance. Not much of a life after all that obedience to an all-powerful master, Fullerton thought to himself.

The swing doors at the far end of the room opened as a wheelchair was pushed awkwardly through by one of the younger nuns. Father Fournier looked up as he approached and showed a faint smile as he seemed to recognise his visitors.

Fournier had a half-folded copy of *Le Monde* on his lap. Fullerton could make out a front page report which was still giving coverage to the recent death of Cardinal Maurice Rousseau, Archbishop of Paris.

'James, it is really nice to see you again,' Fournier said quietly.

Fullerton looked at the old priest and replied:

'I'm Michael, James's brother. Don't you remember me

from my student days in Paris? You should also remember Marguerite; she used to come and listen to your lectures as well.'

Father Fournier looked back at his two visitors for a moment before replying.

'*Michael* Fullerton! Of course! You look so much like your brother. Now I remember you. It was a long time ago but I do remember the long afternoons and sometimes evenings we spent talking about the world and its many fascinations. I don't see many of my friends any more; most of them have died. This is the price you pay for getting as old as I am, I'm afraid.'

'How is James?' Fournier continued. 'He has been a good friend to me over recent years. I owe him a lot for his kindness and his generosity.'

This remark surprised Fullerton.

'James was fine when I saw him last,' he said, not wishing to upset the old man with the true picture, or indeed, to let Marguerite into his secret.

Fournier spoke again.

'Life seems so very complicated these days. Everything was so simple when I was younger. It is reassuring to know that truth still remains the one constant measure of human existence. It is a pity that this church to which I still think I belong, cannot break free from its unchangeable dogma and embrace a doctrine that sets the will and freedom of man at its centre.'

Fullerton felt that he was listening to one of Father Fournier's lectures again all those years ago. The quiet calm of this old man's thoughts still held an unmistakable force that had caused so much embarrassment and created such a challenge for the Catholic Church over the years. He could see how this man's own philosophy and personal conviction had been readily adopted by so many learned individuals and come to form the world-wide organisation known simply as the ADF. The ADF had of course outgrown these early ideals, but Fullerton could not take his eyes off his old friend as he continued to speak. 'The church is very kind to me and has provided me with somewhere to live out my latter years. I am really quite well looked after. I do not want for anything and fare a great deal better than some of those who are staying here.'

What Fullerton didn't know at this precise moment was that his brother was contributing a significant amount to the local parish and indeed diocese, in exchange for the total wellbeing, acceptance and upkeep of his own dear friend and ADF founder.

Marguerite asked Fournier a question.

'Pierre, would you do what you have done all over again if you had your life to live afresh?'

The old priest smiled, almost laughed in fact, and looked back at this young woman.

'I wouldn't change one action or one word, my dear,' he replied. 'My only regret is that I was not able to convince enough people of the truth of my convictions. I still write some articles for the newspapers, but I don't think that they are ever published these days. I am not one of this church's most favoured members. Indeed, officially I am not even a member; those two saw to that.'

Fullerton wondered who Fournier meant by 'those two' but assumed that he must be talking about the staff at the Abbaye.

'I will continue to write what I can whilst I am still able,' Fournier continued. 'They can't stop me from doing that. They know that I still have important friends, people of influence. People like your brother, Michael. Eventually, people will see the truth for themselves.'

One of the older nuns approached at that moment and politely suggested that Father Fournier should not overdo things and become too tired.

Fullerton detected a degree of hidden authority in her voice; he didn't know why he had that sensation, but it troubled him.

'We will not stay too much longer, Sister,' Marguerite replied.

Fullerton cast a knowing glance in Marguerite's direction.

'Pierre, it has really been wonderful to see you again after all these years. Is there anything that I can do for you; is there anything that you need?'

Fournier thought for a moment.

'Your brother is more than kind in that respect. I think that I must owe him an awful lot. Please thank him from me when you see him.'

'I will tell James that we have had this discussion and that you are looking extremely well,' Fullerton replied.

'Tell James to be careful won't you,' Fournier added.

Fullerton was quite unnerved by this last remark, but didn't feel like provoking a more detailed response. They had overstayed their welcome and it was time to leave.

'Good-bye Pierre, we hope to see you again sometime soon,' Marguerite said.

They both stood up.

The same nun came back and adjusted Fournier's blanket in his chair before wheeling the old priest back the way he had come. Fullerton and Marguerite watched him go until he was out of sight.

They walked back through the Abbaye and out into the late afternoon sunshine. Marguerite phoned their ever patient taxi driver who soon appeared and drove them back into the city.

'They are watching his every move, you know. I bet that our visit is reported to their superiors without delay,' Fullerton said to Marguerite as they continued on their return trip. 'I wonder if we will ever see Pierre again?'

Marguerite remained silent. She didn't want to provide an answer.

The next two days were spent in a very leisurely fashion with lots of conversation, nice meals and each one enjoying the other's company.

The time for Fullerton's return journey back to England and Oxford came all too quickly that Sunday afternoon.

He and Marguerite definitely decided that this was something that they should both do on a far more regular basis.

Marguerite decided to come and see Fullerton off at the train station.

'I am worried about Pierre,' Fullerton said. 'There is something going on that we don't know about.'

'I will see what I can find out about the Abbaye and let you know if anything comes up,' Marguerite replied reassuringly. She didn't tell Fullerton but she shared his suspicions but couldn't explain the reasoning.

'I had better get on the train,' Fullerton said, trying not to be too abrupt. He hated goodbyes and always felt uncomfortable at these moments.

'Let's stay in touch, Marguerite,' he added.

'Yes, I would like that,' she answered.

'This visit has been wonderful. We will do it again and soon. Bye!'

Marguerite watched as Fullerton turned his back and walked briskly away down the platform. She watched him go until she could see him enter the train. He hadn't turned round.

Chapter 20

October 5th, 2008. Oxford and Geneva.

James Fullerton died at his home just outside Geneva at 11.20 pm on the evening of Sunday, October 5th. Those present were his private physician and two close confidants; not even Harry Matthews, his 'trusted' assistant, was involved.

At 1.00 am early the following morning Michael Fullerton was woken up by loud knocks on his front door. The sound echoed in the stillness of the countryside.

Fullerton, now fully awake, went down the stairs and opened his front door.

Two men were standing there wearing dark overcoats.

'Professor Fullerton?' the first man asked.

'Yes, I am Professor Fullerton. What on earth do you want at this time of night?'

'We work for your brother. We have been sent to escort you to Geneva. Please get ready as soon as you can.'

Twenty minutes later Michael Fullerton found himself on James's private jet that had arrived at the Oxford municipal airport only an hour or so earlier. He had been collected from his home in Witney by the two unnamed men and driven directly to the airport and the waiting plane.

Fullerton needed no one to tell him what must have happened and why his presence was essential. He could sense the wheels being put in motion.

Two hours later, the plane landed at Geneva International

airport and Fullerton was fast-tracked through the VIP arrivals section and out into a waiting limousine. Forty minutes further elapsed before Fullerton found himself being driven through a large pair of wrought-iron gates to a large country estate. The gates seemed to know when to open as the limousine approached. Everything seemed so well planned and coordinated.

Fullerton could only make out the silhouettes and shapes of the scenery on the drive from the airport through the darkened glass of the car windows, but he guessed that they must be somewhere along the north side of the lake. He occasionally caught sight of water on his right-hand side between the vegetation and the screening of other walled properties.

The car continued slowly now along a winding paved driveway which was lined by a regimented row of tall trees on either side. Beyond the trees Fullerton could just make out the silhouettes of further forested areas which obviously provided a convenient level of privacy to the property from the main highway.

Lights appeared and the driveway broadened out in front of a very extensive two story white-painted mansion. There were flowerbeds and extensive shrubberies and over to the right of the mansion, a second smaller building which Fullerton recognised as a large multi-car garage.

The car came to a halt and Fullerton climbed out and could now see that the property was indeed a very impressive and expansive structure. He was met at the front door of the building by yet another man that he did not know. Behind him were the two men who had accompanied him all the way from Oxford.

'Michael, welcome to *Bellerive*. My name is Francesco Baldini. Please come in. I'm sorry about the rush to bring you over here, but time is very much of the essence,' he said as he walked back inside.

Fullerton said nothing as he entered through the front doors of his brother's mansion. His eyes took in the opulent surroundings of the interior hallway as he was ushered into one of the main living rooms.

'Please take a seat,' Baldini continued as he also sat down. The other two men conveniently disappeared and the two of them were alone.

Fullerton studied him. He was of slim build, tall, probably in his early sixties with thinning white hair and an expensive taste in suits. Fullerton detected an Italian accent.

'First of all, please call me Francesco; I have been a very close friend and confidant of your brother's for many years.' He coughed a little to clear his throat. 'It is with deep regret that I have to inform you that your brother, James died late last night. This moment, as you know, has been expected for some time. Death always seems to come partly as a surprise when it does actually happen. You already know what must now happen. Your brother has discussed this all with you I understand. What we need to do now is to put the plan into action and much has already been done in that regard.'

Baldini turned to glance at some notes that lay on the table beside him before continuing.

'As it is now 5.00 am, I suggest that we all get a few hours' sleep. We have a lot of things to deal with in the morning. I will show you to your room.'

Fullerton ascended the winding staircase and was shown into one of the numerous guest bedrooms.

'You should find all you need. Goodnight.'

'Goodnight,' Fullerton replied. His hastily packed suitcase was already on his bed. Nothing to do now except to do as he was told. For now, he was left alone with his thoughts.

The morning could not come too quickly for Fullerton; he slept intermittently as all kinds of thoughts flooded through his head. The event that he most regretted had finally arrived and he knew that he would need all his energy and nerve in the following days.

He showered and dressed and descended to the main living room where he had met the Italian the night before. He somehow didn't feel at all tired; it must be the adrenaline, he thought.

Baldini was already sitting at the large desk in the enormous bay window and had quite a number of papers spread out in front of him.

'Good Morning, Michael, or should I say James from now on; please help yourself to some coffee and croissants; it's all over there on the buffet table.'

Fullerton decided that some strong black coffee would indeed be most welcome.

'First of all, 'James', you need to understand what is happening right now. Your brother passed away at 11.20 pm last night. He was quite comfortable and in no pain, the doctor saw to that. I am Francesco Baldini and also a member of the ADF. I think that should explain enough about why I am here right now.'

'Can I see my brother?' Fullerton asked.

'Yes, of course, but please let me let continue for the moment.'

Baldini continued 'The whole success of this exchange is based on our ability to execute as seamless an exchange as possible. As you know, your brother was an extremely important and influential man. We must all cooperate as a team to ensure that this transfer of identity is total, unnoticed and complete.'

'Your brother left an envelope for you in my keeping before he died. I give it to you now. Please sit down, open it and read it.'

Fullerton took the white envelope, placed his coffee cup on the side table and sat down on the sofa.

The envelope just had one word written on the outside: 'Michael'. He opened the envelope and took out the single folded piece of writing paper; he recognised James's handwriting even though it was a little uneven, and started to read.

Dear Michael,
If you are reading this note, then I am already dead. It will have been handed to you by one of my closest friends, Francesco Baldini. You can trust him as you could and did trust me. Listen to all he has to say and cooperate fully with his instructions.

I'm sorry that we did not meet one last time, but such is life; I do hope that you will forgive me for asking you to make such a sacrifice but I always knew that really we were one and the same when it came to matters of such importance as this.

You are now James Fullerton and with that name you have inherited much power and wealth. Use it for the good of your fellow man and do not think too unkindly of a brother you never really knew.

I always envied you, Michael. You always had that inner quietness that I never could find. Be strong, be happy and God be with you.

Your brother,
James.

P.S.
Go to my safe. In it you will find a key. This will give you access to my safety deposit box in the Banque National de Paris in Geneva. You're going to need it one day. Do not lose it!

Fullerton paused for a moment and wiped the tears

from his eyes that had formed as he read his brother's last thoughts.

'I would like to see my brother now,' Fullerton said to Baldini.

Without saying a word, Baldini led the way up the broad staircase and opened one of the bedroom doors on the landing.

'I will leave you alone. Call if you need anything at all.'

Fullerton entered his brother's bedroom and walked slowly over to the bed where his brother's body still lay. He sat down on the edge of the large bed and stared at his brother for a moment. Fullerton placed his hand on top of his brother's folded hands. How cold they were, he thought.

His brother seemed very much at peace; the strain of his illness had left his face now. James's race had been run, now it was up to him to continue. I only hope that I can carry this off, he pondered. What if he was uncovered as a fraud? There would be many acquaintances that knew his brother extremely well and who would be sure to notice even the slightest differences of speech, mannerism or familiarity.

Fullerton leaned over and kissed his brother on the cheek.

'Goodbye James; I always loved you.'

Baldini was waiting downstairs for him when he returned to the main living room. He was in discussion with the two other men to whom Michael had not been introduced.

'Come in, James,' Baldini said. 'These two associates of mine will be involved in the logistical side of things and have been entrusted with the safe transfer of your brother's body back to England.'

The two men left the room to perform their assigned duties.

'James, please come over to the table, there are a number

of formalities which need to be sorted out right now before we do anything else.'

Fullerton spent the rest of the day in intense discussion and briefings with Baldini and a number of other close associates of Baldini's. Everything had been planned right down to the smallest detail. Fullerton had practised James's signature endlessly and had even got used to his taste in clothes. Luckily, the two brothers were more of less the same build and so this particular potential problem area was quickly taken care of.

Fullerton found that he liked the kindly Italian as he listened to endless briefings about James's business affairs. James himself had made many arrangements himself, before his death, to give his brother the least amount of difficulty. Careful notes had been left for him to refer to on any number of situations and detailed accounts had been left as to his retrenched business dealings.

Baldini had, with James's agreement before his death, conveniently distanced all of James's close staff and in most cases this had involved either a dismissal or a lucrative transfer to some other part of the Fullerton empire.

House staff had been completely replaced in Geneva and it would be up to James's new executive assistant to effect any new appointments. Fullerton informed Baldini that this might take some time. Baldini replied that he would continue to cover certain communications aspects for him over the next few weeks whilst he became more familiar with all that James had been involved in.

'We have already initiated some press reports about "your death in London", Baldini informed Fullerton. 'Apparently you were taken ill very suddenly in your house in Witney after returning from Switzerland.'

'What else do they say?' Fullerton asked.

'Not too much. Needless to say, we did not involve too many operatives in the process; just our own doctors and an ambulance crew. It all happened too quickly for anyone to even notice what did or did not happen. Your body should already be on its way to the funeral home by now,' Baldini continued.

'Have my children been informed?' Fullerton asked.

Baldini looked over at him and replied thoughtfully:

'Yes, I think that they will know about your death by now.'

The full weight of what Fullerton had done seemed to press down on him at this precise moment. What would his two children be going through? Richard might be away abroad and so wouldn't necessarily know yet. In any case, he wouldn't show his feelings and would deal with it in the same way as he had dealt all his other problems. He would be able to reconcile the fact that people did sometimes just die prematurely. Louise – she was the one he was most worried about. Louise had always been close to her dad, as daughters seem to be, but she was the one child of his that would find this the hardest to accept. It would undoubtedly take her a long time to recover from yet another bereavement.

Chapter 21

October 6th, 2008. London.

Professor Michael Fullerton's very untimely death had come as a complete shock and surprise to everybody. The cause of death had been given as heart failure. He had apparently just returned from a two-day trip to Switzerland the previous evening and having only just returned home, complained of chest pains. He had allegedly called his doctors the following morning who had then visited him at his home in Witney where he underwent an extensive examination.

The official word from the university stated that they had been informed by the doctors that Professor Fullerton had suffered a series of attacks later that morning from which they had been unable to take any corrective action.

Professor Fullerton had been pronounced dead in the ambulance on the way to the nearest hospital at 2.15 pm. Authorities had been notified by the attending physicians. The two doctors had been present both before and at the time that death had occurred and had both certified that the cause of death was from a final massive heart attack. There was, therefore, no problem with the issuance of the death certificate.

An ambulance had initially taken the body to an undisclosed location and subsequently to a local undertaker. An undertaker in Hemel Hempstead had then subsequently been notified and the body taken to their funeral chapel in readiness for a funeral in St Albans.

His next of kin had been informed as had the university authorities and his brother in Geneva had been asked to accept the responsibility for making all the necessary, immediate arrangements.

'I've just been told of my father's death. I must speak to my uncle immediately!' Richard demanded, not knowing why his uncle had even been involved.

'We are sorry, but your uncle is not at home at present,' came the somewhat impersonal reply.

'Please ask my uncle to return my call as soon as possible.'

Richard placed a call to the offices of Mortimer & Begg in Oxford.

'Mr Price, please,' Richard asked.

'Stuart Price here.'

'Mr Price, Richard Fullerton speaking. I was under the impression that both myself and my sister were the joint executors of our father's will. I now hear that my uncle is in control of everything.'

Price listened to Richard's questions.

'Yes, Richard, that is the situation as I understand it to be. It certainly was three months ago when I last met your father,' Price said in response to the rather confused and upset caller. 'Your father had cause to instruct me in the drawing-up of a new will in August last. At that same time he had decided to make certain changes.'

'Why was I not informed?' Richard demanded.

'That I cannot say, Richard,' Price replied. 'Your father did not instruct me in anything other than the preparation of the new will. I cannot comment on the reasons why he apparently chose not to inform his immediate family. I will of course keep you and your sister informed regarding this new will, but for the meantime I would suggest that you make contact directly with your uncle regarding his involvement. I also suggest that we should all meet sometime after your father's funeral and when you two have had a chance to get over the shock.'

He went on.

'I would be grateful however, if you could provide me with the contact details for your sister. Please call my secretary if you need anything in the meantime.'

With that the conversation was at an end.

Two days later, Michael's two children drove from London to Hemel Hempstead and the funeral home where their father's body was being kept in one of the private viewing rooms. The two of them had both decided to pay this last visit to see their father and wanted to make this last act together as a family.

Louise had been particularly upset but had indicated to her brother that she wanted to come with him if he decided to visit the funeral home.

They were met at the funeral home by one of the directors, a rather cadaverous looking man. Richard wondered why all these undertakers seemed so Dickensian in their looks.

'Do you know why you were selected on this particular occasion?' Richard asked.

'We were contacted by a Mr James Fullerton, your uncle I believe, who stated that he had the legal responsibility for making all the funeral arrangements,' the funeral director replied tactfully.

Richard thought no more of it and turned his attention to Louise who had started to cry again.

'Please be good enough to both follow me,' he informed the two of them as he entered the Chapel of Rest. 'Your father is in Chapel Number 3.'

Richard and a now weeping Louise slowly entered the door of the chapel in which their father's coffin had been placed on some kind of raised platform.

'Stay as long as you like, there is no time limit,' he whispered and quietly slid out of the room.

The two of them inched forward to the rim of the coffin and stared at their father's face. His hands had been arranged together on his chest and his face was strangely white, the signs of beard stubble showing on his chin and cheeks.

'I didn't know that a heart attack could change his facial features so much,' Louise whispered as she continued to sob. 'It almost doesn't look like him,' she added.

'Did you know anything about dad's health Richard?' Louise asked her brother. Richard gave no reply and they just stared at their father and nodded in silent agreement that he had aged remarkably, even since their last meeting.

'I reckon that dad knew he was ill and just didn't want us to know that he had some kind of a heart problem. So typical of dad,' Louise said.

Louise took a small box out of her coat pocket and opened it. Inside was a single gold band. It had been her mother's wedding ring which her father had given to her. She placed the ring between her father's cold hands and said:

'Now you have something to remind you of mum.'

Richard was the first to leave the chapel. Louise remained a couple of minutes longer.

'Why didn't you tell us you were so ill?' she said, addressing the lifeless body. 'I would have come and looked after you; you know I would.'

Louise left the chapel in silence and returned to the front of the funeral home where her brother was waiting and the funeral director was completing some paperwork for another client.

'Thank you,' Richard said, 'My father looks at peace now.'

The return journey to Muswell Hill was made in silence. Neither of them had anything to say. It had all taken them so much by surprise.

133

Chapter 22

October 15th, 2008. St Albans.

The day of the funeral was an extremely dull and rather cold October day in St Albans.

The funeral cortege was due to leave from the funeral home in Hemel Hempstead at around 11 am and the service in the abbey was booked for 12 noon. Close family members had been asked to assemble at the funeral home no later than 10.45 am.

Those same family members had assembled at Richard's apartment in Muswell Hill some hours earlier and arrangements had been made for them to journey out of town through Barnet and on to Hemel Hempstead. Richard and Michelle, Michelle's parents, Louise and a couple of her close friends.

'Uncle James could at least have returned my call,' Richard grumbled. 'We haven't heard a single word from him; I don't understand why he is being so callous.'

'I thought he might have found time to attend his own brother's funeral,' Louise remarked.

Two large, black limousines had been organised and arrangements had been made for them to leave their own transport at the side of the premises.

The hearse was ready and waiting and Louise started to cry again at the sight of the coffin. All being ready, the hearse moved slowly off and the two limousines followed behind. As the cars reached the crest of the hill on the south-west side of the city, the cathedral came in to view on the hill opposite. The old buildings which huddled around the cathedral and abbey church of St Alban, with their preponderance of black and white timbered façades and dark roofs, seemed to match the sombre mood of the occasion and the slate-grey sky gave the day's events a suitably sad backdrop.

The cathedral, or Abbey Church as it was known locally, still retained its imposing position on the city skyline and was visible from miles around. The Fullerton family had had close connections with the city for over two hundred years, Michael and James's parents having been married in the cathedral in 1953 by the then Dean.

The funeral cortege drove slowly up the narrow winding streets as they approached the abbey itself. The cars slowed almost to a stop as they drove through the gate and on into the cathedral grounds.

Just as the local clock tower indicated exactly 12 o'clock the cars came to rest outside the magnificent Victorian façade which made up the western end of the cathedral. They climbed out and walked across the paved courtyard and in through the door leading to the beginning of the long nave. Once inside, they walked down the centre aisle as far as the altar. They were overcome by the considerable number of people who had already assembled.

Michael was well known in both university and business circles and this was borne out by the sheer number of those in attendance.

Oxford dons, some also from Cambridge, his old school friends, business friends and representatives from many professions and overseas institutions as well had all made the effort to attend.

The family group were escorted to the front few pews which had been left empty for them. They all sat down quietly and sensed that they were the focus of many of those present.

The organ started to quietly play some haunting piece of music by Edward Elgar and the congregation all stood as the six bearers slowly carried the coffin up the long central aisle.

The service was conducted by the Dean himself who had known Michael from his own days of study at Oxford. The service was taken directly from the Book of Common Prayer as Michael had wanted. He had been known to extol the virtues and mystery of the sixteenth-century language that it contained.

The short service over, Michael's children received the usual expressions of sadness from more people than they knew. They had followed behind the coffin as it was carried down the long aisle and out through the main entrance to the cathedral and had to endure the numerous expressions of condolence for the sake of good manners and what was expected of them.

The burial service had been arranged to take place in the churchyard of the parish church in the nearby village of Kimpton where Michael and James had grown up. Richard, Michelle and Louise and her friends climbed back into the chauffeur-driven funeral cars and the cortege once again slowly moved off out of the cathedral precinct, past the old school round the small cemetery and on up the hill into the centre of St Albans. It then turned left and passed through the market place and on in the direction of Kimpton.

The car carrying Michael's children arrived at the churchyard gate and stopped outside; the vicar had been notified and so was waiting for the arrival of the funeral guests. Michelle and Louise engaged the vicar in polite conversation; Richard was scrutinising the various guests as they also arrived, having left their cars down the narrow lane by the vicarage.

The family had invited all the guests to attend the

burial but some had perhaps felt that too large a crowd would be impracticable and unwanted and so had not made the journey from the abbey.

Richard thought that he knew most of his father's university friends but there were quite a few people that he did not recognise.

It was a brief service around the graveside and the vicar was most kind in his thoughts to the immediate members of the family.

They viewed the selection of wreaths that had been received. One in particular caught their attention. It was an arrangement of white lilies with the following inscription. 'To my brother, a friend indeed'.

'I don't know why he bothered to send a wreath – too busy to come himself!' Richard remarked. A comment that for the moment seemed to echo all their thoughts. Only a few of the people who had attended the service in the cathedral had come out to Kimpton, mainly his academic colleagues. Michael's two children thanked the vicar again, spoke briefly to a couple of Michael's Oxford faculty and climbed back into the limousine for their solitary journey back home.

Chapter 23

October 15th, 2008. Geneva.

At the same time as the funeral was taking place in St Albans, Michael Fullerton opened the patio doors to his bedroom and stared out across the lake from the vantage point of the expansive first floor veranda of James's extensive twelve-bedroom mansion. The water at the lake's edge gently lapping around the footings of the boat house was reasonably calm; there was a slight breeze but only enough to provide some slight movement to the top branches of the trees near the water's edge. He wondered how the funeral was going and who had been there.

It had been his initial intention to attend his brother's funeral. He had been brought to see the potential risks involved and the likelihood of a possible catastrophe had his emotions got the better of him and he had been recognised as being more than Mr James Fullerton. In any case, it was deemed unlikely that his brother would have attended.

Fullerton realised that there was just too much hanging on the complete and total success of this exchange. He had just inherited a business empire that needed some seriously hard work if he was ever going to convince his business associates. This was where close friends were going to prove invaluable.

He went back downstairs and saw Francesco Baldini in deep conversation with someone on the telephone in James's former study.

'Yes, I will inform Mr Fullerton that you called and need to speak with him urgently,' Baldini was saying. 'As soon as he has a free moment I will ask him to phone you back.'

Baldini replaced the receiver and looked up as Michael entered the room.

'He can wait,' he said.

'Michael, following our discussions this morning, we really need to get you up to speed with all of James's various activities. We've been at this for a week or so now but it is still going to take some more work on your part. I have bought us some further time by announcing that you are now suffering from a serious bout of flu and will likely be out of action for at least a further week. Incidentally, one of my contacts phoned about half an hour ago. He had just attended the funeral in England. Apparently, the funeral went off without a hitch.'

'When exactly did I supposedly die?'

'You died in Witney, at your home, on October 5th, shortly after your return from Geneva,' Baldini replied. 'My people took care of all the details and the chronology as well as transferring the body,' he added with a look that was meant to make everything he said sound trivial and inconsequential.

'So, James was in my coffin then?'

'That's correct, I'm afraid,' Baldini answered quietly.

Michael Fullerton was slowly but surely beginning to comprehend the extent of the resources involved and the covert operations that had been mounted just to engineer and control the logistics of this whole exchange process.

'Michael, as you have influence on the operations of Axxon through your holding company, I am thinking that you will need to surround yourself with a layer of intermediaries for the next few months. At least until you

139

feel comfortable with your new affairs. We are also going to have to start calling you "James".'

'Yes, good idea,' Michael Fullerton answered. He definitely needed to build up a group of close confidants and a capable assistant in particular, but whom could he possibly choose? Whom could he trust?

Chapter 24

December 1st, 2008. Cannes.

An urgent meeting had been called. These meetings seldom took place and when they did, they were only in situations of extreme crisis. Meetings were risky affairs and the group knew that their activities at these gatherings could be easily monitored. In order to minimise any attention from the outside world, they were invariably held at a different geographical location each time. In this instance additional precautions were taken and the individuals knew that they were to use exclusively private means of transportation so as not to draw any attention at all to their movements. As all the senior members in the ADF were leading businessmen, their movements could quite easily be concealed in this way and suitable decoy plans could be put into effect so as to misdirect any prying eyes and ensure that nothing at all unusual was happening that might raise their suspicions.

This particular meeting was being held in the South of France. A quorum of members was always needed; this allowed some further flexibility on the part of those other Council members in case situations arose that required their particular talents elsewhere.

Five of the seven key members had indicated their intentions to attend the Cannes meeting; their host on this particular occasion was apparently ill and confined to his bed and word from another member had not yet been received. News had, however, reached them on their arrival that this individual had apparently been indefinitely detained in the Far East for, as yet unknown, business reasons.

All of the members had now arrived by either private or chartered planes at Cannes–Mandelieu airport and had gathered at James Fullerton's villa just outside the city. Their host had been unable to attend the meeting at the very last minute due they were told to a recurring illness which had confined him to his home in Geneva.

The Council had convened this rare meeting because all knew that some specific action had to be agreed to counter the pressure that was being exerted on the ADF by the intelligence services.

In James Fullerton's absence, Francesco Baldini had assumed his mantle as host and had flown in from Milan following a visit with his sick friend in Geneva.

'Welcome, gentlemen,' Francesco Baldini said as the other four senior Council members of the ADF gathered together after having relaxed for an hour or two in the spacious facilities offered by the villa.

'I have, as you know, spoken very recently with James and he shares our collective concern about the apparent success of the intelligence agencies, particularly from France and Britain, in both infiltrating our membership, albeit at a much lower level, and in their relentless fabrication of false news stories about our operations. We are all naturally concerned about these recent developments and James has been tireless in his attempts to uncover those individuals in our midst who have chosen to hijack this organisation's ideals and to supplant them with a far more dangerous and extremist approach.'

'We are gaining a very bad reputation in Germany right now as a result of the attack on one of our leading politicians. The German press needed no second invitation to put the blame onto the ADF,' came one response.

'The death of the French Ambassador in Montreal earlier this year didn't do us any good either in North America,' came a second remark.

These sentiments were echoed around the room with the others nodding their heads in agreement.

'Gentlemen, gentlemen!' Baldini almost shouted as he brought the meeting under control once more. 'We are aware that shared information about a number of our more important activities is being used in conjunction with the most ruthless of blackmail techniques to potentially disgrace certain prominent business leaders and politicians. James and I, as you all know, have been extremely active in recent months and it is my present understanding that James has been particularly successful in his own secret endeavours. More than that I cannot say at the moment. He has not even confided in me as to the amount of progress made in his own secret investigation. If James feels that there is a need for total secrecy, then he must be playing a very dangerous game with these people. For the moment you must all be patient and, above all, extremely careful about the people you talk to and the amount of information that is passed between you and your ADF colleagues.'

Baldini took a breath and continued.

'I am therefore asking for the following safeguards to become official ADF policy. Namely, that we all agree to an immediate information blackout; all information passed between ADF members is on a strictly need-to-know basis; all communications between us and our immediate associates is to be monitored and recorded.' If there is any leakage of information either to or from our members to the intelligence community, we will then be able to more quickly pinpoint its source. I will of course keep you all fully informed of any developments and in the meantime I would ask that you relay any contravention

143

of these new rules to all those others here present by the usual secure channels.'

Following this first session, the meeting then broke up and Council members used this rare opportunity to compare notes verbally on the effectiveness of their various local policies and to arrange for closer cooperation between the international regions.

Baldini went back to his own suite of rooms in the Fullerton villa and made a phone call to Geneva on Fullerton's private number.

'James, this is Francesco. I am still in the meeting with the ADF Council, but have just slipped out to give you a quick call.'

'Thank you for that. How's the meeting gone so far?'

'Everybody is feeling very edgy and under pressure right now, but they have agreed to the necessity of tightening up our organisational structure, particularly regarding communications.'

'Well, that should at least improve matters and make it more difficult for the intelligence services to acquire information. Thank you for taking over my role, right now. Did anyone comment on my absence?'

'No, no comment at all. I think that I sounded suitably convincing about your illness. Indeed, if anyone knew more than they were admitting, regarding James's illness, they would have expected what I had to say on that particular subject.'

'Give me a call when you are back in Milan, Francesco,' Fullerton said.

'I will certainly do just that. Bye for now.'

Baldini walked back from his suite into the main hall of the villa and rejoined some of his ADF colleagues. A further formal session had been arranged for later in the day. In the meantime, he wondered what they must all be thinking and what the future held.

Chapter 25

December 12th, 2008. Paris.

Fullerton had telephoned Marguerite a couple of days earlier and informed her that he was shortly going to be in Paris. He hoped and prayed that Marguerite had not seen or heard anything about his supposed funeral in October. She showed no surprise at all at receiving his call and so he said that he would call her from the airport when he arrived. Fullerton flew to Paris onboard the corporate jet. He needed to spend time with Marguerite and explain the whole situation to her face to face. He had no way of knowing what her reaction would be and therefore decided that both the timing and the location had to be perfect.

Why not invite her to join him on the Amalfi coast or anywhere nice and warm at this time of year? They could relax, catch up on their news and generally see how they would fit in together.

Fullerton had, however, decided that a low-key visit was preferable for this explanation and proposition. For Marguerite to consider the prospect of joining the high-stakes corporate world that he was now living in, never mind the shock from his explanation of the exchange, was going to be a very tall order indeed. All he knew was that, deep down, he had to give it a try. Besides, Marguerite was becoming more than just a friend.

Fullerton's private plane touched down at Charles de Gaulle airport in late afternoon. He was starting to become quite comfortable with his new role and his own background in economics was serving him very well in terms of his business decisions. He had set up several advisory groups to review and report on the most appropriate actions to be taken with his various business interests, but this in essence was simply a front to divorce him further from a front-line role. Many of his associates were intrigued with this seemingly sudden change in working style but did not voice their opinions to the great man himself. They all knew better than that.

Fullerton sat back in the taxi which he knew was not going to take too long to convey him from the airport into the centre of Paris and the Boulevard Saint-Germain.

Marguerite had occupied the conveniently situated apartment on the Boulevard Saint-Germain for a long time. Her work at the Sorbonne necessitated a convenient local address and this one suited her just fine. Fullerton had just telephoned to say that he was at the airport and would be with her in about an hour and so she busied herself with tidying up and making herself suitably presentable.

Marguerite was what the English would describe as a typical fashionably cultured Frenchwoman. She was forty-seven years old and had a younger sister named Marie who lived with her husband in Toulouse and also a younger brother who was in the French diplomatic service and presently posted on the staff of the French embassy in Japan.

Fullerton's taxi joined the Péripherique and merged quickly into the streaming Parisian traffic. Driving in Paris was definitely an art.

Fullerton could see the imposing outline of the Arc de Triumphe ahead of him now. They soon skirted round this impressive structure and onwards down the Avenue des Champs-Elysées. The taxi turned right when it reached the Place de la Concorde and rumbled over the Pont de

THE FOURNIER DOCTRINE

la Concorde and Fullerton gained his first view of the
river Seine again. This river with its stone embankments
was one of the features that he most liked about Paris.

Fullerton observed that he was already on the Boulevard
Saint-Germain and spoke to the driver.

'*Boulevard Saint-Michel, s'il vous plaît.*'

The taxi driver duly complied. Climbing out, Fullerton
had only to cross over the road to reach Marguerite's
apartment.

He rang the button 'Mme M. De Saulx' on the intercom
and waited for a reply.

'*Allo,*' a voice answered.

'Hello, Marguerite, it's Michael,' he shouted above the
noise of some passing traffic. The door mechanism buzzed
and then clicked open and Fullerton climbed up the late-
nineteenth-century staircase to the second floor.

Marguerite was looking lovelier than ever; Fullerton had
not seen her for a couple of months but she appeared
to him now as a person who encapsulated all that vitality
and allure that only French women seemed to possess.

'So, nice to see you again, Michael,' Marguerite said in
English with the same pronounced French accent.

What was it about French people speaking English that
seemed so sexy, Fullerton thought to himself?

She came up to him and gave him a salutary three
kisses on his cheeks and after studying him for just a
second or so, invited him into her apartment.

'Do you have somewhere to stay, Michael?' she asked.

'Yes, I have a room at the Hotel Saint-Michel just round
the corner,' Fullerton replied.

'What would you like to do this evening?' she asked.

'Well, I thought that we could walk down to my hotel
so that I can check in and leave my luggage and then
perhaps we could find a nice little restaurant somewhere
nearby.'

'I would like that,' Marguerite said. 'It is still quite early, but perhaps I could telephone a restaurant and make a reservation for about 8.00 pm,' she added, looking at Fullerton.

Fullerton nodded.

'You could help yourself to a drink while I use the telephone,' Marguerite said. 'Help yourself; there is some nice white wine in the fridge.'

Fullerton went in the direction that Marguerite had pointed and found the fridge in her tiny eat-in kitchen. The glasses he could see in a glass-fronted cabinet next to the cooker and taking two of them, poured some nicely chilled wine into both.

Returning to the sitting room he heard Marguerite in conversation with the restaurant that she had chosen and concluding the booking in the name of De Saulx.

'I have made a reservation at another nice little restaurant that I sometimes go to with my friends from the university. It's not too far from here, so we can walk. It will be a nice evening to walk, I think.'

Fullerton observed Marguerite as she spoke. He took in her shape and wondered now why she had never married. She somehow seemed fragile and alone and Fullerton wondered what kind of existence she had these days and just how he was going to choose the moment to tell her what he knew he had to tell her.

For now he was happy just to enjoy her company and catch up on some of the events that had happened in her life since they had met last.

Seven o'clock soon arrived and Fullerton and Marguerite left her apartment, crossed over the Boulevard Saint-Germain and round the corner onto the Boulevard Saint-Michel. It was only about a quarter of a mile to the Place Saint-Michel and Fullerton's hotel and they covered this distance in no time.

Fullerton checked in and asked Marguerite to wait for him in the rather tiny hotel reception area while he hurried into the equally tiny lift and ascended to the fourth floor. He landed his case on the bed, opened it and unpacked. After having literally splashed some water over his face, changed shirts, looked at himself in the mirror and dashed on some cologne, he headed back to the lift and the hotel reception.

Marguerite was glancing through some fashion magazine as he exited the lift.

'Right, I am ready for anything now. Which way are we going?'

'I thought that we would go to one of my favourite places; it is about ten minutes away,' Marguerite replied and took Fullerton's arm as they retraced their steps back along the Boulevard Saint-Michel.

Le Mesclun was a small restaurant tucked away down a narrow alley which joined the main boulevard. Marguerite entered with Fullerton close behind and introduced herself to the owner who indeed remembered her from her previous visits.

They were given a table in the rear courtyard and Fullerton found it most delightful. 'I hope you like this place,' Marguerite said.

'It is just lovely; another courtyard.'

Both Fullerton and Marguerite decided to remain on white wine and Fullerton chose a fine Bordeaux.

The waiter came over and indicated that the specialty that evening was grilled salmon. They both decided that they would go with the recommendation and handed back the menus without looking further.

'You remember that I have a twin brother, don't you, Marguerite?'

'Yes, I remember that you used to talk about him a lot when we were students here a long time ago, and you saw him in London in April. What is he doing these days?'

'He went into business and became both very successful and rich,' Fullerton stated. 'We haven't seen each other much at all; we were two different people, even though we were twins and identical twins at that, we never really saw eye to eye. He went his way, I went mine.'

Fullerton took another sip of wine and replaced the glass on the table.

'Anyway, he died recently in Geneva,' he said slowly.

'Oh, Michael, how awful; I'm so very sorry.'

Fullerton continued. 'He had a very aggressive cancer. As you've remembered we had to leave Rome in somewhat of a hurry last April and fly back to London? Well, that was all to do with my brother's health. I couldn't tell you anything at the time because I didn't know anything,' he continued. 'James was in London to see his doctors amongst other people and I met him the morning that we arrived. He left his whole estate to me; he was not married and therefore had no family except me, but there was a complication.'

Fullerton paused at this point in his story again to allow Marguerite time to take in what he had just said but also to allow him to think of the most appropriate words for the next part of his story.

Marguerite sat forward in her seat.

'Marguerite, you must promise me not to divulge to a living soul what I am about to tell you.'

'OK, I promise,' Marguerite replied, starting to become a little alarmed.

'The complication, Marguerite, was that he needed me to take his place, not just carry on with his business but literally take his place, become him. Take over his identity.'

'*Mon Dieu!*' Marguerite exclaimed. 'I can't believe that James would have orchestrated all this without there being a much more important reason.'

'This was James's idea from start to finish. He planned all the details before his death,' Fullerton replied. 'You are officially having dinner with James Fullerton, CEO of Brentmark Holdings; my business empire is based in Geneva and for all intents and purposes, I am in Paris on business. Poor old Professor Fullerton died from a heart attack recently, shortly after he had returned from a short trip to Switzerland. His funeral took place eight weeks ago in England.'

Marguerite sat totally at a loss for words. Then she said: 'I heard nothing at all about all this otherwise I would have gone to the funeral.'

'Under the circumstances I'm glad that you hadn't heard about it. I was worrying about what you might have heard.'

'What about your poor children?' Marguerite whispered at last.

'That has been the hardest part of this whole wretched business. They think I'm dead and that their uncle couldn't even be bothered to fly over to England for the funeral.'

'Oh, How awful! There must be more to this than what you have told me,' Marguerite responded. 'Who could make such a terrible sacrifice?'

Marguerite looked at Fullerton as she said these last few words and saw the tears flooding into his eyes.

'Oh, Michael,' she whispered, 'I'm so sorry, this whole situation must be appalling for you; it must be something very important for you to have become part of all this.'

Fullerton pulled himself together, looked directly into Marguerite's eyes and spoke softly to her.

'Yes, it really is. I don't yet fully know what I have got myself into but I just had to support my brother. I need you to come and live in Geneva.'

With the meal over, Fullerton settled the bill and the two of them decided to walk back down to the river. Marguerite continued to hug Fullerton's arm. They walked along the left bank and crossed onto the Pont Neuf. They stopped in one of the many alcoves on the bridge and stared down the river as it continued to flow beyond the Pont des Arts.

'James was a more complicated person than even I thought he could be; as well as all his various business dealings and the fortune he had amassed, he had one final secret.'

Marguerite sat silently, waiting for Fullerton to continue.

'It appears that he is also a key member of a discreet business organisation that goes by the initials, ADF,' he said carefully

'Tell me about it?' Marguerite asked.

'ADF stands for L'Agence de la Doctrine de Fournier. From what little I know, it is a multi national organisation that has existed in some form or other since the early fifties and apparently bases its ideology on the writings and philosophy of Pierre Fournier, hence its name.

'What else do you know?' Marguerite said.

'I simply don't know anything more at the present moment. James felt that it was sufficiently important for me to assume his complete identity and so there is obviously more that I don't yet know.'

The two of them sat down in the alcove and Fullerton took Marguerite's hand in his.

'I really need you to come, Marguerite.'

Marguerite leaned her head on his shoulder but said nothing.

December 13th, 2008. Paris.

Saturday morning was a lovely clear day and so Fullerton arranged to call for Marguerite early so as not to waste the little time that they had together.

A trip down the Seine was the order of the day and

so they took a taxi to the departure point near the Eiffel Tower and bought tickets on the next departure. Having some time to wait they decided to stroll across the road and underneath the huge base of the tower itself. Fullerton marvelled at the complicated mass of interlocking steelwork rising up into the sky and wondered how it ever came to be built all those years ago. The crowds were already starting to accumulate and lines had already formed for the lifts. Even the entrance to the stairs, where hardy individuals could climb to the various levels on foot, had a long queue of people waiting.

They continued past the confines of the tower and walked part of the way along the long pedestrian avenue leading to the Ecole Militaire.

Fullerton and Marguerite just walked along deep in the enjoyment of each other's company.

Fullerton looked at his watch. We'd better hurry back to the river or we'll miss the cruise.'

They made it back with a couple of minutes to spare and took their place on the front section of the boat. The cruise down the Seine was a popular activity for tourists and the attractive young woman who was giving the commentary in several languages seemed particularly enthusiastic on this trip. The boat glided under bridges and past buildings of note – The Louvre, the Musée D'Orsay and eventually took the right fork as the river divided around the Ile-de-France and the cathedral of Notre Dame came into full view before it disappeared temporarily above the high embankment.

They took in the scenery of the river and the outlines of the various buildings as they passed by, but spoke little for the entire voyage. They each had some serious thinking to do and though they enjoyed conversation, this precise point in their renewed relationship did not somehow seem the right time to engage in serious discussion.

The voyage was soon over and Fullerton hailed a taxi to take them both back to Marguerite's apartment. He had the taxi stop on the way and wait outside his hotel whilst he checked out. Marguerite had told Fullerton that she would prepare some lunch and they could stay at her place until it was time for Fullerton to head back to the airport and his return journey to Geneva.

Marguerite wanted so much to explain her thoughts to Fullerton but her head told her to wait and allow time to sort out her conflicting feelings.

Chapter 26

Fullerton had been purposely avoiding any direct phone calls with other Agency members since he had taken his brother's place in early October. A decision that had been made for the moment at least. Fullerton should continue to play the part of a dying man.

Whoever was responsible for poisoning his brother would expect him to be very seriously ill at this point in time. Baldini had provided him with a report on the meeting in Cannes which had been sent to Geneva for James's attention, but Fullerton had decided against attending any meetings for this very reason and the fact that he hadn't yet figured out who or what was involved and what type of game they were all playing.

This particular group of individuals did not normally entrust any external communication between regular members to the normal forms of communication in any eventuality. E-mail encryption was the preferred means. A rather nondescript brown envelope had, however, arrived whilst Fullerton was away, signed for and placed in Fullerton's study in readiness for his return from Paris.

Fullerton returned to Geneva from his all too short but eventful visit to Paris on the Saturday evening. He had left Marguerite with a lot to absorb and contemplate. Her safe, secure little world was being dismantled and he knew that she would need some time to arrive at a decision.

Fullerton scanned through the usual pile of mail that had accumulated on his desk in his absence. Most of it he could deal with later; some things he had to deal with now. He was intrigued by the brown envelope that had been sent recorded delivery and signed for by Baldini himself in his absence. It carried an unknown crest on the outside. The blue logo showing a hovering eagle left him none the wiser as to the sender.

Fullerton opened the envelope and found that inside was a single blank sheet of paper, blank except for a single line of numbers:

102 – 137 – 644

Fullerton had no idea as to the meaning of this sequence. There was nothing else written underneath. He had spent a lot of time going through James's personal effects, business papers but had found nothing that could be considered any help in solving this mystery.

One place that he hadn't yet visited was James's bank and his safety deposit box. He was reminded at that moment of his brother's words to him in London when he was told about the key.

'You're going to need it one day. Do not lose it!'

Fullerton guessed that there must, quite obviously, be items of importance in that box. He knew that this coded message could only be deciphered if he was in possession of the necessary codebook and as he had looked everywhere else, there must be an answer contained in whatever was still safely stored in the bank vault in Geneva. For this he had to visit the BNP Paribas (Suisse) in Geneva and James's safety deposit box. He checked to ensure that he still had the key that James had left in his safe.

Membership of the Agency was exclusive, secretive and by invitation only. Any prospective members would be scrutinised carefully and judged ultimately by existing members according to their political commitment, sphere of influence and many other determining factors. Even after becoming a member, not all the Agency's knowledge was for them to know.

Whoever had sent him this envelope and the coded message was obviously an insider. But why had it arrived by recorded delivery and not in the usual manner? Fullerton knew that he had to visit the bank in Geneva without too much delay. He consulted his diary and phoned the bank to arrange a visit for the following Tuesday.

The intercom rang. He picked up the receiver and listened to a member of his staff speaking.

'I have a Madame De Saulx on the line from Paris. Do you want me to take a message?'

'No, put her through.'

'Hello? Hello, Marguerite. Could you call me back on the following number?'

His private phone rang.

'How are you feeling?' Fullerton asked awkwardly.

'I'm fine,' Marguerite answered. 'Are you free to talk for a few minutes?'

'You have my undivided attention, Marguerite,' Fullerton replied.

'I have been thinking about what you said here on Friday. I have a lot of questions to ask you but I don't want to ask you over the phone.'

'Come to Geneva, then. I'll have my people collect you in my private jet.'

'Private jet, eh?'

'When can you come?' Fullerton asked anxiously.

'On Wednesday?' Marguerite suggested.

'That's perfect; I'll have my secretary contact you with

all the details. We'll pick you up and bring you right here.'

'OK,' Marguerite answered. 'Look forward to seeing you again on Wednesday.'

'I'll have to show you Geneva whilst you are here; can't wait. See you soon. All my love.' He sat back and replaced the receiver.

He stared out of his window and thought of the coming week.

Chapter 27

December 16th, 2008. Geneva.

The short drive into the city centre from *Bellerive* took the usual thirty or so minutes. His chauffeur-driven car came to a halt in front of the bank's impressive French renaissance façade. Fullerton climbed out and walked up the steps and into the central atrium of the bank.

'*Bonjour, Monsieur Fullerton,*' came the salutation as he was recognised by one of the managers who happened to be passing by. 'Can I be of assistance this morning?'

'Yes, I need to obtain some papers from my deposit box.'

'Please follow me.'

He followed the man as they walked towards the rear of the atrium and down a wide flight of marble stairs leading, Fullerton assumed, to where the bank's vault was located.

'I will leave you in the capable hands of my colleague,' the manager said as he walked up to a large desk. 'He will take care of you from here.'

'This is Mr Fullerton, please look after him.'

Fullerton now followed the second official. They passed down a brightly lit hallway and in through a huge time-lock doorway. Fullerton completed the security procedure with the aid of his coded key and duly added James's signature to the appropriate place on the register.

The bank official removed a long thin box from its place of safe keeping and placed it on the table in the centre of the room. Fullerton observed that there must have been several hundred such niches for similar boxes.

'I will leave you now,' the official stated. 'Please let me know, Mr Fullerton, when you have finished.'

Fullerton sat down at the table and opened the box. There were a number of items of jewellery and papers inside. He removed the entire contents and placed them one by one on the table.

He wondered why James had gone to the trouble of keeping some of his possessions in the vault of this bank. He had a large safe back at the house that could easily hold these few extra items.

Amongst the papers was a file with the blue logo of a hovering eagle in the top right hand corner. Fullerton opened it and scanned the several pages it contained. He quickly realised that these pages contained the code-breaking information that he needed back at the house.

There were various other papers that Fullerton ignored. The one that attracted his complete attention was a file containing some newspaper articles. Fullerton realised that they were all articles that he, Michael, had written over the years and which had been published in various newspapers and magazines.

So my brother was human after all, Fullerton thought to himself.

The jewellery consisted of an extremely expensive-looking bracelet, a pair of equally expensive-looking ear-rings and a large gold medallion about five centimetres in diameter upon which was an engraving with the letters ADF on it. On its reverse side was the name: JAMES P FULLERTON.

Michael slipped the medallion into his right-hand jacket pocket. It felt strange to be going through all his brother's effects, but they were his now. He looked again at the various items as he placed them all into his briefcase.

He advised the bank official that he had completed his examination and that the box was ready to be returned. Exiting the bank, he found his car and driver parked a short distance away and issued instructions to return to *Bellerive*.

Once Fullerton had returned and entered the privacy of his own office, he emptied his briefcase of the items it contained, collected the jewellery and the medallion and, opening his own safe, placed them safely inside.

The papers he spread out on the top of his desk and located the 'blue eagle' folder. The contents arranged in sequence according to an itemised list at the front: telephone numbers, names and addresses and passwords for the name of each of four individuals

Classifications of numbers which stood for coded identification of locations, events and items for some kind of pre-planned agenda or activity. Michael now started to decode the numerical sequence that he had recently received.

He located the note he had received with the coded sequence:

Meeting Number: 102.

He could see that this was purely a sequence number to allow any missing messages to be exposed.

Location: 137.

Fullerton referred to the second grouping and his eyes scanned down the list. He could see that this particular number stood for Milan.

Name: 644.

The third grouping listed names of various politicians and

161

dignitaries. Again Fullerton's eyes ran down the list until he spotted the number. This stood for the current German Foreign Minister, Gerhard Brecht.

Fullerton referred back to the first page he had looked at which contained the names and coded contact details of four individuals together with their encryptions.

Fullerton needed to find out what the relationship had been between his brother and these individuals, but he couldn't just pick up the telephone and dial any of the numbers.

On the front of the folder was the word 'MARTIN' written in capital letters and underlined presumably in his brother's handwriting.

Who or what was 'MARTIN' Fullerton wondered.

Chapter 28

Marguerite arrived at the airport in Geneva on Michael's private jet as had been arranged. Fullerton was waiting for her as she came through airport control. They just smiled as they caught sight of each other and gave each other a big hug.

'Welcome to Geneva,' Fullerton began. 'Was everything taken care of for you on the flight?'

Marguerite said that she had never flown on a corporate jet like his before and so wasn't sure how to answer him. She did add that she had enjoyed the experience.

'Well, get used to it; this is going to be your life from now on,' Fullerton said teasingly.

Marguerite had only brought two suitcases with her as Fullerton had told her that all her moving arrangements could be taken care of in due course.

The car was waiting for them as they exited the terminal and they both climbed into the rear of the large, elegant Mercedes.

'It will take us about forty minutes to reach my house; the traffic will be a little heavier than usual at this time of day.'

They looked at each other from time to time and passed the journey talking of mundane things of no real importance. They both knew instinctively that the important questions could wait for the moment.

The Mercedes passed through the entrance gates and

on down the driveway. Fullerton wondered what Marguerite would think of the house when she first saw it through the trees.

'You didn't tell me that it was this big, Michael!' Marguerite exclaimed.

'Wait until you see round the inside and the view of the lake,' Fullerton said proudly.

Marguerite was shown round the house and that was followed by a walk down by the lake.

'Have you thought about what we discussed in Paris?'

'Yes, I have thought about little else. Why do you want me here?' she asked pointedly.

'Now that I have all my brother's business activities to look after, I need people around me that I can trust and rely upon. In particular, I need an executive assistant. Somebody who knows me and can handle a lot of my affairs.'

'Where would I live?' Marguerite questioned. 'What about my life in Paris? I have a good job there that I like and it gives me a comfortable living.'

'Marguerite, look at me' Fullerton responded. 'I have inherited a huge financial empire that I am only just starting to understand, so anything is possible. Money is no object. Name your price! I want you to be in my life again, is that simple enough for you?'

Marguerite smiled and looked up at Fullerton. 'I think that I knew the answer to your question before you left Paris. Of course I will come, but I still have some conditions.'

'Name them,' Fullerton said confidently.

The two of them continued their walk along the shore of the lake and discussed some of the more mundane practicalities.

December 20th, 2008. Paris.

Ives Rousseau stood in front of one of his long office windows at Place Beauvau and looked out onto the sunlit courtyard. The death of his brother three months ago was still a source of great sadness to him. Cardinal Maurice Rousseau, Archbishop of Paris had died on the 6th September after a short illness. Ives, however, knew that the illness had been greatly aggravated by the stress and moral pressure brought upon him from the powers that be in the Vatican.

Rousseau contemplated, yet again, what action could be taken against the person that in his mind had caused all the problems for both his brothers. This elderly priest would be made to atone for his older brother Charles's untimely removal from the Bishopric of Laval all those years ago as well as for the embarrassment and worry caused to his other, more eminent brother Maurice. The Cardinal would never have agreed to his plan whilst he was living, albeit that he held an intense dislike for the troublesome priest, but now that the Cardinal had passed away, there was nothing to stop his brother or his intended course of action.

Rousseau contacted the only person that he knew who could 'interpret' his concerns and implement his wishes. Picking up the phone, he dialled a certain number.

'Armand, this is Ives Rousseau, please arrange to visit me at my country estate this coming weekend. I have something important to discuss.'

December 23rd, 2008. Geneva.

Only a few days later, Marguerite found herself already comfortably installed in the lodge on the perimeter of

165

the property. The lodge was a nice structure with its own view of the lake. It had been used by James to house some of his own staff, Harry Matthews in particular, but as Matthews had been told that his services would no longer be required and rewarded handsomely for his past services, it was now the obvious place in which Marguerite could place her own possessions and know that it was her own space.

She had not spoken to any of her friends and family since her arrival except for the few calls she had made to a certain number in Paris. She was due to make another one shortly but felt that it could wait a day or so.

She had spent the past few days unpacking most of her limited personal possessions, but they seemed lost in the much bigger accommodation. Michael had told her to order anything she needed in the way of furniture and fittings, but she hadn't had the time to think about that. This was all going to be so different from before.

The phone rang on the desk in her living room. She picked up the receiver.

'Hello?'

'Hi, Marguerite it's me,' Fullerton said. 'Can you come right over to the house, we have some things to discuss?'

'Give me five minutes.'

'OK,' Fullerton replied. 'Bring your desk diary with you.'

When Marguerite arrived at the house she walked straight into Fullerton's study. He had just finished a call and was replacing the receiver.

'Come in and sit down. We have lots to go through but first I need to ask you something. You remember me talking about my children? Well, I have written to them.'

'What did you say?' Marguerite asked with a worried look on her face.

'I was my usual abrupt self and told them I would call them when I was next in London.'

'And will you?' Marguerite said staring intently at him. 'Do you think they know anything?' she added.

'They won't know about James and you know they don't know about us. On that subject, I promised Evelyn that I would never divulge that secret. Now that she is no longer living I find that it is a whole different ball game. A lot of water has passed under that bridge, Marguerite. It was long ago; we were young and foolish and I don't know how Evelyn had the strength to deal with it all her life.'

Marguerite came over and stood close to him.

'Are you going to meet them?'

'Now that I have the opportunity, I just don't know. They think I'm dead and their uncle doesn't care. How do children deal with the fact that their own father has deceived them in the worst possible way, twice?'

'You will know, Michael, it will either feel right or it won't.'

Fullerton collected his thoughts and remembered that someone else had used that phrase before. He turned his attention to the matters in hand.

'I must go into Geneva again tomorrow morning, to the bank. I have to deal with some financial matters. It will only take the morning. Right now I need to fill you in on some of James's affairs. Let's go into the living room where we can be more comfortable.'

They went and sat down. Fullerton resumed.

'First of all, I have a number of business trips to make in the next few weeks; obviously you will be coming with me as my executive assistant. What's more pressing is that we must find out more about James's precise involvement in this ADF organisation. Can you make some arrangements for us both to travel to Bonn tomorrow morning? Make reservations in a nice hotel in the centre of the city for two nights returning here on Friday, the 26th.

'Who are we meeting in Bonn?' Marguerite enquired. I'll give you some details on the people that we'll be meeting there; I need you to check up on their latest corporate activities. Baldini can give you all that.'

'Not a problem,' she replied.

'I also have some other calls to make so can we meet back here around 12.30 pm for lunch and then we will go for a cruise on the lake. There are some really lovely views from out on the lake, you'll enjoy it.'

Marguerite left the house and returned to the lodge. She thought that she would make that call to Paris now.

Chapter 29

Fullerton had decided to take the bold and somewhat dangerous step of making contact with his two children. He had received much advice to the contrary, but it was Marguerite who had real misgivings in this endeavour.

He had sent a letter of condolence to his children purporting, of course, to have come from their uncle and so further contact now was, if not expected, at least an action that the two of them could reasonably deal with.

Being very careful not to write or say anything that could be recognised as being facts known only to their father, Fullerton sent the two of them simple messages about wishing to meet on one of his next visits to England.

'I would be very pleased if I could meet with you and make up for the long period of absence between us.'

This sentence seemed to Fullerton to convey a suitable mix of warmth and the need to fill the void left by their father.

His letters had duly been sent and three weeks or so had now passed without any word of reply. It was therefore with quite some surprise when he saw a handwritten letter, postmarked London, which had arrived in his morning delivery. He looked at the reverse of the envelope and could see the little label bearing his son's Muswell Hill address.

The single page contained a quite short note.

'I would be willing to meet you in London at your convenience. My mobile # is: 07797 444312.

No word about his sister. Still, this was a promising start.

Fullerton decided to wait a while longer before replying in the hope that he would hear from his daughter. He wondered what they must be going through and how they had managed to deal with their father's death.

He, Michael, had not been a particularly rich man, unlike his brother, James and so he had recently seen to it that his 'former' estate, which largely consisted of his house in Witney and some modest savings, had been conveniently enriched. He had arranged, during his earlier contact with his brother, for a life insurance policy to be put in force to the value of half a million pounds. This ensured that both his children would be comfortably better off as a result. The funds for this, of course, came from James's cash holdings but all the written documentation showed Evelyn's name as the policyholder so as to create no suspicion in relation to his sudden demise.

He stared out of his study window and across the large expanse of lawn to the lake. It was at times like this that he struggled to come to terms with the enormous sacrifice that he had made.

'I damn well hope that this is all going to be worth it,' he said to himself and he realised that all the wealth and power that he had recently inherited was of small consequence when balanced against family, good friends and strong personal relationships.

He hoped that he could become a kindly uncle and establish a new arrangement with his children but also recognised all too well that this was a big ask and the practicalities of ever achieving this ideal were potentially fraught with failure and rejection.

Chapter 30

January 20th, 2009. Paris.

The car continued driving south past the sleepy little villages in the central Burgundy region of France. One of the occupants dialled a number on his mobile phone and waited for a reply.

The voice at the end of the phone answered, '*Oui, j'écoute!*'

'Is that you, La Croix?'

The voice again answered with '*Oui.*'

'Benoit is playing for both sides at the same time. Find out exactly who he is talking to and what they are interested in,' the caller barked out and ended the call.

La Croix replaced his mobile phone in his coat pocket and continued cooking his omelette on his kitchen stove. He pushed the omelette onto a plate and walked over to the small table in his main living area and sat down. His tiny apartment on the Rue Blomet was on the fifth floor of a rather dilapidated building in the Quinzième Arrondissement of Paris. He had chosen it not for its location; this was not one of the best parts of the city, but for its accessibility and relative anonymity. In any case, he did not stay there for more than a couple of days at a time; he was always on his own and so nobody needed to know.

So Jean-Claude Benoit, an agent working for the DGSE had been scratching more than one back, La Croix thought to himself. La Croix wasn't his real name. He had used this name now for over three years and it had served him well in his particular profession. Secrecy was all important and his various contacts only knew his cover name and certainly not anything more about him. He even changed his 'business' mobile phone on a regular basis so as avoid his movements being tracked.

La Croix knew all about the so-called Action Department of the DGSE from his former days serving in a French military commando unit. They had regular interactions with the action wing of the DGSE and their many covert agents.

He also knew that Benoit was currently posing as a French diplomat stationed in Germany. His sources had kept him very well informed as to all those people who had recently been in contact with a certain Professor Michael Fullerton.

He was going to enjoy taking a closer look at the activities of that fat little man Benoit from now on and, in particular, those people with whom Benoit was involved.

La Croix took his phone out of his pocket once more and dialled a number. The number rang and a voice answered in French.

'Just listen,' La Croix said. 'Get me all you have on the activities of a certain Mr Jean-Claude Benoit; I need this urgently.' He pressed the button on his phone, ended the call and replaced the phone once more in his jacket pocket.

He was in Paris for a further two days; his brief trip had begun in London and he had to be back there again by the weekend. He was meeting tomorrow with someone whose name had seemed vaguely familiar to him. He had recently received word from his superiors that this particular individual could be most helpful to him in his recent investigations. This person was apparently quite an elderly man, in his eighties in fact, and living in a home just outside Paris that catered for retired Catholic priests. The name of that individual was Pierre Fournier.

La Croix journeyed out to the small town of Crecy-La-Chapelle on the eastern outskirts of Paris early the next morning. He had no difficulty finding the Abbaye de Saint Jean, and the Catholic rest home. It was well known in the town. It was the usual turn of the century brick structure, greatly in need of some serious renovation work, aptly situated in a walled enclosure that seemed somehow to convey a sense of faded former grandeur. Ignoring the antiquated bell mechanism, he pushed open one of the large, elaborately embossed wrought iron gates which groaned on its rusty hinges and walked the fifty or so metres to the front entrance. Knocking three times, he stepped back and surveyed the rest of the property. He thought that it must have been a church school building at some previous point in its history but was now looking quite the worse for wear. The property seemed quite extensive and no doubt this rather insignificant refuge provided a safe and secure place in which elderly priests could exist and see out their days.

The door opened and La Croix was greeted by a middle-aged nun.

'*Bonjour, Monsieur, puis-je vous aider?*' she asked quietly. La Croix replied to her in French that he wished to visit with a certain Fr Fournier if that was at all possible.

'I am Sister Marie-Therese, will you please come in.' La Croix followed her into the rather austere hallway and an equally austere waiting room. 'I will go and see if Father Fournier can see you, please take a seat.'

La Croix did not have to wait long and had only just finished studying the various religious pictures on the walls, including a large one of the new pope when Sister

Marie-Therese returned to say that Father Fournier was not quite himself, but could see him for only a few minutes. La Croix followed the sister back into the hallway and down another corridor into an area where there were a number of old residents already seated. This place was full of corridors, La Croix thought to himself.

'Father Fournier will be with us presently,' Sister Marie-Therese said. 'He will be coming through that door over there in just a moment. Please come into this office where you will be private.'

La Croix went over to where the sister had pointed and sat down in such a position so that he could focus on the door in question.

Father Fournier entered under his own steam but with a little help from another sister. He was a frail-looking man, stooped forward and walking slowly with the aid of a stick. La Croix noticed immediately that, whilst Father Fournier was showing every physically outward sign of his advanced years, his eyes retained an astonishing clarity and focus.

The sister helped Father Fournier to sit down in the raised chair opposite La Croix and then left the two of them alone. La Croix noted that the door had been purposely left partly open. No doubt someone was listening.

La Croix leaned forward and shook the emaciated hand of the elderly priest.

'Thank you for seeing me at short notice,' he said. 'My name is Thierry Leblanc. I have a few questions for you about the assistance the church is giving to retired priests such as yourself.'

The old priest looked across at the young man sitting opposite him and studied him intently.

'Why are you interested?' he asked.

'I am an investigative journalist and I need to know as much as possible about the retirement conditions for people like yourself.'

'We are looked after very well. The sisters are very kind and do as much as they can to make our lives as comfortable as possible,' Fournier replied.

La Croix stood up and went over to close the office door. There was a rustle of skirts outside as their listener vanished.

La Croix chuckled to himself and sat down again.

Leaning forward, he resumed.

'What can you tell me about an organisation that carries your name, the ADF?'

Fournier smiled as he thought about all those many years of struggle and sacrifice that he had made in the early years to promote his own writings and ideas.

'I am afraid that I cannot help you, young man,' Fournier replied, continuing to study La Croix's face. 'It has been many years since I had anything to do with all that.'

La Croix wondered what the old man meant by 'all that' but didn't push for a further explanation.

'Do you know anyone that I could talk to about the current activities of the ADF?' La Croix asked.

Fournier again studied his young inquisitor and continued to smile.

La Croix decided that this old man couldn't provide him with anything useful and that he was starting to waste his time.

'Thank you for your willingness to meet with me, this morning, Father,' he said briskly and shook the old man's frail hand. He stood up and made his way to the door.

The old man looked again at his young visitor and was struck by his resemblance to a man he had known many years before.

Fournier beckoned with his hand for La Croix to come back nearer to him. In a low voice the old priest said, 'You should talk to my old friend James Fullerton in Geneva, you know.'

175

La Croix felt a sudden shock go through his body as he heard the name. This was the second time in as many days that he had heard this name mentioned.

La Croix shook the old man's quivering hand once more, gave the old priest a final look and with it, a half smile, and left the room, partly closing the door.

A nun soon appeared as if on cue and gave him a searching look that seemed to challenge the true purpose of his visit. La Croix journeyed back into Paris. His mission had gained a sense of urgency and he knew what he must do now.

La Croix knew a lot about the lobbying activities of the ADF and that James Fullerton was probably one of its most active and influential members. What came as a surprise to him was the fact that the old priest he had just visited would readily remember him and provide apparent strangers with his name.

Was this a piece of innocent, confused advice from the old priest or was this relationship more than he could presently comprehend. He was sure that Fournier was being watched and his visits recorded.

He would advise his superiors and await their instructions.

As for Benoit, he would wait for his associates to call him back with any useful facts.

Chapter 31

The German Foreign Minister had been found shot dead in his office building in Bonn. It had been a carefully executed operation, undoubtedly planned using insider knowledge. The event had made the headlines in all the national and international newspapers and all TV news programmes were running reports live from the scene.

Fullerton had only just landed at the Geneva International airport and as he and Marguerite walked through the terminal they saw the latest news flashed up one of the numerous TV screens. They both stood still and looked at the broadcast footage and the ticker-tape sub-titles. There was no sound so they couldn't hear the commentary.

'German Foreign Minister Brecht shot in Ministry building three hours ago.'

'My God' said Marguerite, 'we were there ourselves this afternoon!'

Fullerton stared at the screen and watched the rest of the broadcast.

'This name is very familiar, I've seen it somewhere before and quite recently.'

Gerhard Brecht had been quite a controversial figure during his time at the German Foreign Ministry. He was known to be very progressive and had created quite a sensation when he had gone ahead with a meeting with the newly proclaimed leadership in Bosnia.

177

'You remember that mysterious note that I received back in December. That was the coded name!'

Fullerton switched 'his' mobile phone back on and saw that he had three missed calls. Once in the limousine, Fullerton checked the numbers to see if they were in his phone memory. Looking at the first of these missed calls he was very glad that he had transferred all his old numbers into James's phone. He decided to return this call; it was from Jason Fletcher in London. How had Fletcher managed to obtain James's mobile phone number? Fullerton paused before returning the call; he listened to the message that had been left.

'This is a message for Mr James Fullerton. Mr Fullerton, this is Jason Fletcher of the British Foreign Office. Please be good enough to return my call at your convenience.'

Fullerton pressed call-return and waited for his call to be answered.

'Mr Fletcher? This is James Fullerton, how can I help you?'

'Mr Fullerton, thank you for returning my call. There is an important matter that we would like to discuss with you in person as soon as possible.'

'Mr Fletcher, I am sorry that I missed your call but I was in the air on my way back from Bonn.'

Fullerton guessed that Fletcher probably knew this.

'Have you seen the TV news?' Fletcher asked.

'I take it you are referring to the recent news from Germany; yes, we saw it briefly in the airport; is that why you're calling?'

'It certainly is. 'This occurrence is of the greatest possible concern to Her Majesty's Government.'

'When would you like to meet?'

'Tomorrow if possible in London,' Fletcher replied anxiously.

'I'll see what I can arrange, Mr Fletcher. I do have

some business to attend to in London. I'll call you as soon as I know my ETA; I take it I can reach you on this same number?'

'That's correct, I'll be waiting for your call; I can come to pick you up when you arrive.'

Fullerton needed to get home as soon as possible and make some calls.

They arrived back at the house about forty-five minutes later. Fullerton went straight into his office and attended to some pressing business matters that his lawyer had left for him to review and sign.

His secretary had taken care of all the routine messages and those that required his particular attention were waiting for him next to his office phone. There was one from Fletcher which he deleted and decided that the other two could wait.

'Marguerite! Call the airport and tell the pilot we are going to Heathrow in the morning and book our usual rooms at the Dorchester.'

Marguerite went into her own office next door and made the obligatory call to Paris.

Chapter 32

January 24th, 2009. London and Bonn.

'Well, this is going to be interesting,' Fullerton said as the plane made its approach into Heathrow.

'How often have you met Fletcher?'

'Just the once, last August I think it was, in London. Still says that he is from the Foreign Office but James thought differently. He reckoned SIS.'

Their plane landed and Fullerton and Marguerite found Jason Fletcher waiting for them in Arrivals with an appropriate sign.

Fullerton had had a long discussion with Marguerite on the short flight over to London and told her about the significance of the name Brecht. They were going to go along with the appearance of assisting the intelligence agencies in order to find out what they knew, or more importantly, didn't know, but not to the extent that they had anything themselves to report.

'Good morning, Mr Fullerton,' Fletcher said as Fullerton and Marguerite walked towards him. The two men shook hands.

Fullerton introduced Marguerite to Fletcher and they went outside to where his car was waiting.

Marguerite tugged at Fullerton's coat as they followed Fletcher outside to his waiting car, and looked in Fletcher's direction as if to confirm that Fletcher had not appeared to be too surprised by Fullerton's appearance. After all Michael and his brother had been identical twins.

Fullerton let Fletcher know that Marguerite was fully in his confidence and therefore he could speak freely.

'My lot are freaking out over this one, Mr Fullerton. They have their suspicions as to who was involved.'

'Well, I don't exactly know what use I can be in all this. I have been talking to some of my business contacts and they aren't exactly laughing their heads off either. Your security people really should be more on the ball,' Fullerton commented sourly. 'Christ! We were in Bonn ourselves when this shooting took place. That doesn't look good from where I am sitting. It could have been me.'

'Where are you staying?' Fletcher asked.

'The Dorchester,' Marguerite replied.

'Right, can I suggest that I drop you both off there directly and we can then meet later with some of my other associates who are working on this.'

Fletcher used his car phone to relay their coordinates to his people and Fullerton dialled a couple of numbers on his mobile as well. One call was to Frankfurt to leave a call-back message and a second one to his lawyer in Geneva.

Fullerton's lawyer was out of the office as was his business colleague and so Fullerton left similar call-back messages for both the German and the Swiss.

Fletcher dropped the two of them off at the front of the hotel and drove off to park his car. There usually was valet parking but no one was in sight and Fletcher didn't want the hassle of waiting until someone appeared.

They both decided to check into their rooms and agreed to meet Fletcher in the hotel foyer in fifteen minutes.

Marguerite let herself into her room and landed her case on the bed. She went into the en-suite bathroom and turned on the tap, took her phone out of her bag and dialled Paris. They would need to know what she was doing in London.

The three of them met downstairs and went over to the nearest lounge area and ordered some coffee.

Fletcher had heard from his people and stated that they would be over to the hotel by 1.00 pm with their latest briefings.

'Well, Mr Fletcher, tell me why my presence is so important to the British Foreign Office,' Fullerton began in a tone of voice reminiscent of his brother's.

'I would prefer to wait until my colleagues arrive, but as they will not be here for a while, I think I can tell you this much,' Fletcher began. 'We have good reason to believe that the motivation behind this killing is not just a coincidence. The German Foreign Minister, Gerhard Brecht, had been intimately involved in some very crucial negotiations with other EU Foreign Ministers.'

'What has all this to do with me?' Fullerton asked, still using his brother's businesslike approach.

'You are a leading figure in the ADF are you not, Mr Fullerton and there is increasing evidence that your organisation, if I can call it that, is directly involved.'

'That is absolute nonsense!' Fullerton exclaimed. 'The ADF is a legitimate group of people who discuss import-ant matters with a large number of individuals across Europe and internationally and use force of argument to correct what they see as badly constructed government policy. I will not believe that anyone belonging to the ADF has any remote connection with this or any other crimes.'

'Well, I hope that the information that my colleagues will be presenting will not come as too big a surprise to you, Mr Fullerton,' Fletcher retorted.

Somewhere in Bonn, La Croix up-ended the glass of lager that was in front of him and walked out onto the street;

he disliked noisy bars but they were useful places to while away the time.

He had been in Germany since the previous Wednesday and had made some interesting discoveries about certain DGSE operatives that were active in Bonn. His own sources had provided him with some very detailed information and it had been his job to authenticate that information and inform his superiors accordingly.

All he knew initially was that certain DGSE and possibly SIS operatives were physically present in Bonn at that time. He also had been informed that certain ADF members had also been in Bonn.

La Croix called a number on his phone and waited for the recipient to answer.

'This is La Croix. Meet me at the corner of Maximilianstrasse and Poststrasse in half an hour.'

The phone went dead and La Croix looked at his watch to take note of the current time. He only had half a mile to walk and would be there in plenty of time; besides, he could observe the scene before his contact arrived.

Back in London at about the same time two other men, also purporting to be from the Foreign Office, arrived and shook hands first with Fletcher and then with Fullerton and Marguerite.

Fletcher asked them to outline what precisely was their latest information.

Fullerton listened intently to the presentation. All that these people knew at the present time was that this apparent assassination had been carried out in a very similar fashion to all the previous ones. A lone gunman was again thought to have been the only person involved. One single, well-aimed shot to the head at close range.

No motive had ever been established for the earlier

killings and no organisation had publicly admitted to the killings.

'This is going to take some careful investigation,' Fletcher remarked. 'Mr Fullerton, we have asked to meet with you because of your involvement with the ADF. From where I stand, it is starting to look like the ADF is involved up to their necks.'

'Gentlemen, this really is getting quite ridiculous. You have absolutely no proof whatsoever,' Fullerton responded. 'There is no way that the ADF is involved and you have no evidence of any ADF involvement. What I would like to know is why the Foreign Office and not the Intelligence Services are involved.'

'They are very much involved, but we are taking the lead in trying to assist our European neighbours,' Fletcher replied.

Now things were starting to become a little clearer, Fullerton thought.

'We are putting a high priority on these events, Mr Fullerton, as are our European counterparts. Why did you think we are going to all this trouble?'

Now that was indeed the very question that he wanted to understand, Fullerton thought to himself. What was their real motivation and who was calling the shots? He had a strange sensation after that last remark from Fletcher that this was no idle enquiry.

Fullerton was then asked a more leading question by one of Fletcher's associates.

'Mr Fullerton, are you aware of any extremist element within your organisation? Maybe there are some of your members that have decided to take the law into their own hands.'

Fullerton had to control himself before answering.

'The ADF remains committed to its original ideals. To those essentially expounded by its founder, Father Pierre

Fournier. We would not tolerate extremists of any variety if we had any, particularly those whom you suggest would take the law into their own hands.'

How was that for a politician's answer, he thought to himself?

'You would inform us should you come across such individuals,' came the next inane comment.

'Gentlemen, I can assure you that you would be the first to learn about anything that I consider to be of direct interest to you,' Fullerton responded tactfully.

'If this is all that you gentlemen have to discuss, I do think that this meeting was a little over-rated and certainly premature,' Fullerton continued. This was just another fishing expedition on their part in the hope that something would be disclosed by accident.

Fletcher looked uncomfortably at his two colleagues as they considered Fullerton's last remark.

'Thank you again for your time Mr Fullerton,' Fletcher said as he now glared at his colleagues as if to convey his annoyance at having arranged what had turned out to be a pointless discussion.

'That was a bit of a waste of time,' Fullerton said to Marguerite as they walked back to their room. 'These people don't live in the same world as we do. They look for suspicion and intrigue in everything they come across and when it does exist they can't see it.'

Chapter 33

January 24th, 2009. London.

Fullerton had discussed with Marguerite the information that Frankfurt had sent over. This was a very serious situation and he recognised that serious action was needed. The discussions with Fletcher and Von Beck all pointed towards there being an extremist element within the ADF organisation. This element was using information that legitimately passed between associates and converting it into the warped justification for their more extremist activities.

'You have to admit, Michael, that what the intelligence agencies are guessing at, we already know,' Marguerite said in a tone that matched her belief.

'Von Beck and Fletcher are just dangling the bait in the hopes that I will confess to being involved. Once I do that, they will never stop squeezing me for more and more details,' Fullerton answered. 'You know that I am right.'

'Someone had your brother killed, Michael and it certainly doesn't look like it was the intelligence agencies. They aren't even really sure that you have anything to do with any of this. They have no motive; quite the reverse in fact. They need you a lot right now because they are obviously getting nowhere!' Marguerite was starting to get a little angry now with Fullerton's apparent lack of awareness of the obvious. 'They apparently want you to give them all you've got, why?' she continued. 'Why do they feel that you are the only one that can help them solve these murders?' I don't think they need you for that reason at all, Michael. You are assuming that they are too clever. I think that they just want to learn all about the Agency's activities so that they can destroy the Agency. These murders are just a front, an excuse to get you to confide in them.'

Michael turned to Marguerite and looked at her intently.

'How do you come to this conclusion?'

'Because I know that this is what they are trying to do.'

'How do you know?'

'Sit down, Michael, here next to me; I have something to tell you. Michael, do you trust me?'

'You know that I trust you, Marguerite; I have told you everything that I know; you are the only outsider that knows who I really am. Even my kids don't know that!'

Marguerite took hold of Fullerton's hand and looked into his eyes.

'There is something that I haven't told you,' she said. 'I was working at the university when we met up again.'

'Yes, I know all that,' Fullerton answered impatiently.

'Well, I had another occupation as well as my teaching career.' She paused. 'I am in the DGSE.'

Fullerton stared back at her.

'Why are you telling me this now?'

'Because you need to know this now,' Marguerite said. 'I was originally assigned by the DGSE to look into the activities of the ADF, but things have changed now. They know that I am now working for James Fullerton and this has proved too valuable for them not to use the connection. They have instructed me to feed, directly to them, all that I know or can find out about any involvement you might have with these extremist elements. They want this information by any means and they don't give a damn about who gets destroyed in the process.'

'My God!' Fullerton said with a total sense of bewilderment. 'And what have you told them about me?' he continued. 'Do they still think that I am James? And if they do, how do they think you managed to become James's executive assistant?'

'I haven't told them anything at all that matters. I told them that I had met you on a couple of occasions at some high-level business meetings and we started seeing each other.'

'At least that part of the story is true. Things have changed between us, Michael. I didn't agree to come to Geneva and work for you just because you asked. I came because I wanted to; I wanted to be near you.'

Fullerton looked at Marguerite and took hold of her hand again and stroked it gently.

'And I wanted you to be near me,' he replied. 'I don't want you to ever not be near me again,' and with that last remark he hugged Marguerite and kissed her neck.

Fullerton hadn't felt like this for a long time, not since Evelyn had still been alive. He knew that he loved this woman and just wanted this moment to last and last.

He pulled back and looked Marguerite full in the face.

'I love you, Marguerite,' he said.

'I know that I do,' she replied and they kissed each other for the first time in a way that only two lovers could kiss.

'I think I started loving you when we were in Rome, you know,' Fullerton said as they stared back at each other. 'I didn't trust my instincts back then; it was still too close to Evelyn's death and she was still very much on my mind.'

Marguerite said simply:

'I have loved you since we were at college together; we both have something to remind us of that. When we met again and decided to go on holiday to Rome, I did not know how you would feel and so I allowed things to take their natural course.'

'Is that why you never married?' Fullerton asked.

'I don't know. I was busy with my career and keeping our secret from my parents, but I suppose that it must have had something to do with it,' Marguerite replied.

'You realise that I probably have only fallen in love with you now that you are rich and famous,' she added with a giggle.

'I thought as much; classic case of the secretary making out with her boss,' Fullerton added with a laugh.

A serious look came over Fullerton's face.

'Where does this leave us with all that is going on right now?'

'We carry on as usual; we keep the SIS on the hook for as long as it is necessary and I do the same with my lot,' Marguerite replied. 'We have to find out who is involved in all of this; people are being killed and I am sure that your brother was getting close to the truth before they found out and killed him as well. We are going to have to be very careful; there are people out there who will stop at nothing to kill you "again" once they find out that their first attempt was unsuccessful. We are going to have to come up with some kind of a plan and I'm sure that we can use the intelligence agencies to do most of the work. Let's finish off what we have to do with the SIS here in London and then we can get back to Geneva and start planning our own surprise.'

'Now I want you to kiss me again,' she added.

Chapter 34

January 27th, 2009. London.

Clayton Andrews had always had a sixth sense when it came to smelling out questionable corporate practices and he had been proved right on a number of occasions.

He had had that feeling again ever since he read the obituary page of *The Times* and observed the large tribute article to a certain Oxford professor.

He opened the left-hand drawer of his desk and took out a manila folder and opened it. There he had kept a copy of that same article.

Professor Michael Fullerton

The sudden death of Professor Michael Fullerton has been announced from Magdalen College, Oxford. Professor Fullerton had just returned from a lecture engagement in Switzerland and was taken ill on his arrival back in London. He had just returned to his home in Oxfordshire and required the immediate services of doctors after feeling unwell.

Professor Fullerton had been a leading figure in the world of international economics and a valued member of the university academic staff.

He is survived by his two children, Richard and Louise, his wife having pre-deceased him earlier last year.

Professor Fullerton's brother is the multi-millionaire

investor and international business tycoon Mr James Fullerton who resides in Geneva.

Andrews stopped reading the article; he had read it and re-read it so many times. There were a number of apparent inconsistencies in this whole sequence of events and Andrews couldn't quite put his finger on what.

He picked up the telephone and placed a call to a person that he had found very useful in the past.

Blake Thomas was a private investigator. Andrews had used him before for certain court proceedings where there had been a need for some confidential and carefully discreet investigative work. He was going to see what Thomas could come up with on this one.

Thomas answered the phone.

'Clayton Andrews here, I have some more work for you, please call in at my office early next week and I will acquaint you with the case details. My secretary will fix the time.'

Andrews replaced the receiver and thought smugly to himself. This could turn into a nice little money-earner if he was even half correct in what he suspected.

Michelle was sat in front of the TV watching the latest news broadcast. Andrew was at play school and didn't need picking up for another hour or so. Richard was away on yet another of his short overseas business trips. These trips were becoming more and more frequent of late and she was starting to regret the job that Richard had taken after leaving the service.

Richard was not the easiest of men to live with, never mind be married to, but he was an attentive father and seemed to be content with his new employment. There were moments when she felt that he had kept a part of himself to himself, a part that she would never know. His mood swings could be quite dramatic, but she put that down to his still incomplete adjustment from the military life to which he had grown all too accustomed.

This was a part of his life that had existed before they met; he had never talked much about it and she hadn't raised the subject either. She had spoken to his father about it but he had not been able to provide any meaningful advice. In fact, she had gained the distinct impression that her father-in-law had seemed in some way embarrassed to discuss his son's early childhood. Evelyn too had been fairly tight-lipped about this as well and now neither of them was around to provide any further moral support or guidance.

Richard was due home in a couple of days, from Egypt she thought this time and she pinned her hopes on an enjoyable few days as a family.

He supposedly was going to be meeting his uncle in the next few days or so and so Michelle hoped that this get-together would provide some means of easing the sense of loneliness that pre-occupied her husband of late.

Blake Thomas showed up at the offices of Andrews, Thompson & Claybourne and asked to see Mr Clayton Andrews.

'Come in, Thomas, sit down,' Andrews said in his official, solicitor's voice. 'I have an interesting piece of work for you. It involves the death of a certain Professor Fullerton last October. I need you to find out all you can about the events surrounding both the time of death, the doctors involved, the funeral and most importantly anything you can dig up on Mr James Fullerton, his brother.'

'Would that be the Mr James Fullerton of the Axxon Group?'

'Yes, it certainly would,' Andrews replied. 'You will be retained by me on your usual terms and you will speak to nobody about my involvement or divulge the reasons behind your investigation, should you be asked. Is that perfectly clear?'

Thomas nodded to show his agreement.

Andrews continued.

'Here is a file with some initial facts in it, see what you can find out and report back to me in seven days. That will be all.'

Thomas left the building and puzzled at the motives involved. He had never really liked Andrews, but work was work and this could prove to be a nice little earner. Little did he know about his client's own similar thoughts.

Thomas decided that he would commence his investigation in the usual manner, death certificate, attending physicians, last known movements, etc. He would even drive down to Witney. He thought that he would go there and chat to the locals a bit, see who would or could tell him anything. A few pound notes pressed into the right palm worked wonders for the memory. After that, he would go to the main library and search all the city newspapers for any relevant articles.

His short visit to Witney and some informal interviews with the local inhabitants proved more informative than he could have imagined. These people saw everything that went on and knew about everybody's movements. Even if they didn't, one of their neighbours filled them in on any juicy gossip.

He specifically asked them about the doctors that had been involved and how they came to be so conveniently available. The locals confirmed that they had not seen any noticeable sign of activity at Professor Fullerton's house although there had been some late-night comings and goings in recent days. They also confirmed that none of the town doctors had been contacted which Thomas thought was very strange in emergency situations like this.

Back at the library, he concentrated on the main broadsheets and went back over the articles printed just after the date of death. Here he drew a blank; there was no record at all of the death at the house in Witney and no articles between the date that Michael Fullerton died and the funeral itself. This in itself was not surprising, but the information that he had gained from some of the locals pointed to some curious chronology. The fact that the doctors who attended Mr Fullerton were readily available in the town; the fact that the ambulance that took away the body was from a private hospital and the fact that all these events seemed to happen with clockwork precision. They certainly seemed all too efficient and far too convenient.

Thomas went round to the private hospital involved and watched the comings and goings of the ambulances. He walked over to the ambulance bay and started a conversation with one of the drivers.

'Oh, no, we don't get involved with transporting dead people; the hospital always uses one of several local undertakers.'

'So, you wouldn't go to, say, somebody's home to collect a dead body then?'

'Why on earth would we do that?'

Thomas started to smell a story and now was becoming convinced that he was onto something.

He decided to go to the airport the following day to see if there was anything unusual in the flights from Zurich. This source of inquiry had proved in the past to be quite informative but in this instance it provided no leads.

194

He decided instead to concentrate on the medical treatment that Professor Fullerton could supposedly have been receiving. Perhaps Professor Fullerton was already seeing doctors on a regular basis, but this thought didn't hold up to much scrutiny. Professor Fullerton had only very recently arrived back home in any case.

Thomas contacted the General Medical Council and asked for details on the two doctors who had signed the death certificate. This information was not readily forthcoming, so again he had to resort to one more of his covert methods of investigation. He knew of several doctors who were in general practice local to the place where he lived and, in particular, one who could be 'leaned on' for a bit of apparently trivial information like this.

This line of enquiry proved to be the icing on the cake; the two names of the doctors involved were found to belong to two rather elderly doctors who were in general practice in the north-east of the country. They were hardly likely to have been on the spot in London just when so urgently required. Thomas, however, decided to be completely thorough and placed calls to the two doctors' surgeries. He pretended to be with a drugs company and wondered if either of them travelled down to London at all. The reply he received confirmed that neither of them had made any recent visits to London or indeed any visit outside of their immediate area for a long, long time.

Thomas wrote up his facts and called his client for further instructions. Clayton Andrews had no intention of discussing any of the details over the phone and so they arranged to meet at a nearby coffee house later that same day.

'OK, what have you managed to find out?' Andrews demanded.

By the time that Thomas had completed his report and

fully explained his activities, Andrews had already started to formulate in his own mind his own particular plan of action.

Chapter 35

Back in Geneva, Fullerton and Marguerite started to compare notes.

'Let's consider what real factual information we have,' Marguerite began. 'We are one hundred percent sure that your brother was murdered. We also know that he was an active member of the ADF and we also know that he had some secret connection with these four other individuals, whose names we now know. They use this blue eagle logo and somehow have the name Martin in common.'

'Your lot, Marguerite, in Paris, have also confirmed to you that the intelligence community is out to discredit the ADF or at the very least to neutralise it,' Fullerton added.

'As both the SIS and the DGSE seem to require our cooperation, what do they think we can provide them with? The ADF is obviously being targeted by the intelligence agencies because their respective governments have given it such a high priority.'

Fullerton paused in thought as he tried to find the missing factor.

'There's more to this than some petty bribery or lurid scandal surrounding some politician.'

'The codes that James kept in his bank safety deposit box appear to allow the receiver of such information advance knowledge of both the location and the individual targeted. We also know that the last coded message that I have received provided Gerhard Brecht's name and a location. What we don't know is why the particular message identifies Milan. Brecht was killed in Bonn.'

'Keep going, Michael,' Marguerite said encouragingly.

'These four people plus now myself, so five people are privy to the names of these targeted individuals before the actual event. Why? One reaches the obvious conclusion that these five individuals comprise some kind of extremist grouping that are somehow responsible for committing these murders?'

Fullerton looked at Marguerite.

'If my conclusion is correct, I just can't believe that James was complicit in this.'

'Well, we should be able to find out what these four people have been up to and where they each were when the latest assassination was carried out,' Marguerite said.

'Easier said than done I'm afraid,' Fullerton replied.

'This name 'Martin' has me baffled. Why would James write this name in large letters on the front of the folder and then place all this stuff in his safety deposit box? Remember, Marguerite, he only told me about the key and where I could find it after his death in October. Why would he do that?'

'Because he knew that his attempts to locate the extremists within the ADF had been uncovered? Why else was he poisoned?' Marguerite ventured.

Fullerton pondered this, then went on.

'James needed me to take over his identity without anybody knowing other than myself and a few very close friends that he trusted. He also must have known what he was asking me to sacrifice for this continuity.'

The two of them sat on the sofa deep in thought and considered where this process of logical deduction was taking them.

Finally, Fullerton began again.

'Marguerite, just listen to this. What if James was killed by the Intelligence Services because they thought he was responsible for the assassination of Marc Roland last March? It would certainly explain why the SIS and DGSE suddenly contacted me and have since wanted me to get to know my brother again and why they kept telling me that he was in serious trouble.'

'But why kill him if they thought that you, by meeting him, could bring them absolute proof?' Marguerite queried.

'No, there is more to this. James was murdered by poison; this is not the work of the intelligence agencies. What if he was actually murdered by one his friends and it was made to look like a government cover-up?'

'OK, but then you have to supply the motive,' said Fullerton. 'We need to find out what these four people are actually involved in and, as I don't yet know how involved James was, I am also not sure how we are going to do this.'

Fullerton looked at Marguerite and a faint smile appeared on his face.

Marguerite was about to say something, then stopped and looked at him.' Why are you smiling?' she said.

'No particular reason.'

Chapter 36

January 31st, 2009. Crecy-La-Chapelle.

The two men had been provided with detailed information on their target and were being paid double their normal fee to take care of this assignment because of its urgency. It didn't seem like a particularly dangerous assignment compared to their previous ones. In fact, they both had a hard time understanding what the possible significance was in eliminating an old Catholic priest, living in retirement in an out-of-the-way rest home in the French countryside.

They had both been employed in this sort of work for many years and had long ago lost the need or the inquisitiveness to know any of the personal details. Money talked and it was just a job of work to them for which they were well recompensed.

In small rural French villages outsiders would attract a lot of attention. If they were to arrive as two strangers with no apparent reason for being there, they might as well nail a description of their activities to the town hall door.

The Abbaye, its layout and accessibility and the movement of its occupants needed some detailed scrutiny, but it all needed to be achieved in one, or at the most two, quick visits.

Their specific instructions included a requirement that their target had to be eliminated in such a manner as to give the appearance of death by natural causes. No reason was given for this and the two men did not query the instruction.

Their plan took the form of a visit by two sanitary officials, sent to the Abbaye by the regional department for health to carry out a routine inspection of the premises. This guise would give them complete access to the buildings without creating any undue attention. It was also a Saturday which should ensure a minimum number of staff to encounter. Once completed and all details decided, a second visit later that same day would be required to achieve their objective.

Arriving in Crecy-La-Chapelle in the early morning, the two men could quickly see that there was limited access to the Abbaye. The main building could be seen through the old iron railings that formed the perimeter of the grounds. A gravel driveway led straight to the front entrance which was flanked on either side by neatly arranged and well-kept borders.

The two men had acquired a nondescript white van which would both serve as their mode of transportation and give the appearance of just another routine tradesmen's visit.

They rang the bell and waited for a response. A few minutes elapsed which they both used to study the façade of the building itself and the layout of the grounds. They noticed that a number of the residents were using the grounds for short walks and on sunny days such as this, to sit outside on one of the many benches that had been provided.

A middle-aged nun soon opened the door and inquired as to the nature of their visit.

'Good morning, Sister. We represent the local authorities and are here to carry out an official inspection of the sanitary facilities.'

'Please come in, gentlemen.'

'I wonder if you could give us a brief tour of the Abbaye so we can better understand the internal layout of the plumbing arrangements. This tour afforded the two men invaluable and detailed knowledge of the internal room layout, both public and private.

Their enquiries quickly established the fact that all the 87 residents had individual rooms on the first floor. All the ground floor rooms were either public areas, offices or kitchen facilities.

'How do you keep track of all these elderly people?' came the searching question.

'During the day, all the residents are free to move about on their own. At night-time our security is quite strict; access between the various zones of the Abbaye then requires the use of pass keys.'

The Sister then made light of this apparent level of security by confirming that 'it is all for the good of the residents and needed so as to avoid any nocturnal wandering.'

The two men completed their initial tour and made an excuse to return to their van.

'This is not going to be anything like as easy as we first thought,' the first man said.

'There cannot be a second visit,' the second man replied. 'We'll need to find our target and eliminate him right now.'

The two men had already agreed that their method of execution was going to be by lethal injection. It would only take a couple of minutes and would require a very short window of opportunity to accomplish. They decided that they would need to locate their target as quickly as possible without creating any undue or unneeded attention by any members of staff.

They had already established from their apparently idle conversation with the Sister that all the residents were either in the public areas or outside. Lunch was set for 12.00 noon in the dining area. The two men decided to wait for the lunch interval to arrive which only now involved a wait of twenty or so minutes. Maybe they would be able to identify their target during lunch when all the residents would be together.

They returned to the Abbaye and decided to inspect the kitchen areas in the context of their sanitation activities and in the hope of obtaining any kind of a lead

The kitchen staff was all busy with their lunch duties and there was a considerable amount of noise as pans were rattled, plates organised and the general background noise of people cooking and making the final preparations to the Saturday lunch menu.

Some of the more elderly residents had already been collected from their various locations and they were already positioned at the appointed tables. Those who could manage to arrive without aid were gradually entering the dining room area.

'*Bonjour, Alain!*' one of the cooks shouted as an elderly priest shuffled past the counter in search of his place.

'*Bonjour, Matthieu!*' a second voice shouted.

'*Bonjour, Pierre!*' the first cook responded to a greeting from another of the residents.

'How's your letter writing going today?'

The two men stopped and looked at the young woman who had just uttered the last remarks.

'Excuse me *Madame* but who was that you were just talking to?'

'That was Father Fournier, he's one of the oldest residents,' she replied.

'Do you know Father Fournier's writings?' she replied. 'He is always trying to get his articles printed in the local paper.'

'Hmm, no *Madame*, I can't say I've heard of him.'

The two men couldn't believe their luck. They had, until a moment ago, doubted if they could locate their

JAMES BUCKINGHAM

target, a certain Father Pierre Fournier, at all, without bringing a huge amount of attention to their real activities. Now they had found him purely by chance.

They watched where Fournier went to sit down and studied him from their safe vantage point inside the kitchen. They would wait until lunch was over before making their move.

Thirty minutes elapsed and the two men, having temporarily left the confines and potential notoriety of the kitchen, returned once more to spy on their quarry. The old priest was still sat in the same spot but looked as if he might be ready to leave shortly.

The two men concluded their contrived form-filling and made ready to follow Fournier as soon as he showed any signs of leaving the dining area.

At length, Father Fournier stood up and, slowly making his way out of the dining room, shuffled down the hallway. He stopped at the open doorway which led out into the rear garden. Looking out, he decided to take a short stroll.

The sun was quite strong for late January and the old priest had always enjoyed being in the open air and pleasant countryside that his various rural parishes had afforded.

Beyond the lawns and the rather attractive flowerbeds was a wall separating the inner grounds of the Abbaye from the less frequented but equally well-tended vegetable garden and orchard. The Abbaye relied greatly on home-grown produce and the orchard produced some lovely cooking apples and berries in season.

Father Fournier decided to visit the vegetable garden; it reminded him so much of his early years as a priest and his rural parish in Brittany. Reaching the gate in the wall, he opened it and surveyed the rows of planted crops, some already harvested and empty.

He turned as he heard the sound of footsteps on the gravel path and peered at the two men who approached him. They seemed intent on speaking with him and so he paused in the archway.

'Father Fournier?' the taller of the two men asked in a polite tone.

'Yes, I am Pierre Fournier,' the old priest replied. 'Do I know you?'

'No, I don't think so, but we would like a quick word with you. Shall we go and sit down over there?'

The old priest assented and slowly made his way over to a wooden bench some distance from the archway.

He enjoyed these surprise visits.

Fournier sat down and one of the two men sat next to him turning slightly sideways so as to appear relaxed and to put the old man at his ease. The second man remained standing behind the bench.

'We have some associates that have a great deal of interest in you, Father, so much so that they have asked us to pay you a visit and let you know just how much they think of you.'

The old priest sat and stared at the apple trees, half listening to the young man next to him. The trees reminded him yet again of his own rural parish all those years ago and his love of the Breton countryside.

The sudden sharp pain as the needle entered his bony right arm forced him back into the present and he turned his head to look as the second man emptied the contents of the syringe and withdrew the point.

'Your friends hope that you will now have a nice sleep!' the tall man said as he rose from his seat.

Pierre Fournier felt a warm feeling come over him and then everything went black.

The two men waited for a few moments for the drug to take full effect. No pulse could be found and the old priest's eyes were staring vacantly into the distance and his head had now flopped over to one side. They arranged the body in such a way as to give the appearance of slumber; not unexpected for a man of Fournier's age.

Returning quickly through the gateway, the two men retraced their steps through the corridors of the building and out of the main entrance. They walked slowly but with purpose down the driveway and to their waiting van.

Chapter 37

February 4th, 2009. Geneva.

The sad news that his old friend and, in many respects, mentor, Father Pierre Fournier had died reached Fullerton from an unknown source.

The note, which was postmarked Paris, just said the following type-written words:

[Father Fournier found dead in the grounds of the Abbaye de Saint Jean on Saturday. He didn't die of old age.]

Fullerton looked at the envelope for a further means of identification. There was none. Whoever had sent this note had intended to remain anonymous.

Why had they told him? Fullerton showed the note to Marguerite for her reaction.

Marguerite contacted her DGSE sources for any information on this subject. She didn't approach it head-on but managed to find out that the local police were considering the case. She made a few further phone calls and soon ascertained who exactly was in charge of the case.

'Michael, I am going to Paris in the morning to meet with the local police who are looking into the apparently suspicious circumstances surrounding Father Fournier's death.'

'OK, you see what you can find out,' Fullerton replied.

'But don't make it look too obvious! I need to attend to some personal matters and I also have to arrange some "business" meetings with my ADF associates and see if I can come up with any useful information from them.'

Both Fullerton and Marguerite had re-arranged their offices in the mansion so that they were now adjacent to each other and could easily converse through the open inter-connecting doorway.

'I need to go to my flat in Paris in any case, Michael, to collect the remainder of my things and to hand back all my keys. I would also like to see a couple of my university friends as well as I haven't been in contact for a while and they don't know that I have moved.'

Chapter 38

Fullerton had searched James's house again and again and had gone through all his brother's belongings and papers except for those few that he had picked up from the safety deposit box. He opened his safe and withdrew the folder in which he had placed these pages.

The exact connection between James and these four individuals still remained a mystery but any direct contact with them had to be ruled out until he knew more about who and what they were.

Fullerton went through each document line by line. He even read the old newspaper articles that James had kept. In amongst the newspaper cuttings was one that he hadn't noticed before. All the others were about himself and his various activities that had made the papers over the years. This one wasn't about him at all; it was quite a long article in the French newspaper *Le Figaro* about the formation of a new political faction by a young Catholic priest named Pierre Martin Fournier in 1957. The date of the article was December 12th, 1958. The last part of the article dealt with the response this action had received from the Catholic Church authorities in Rennes and the resulting excommunication of the young priest.

Fullerton read the article again. There it was – the name 'Martin'. He, himself, had known Father Fournier quite closely when he was a student in Paris in the 1970s but had never known him as anything other than Pierre.

Was this the same Martin that was written on the front of James's folder containing all the secret codes?

The phone rang, Fullerton picked it up.

'Mr Fullerton, there is a Jason Fletcher on the line for you.'

'Put him through.'

'Mr Fletcher, what can I do for you?' Fullerton said, trying quickly to remind himself of what the discussion had been when they spoke last.

'We have some interesting information for you,' Fletcher said.

'Do you know anyone by the name of Steven Fellowes?'

'No, not to my knowledge,' Fullerton replied. 'Should I?'

'Well he says he knows you and quite well; certainly by his account,' Fletcher continued.

'We have good reason to believe that Fellowes is possibly one of the most active members of your Association right now. You might want to make some enquiries about him from your end.'

'Thank you, I will look into it and let you know,' Fullerton replied.

Fullerton did indeed recognise the name Fellowes, but managed convincingly to convey his ignorance of the man, since he, Michael, had as yet not met with one of his brother's secret associates. If these four individuals were all ADF members, perhaps his good friend Baldini could shed some light on their activities.

Fullerton placed a call to Milan, only to be informed that Sgr Baldini was not at home and would not be returning until the weekend. Fullerton made a note to call his friend again in two days' time and ask him to use his very efficient information network to discover the activities of both Fellowes and the other three on his brother's list.

Chapter 39

February 5th, 2009. Paris.

Marguerite arrived in Paris on a scheduled flight from Geneva. Fullerton had needed his plane for his own activities. She took a taxi from the airport to her apartment on the Boulevard Saint-Germain, collected some post from her box on the ground floor, climbed the stairs and let herself in to the apartment.

It was quite obvious as soon as she walked in that something was very wrong. Her hall carpet had been ripped up; the two pictures that were on the wall had been pulled off, broken and discarded on the floor.

She walked on into her living room and found a similar state of destruction there too. She had removed most of her belongings to Geneva but the larger items of furniture which had been in the flat and which she had no further use for, had been totally demolished.

Marguerite put down her bag and took out her phone and called her DGSE contact.

'Roger, this is Marguerite. I have just arrived back at my apartment on the Boulevard Saint-German; it has been totally ransacked. What the hell has happened?'

'We haven't been anywhere near your apartment, Marguerite. Give me fifteen minutes and I will be with you,' Roger replied.

Marguerite thought of calling Fullerton but knew that he would be in meetings most of the day and so put her phone back in her bag.

She continued to look round the wrecked apartment. Whoever had been responsible for this action had been very thorough. They had searched absolutely everywhere. Even the kitchen drawers had been dragged out and left on the floor.

She went back downstairs to the apartment where the concierge lived. Marguerite knocked on the door and waited. The door opened and the old lady greeted Marguerite with a smile.

'*Madame*, have you seen or heard anyone entering my apartment whilst I have been away?'

'There were two men dressed like removal men who said they had come for the rest of your belongings and needed a key. They looked OK and so I let them have my pass key. I didn't see them come down as I had to go out shortly after they arrived.'

'When was this?' Marguerite asked.

'Let me think now; it would have been last Friday, because that was the day I went to my sister's house in Mantes.'

'Thank you, *Madame*,' Marguerite replied and turned to go back up to her apartment.

Marguerite studied the desolation in her apartment; this was a professional job. She had had some experience of this kind of search in the DGSE and knew that only this detailed a search would have been undertaken if whoever did it had some really good intelligence.

The strange thing in this case was that she knew that there was nothing in her apartment to find no matter who it had been.

Roger arrived and came in through the open door of Marguerite's apartment.

'Someone has given this place a thorough examination,' he said.

'That was what I was thinking, Roger,' Marguerite replied.

'It definitely was not any of our agents,' Roger said. 'I

have already informed our people of this and they will make some enquiries. What were they looking for?'

'My thoughts exactly,' Marguerite replied.

'Whoever it was didn't know that I had moved most of my possessions to Geneva already,' Marguerite added.

'When exactly did you move?

'Last month, didn't I tell you? James arranged it all for me.'

'Well, if you don't need me for anything else, I will get back and see what I can discover about the identity of your visitors,' Roger said as he walked towards the door of the apartment.

'No, nothing,' Marguerite replied. 'I won't be here long myself; I was only going to arrange for the rest of the old furniture to be taken away. Not much left though worth collecting out of this mess.'

Once in the street, Roger called his office on his mobile phone.

'Gaston, it's Roger. Listen! I have just left Marguerite. She knows nothing and has no idea who entered her flat. I've told her that we weren't involved and that we will investigate. No, there's no way she will find out that it was us. We made too much of a mess.'

Marguerite called one of the local removal firms and asked them to just take everything in the apartment and sell anything if it was worth the trouble.

She pushed her key under the concierge's door and shut the main entrance door to the building behind her. She felt a little sad at leaving this place for the last time but glad that it was going to be for the best.

She had arranged to meet two of her university colleagues for an early lunch just round the corner and so walked eagerly along the pavement to towards the restaurant. She didn't notice the two men sitting in the grey Peugeot across on the other side of the tree-lined Boulevard.

213

Marguerite arrived at the restaurant later than she had planned. Her two friends were already there and were just about to phone her to see where she was.

'Sorry I'm late,' Marguerite said. 'I had a bit of a problem at my old apartment.'

'Well you aren't going to believe what we have been through this morning. We have both been interviewed by some security people. It was most embarrassing, being called into Mr Monet's office and asked questions by these people.'

'What did they want to ask you?' Marguerite added innocently.

'This was the strange thing about it,' one of them replied. 'We were both interviewed separately by these two men in Mr Monet's office and asked the same questions.'

'Oh, do hurry up you two and get to the point,' Marguerite said.

'We were asked how well we knew you, Marguerite. They wanted to know how often we met outside of work and what we did or discussed when we did meet.'

'That's really strange,' Marguerite said. 'What did you say to them?'

'Well, we didn't have anything to say to them really. Are you in some kind of trouble, Marguerite?'

'No, not at all,' Marguerite replied not very convincingly.

'Oh, Marguerite, you can trust us you know.'

'Listen, both of you. There's something going on, but I just can't tell you about it right now. You must promise me that you will say nothing to anyone. It's very important!'

'Well that's going to be really easy seeing as how we don't know anything anyway!' came the reply and they all laughed and continued with their lunch.

Lunch over, Marguerite kissed her girlfriends goodbye and hired a taxi to take her out to Crecy-La-Chapelle. She had telephoned the local police earlier and identified herself as working for the DGSE. Arriving at the tiny local *gendarmerie*, she went in and asked for Inspector Le Blanc.

Inspector Le Blanc was most polite and went through all the details of Father Fournier's case so far.

'This is a very strange case,' Le Blanc began. 'Father Fournier had been found out in the garden of the Abbaye early in the evening. He had sat down on one of the benches near the orchard and had apparently gone to sleep. He was found later that evening by one of the sisters who had noticed that Father Fournier was not in his room. She thought that he was just sleeping but did wonder as it was a rather chilly evening and her first concern was that Father Fournier would catch cold. The Sister walked right up to Father Fournier and gently touched his arm in order to wake him up without giving him a fright. Father Fournier just flopped over sideways on the bench as the Sister screamed for help.'

'Did anyone see anything or hear anything out in the garden?'

'We have spoken with all the sisters on duty that evening and none of them heard or saw anything.'

'Had Father Fournier received any visitors recently?

'We are looking into that at the moment,' another officer replied.

'Do we know how he died?' Marguerite asked.

'No, not yet. We are awaiting the results of an autopsy right now.'

'Why is an autopsy being performed?'

'Because the attending physician noticed that Father Fournier's eyes were quite bloodshot and there was some bruising to the side of his neck.'

'Why is this case of interest to the DGSE?' Le Blanc asked.

'That I cannot tell you, Inspector,' Marguerite replied. 'Is there anything more that you can tell me at the present time?'

'I think not,' the Inspector replied. 'I will of course notify you of the progress of our investigation.'

'Thank you, Inspector.'

She decided to have a look round the building and grounds so that she could better understand what might have happened. Apart from the main building block, there were a number of other smaller structures, some attached to the main block and others separated by enclosed corridors or external pathways.

The grounds turned out to be quite extensive with a walled vegetable garden to one side, a large expanse of crudely mown lawn in the centre and a high privet hedge separating the lawn from the apple orchard. All of this was contained within a high, partly crumbling brick and stone wall which made up the perimeter of the establishment.

'Can you show me where Father Fournier was sitting when he was found?' Marguerite asked the attending nun.

It struck Marguerite as quite strange that the old man would have been sitting on a bench some considerable distance from the main building, particularly at that time in the evening.

No doubt the Inspector would investigate that particular aspect.

Access to the grounds of the Abbaye was also limited to two routes, one external wrought iron gate which Marguerite was informed was rarely opened and normally kept locked and the main access gates from the Abbaye itself.

Marguerite had not provided the Inspector with the details of the anonymous note that Fullerton had recently received. She knew that there must be a reason why

Fullerton had been singled out for this particular attention and both she and Fullerton needed to solve that mystery first.

Marguerite decided that there was nothing more to be gained by staying longer at the Abbaye and so located her patient taxi driver and returned to Paris.

Chapter 40

Marguerite's phone rang and her secretary announced that she had an Inspector Le Blanc on the line.

'Good Morning, Inspector. Do you have any further information?'

'That's why I am calling, *Madame*. I have to inform you that there have been some very interesting discoveries. You must keep what I am about to tell you in the strictest confidence however. Firstly, and most importantly, the results of the post-mortem on Father Fournier's body revealed a very high dose of barbiturate poisoning. He was not receiving any medication from the nuns in the Abbaye and the pathologist was certain that it had been administered by a single injection into his right arm where there was some local bruising. The marks around the neck are thought to be the result of the limited struggle that the old man put up against his assailant.'

'So you are treating this as a case of murder, Inspector?'

'That is correct, *Madame*.'

'*Madame*, I would ask you to keep all this information in the strictest confidence. You would not be receiving any of this if it had not been for your close connection to Mr James Fullerton. I could not provide you with this knowledge even knowing that you are in the DGSE with whom we have been asked to cooperate.'

That last remark struck Marguerite as quite odd. She had told nobody of her intention to visit the Abbaye and

218

she doubted that the police inspector had gone to the trouble to inform the DGSE about what he must have thought was a routine police matter.

'Inspector, were you contacted by one of my colleagues in Paris?' Marguerite asked.

'No, *Madame.* I received no such call from the DGSE. These instructions came from a very senior level within my own organisation. I was instructed to make only a certain amount of information available to you directly and without delay. That is why I have called you now.'

'Thank you, Inspector, you are most kind. Please continue to keep me informed,' Marguerite said, still not understanding what forces were in play over this incident.

Chapter 41

March 13th, 2009. Geneva.

Fullerton pulled out his brother's diary for 2008. He noted numerous business meetings and social engagements. There must be something in all this detail that could shed some light on the activities in James's life leading up to his death.

His private phone rang and Fullerton picked it up.

'James, this is Armand, I have the information we will need before next Thursday's meeting in Brussels.'

'That's very good news, Armand; send a copy over as soon as you can so that I can go over it before Thursday.'

Fullerton put the phone down and wondered who on earth Armand was. He was not one of his regular business contacts. After five months running James's business affairs he had become sufficiently familiar with all the regular business contacts to not only recognise their names but to have direct conversations with them. But this person who called himself Armand was not one of them.

Fullerton looked in his diary and saw that the only engagement that had been confirmed by Marguerite for Thursday was an early afternoon meeting in Strasbourg with the European Commissioner for Trade. Fullerton knew that his brother had not met this particular individual previously and needed to understand the background situation.

He picked up the phone.

'Marguerite, I need to find out everything we have on Mr Gaston Cormier, the EU Commissioner.

'I'll see what I can find out and call you back.'

The phone rang again, this time it was one of his staff.

'I have a Mr Clayton Andrews on line two for you.'

'Put him through.'

'This is James Fullerton, what can I do for you Mr Andrews?'

'Mr Fullerton, I'm afraid that you and I will need to meet in the very near future. There are matters concerning your late brother that have come to my attention and I feel sure you will find them of significant interest.'

'What on earth could you possibly need to talk to me about concerning my late brother? Fullerton replied trying not to sound too defensive.

'As your solicitor, Mr Fullerton, there are significant legal issues that will need some kind of satisfactory resolution. Shall we meet in the next week or so?'

Fullerton had never liked this individual and thought back to their first meeting. Now, again, he felt somehow uncomfortable with this discussion but didn't know why.

'I will have my staff confirm some suitable dates with your secretary in due course, Mr Andrews,' Fullerton answered in an official tone and replaced the receiver.

He returned to his work in hand and decided to forget about Andrews at least for the moment.

Thursday's meeting in Brussels and the call from his 'friend' Armand again occupied his thoughts. Fullerton, for no particular reason found himself referring to the 'Martin' file once more. There, in bold print was the name Armand Dubois – one of his brother's four mystery contacts.

It looked like at least part of this puzzle was about to reveal itself. He wondered what this information would contain and how he was going to react to its content. One way or another, something was undoubtedly about to explain his brother's secretive association with these individuals.

Chapter 42

March 14th, 2009. Geneva.

The encoded e-mail was waiting in Fullerton's Inbox. Fullerton printed it off and translated it using the code book he had retrieved from James's bank deposit box.

Mr Gaston Cormier, the EU Commissioner for Trade had apparently been the subject of some intense lobbying pressure by the ADF for about a year and a half with little or no satisfactory progress.

Here were the agenda items for the meeting in Stuttgart carefully presented and a concluding strategy outlined.

Fullerton would be joining Steven Fellowes and Armand Dubois at this meeting. Fullerton knew that Fellowes was also one of the members of James's secret group. He also remembered hearing Fellowes's name mentioned earlier by Fletcher.

He decided that he should do some homework himself on Cormier before the imminent meeting.

Chapter 43

March 19th, 2009. Brussels.

As all three of them would be arriving in Brussels from different locations, it was agreed that they would meet at the airport for a preliminary, face-to-face discussion. The meeting at the EU parliament had been arranged for 11.30 am. The last person to arrive was going to be Fullerton from Geneva at 10.15 am and so they would have approximately an hour to run over the details.

Dubois and Fellowes were waiting for Fullerton as he came through the Arrivals area. Fullerton had wondered how he would recognise these two individuals at the busy airport but rightly assumed that they would recognise him and therefore make themselves known to him.

'Good morning James, good flight?' Dubois asked as they approached Fullerton across the busy arrivals gateway area. Fullerton was quite thankful that this had afforded him a few extra seconds to appear less than a complete stranger. He gave the appearance of knowing who he was talking to in the hope that the identity of each man would soon become clear.

'Let's find a convenient spot where we can have our discussion; we need to show our esteemed politician what we are capable of,' Dubois continued.

'James, I believe that you and Steven already know each other. Steven is usually my main contact and has done some really good homework on this man Cormier,' Dubois added.

Fullerton immediately picked up on this last remark and said, 'Yes, we do', as he acknowledged the man he now knew to be Fellowes.

Fullerton was glad that Dubois, whose identity he also now knew, was doing all the talking; every minute comment was all invaluable information.

'It's been a while since we last met, James,' said Fellowes volunteering further useful facts. Fullerton continued to say nothing.

'Right, is this spot OK for you James?' Dubois said as they came across a small seating area that afforded sufficient privacy.

'This will do fine, Armand; tell me what you have in mind?' Fullerton said, posing a suitably leading question.

'We have almost given up on our friend Cormier; he is just playing politics and treating us like idiots. This is the last opportunity we are going to give him before we start with plan B.'

'Cormier is basically still refusing to grant any of our requests for favourable trading status. This all ends right here today. Steven has all the dirt on this particular individual.'

Dubois looked across at Fellowes.

'Give James a quick run down on our friend Cormier?'

Fellowes looked around to ensure that no one could overhear what he was about to say.

'Mr Gaston Cormier is a prime candidate. We have found out that his present flamboyant lifestyle has and is being funded through illegal bribes, mainly from the eastern European member states but not exclusively. He is "happily" married with a wife and two children who presently live in Lille. His two mistresses are however well concealed, one just outside Brussels and the other in Strasbourg.'

'Obviously not well enough concealed,' Fullerton commented to some amusement.

'He either gives us the agreement that we want on these trade issues today in this meeting or we advise him of the possible consequences,' Dubois added with a knowing wink of his eye. 'We will allow the meeting to progress a sufficient time in a normal businesslike manner and then I will ask if we could have a few words in private with him. We don't want all his bureaucrats to hear all the good stuff, do we? James, you usually like to handle this part of the meeting; shall we just leave you to pick the right time to put the writing on the wall?'

'As you two have all the specifics at your fingertips on this one, why don't you take the lead? I'll add anything that I feel needs to be said,' Fullerton said, expertly extricating himself from an otherwise complicated situation.

'That's fine by me, James,' Dubois replied. 'Now I think we should find a taxi and make our way to his office.'

The three men left the Parliament building and hailed a taxi to take them back to the airport.

'I think we gave our friend Mr Cormier enough to contemplate for a couple of days,' Fullerton chuckled as if he was enjoying the whole sordid process.

'Well, he certainly knows what the consequences will be if he doesn't cooperate. I thought he took everything quite calmly,' Fellowes added.

'I think we will know soon enough what his decision will be,' Dubois said somewhat triumphantly.

They arrived at the airport and Dubois took Fullerton on one side so that Fellowes was out of earshot.

'I will send the usual emails to Breton, Levert and Deschamps. They will want to know the latest information.'

Here were some names that Fullerton had not heard before. He could not believe his luck, however. A picture was now starting to form in his mind. Four people, of whom Fellowes was one, plus his brother to some degree as yet undetermined, were at the very least involved in serious blackmail activity. He didn't as yet know what Dubois's role was in all this and how these new people fitted into the puzzle, but there was obviously a distinct and ongoing connection. Fullerton felt sure that this process was part of a well-oiled machine with some far-reaching consequences, involving a considerable initial financial outlay but with enormous financial benefits. What he needed to ascertain now was the extent to which these other four individuals were involved and just how far this activity had affected other possible ADF clients.

He decided to bring Marguerite up to speed on all this and see if she could shed any light on the whole process from her contacts in the DGSE.

Chapter 44

March 25th, 2009. London.

Fullerton's business interests had kept him quite busy over the past ten days and this latest trip to London was no exception. He needed to reorganise some of his financial dealings as well as consider at least one potentially lucrative acquisition. There was also the meeting with Clayton Andrews that he had put on his agenda for this London visit.

Fullerton had engaged the professional services of a different law firm in London for the changes that he was about to make. There was something about Andrews that he didn't like and until that particular matter had been resolved, he thought it would be both prudent and more effective if he isolated Andrews from his business affairs for the time being.

The new firm of solicitors, Cromwell Whitegate, had been strongly recommended by one of Fullerton's new but influential business associates and from his initial discussions, seemed to prove themselves worthy of that same recommendation. Fullerton had given them some detailed instructions on his latest business reorganisation as well as some due diligence work to carry out regarding the potential acquisition. Their senior partner, a Mr Benjamin Taylor, had undertaken to perform the necessary work himself.

Fullerton went back to the Dorchester after a satisfactory day in discussion with Cromwell Whitegate. He checked into his room and phoned Marguerite, who had not come with him on this particular trip. He had grown used to her presence; she provided him with the company that he now found he needed and business trips like this one, where he was without a confidant, seemed all too lonely and even boring at times.

Her voice at the end of the telephone was a poor substitute for her actual presence but he needed to run through a number of business matters with her and to hear how she had progressed with some of her investigations.

'Hello, Marguerite. How was your day?'

'My day has been quite busy actually, Michael. By the way, the valuation on that company in Frankfurt has arrived. I have given it a preliminary look and their work seems to be very thorough.'

'That seems promising then,' Fullerton replied. He visualised Marguerite sitting at her desk in the office next to his and decided that phones were merely a means of conveying information. They made other, more personal kinds of conversation too clinical and impersonal.

'I should arrive back in Geneva on time tomorrow evening and so will see you then. I have something that I want to discuss with you,' he found himself saying.

'That sounds ominous.'

'Oh, I don't think you will find it too hard to understand,' Fullerton said.

'Anyway, got to go, see you tomorrow. Bye,' and with that rather starchy farewell Fullerton ended his quick call to the woman who he now knew was very important to him.

Fullerton had arranged for Clayton Andrews to meet him at the Dorchester the following morning. He had purposely chosen the venue for the meeting so as to place his former solicitor at some slight disadvantage.

Fullerton's phone rang in his room and the hotel reception advised him that there was a Mr Andrews in the foyer waiting to meet with him. Fullerton asked the caller to notify Mr Andrews that he would be down in five minutes.

'Good morning, Mr Andrews,' Fullerton stated in a suitably businesslike tone. 'Shall we sit over here?'

Fullerton listened as Clayton Andrews made his ingenuous opening remarks and then ran through his litany of piecemeal evidence that some private investigator had obviously been hired to produce. Some of the facts were quite close to the truth but most of what Andrews had to say was quite circumstantial and uncorroborated. The conclusion that Andrews had arrived at, however, was unwittingly deadly accurate. Andrews was sitting there and telling him to his face that he was an impostor and had somehow taken his brother's place.

The exposé ended with the inevitable suggestion that a certain financial arrangement could be considered in order to obtain his continued silence on the subject.

'Mr Andrews, this whole notion of yours is a complete fabrication; I strongly suggest that you investigate the dealings of whoever supplied you with such ridiculous information. Furthermore, if I hear anything further from you on this matter, I will have to consider my position.'

Andrews stared at him.

'In that case, might I leave you with this envelope and its contents which I am sure you will realise are more than justified under the circumstances,' he said with his usual, but now more pronounced, sneer.

'Good day Mr Andrews,' Fullerton snorted and left his adversary to his own devices.

Returning to his room, Fullerton mulled over the discussion that he had just had with Andrews. He was angry, not so much about the details of Andrews's cheap blackmail attempt, but more at his own over-reaction to the revelations. He should have remained much more calm and composed. He felt that he had almost convinced Andrews that his suspicions were well-founded and could now only have reinforced the certainty that Andrews obviously entertained.

Fullerton opened the envelope that Andrews had handed him. The single sheet of paper just contained the phrase 'Five million pounds'. So Andrews thought he could expect that kind of sum for his silence. Well, he was going to have to think otherwise; Fullerton was not going to be blackmailed by some petty, crooked London solicitor. Whatever he did, however, would need to be carefully thought out. Andrews still knew an awful lot about his corporate affairs.

Fullerton was also forced, by this action, to consider his own role in the ADF. Was he not just being a simple blackmailer, similar in approach to Andrews?

It was at this particular moment that Fullerton instinctively knew what his brother had been attempting to achieve and in all likelihood why he had been murdered.

James, for all his business acumen had, in all probability, been unwittingly drawn into a seedy world of political intrigue and eventual blackmail by his own sheer determination and drive to see the success of the original ideals of the ADF as espoused by Father Fournier. These same ideals had now been hijacked by a small group of, in this instance, four other powerful men, who added the sinister world of blackmail and possibly murder to ultimately ensure the success of their misguided aims.

Fullerton now knew exactly why his brother had purposely revealed his apparently questionable activities to his brother after his death. James somehow knew that the only person to right the wrongs and continue to redress the balance was his own twin brother.

There was, however, one issue that was not going to allow all his and his own brother's good work to come to nought and that was the Andrews situation.

Fullerton completed his business in London and arrived back in Geneva later that same evening and was met in the hallway by Marguerite, who gave him a big hug and a kiss.

'Did you have a successful trip?' she asked innocently.

'It was quite interesting,' Fullerton replied. He did not want to get into any immediate discussion about Andrews or even tell Marguerite about his own recent conclusions about James's activities. That could wait until the morning when both their minds were fresh.

'Right now I have something far more important to discuss with you,' Fullerton found himself saying. 'Come here and sit down beside me; I need your undivided attention.'

'I was right, this does sound ominous,' Marguerite smiled.

'Imagine we are still sitting on that seat watching the Seine flow past with only each other to concentrate on and no worldly concerns yet to spoil the moment.'

Marguerite said nothing but looked at Fullerton with a certain vulnerability showing in her eyes.

'Marguerite, you know who I am and what I am; you also know what I have sacrificed to help my brother and you have known me ever since we were young happy-go-lucky students in Paris. We shared our love once and have a son to show for it. I don't know what the future will hold and I have only a small grasp of what my brother's activities are going to show as I try and piece this puzzle slowly together. What I do know is that I do not want to be continuing with all this by myself. If you love me as much as I know I love you, I need you to answer this next question very carefully.'

'Marguerite, Will you marry me?'

'Oh, Michael, you know I will,' Marguerite answered and kissed him.

Chapter 45

La Croix had returned to Bonn for a very specific reason. He had received the information he had expected and now it was time to put in another appearance.

He would only be in the city for less than twenty-four hours. What he had to do should take a lot less than that if everything worked out as he planned.

This time he had driven all the way to Bonn from Paris and found that several hours alone in a car allowed him to formulate his plan of action without any distractions.

He had arranged to meet Johannes Von Beck. Until this moment, Von Beck had been in the employ of the DGSE in Germany, but his activities involving the exposure of certain ADF members had been brought into question.

La Croix knew that the information that had been passed on to him by his superiors was 100 per cent accurate. Even if it wasn't, when he received specific instructions, his superiors knew that they would be carried out to the letter.

Von Beck had been under suspicion, it appeared for some time, but now there was no doubt as to his current activities. Blackmail, bribery and complicity in the murder of two influential politicians required an equally strong and suitably discreet response. This is what he had been trained for and now he had been called upon to act.

La Croix had arranged to meet Von Beck in one of Bonn's city centre bars. This kind of public place would

233

allow Von Beck to feel at ease and reduce the likelihood that he would suspect anything other than a simple exchange of cash.

La Croix had arranged to meet Von Beck at 9.30 pm that evening. The bars would all be busy and there would be plenty of people frequenting the numerous drinking establishments.

Von Beck was a middle-aged man with white hair and a small mole on his right cheek just below his nose. La Croix could therefore easily recognise his quarry without initially revealing his own identity.

The bar that La Croix had chosen was one that he had visited on an earlier assignment and it suited his purpose again on this occasion. There were three different levels, each with its own drinks counter where the usually young drinking crowd could move around and circulate without attracting any particular attention. At this time of night La Croix knew that it would be full to capacity.

La Croix left his car at a discreet distance about two streets away and walked the short distance in between in about three minutes.

He waited outside for a few moments and then entered the premises, passing the two heavy-set men on the door without notice.

A quick tour round the three levels assured La Croix that his quarry had not yet arrived and so he stationed himself at the foot of one of the staircases where he could survey any new arrivals.

He was not kept waiting for more than five minutes when he saw Von Beck walk in, make his way to a gap that formed along one of the counters and wait for one of the scantily clad girls to serve him.

Von Beck was casually dressed with a heavy dark cotton shirt and grey trousers. He seemed to know his way around and even spoke to a couple of the other drinkers. One of the drinkers engaged Von Beck in a brief conversation. More than just a casual chat, La Croix thought. La Croix watched the two men discuss something. He assumed that this was probably one of Von Beck's regular haunts. Once served, the two men moved along the bar and appeared to be studying the other revellers. La Croix waited until Von Beck and the unknown man had ascended to the middle level before continuing his survey of the premises.

La Croix was aware that the establishment had toilets situated on all three levels. The upper two levels had fire exits just to the side of the toilet blocks. La Croix ascended the stairs, walked to the rear of the building and passed through a pair of swing doors that led to the toilets on that level. Checking that he was alone, he moved over to the nearest fire exit and checked that the crash-barrier-styled door would open.

Returning to the bar, he observed the two men still in conversation. The unknown man finally shook hands with Von Beck and left the establishment by the front entrance. La Croix moved up alongside Von Beck.

'I believe we have some business to conduct this evening, Herr Von Beck,' he said quietly.

Von Beck looked round to see who had spoken. He studied La Croix intensely.

'I believe that you have something for me?' Von Beck replied in an insolent tone of voice.

'I trust that you also have something for me?' La Croix replied.

Von Beck placed his glass down on an adjacent table and moved to pull a package out of his left rear pocket.

'Not here!' La Croix muttered, taking Von Beck's arm. 'I think we should be a little bit more discreet. Follow me.'

La Croix led his quarry into the men's toilet. There were two other occupants just on their way out.

It was all over in a split second; the stiletto knife slid into Von Beck's back; his scream was stifled by La Croix's left hand as he was forced against the tiled wall. A second thrust saw the knife bury itself up to its hilt in Von Beck's upper chest.

La Croix quickly allowed Von Beck's body to slide to the floor. He removed the thick envelope from Von Beck's now lifeless body before leaving the room. A cleaning trolley was conveniently sitting outside the entrance and La Croix quickly pulled it out of its corner so as to block the entrance. One minute later and he had descended the rear escape stairs and out into the crowded street once more.

Once back in his car, La Croix paused for a few moments; he took a deep breath and drove slowly away. All that training had proved its worth yet again, he thought to himself. Once out of the city and back on the autobahn, La Croix made the expected phone call to his superior.

Five hours later and La Croix was back in Paris at his little apartment. He decided to visit one of his local all-night clubs and unwind before trying to get any sleep. He had to be in London by the following evening and so could afford to sleep in late. The Eurostar train reservation was not until mid-afternoon and the cross-city journey from his apartment to the Gare du Nord would not take that long.

Chapter 46

Fullerton caught up on all his recent post and business dealings and scheduled a couple of meetings for the following week. He still used one of Baldini's close confidants as his key member of staff. Marguerite was now proving invaluable in her ability to fully execute most, if not all, of Fullerton's confidential business dealings.

Later that morning, Fullerton unlocked his safe and reached for the manila folder containing all the information that James had deposited in the bank. Two larger files containing various corporate statements also tumbled out of the safe and spread their contents on the carpet.

'Damn these papers!' Fullerton cursed under his breath and collected them up as best he could.

'Marguerite, can you come in here and re-sort these documents. You know how I hate getting everything in a mess and can't put my hands on things when I need them.'

Marguerite came in from her room next door, smiled at him, gave him a kiss on his head and walked back into her office.

Fullerton turned to close the safe door when his eyes chanced upon a panel near the bottom. Removing some of the remaining folders, Fullerton saw that there was a small compartment in the base of the safe which required a small key to allow it to open. The key-hole was quite small and almost round; it obviously needed a miniature

237

key of the sort usually only seen in use on fine antique furniture.

Turning back to James's desk, Fullerton remembered seeing a small key in one of the many compartmental drawers. A brief search located the little key which Fullerton then tried out in the safe.

Sure enough, the lid sprang open to reveal the first couple of inches of a red file folder. Carefully removing the folder and its contents, Fullerton looked again in the compartment for any further documents. It was now empty.

Placing the red folder on his desk, Fullerton opened the cover.

The first dozen or so pages were stamped TOP SECRET and quite clearly belonged to various British Government departments. Behind these pages were three further pages containing names, what appeared to be communication codes and addresses in several European cities.

'Marguerite! Come in here.'

'What do you think that all this means?' he asked, showing her the red folder.

Marguerite studied the pages while Fullerton explained how he had found them.

They both looked at each other for a moment in silence.

'What has James been involved in?' Fullerton said as he started to study some of the written contents.

'Stop a minute!' Marguerite said as Fullerton was about to turn to the next page. 'This page has DGSE top level security; I haven't seen anything like it before, but I do recognise the security level.'

'These others are British Government papers, more specifically Foreign Office,' Fullerton exclaimed as he continued leafing through the papers. 'My God, this one is discussing termination options against certain foreign dignitaries and has been initialled in ink at the bottom! CFS if I am not mistaken.'

'Good God! You don't think that stands for Charles Stevenson do you?' Marguerite exclaimed.

Fullerton removed his glasses and looked up at Marguerite in absolute astonishment. James Fullerton was quite obviously either involved in or aware of some very, very secretive and important government discussions clearly relating to foreign powers. Not only that, the French Government was also clearly implicated.

'Why was James involved in all this and more importantly who was he working for? He can't have been working for both governments?' Fullerton said incredulously.

Marguerite picked up a couple of the DGSE stamped pages and studied their contents, which were written in French.

'I don't think I like what I am thinking, Michael,' she said. 'These papers are liaison documents produced by the DGSE and dealing with some very critical policy decisions that have been taken by the British and French Governments. Why would James have these documents in his personal possession?'

'I was about to say exactly the same thing, but the other way round,' Fullerton replied. 'James was somehow receiving top secret information. Was he privy to this information in order to perform some kind of double agent function?'

'No, we don't know that. We do know that he was in possession of some very sensitive documents and people have been killed for less than this.'

'You don't think James was found out and eliminated by external government forces?' Fullerton said.

'I don't know, Michael, but what I do know is that James appears to have been playing a really dangerous game.'

Chapter 47

March 31st, 2009. Paris.

He glanced over at his private mobile phone as it started to ring in its usual melodious tone.

'*Oui, j'écoute!*' he said as he put the phone to his ear. La Croix knew that this would be one of his contacts phoning him at the agreed time.

'Benoit is involved,' came the abrupt statement.

What do you want me to do?' La Croix asked.

'He is running scared now that he has heard about Von Beck. We need him to understand that his life will be spared on one condition. He must on no account provide Dubois with any more information. He needs to be convinced that his life expectancy will be longer if he now works with us rather than against us and for his own financial gain. Please make sure that he fully understands this.'

La Croix needed no further explanation. The phone line went dead.

Later that same afternoon, La Croix waited on the corner of the Rue Mathieu and the Rue des Rosiers in the Saint-Ouen district where he could keep a close eye on the building that Benoit called 'home'.

He had already visited the building and ascertained that Mr Benoit was not home and according to the very sociable concierge, usually came home around 5.30 pm when he was not out of town.

La Croix crossed the street and sat down outside a rather seedy café and ordered a cognac. He could still observe Benoit's building and thought that he might as well enjoy a drink while he waited.

The predominantly blue-collar neighbourhood soon started to fill with a variety of people of all nationalities as they trudged home from their nearby menial jobs. La Croix wondered why Benoit had remained living in this area when he could quite easily have afforded somewhere more congenial. No accounting for tastes, he thought.

It had now been some two hours since La Croix had taken up his watch and still no signs of Benoit. He decided to pay the concierge another visit.

The concierge spoke in limited French with a heavy Moroccan accent. But she did inform La Croix that Mr Benoit had indeed returned home and was upstairs in apartment 413.

La Croix thanked her for this information and climbed the stairs to the fourth floor. There were children running along the hallways and sounds and smells of African cooking wafted down the corridor on the slight breeze.

Finding apartment 413, La Croix knocked on the door and waited.

Benoit's chubby round face duly appeared and he stared at La Croix as he finished eating a rather disgusting piece of salami.

La Croix wasted no time in informing Benoit that he worked from the same organisation as he did. Benoit seemed to relax but was surprised by the unexpected evening visit.

'I don't know who you are, my friend, but I am sure that this could have waited until tomorrow.'

La Croix said nothing and pushed past his fat friend and walked into the apartment.

'I didn't ask you to come in,' Benoit protested.

241

'No, that's right you didn't,' La Croix muttered as he pushed the door shut with his foot. 'I have something to tell you.'

'Well, whatever it is, be quick. I'm cooking!'

La Croix looked at Benoit for a moment and then grabbed the fat little man by his shirt collar and shoved him into a dilapidated armchair.

'I will talk, you will listen. Do you understand?'

Benoit nodded his head as he stared up at La Croix from the chair.

'There are people that are becoming quite concerned about you and your association with a man by the name of Von Beck. As you probably know Mr Von Beck upset my associates and, unfortunately for him, met with a rather nasty accident just recently.'

Benoit's face turned pale and his sausage slipped from his mouth onto his large stomach.

'You are asked to refrain from your current activities and to stop providing certain people with privileged information. The consequences of your not agreeing with this request would be most unsatisfactory and you could put your health at great risk. Do I make myself clear?'

Benoit said nothing at all and just nodded his complete compliance.

'That is very wise,' La Croix said. 'There will be no second visit by me or anyone else should you choose to disobey this request. You will just read about yourself in the local obituary notices. Do try and work hard for the people who pay your salary. It would be for the best.'

La Croix turned and left the apartment. He felt sure that Benoit had understood the message.

Chapter 48

April 2nd, 2009. London.

Clayton Andrews felt quite pleased with himself. His meeting a few days earlier with James Fullerton had been quite productive. Mr Fullerton's reaction and anger at his 'proposal' seemed to at least partly authenticate what that idiot Thomas had managed to come up with.

A classic case of where there's smoke there's fire, he mused. What must be done now was to decide on the next course of action. Fullerton was not going to just pay up and hope that the matter would go away.

Andrews stared out of his window and considered his options. Fullerton would pay up: not likely, at least in the beginning. Fullerton would bluff and do nothing: again not likely. Fullerton couldn't afford any public scandal or notoriety. Fullerton would offer him a lesser amount: No, why would he admit to there being any truth in the facts provided to him?

No. Fullerton would probably take some direct action, possibly even intimidation. He would never agree to a financial settlement.

Andrews decided that he would beat his adversary to the punch. I wonder what the intelligence community would make of all this evidence, he thought. There was certainly enough detail to stir up some interest.

Thomas had, as part of his investigation, established that James Fullerton was now a naturalised Swiss citizen living in Geneva but with a lot of business dealings in France.

A tip-off to the French police, in a country where he could be the most vulnerable. That would deflect any attention at all from himself as being the source. The French authorities would more than likely feel that it came from a business adversary.

He would carefully select what factual information he had and also conveniently add sufficient fabricated details to cause quite a stir where it would do the most damage.

His mobile phone rang. La Croix answered it with his usual, *'Oui!'* It was a call from his 'employer'.

'A situation has arisen that we need to understand,' the voice said. 'Some information has been passed to us by the French police in Paris which needs your particular attention. Please arrange to come in for discussions.'

The line went dead.

La Croix was in London but knew instinctively that his superiors did not waste their time, or indeed his, on matters of insignificant detail. Whatever it was required his prompt attention.

La Croix checked on the Eurostar schedule and selected a journey time that would place him in Paris in a little over three hours.

The journey to Paris was uneventful and La Croix made his way from the Gare du Nord to the offices of the DGSE on the Boulevard Mortier.

He was duly ushered in to the office of his superior, Pascal Lefevre.

'La Croix! Come in, sit down over there. I have some rather strange information that has been passed to this department by the police here in Paris.'

La Croix asked if he could smoke. He took a cigarette out of a packet in his jacket pocket and lit it. He studied

Lefevre, looking for some kind of reaction in connection with this rather urgent summons, but detected none.

Lefevre walked over to where La Croix was sitting and handed him a thin folder.

'The pages you will find in this folder were mailed anonymously to the Prefecture here in Paris yesterday. It is only because a good friend of mine happened to contact me about this matter that I even know of its existence. You will see that there is a great deal of information concerning a certain James Fullerton, not to mention some quite disturbing allegations as to his exact identity. Please read all this information here in this room and I will return in one hour to discuss the matter in some detail. In the meantime, I have an important meeting with the Director.'

La Croix relaxed a little after Lefevre had left. He had worked for Lefevre for a couple of years now. They had only met on a few occasions and during that time La Croix had decided that he did not particularly like him. Lefevre was a typical intelligence officer who had made a career out of being the ever-dutiful civil servant. He had never been 'in the field' and had never found himself in a position where he had had to make important decisions. All the 'instructions' that had come to La Croix from Lefevre over the years had in fact come from a far more senior level. La Croix was employed because he did what he was told without any questions and carried out his covert assignments with military precision. This was the life that La Croix knew and understood; it suited his temperament and besides which, his military training had produced a perfect operative for this line of work.

La Croix started to read the documents and immediately wondered who had spent the time compiling such allegations. What was the purpose behind it all? He studied the details with some interest. The allegations inferred

JAMES BUCKINGHAM

that there had been some kind of very coincidental activity surrounding both the sudden death of Professor Michael Fullerton, his meetings with his estranged brother and the involvement of British Intelligence.

La Croix already knew that James Fullerton had been meeting with both SIS and DGSE operatives and so he could not see what value there was in any of this supposedly important information. It was, in any case, all conjecture and contained no substantiated proof of any of its assertions.

Lefevre returned to his office sooner than expected and after returning some documents to one of his filing cabinets, came over and sat down opposite La Croix.

'Well, what do you make of all this?'

'Nothing at all, if you are looking for my honest opinion,' La Croix answered. 'There is nothing here that I didn't already know. I suggest that we waste no further time discussing it.'

'I have been asked by my superiors to make you aware of its contents and that is what I have done,' Lefevre replied, obviously offended by La Croix's evident lack of interest.

'They 'suggested' that you make some enquiries as to the author of such facts if only to understand the motivation behind it all.'

'I'll see what I can discover when I return to London,' La Croix answered. 'It shouldn't be too difficult to discover who the sender is.'

Chapter 49

April 17th, 2009. Geneva and London.

Fullerton had thought about his meeting with Andrews a week or so earlier in London and decided that it was time to take the bull by the horns.

He picked up the phone and dialled Andrews's office number in London. The number rang a couple of times before being answered by the firm's receptionist. 'Andrews, Thompson & Claybourne, can I help you?' the young lady's voice stated.

'Clayton Andrews, please, this is James Fullerton calling from Geneva.'

'Just a moment, sir,' the young lady replied.

Fullerton had a couple of moments to concentrate on what he would say and to decide on the most appropriate tone of voice.

'Clayton Andrews,' the voice answered.

'Mr Andrews, this is James Fullerton. I am calling you in response to our meeting in London about three weeks ago. No doubt you will recall our main topic of conversation.'

Fullerton had decided in that instant to carry out a normal businesslike conversation with Andrews if at all possible. He could still remember how he had over reacted during their earlier meeting and knew that he would not make that same mistake again.

'Mr Fullerton, thank you for calling. Yes, I do indeed remember our last meeting. What can I do for you today?'

Fullerton was mildly annoyed at the almost triumphant sound in Andrews's voice.

Realising that the call was most likely being recorded, Fullerton remained suitably vague with his comments.

'Mr Andrews, I am just calling to advise you that I will not be taking you up on your earlier proposal as it does not fit in at all well with my other business plans.'

'Well, I am very sorry to hear that Mr Fullerton. It was, I felt, a very well-thought-out proposal. I trust that you have considered all the various consequences?' Andrews replied, equally vaguely.

Fullerton thought just how much he detested this crooked solicitor and wondered how his brother had managed to work with such a criminal.

'Yes, I have considered all the options and will not be considering your proposal further. Good bye.'

With that, Fullerton replaced the receiver. He felt that he had dealt with the matter in a suitable manner.

Andrews replaced the receiver and sat staring into the distance. At that precise moment his secretary called him on his intercom to remind him of his next appointment.

'Tell him to wait!' Andrews snapped back.

'I'll teach that son of a bitch what I am capable of,' he said to himself. He picked up his private phone and dialled a number that he hadn't used for a while.

'I'm looking for Seamus O'Malley. Can he still be reached on this number?'

'You're talking to himself,' the voice replied.

'Seamus? This is Clayton Andrews, I have another little assignment for you. Can we meet at the usual place sometime this evening?'

'That we can. How about 8.00 pm. You can buy me a couple of whiskies.'

Seamus O'Malley was a small-time thug, sometime arms dealer and well known to the local London authorities. 'See you at eight,' Andrews said.

The Old King George pub in one of the less respectable parts of Whitechapel had been in existence since the late eighteenth century and was not the sort of place that anyone who was not local to the area would dream of entering. It had always been a meeting place for the criminal element and had in its time played host to a number of notable gangsters.

Andrews decided to take a taxi over to the Old King straight from his office. He found O'Malley already well positioned at the far end of the long bar with a whisky glass in front of him.

'Mr Andrews, so it is,' O'Malley responded as Andrews walked down the bar towards him. 'What'll it be?'

'Nothing for me,' Andrews replied. 'This won't take long.'

O'Malley sat back and listened as Andrews provided what information he had on a certain Mr James Fullerton. He couldn't help despising Andrews for his 'holier than thou' attitude. After all was said and done, Andrews was just a crooked solicitor whose own personal greed and envy of others had turned him into this rather pathetic individual.

O'Malley knew Andrews only in the briefest sense. Andrews had seen to it that their relationship on previous occasions had been kept at a suitable arm's length. O'Malley had proved useful to Andrews in the past when some strong-arm tactics were required to facilitate the 'adjustment' of witness testimony and the furtherance of Andrews's own professional success.

'OK, I get the picture,' O'Malley said. He didn't need

Andrews to drone on any longer. 'You want me to use this information in any way I can to discredit this man Fullerton and should any financial transaction take place, you presumably want a cut.'

'I will pay you twenty per cent of any money that Fullerton eventually agrees to pay me for keeping silent. I will of course continue to be the only person to contact Mr Fullerton directly on the subject of money but I leave it to you to arrange the "necessary persuasion".'

'You know, Andrews,' O'Malley commented, 'you really should be careful not to bring the legal profession into disrepute.'

Andrews smirked and handed O'Malley the file folder containing all the information on James Fullerton.

'I will expect you to produce some results without delay.' Andrews stood up to leave.

'I always do, I always do,' O'Malley retorted with a smile.

After Andrews had left the pub, O'Malley spent a few moments in thought. He knew exactly who he would call to work on this one; someone who had been very helpful to him in the past.

Chapter 50

June 5th, 2009. Normandy.

The little Normandy town of Vernon had been chosen as the venue for the wedding. Most of Marguerite's friends were living and working in Paris and so Vernon had been chosen for convenience and particularly since her parents lived there, and her father's family had been in the area since Napoleonic times. They had a modest house on the Rue Claude Monet which served as the centre of operations for Marguerite's side of the affair.

Fullerton had flown in from Geneva the previous evening with his close friend and confidant Francesco Baldini. They were both staying at the Hotel Normandy in the centre of the town, conveniently situated for the Town Hall.

Fullerton had invited both his children to the wedding but had only received a reply from Louise. She had decided to drive over to Normandy using the Channel Tunnel and was staying in a local Chambre D'Hôtes.

Marguerite's sister, Marie and her husband had driven up from Toulouse and were also staying with her parents and so the house was literally bursting with family members.

Marguerite's brother, Henri had managed enough leave from the French Embassy and had flown in from Japan two nights earlier.

The civil ceremony was due to take place at the town hall at 12 noon and that Friday morning was all excitement and activity.

The big day had finally arrived. Marguerite had been

staying with her parents since the previous Friday and had enjoyed their company immensely.

All the arrangements had been made remarkably quickly since the surprise announcement at the end of March and now there was nothing more to do.

'*Es-tu prête, Marguerite?*' came a shout from her father. '*Il faut partir maintenant!*'

'I am just coming, Papa, won't be long,' Marguerite shouted from an upstairs bedroom.

The car was waiting outside in the street for the two of them. Her sister was her only bridesmaid as Marguerite didn't want this event to be too ostentatious.

'Here I am Papa!'

Henri De Saulx de Tavannes stared at his older daughter and couldn't find any words to say.

'Do you think it all looks OK Papa?' Marguerite questioned.

Again Henri could only continue to stare at his daughter.

The two of them went into the street and Marie helped her sister get into the car before getting into the second one behind.

The cars then moved off towards the Town Hall and the expectant guests.

Fullerton had made his way to the Town Hall on foot from his hotel and was greeted by many of the assembled guests. Only close friends and family had been invited to this civil ceremony and his eyes searched the room to see who was present.

As Marguerite had not yet arrived at the Town Hall, Fullerton continued to survey the other people present. No sign of Richard he noticed.

Fullerton and Baldini stood together near the large rather ornate table in the centre of the room upon which there were several leather-bound document cases and an array of floral decorations.

Fullerton turned and saw Louise sitting near one of the large casement windows, almost concealed by an enormous French 'tricolore'. He looked at her and nodded. This was the first time he had seen his daughter in twelve months and he had been dreading this particular moment. He had rehearsed this moment many times and knew that he had to conceal a multitude of emotions; but when the actual moment arrived, he forgot about all his fears.

'You must be Louise,' Fullerton said to his daughter. 'Thank you for coming.'

Louise stood up and shook her 'uncle's' hand somewhat formally. Fullerton felt that she was looking at him with a strange hint of recognition in her eyes.

'Why did you not come to dad's funeral?' Louise interjected.

Fullerton had not anticipated this rather obvious question and certainly not at this particular moment.

'I was away on business in the Far East at the time and couldn't return in time,' Fullerton said and hoped that it sounded convincing.

'I never knew that identical twins could look so alike,' Louise continued.

'Well I can't comment on that remark, Louise, as I hadn't met your father in recent times.'

'Is your brother coming, do you know?'

'Yes,' Louise answered. 'He phoned to say that he would be a little late arriving. He has a job in London that takes him away an awful lot. Michelle is always complaining about him being away so much.'

At that moment, the doors at the end of the room opened and Marguerite entered with her father and sister.

Fullerton stared at her and thought that she looked absolutely stunning.

Marguerite walked over to Fullerton and gave him a kiss.

'You look beautiful,' he said.

'Is everybody here?' Marguerite asked her mother.

Her mother nodded a reply.

'Richard is not here yet,' Fullerton said. 'I don't want to begin until he has arrived.'

Louise took the hint and pulled out her phone to try her brother's number. It proved to be a redundant call as Richard appeared through the double doors with his phone in his ear.

'He's here now,' Louise informed the group.

Fullerton turned round to look at his son as he walked up to them. Fullerton glanced over at Marguerite but she hadn't yet noticed her son's arrival and was in deep conversation with one of her mother's old acquaintances.

'Richard,' Fullerton said warmly, extending his right arm for a handshake.

'Uncle James,' Richard replied.

Their hands remained clasped for quite some time as they both looked at each other.

Richard had his mother's eyes but that was where the similarity ended. He also looked very imposing, wearing a suit which made his physique more pronounced. Fullerton knew that this was down to his years in the army.

Fullerton looked over to the door as the mayor and his two companions entered the room and the noise of conversation ceased. He had always been intrigued by the French civil marriage service; it was more like a visit to a lawyer's office than a marriage.

The words said, the signatures completed, Fullerton took hold of his new wife's hand and gave it a slight squeeze. Marguerite had been gazing across the room at her own son Richard. Fullerton caught her gaze and said:

'Let me introduce you to my nephew and niece, Marguerite.'

Introductions over, the invited family members were made aware that there was another ceremony about to commence and that they should make their way to the exit as quickly as possible.

Fullerton hadn't yet met many of Marguerite's family, but acknowledged both her parents whom he had met on a previous occasion some three weeks earlier.

Fullerton and Marguerite climbed into the car outside the Town Hall and were driven the short distance to a rather imposing town house on the Boulevard du Maréchal Leclerc.

This impressive property commanding an excellent view of the river belonged to an old friend of Marguerite's father. The grounds provided a delightful setting for a marquee and were just made to be used for wedding receptions.

Richard and Michelle had been invited to drive over to the reception with his sister. All the conversation was focused on the wedding activity; Richard, however, was far more interested in the two men in the dark blue Citroën which had been parked opposite the Town Hall and was now following them at a very discrete distance.

As they all climbed out of the car which had stopped just short of the very impressive entrance to the town house, Richard glanced in the rear view mirror and observed that the Citroën had also stopped about 250 metres further back on the opposite side of the Boulevard. Richard could now clearly see the silhouettes of two men.

The rest of the family had walked on ahead and had passed through the stone entrance gateway. Richard paused, stared back at the Citroën and its two occupants and started to walk back down the Boulevard towards the stationary vehicle.

When he was only about fifty or so metres away, the car reversed into a nearby driveway and departed at some speed in the opposite direction. Richard smiled and retracing his steps, rejoined the celebrations.

The marquee had been placed in a lovely setting to the side of the expansive property with an unobstructed view out over the river. The afternoon had turned out sunny after some early rain and everything looked perfect for a wonderful reception.

Fullerton and Marguerite were, of course, the centre of attention and were standing in the marquee when Richard finally had made his way through the house and out into the rear garden. Marguerite's hosts had gone to extraordinary lengths to create a delightful setting. Richard rejoined his wife and sister who were strategically stationed close to where they had a nice view of the river and the table from which a selection of wines could be obtained.

'What kept you, Richard?' the ever observant Louise asked. 'I thought you were right behind us when we came in.'

'I was, but I had to go back to the car for something.'

Richard's sister looked at her brother with a quizzical gaze; she had always found him to be all attention one minute and completely lost in his own thoughts the next. She felt that she knew him really quite well but there were times when she wondered whether she knew him at all.

'Have you seen Uncle James yet? You really should go and find him and Marguerite before you do anything else.'

'Er, yes, I'll go and find them right now,' Richard said, thankful that he didn't have to make any further polite but meaningless conversation with his sister.

Richard was still thinking about the two men in the car outside. His gut feel told him that they were government agents; he had long gained a sixth sense about such things but he wasn't sure and that really annoyed him. Obviously, they didn't want to enter into any kind of a conversation with him and must have wondered who he was.

'Hello, Uncle James,' Richard said as he and Michelle approached the newly-weds. 'What does it feel like to be married at last?'

'Hello Richard, thank you for coming. Marguerite is especially pleased that you were able to make it to the wedding.'

'Marguerite!' Fullerton's new wife turned round from a conversation she was having close by with a family friend and gazed at Richard.

'Hello Richard,' Marguerite said in an almost hushed voice. 'It's been a very long time since we last saw a lot of each other hasn't it?'

'Over twenty years, I think,' Richard replied. 'You don't look any different than you did when we last met. I remember my father and mother bringing me to your house that first time.'

Fullerton looked at his son talking to Marguerite and memories flooded back into his mind.

'Uncle James, can I have a quick word with you in private?' Richard asked.

'Of course,' Fullerton replied. He grabbed the arm of Marguerite's father who happened to be passing and asked him to organise another drink for his own daughter.

The two men walked on across the lawn to a spot where they couldn't be overheard. Richard began.

'There were two men in a Citroën out in the street; they had followed us from the Town Hall. Do you have any idea who they might be?'

Fullerton took a little intake of breath and then paused before he said anything back.

'Two men, you say, in a Citroën. Can't think who they might be, nothing to do with me that I know of.'

257

Fullerton winced as he realised that his answer was totally unconvincing.

'Maybe they needed to see my marriage licence,' he added with a forced laugh.

Fullerton knew all too well who might be watching him, but he was not going to explain anything to his son and certainly not at this particular time and place.

'Let's go and find our hosts; you really should meet them. They've been so very kind in donating their house and grounds for the wedding.'

Fullerton led his son off in search of Mr and Mme Colbert, managing to achieve a complete change of subject.

Chapter 51

June 9th, 2009. Avignon.

Fullerton and his new wife decided on the spur of the moment to take a week in southern France following their wedding even though there were many pressing engagements and business dealings to attend to back in Geneva.

They flew down to the airport in Cannes and drove out of town to Fullerton's villa. Fullerton wanted Marguerite to at least see it and spend a couple of nights there but had acceded to Marguerite's wishes and had reserved a room in the *Hôtel Cloître Saint Louis* in Avignon before they had left Vernon.

Fullerton had suggested his own villa just outside Cannes for the whole of their stay but Marguerite wanted them to be completely on their own without any prying eyes of staff to worry about.

It was quite warm for June and the car journey from Cannes had been quite tiring. As they reached Avignon, they could see that it was already welcoming its usual flood of tourists.

They literally just dropped their bags in the hotel room and decided to take a stroll around the central square which was dwarfed by the huge stone structure of the Palais des Papes.

Fullerton felt as if thirty years had been stripped away and he and Marguerite were young students again.

It had indeed been nearly forty years since Michael had been in Avignon, when he was still in school in England.

Not much had changed, particularly in the centre of town. The cafés were still as busy as ever and the roving musicians and performers seemed to be getting in some much needed practice before the annual music festival in a few weeks' time.

'Let's sit down and have a coffee,' Marguerite said. 'I feel like just relaxing and watching the people go by.'

Two coffees duly ordered and delivered, Fullerton and Marguerite enjoyed the mid afternoon sun and the hustle and bustle of this ancient town.

'What did you think of Richard?' Fullerton asked. Marguerite paused before answering and then said, 'He is very much like his father, isn't he?'

'What do you mean by that?'

'He has that *je ne sais quoi* about him, Marguerite replied. 'He has your same depth of personality.'

'What was it like, Marguerite, to see him again after so many years?'

'He is a grown man now; nothing like that young boy who went to school in Paris and thought of me as some kind of honorary aunt.'

'He has always been a very quiet individual,' Fullerton added. 'I never felt that I fully knew what he was thinking. His time in the French army has changed him in some respects. He seems to be happy in a strange sort of way.'

'What do you mean, Michael?'

'Richard gives the appearance of being content; after all he has a lovely wife and young son. But there is a part of him that will, I think, be always kept secret. I sense that Michelle would know what I mean.'

'He is still travelling a lot with his job and I do know that Michelle wishes he would find something closer to home and without all the absences.'

'What did Louise have to say? Did you speak much to her?' Marguerite asked.

'Not too much; I couldn't afford to take the risk of letting down my guard. I sensed that she already felt that there was something strange about our interaction, limited as it was.'

The binoculars surveyed the busy square and focused in on the couple sitting at a table drinking coffee and chatting to each other.

'They arrived in Avignon a couple of hours ago; your informant was worth his money. They have just sat down in the main square and have ordered coffees. I have already checked out their hotel. They are in one of the front rooms overlooking the boulevard, Room 217. I will call you when I have completed the assignment.'

The man replaced his mobile phone in his shirt pocket and continued to observe the couple in the square.

'Shall we take a bit more of a walk?' Fullerton suggested. 'Let's walk up the steps to the palace gardens. It will be a bit cooler up there and the view over the river is wonderful.'

After quite a climb they came to a lookout point which provided a panoramic view of the sweeping bend in the river.

'We can see the River Rhône for miles from here,' Michael said. 'Look, there is the old bridge and over there in the distance is the town of Chateauneuf. One of my favourite wines!'

'Let's take a trip down the river while we are here, Michael. It would be such a nice way to see some of this wonderful scenery.'

'I will find out what we can do when we get back to the hotel.'

They continued their walk through the gardens and ended up down almost at the river's edge before climbing back up into the town from the old bridge.

Reaching their hotel once more, Fullerton had enquired both about the possibility of a boat trip and recommendations for a suitable restaurant for dinner, later that evening. The hotel manager had suggested a little restaurant conveniently away from the main tourist areas and also would be checking out which boats would be available in the morning.

Marguerite decided to go up to the room and have a shower.

'OK, I'll see you in the room in ten minutes or so; I just want to find this restaurant that has been recommended. It's apparently just around the corner.'

Fullerton left the hotel entrance and turned left in the direction of the centre of the town. He had not gone far and he didn't know why but he gained the distinct impression that there was someone following him. He paused at one of the numerous café restaurants to inspect the published menu. The reflection in the glass-fronted window provided an excellent image of passers-by and Fullerton could see that he did indeed appear to be under observation.

Marguerite unpacked her case and hung most of her clothes in the fitted wardrobe. She had not brought all that much with her as they only expected to be away for six nights and unlike Geneva, they were able to wear lightweight clothes given the warm weather.

The doorbell rang and she walked over to it and opened the door. Two men forced their way into the room and dragged Marguerite backwards, throwing her onto the bed.

'Hold her steady,' the heavy-set man said to his accomplice in French.

Marguerite found her arms forced back behind her so that she was now lying on her front with her face pressed into one of the pillows. She was powerless to move or even cry out. She felt the sharp prick of a needle as it entered her thigh. Seconds later, her mind was drifting into unconsciousness.

Fullerton found the restaurant on the narrow side street. It was a quaint little establishment with a couple of tables positioned outside and just off the pedestrian walkway. He peered through the closed door and could see some nicely furnished tables and a typically Provençal décor. The published menu contained some quite intriguing dishes and Fullerton thought that this place should indeed receive their custom later that evening.

'Could I please make a reservation for two at around 8.00 pm,' Fullerton requested and received a polite nod in return. Having left his name, he returned to the hotel, quite pleased with himself as it would make for a nice evening.

The walk back to the hotel was made with a feeling of accomplishment and this time he did not sense that he was being observed. Maybe he had imagined the whole episode.

Fullerton saw the hotel manager as he entered the reception area and went over to compliment him on his recommendation.

Walking up the stairs to his room, Fullerton thought about just how much he was enjoying this little break. He must do it more often he said to himself.

Fullerton knocked on the door of room 217 and waited for Marguerite to open it. He hadn't had time to even think of needing a second key.

He knocked a little louder the second time and again waited for the door to be opened.

Fullerton put his ear to the door but could hear nothing. Maybe Marguerite had the shower going and the bathroom door shut and couldn't hear his knock. Returning to the hotel reception, Fullerton asked the girl for a second key which was duly provided.

Reaching his room once more, Fullerton unlocked the door and went in to the room.

'Marguerite?' he called. The room was empty as was the bathroom. He turned from his inspection of the empty bathroom and his eye caught sight of a shoe which was partly covered by the turned down bedspread.

Marguerite's body had been pushed underneath the bed with only a foot visible from the far side of the room.

Fullerton rushed over and carefully eased Marguerite's inert body out from under the bed.

He felt her pulse which was present but very weak; her breathing was also low and quite erratic.

Picking up the phone, Fullerton called the hotel reception.

'This is an emergency, I need a doctor and an ambulance urgently. My wife has suffered some kind of attack.'

'Let us take over please,' the paramedic said to Fullerton. 'Your wife seems to be experiencing some kind of shock. Does she take any kind of medication?'

'None whatsoever!' Fullerton replied. 'She is perfectly fit and active.'

'We are going to take your wife to the nearest hospital for some further assistance. She is in a comatose state and would appear to be experiencing some kind of breathing difficulty. We are setting up an oxygen supply.'

Marguerite had already been placed on a stretcher and was now rushed down to the waiting ambulance. Fullerton followed and climbed into the ambulance behind the stretcher. All Fullerton could do was sit and stare at the apparently lifeless body of his wife as the sirens blared and the vehicle sped through the city streets.

An hour later as Fullerton was pacing up and down in the waiting area of the hospital emergency wing, he was approached by two doctors, one of whom had been treating his wife.

'Mr Fullerton?' Fullerton nodded. 'Your wife has been extremely lucky; one of our nurses had noticed a small area of bruising on your wife's left thigh together with a needle puncture wound.'

'What are you saying, doctor?' Fullerton gasped.

'Someone has tried to harm your wife, possibly with an injection of some kind of barbiturate. We will know exactly what very shortly after the results come back from the blood tests.'

'She is presently stable but being monitored very carefully. I'm afraid that you will not be able to see her for a while yet and certainly not until we have identified the drug that was used.'

The two doctors left. Fullerton sat down and stared at the wall opposite.

'Please God, don't take my wife away, let her live, please let her live,' he prayed.

Three hours passed in what, to Fullerton, seemed like a haze of disbelief and anxiety. What was going on? What had happened to his wife in the space of no more than fifteen minutes?

Fullerton went outside for a breath of fresh air; he did not go far in case he was needed. This holiday had suddenly turned from being one of the most special moments in his life to possibly the worst.

His phone rang.

'Is that James Fullerton?'

265

Fullerton answered with a hushed 'Yes.'

'This is what happens to someone who has caused us a lot of trouble. Think hard about what you do from now on or your wife won't be so lucky next time.'

'Who is this?' Fullerton shouted but the line had gone dead.

Fullerton returned to the emergency department and sat down in the same seat he had vacated several minutes earlier. He watched the hospital staff come and go, pre-occupied in their various duties.

He thought about his own life, his children and just how their bereavement must have affected them. Fullerton decided in that moment that he would change his whole life around. There were people in his life that were more precious to him than he had hitherto realised – far more precious in fact. He was going to use every resource that his brother's financial strength had made available to him in the fight that he had undertaken. He needed Marguerite more than he had ever thought possible and would give away all his wealth in an instant for a guarantee of her safe recovery.

'Mr Fullerton,' a voice stated behind him. 'You can see your wife now if you wish.' It was one of the intensive care nurses who had come to find him.

Fullerton followed the nurse down the corridor past a number of rooms that seemed to be bulging with all kinds of technical equipment.

The nurse opened a door at the end of the passageway and motioned for Fullerton to enter. She smiled at him as he passed.

Marguerite was lying in the bed with her eyes closed and her arms by her side. Fullerton did not know what to think or do. The nurse had disappeared and so there was no one to provide him with any comment or information.

He sat down beside the bed and placed his hand in hers and gave it his own little squeeze. He thought he felt her respond and give him a little squeeze of her own but couldn't be sure.

He must have been in the room for about ten minutes, deep in his own thoughts. When he looked over at Marguerite he saw that she was looking back at him with a slight smile on her face.

'Oh Marguerite! What happened?' he said. 'I love you so much, darling.'

'Love you too,' she mouthed in silence and smiled some more.

'I thought I had lost you for ever,' Fullerton said, his eyes welling up with tears. 'I didn't know just how much I love you until now.'

One of the doctors entered the room and Fullerton turned to look at him.

'Your wife has been very lucky, Mr Fullerton. It was touch and go for a while earlier on. We've had some very fine technicians working on your wife's blood samples and it was sheer luck almost that they quickly identified the drug that had been injected into your wife's leg.'

'My wife was intentionally poisoned? Is that what you are telling me?' Fullerton said incredulously.

'It would appear so, Mr Fullerton. We must officially notify the local authorities in due course,' the doctor added.

Fullerton turned back to look at Marguerite. She turned her head to survey her surroundings.

'I feel quite light-headed and can't put my thoughts into words,' she whispered.

'This is a likely side effect of the antidote that we have given your wife; it is nothing to worry about at all. Your wife will be just fine in a few hours from now,' the doctor said reassuringly.

'Thank you for everything doctor.' Fullerton replied.

The doctor left the room. Fullerton followed him and spoke to him again, this time in the corridor.

'I don't want any report of this reaching the authorities under any circumstances. It is very important that no word of what has happened to my wife is made public. You do know who I am!'

'Yes, I quite understand Mr Fullerton, but I must complete the necessary records,' the doctor replied.

'Then make it look like a case of severe stomach upset or something equally less severe. I want no mention of an attempted murder. I think that a suitably large donation to the hospital could be arranged to fully demonstrate my thanks,' Fullerton stated quite forcefully.

Fullerton returned to Marguerite's room. He was not going to take any chances. He would remain with Marguerite until she was fit enough to leave the hospital.

Fullerton arranged for his own plane to fly up to Avignon from Cannes and organised a private limousine to be on standby for later that night and ready to collect them at a moment's notice from the hospital.

Shortly after 2.00 am with the medical staff giving Marguerite the all clear, Fullerton called for the limousine to come to the hospital.

Slipping quietly out of the hospital without any fuss, Fullerton and his still drowsy wife were driven the few miles to the local municipal airport and their waiting plane.

Chapter 52

Fullerton decided that there was one way to flush out the perpetrators of the attack on Marguerite. He would use both his network of contacts and his considerable financial muscle to get someone to talk.

Before he did any of this, he needed to work out exactly what the motives were.

Marguerite had spent most of the past month recovering from the ordeal in Avignon. She said that she was feeling better but Fullerton could see that the effects of the attempted poisoning and the shock of the attack were still affecting her quite considerably.

The local Swiss doctors had been most attentive and had prescribed a combination of rest, relaxation and medication, designed to eliminate any lasting effects of the drug that was used by Marguerite's attackers.

Fullerton had been busy with his business affairs over the past couple of weeks but had spent some of his own free time attempting to come up with some kind of rationale for the attack. Why Marguerite and not him? How had these people known of his movements because the honeymoon destination had not been publicised or even mentioned to all but a few close friends and acquaintances.

Marguerite was in the drawing room when Fullerton came in. He had decided to give his business affairs a rest and see what his wife was up to. She was curled up on one of the sofas and appeared to be engrossed in a book.

'How are you, darling?'

'Hello Michael, I'm fine really. It has all been fine since those pills the doctors prescribed did their job.'

'You still look quite tired to me.'

'Yes, I am a bit but I do really feel much better than I was only a few days ago.'

'Are you up to a brief talk about what we need to do next?'

'Yes, of course, what did you want to discuss?'

'Well, I have been thinking about what happened in Avignon and who knew about our travel plans. These men, whoever they were, did not just arrive there by chance, they had been given orders by somebody and presumably that somebody knew all about our movements.'

Fullerton tried to avoid the necessity of going into the details of the actual attack for fear of upsetting Marguerite again but he knew that any information that Marguerite could provide about the identity of her assailants would be extremely useful.

'It might be a good idea, if you feel up to it, if we listed all the people who knew about our honeymoon plans and when they knew it. It is hard to believe that anyone we know and had invited to the wedding, could possibly have any involvement in this at all, but we do need to consider all possibilities.'

'I can work on this on my own if you like, Michael. It would give me something specific to do and I do feel up to it.'

Fullerton saw that this would be an excellent way for Marguerite to confront her anxiety over what had happened.

'If you really feel that you can handle this task, I will be delighted,' Fullerton responded.

'If we can piece together the "who knew what and

270

when" we may be a long way towards identifying the actual individuals involved.'

'I will spare no expense to find out who and what we are up against, but we do need to tighten our focus first.'

July 16th, 2009. Geneva.

Marguerite had agreed with her husband's notion that some good, honest work would help to take her mind off her recent ordeal and so she had spent quite a bit of time putting her intelligence training to good use.

She worked, as Fullerton had suggested, on the theory that whoever had been involved in her attack in Avignon must have had prior knowledge of their honeymoon plans and their detailed movements.

Marguerite's list of guests at both the church and the more intimate gathering afterwards, had not yielded any plausible leads at all. Apart from family, who had no idea at all as to their covert activities, their close friends could just not have been the ones to divulge any useful details. Only a very few people knew of their honeymoon plans and even fewer knew of the last minute changes in destination. They had only decided to pass up Fullerton's villa on the coast in favour of Avignon at the last minute.

Fullerton had made the hotel reservation from Mr Colbert's study just before they left Vernon and notified his pilot that after flying down to Cannes, they would need to be picked up again from the local airport in Avignon some ten days later. Fullerton had, of course, provided Jacques, their pilot with their contact address in Avignon.

Marguerite considered what she had discovered for a moment. Jacques had been working for the Axxon Group for about ten years and had an unblemished record.

271

No, it couldn't be Jacques, she thought. Her intelligence brain now took over from her emotional deliberation and told her that their pilot was an all too obvious target, if someone wanted to obtain this kind of information. Who better than the personal pilot to provide up-to-the minute travel arrangements. Anyone wanting this information would automatically know that the pilot would need to file his flight plans and therefore be the first to hear of any last-minute changes of plan.

OK, Marguerite thought to herself. If Jacques was the leak, and only if, who would have 'contacted' him? Who would want this information?

'How well do you know Jacques?' Marguerite asked Fullerton.

'Not that well at all; he had been with my brother for a number of years and has carried out his duties as a private pilot should. Why do you ask?'

'I cannot come up with any other possible source for the leak of our plans to go on to Avignon. He is, you must admit, the obvious choice for informant.'

'Go on.'

'Nobody else knew that you had made a reservation at the hotel in Avignon, did they?'

Fullerton thought through his activities and movements in the hour or so remaining of the reception before they left their guests and drove to the airport.

'After I had made the hotel reservation in Avignon, I came over and told you.'

'You said later that you had contacted Jacques and given him this information.'

'Yes, I did,' Fullerton replied. 'The only other person that I spoke to about our change in plans was Richard because he and I were catching up on some family matters.'

'Now that I come to mention it, Richard did make a somewhat strange remark just before we left the reception.'

'What was that?' Marguerite asked, all ears.

'He and I had had a brief conversation out on the lawn. He told me that he had noticed two men in a Citroën who had been following us apparently from the Town Hall to the reception and that they had driven off when he walked back to see who they were.'

'When we came to leave the reception, he said that he had noticed that the guests were not the only people attending the wedding. I assumed at the time that he had possibly meant local press photographers.'

'What else could he have meant?' Marguerite asked.

'Maybe I am just imagining things,' Fullerton replied. 'This whole business needs sorting out once and for all. I think that the real target in Avignon was me, but that whoever was there in Avignon had decided to send me a very strong warning that I am getting too close for my own good...'

Chapter 53

Fullerton had, some time ago, instigated a private medical report into the possible methods, resultant effects and time frames involved in poisoning using radio-active substances. The very long-awaited results had now arrived and the report was on his desk.

There was a lot of clinical and medical terminology used in support of all the analyses. The conclusions which had been purposely written in layman's terms proved conclusively that a radioactive substance could only have been administered undetected if it had been ingested as part of a person's normal food intake.

It also concluded that the time frame between the actual act of poisoning and the first time that the victim would have noticed any significant discomfort would only have been a matter of hours.

Fullerton took out James's personal diary for March and April and searched for any doctor's appointments. There were several with local specialists in Geneva. This all seemed compatible with James's own statement to him of having felt unwell 'for five weeks'. Fullerton searched James's diary going backwards from that particular date. James had apparently made two visits to London in the same five week period. Fullerton noticed that both had been for different reasons and with different individuals.

The first visit had been a one-night stay to see his London bankers, his solicitor and for a dinner engagement.

The second trip, about a week after the first, had been to visit a private consultant in Harley Street. No doubt this meeting was at or about the time that James had started to feel distinctly unwell. James had flown in from Geneva on his private plane and had left again later that same afternoon. He hadn't even stayed overnight at the Dorchester as was usually the case whenever he visited London.

'It is quite apparent that James had to have been poisoned whilst attending some public function during the day or dinner engagement on that first visit,' Fullerton surmised.

'James had a dinner engagement with some people at a restaurant in Knightsbridge on that Saturday evening. That could most likely have been where it happened. We need to find out who James's dinner guests were that evening and who else had prior knowledge of the engagement. This had to be well planned beforehand,' Marguerite added.

'I have already found that out,' Fullerton replied. 'James had arranged to meet with a man by the name of Thornton. It was written in his diary.'

Fullerton looked at his watch; it showed just after 10 am.

'If we delay our flight to Germany until later this afternoon, I think we can put our time to some very good use. Call the airport and inform the pilot that we will be flying to London shortly and then on to Germany about three hours later than planned.'

'What do you have in mind?' Marguerite asked.

'I think that I might just know the person to find out about our Mr Thornton,' Fullerton answered.

Fullerton pulled out his phone and dialled Jason Fletcher's number.

'Jason Fletcher here,' the voice answered. Michael realised

that Fletcher would not have recognised his own phone number as he had transferred all of his numbers to a new phone.

'This is James Fullerton speaking, I think we should meet each other,' Michael said in a controlled tone of voice.

'Mr Fullerton?' Fletcher answered trying desperately to understand why he should be receiving an unexpected call from James Fullerton.

'Mr Fletcher, circumstances have changed since our last meeting. I think there are some issues that need discussing. Shall we say one o'clock at the Dorchester Hotel?'

'Er, yes, that will be fine, I look forward to meeting you, Mr Fullerton,' Fletcher replied, still in shock.

'Mr Fullerton,' Fletcher said looking at Fullerton with some degree of familiarity mixed with nervousness.

'Excuse me for staring but I knew your brother Michael slightly; we had cause to meet last year on a Foreign Office matter. You really do look so much like your brother, I can't believe the similarity. I was very sorry to hear of your brother's untimely death, a sad loss of a fine academic.'

'That is quite all right, it was a great shock to me also; please may I introduce my wife Marguerite,' Fullerton replied turning to look at Marguerite.

Fletcher eyed Fullerton's glamorous wife before shaking her hand.

'Mrs Fullerton, it is extremely nice to meet you again,' and looking back at Fullerton added, 'but I have no idea why you would want to meet me unless it is to discuss your brother's activities.'

'And what would those activities be?' Fullerton retorted.

'I met with your brother only the once; the Foreign

Office had decided to seek your brother's advice on an economic matter,' Fletcher replied somewhat anxiously.

The answer Fullerton knew all too well was a complete lie, but he decided to ignore it for the time being. He had more important things to squeeze out of this man.

'As you know, Mr Fletcher...' Fullerton began.

'Please call me Jason,' Fletcher interjected.

'As you know, my brother and I were not particularly close, but we did meet on a couple of occasions just before he died. I wasn't aware that he knew Thornton.'

Fullerton purposely constructed the sentence so as to make the connection between his meeting with his brother and the name of Thornton and to leave Fletcher with the impression that both his and Thornton's name had been passed between them.

'Thornton? Hmm, yes. I am assuming that you are referring to Alex Thornton,' Fletcher replied, suddenly feeling very uncomfortable with this whole line of questioning. He had been caught quite unprepared and had no way of knowing why Fullerton would be asking him about a very senior member of the Intelligence Service. It was not at all his place to confirm or deny the names of SIS personnel but something inside told him that Fullerton, by reputation, knew a lot more than he was conceding.

'I also wanted to ask you who you work for, Mr Fletcher?' Fullerton continued. Marguerite sat silent and watched the younger man's body language which gave some very clear signals as to his present discomfort.

'I work for a small department connected to the SIS; we provide liaison and support services between the Foreign Office and other overseas governments,' Fletcher said, trying to recover his composure.

'What do you know about this man Thornton?' Fullerton continued, keeping up the pressure.

277

'Nothing at all really,' Fletcher replied. 'He holds a senior position of some kind but I cannot add anything further.'

'Do you know where he might be reached?'

'No, I don't, but I could make some enquiries and let you know.'

Both men knew that there would be no enquiries made and no further information either forthcoming or provided.

'Thank you very much, Mr Fletcher for meeting us at such short notice,' Fullerton added as he rose from his seat. Marguerite also stood up and the three of them shook hands and made their way to the hotel entrance.

'Goodbye, Mr Fletcher,' Fullerton said as they reached the curb of the hotel driveway.

Fletcher had half turned to walk away when Fullerton said:

'How is your colleague Von Beck?'

Fletcher froze for an instant, then, turning back to face Fullerton, replied:

'I'm sorry, I don't think I know anyone by that name. Goodbye, Mr Fullerton.'

A taxi pulled up in front of the hotel at that precise moment at which Marguerite signalled her intention to hire. Fletcher took full advantage of the slight interruption and walked briskly off down the road.

Fullerton and Marguerite climbed into the taxi and gave the driver the appropriate instructions for the airport.

'What a strange man,' Marguerite said. 'He was most uncomfortable with the whole discussion.'

'Yes, he probably said more than he now knows he should,' Fullerton added. 'He must be wondering why I have such an interest in Thornton. I think we can safely assume that Thornton, whoever he actually is, will know about this discussion very quickly and if he was involved in my brother's murder then he must still be wondering why I am walking around apparently quite healthy.'

Chapter 54

August 8th, 2009. London.

The call from Seamus O'Malley came just as La Croix was about to leave on one of his overseas trips. The name of Fullerton which O'Malley mentioned changed all that. The two men had never met but they had both been involved in some very difficult situations in the past which had formed a kind of bond between them.

La Croix had provided O'Malley with some very convenient help and now it was time for O'Malley to see if he could return the favour.

'What do you know about a man called James Fullerton?' O'Malley asked.

'I know quite a lot about the man in fact, Seamus,' La Croix replied.

'Well I might have something that you will find very interesting in that case.'

O'Malley mentioned the meeting he had recently had with a crooked solicitor by the name of Andrews and the apparent failed blackmail attempt that Andrews had initiated.

'I would be most interested in receiving anything you have on Mr James Fullerton,' La Croix replied, 'and the involvement of this man Andrews as well.'

La Croix provided O'Malley with an address so that the information could be sent over to him and the conversation was over.

* * *

Two days later La Croix put in a call to Clayton Andrews at his office. La Croix had made the connection between Andrews's petty blackmail attempt and the same information that had been anonymously sent to the Paris police authorities.

'Mr Andrews please,' La Croix said when the receptionist answered the phone.

'Who may I say is calling?'

'Tell Mr Andrews that it is a friend of Mr O'Malley.'

'Clayton Andrews here,' the voice answered. 'Who am I speaking to?'

'My name is irrelevant Mr Andrews, but you can call me John Smith.'

'Do I know you?'

'No, but I know all about you, Mr Andrews. I know where you live, I know where your wife works, I even know where your two children go to school. You have got yourself involved in something you know nothing about and I have powerful friends who do not want to see your petty attempt at blackmail go any further.'

'I don't know what you are talking about, Mr Smith, if that is your real name which I doubt,' Andrews answered bluntly.

Andrews was about to add a further comment but was interrupted by La Croix.

'Mr Andrews, please listen very carefully to what I am about to say because it will not be said again. If you make any further attempt to contact Mr Fullerton in this pathetic attempt to extort money, you and your family will suffer the gravest of consequences. If you do, you will come home one evening to find your wife and family dead. Do you understand?' There will be no warning, no second chance to amend your ways and nothing but horror for you to contemplate.'

La Croix replaced the receiver of the public telephone

without waiting for a reply from the now shell-shocked solicitor. Andrews would not be making any future attempts he thought to himself.

Clayton Andrews replaced his receiver and sat back in his chair for a moment.

So James Fullerton thinks I have made a pathetic attempt to scare him off, he thought. He smiled at what he felt had been a very amateurish approach over the telephone. People used the telephone to make threatening remarks; it allows for the caller to sound menacing with complete anonymity.

He thought that Fullerton could have come up with a much better, and more intelligent, response than employing some cheap thug to call him up at his office and make all those threats.

Nice try, Mr Fullerton, Andrews thought to himself. Obviously he was getting rattled, otherwise he wouldn't have bothered with this cheap attempt at intimidation.

Andrews picked up the phone and called James Fullerton's number in Geneva. After a few minutes' wait he was put through and he heard James Fullerton's voice.

'James Fullerton here, what can I do for you, Mr Andrews? I thought that we had completed all our discussions.'

'Nice try, Fullerton but you will have to do better than that.'

'I have no idea what you are talking about. We have nothing further to discuss and I will ask you not to call me on this number again. Goodbye, Mr Andrews.'

Fullerton replaced his receiver before Andrews could add any further comment and wondered what had provoked that sudden, strange call, quite out of the blue.

Andrews stood up and paced around his office, absolutely fuming. Who did Fullerton think he was? Did he not think that he, Andrews could cause him a lot of trouble and potential embarrassment?

He decided to contact his 'friend' O'Malley again and find out what he had been able to come up with.

'Seamus, Clayton here. What have you managed to find on our Mr James Fullerton?'

O'Malley listened to the crooked solicitor rant on for a bit before interrupting him and saying:

'Clayton, my old friend, you really must let me do my work in my own way and in my own time. Your relationship with Mr James Fullerton requires some special attention and it will take quite some time for me to achieve the result that I want.'

'I need something big on this bastard and quick; I am paying you a lot of money to get results and so far I haven't seen very much for my money,' Andrews shouted.

'I think that I can safely say that you will be seeing the results of my investigation quite soon now,' O'Malley answered. 'Leave it with me for a few days and I'll get back in touch with you then.'

'All right, but I want some something significant real soon,' Andrews added and rang off.

O'Malley, having now confirmed in his own mind that he really had quite an intense dislike for this warped little man, picked up his phone again and dialled a certain mobile phone number again from memory.

The number, after ringing a few times, kicked over to its voicemail service.

'This is O'Malley. Give me a call back as soon as you receive this message.'

Chapter 55

La Croix knew the leafy suburban streets of Wimbledon like the back of his hand. He had had many previous assignments that had brought him to this particular part of south London and the particular address he sought on this particular occasion was not at all difficult to locate.

The address that he had acquired, after some minimal detective work, turned out to be an extremely nice detached property, set back from the street in a very attractive setting. He imagined that this whole neighbourhood which was comprised of equally extensive detached properties with manicured lawns and immaculate landscaping was owned by professional 'city types' who had made their money through providing expensive advice and services of one kind or another to their well-heeled clients.

The impressive iron gates that marked the entrance to this particular dwelling were electrically operated and covered by CCTV surveillance on both sides.

La Croix always wondered what these individuals had to hide if they needed to resort to all this excessive secrecy.

He knew that Andrews usually arrived home around 6.30 pm each evening after a short train ride and an even shorter walk. He also knew that Andrews had a wife and two teenage children and that Mrs Andrews worked part-time for a local estate agent whilst the children attended the local grammar school. This personal visit to Wimbledon, whilst everybody was out of the house, was to reconnoitre the property and to assess the actual approach to be made.

La Croix was aware that his previous verbal warning had been sneered at; his old friend O'Malley had brought him up to speed on Andrews's response. This second visit was going to be the second and last time that he would be wasting his valuable time on this particular individual. He decided that he would observe the estate agent's office in the town and even make himself known to the unsuspecting Mrs Andrews that same afternoon. He needed to know what sort of woman she was as his visit to the house that evening, when everyone would be home, was going to use her as the principle target for his 'persuasion'.

He found the office of Ridley Scott in the High Street opposite the local supermarket car park. This space provided him with an ideal vantage point from which to observe the comings and goings from the agency. La Croix could easily see that there were two women seated inside the agency attending to the day's business activity. One woman was in her early twenties and the second, he guessed to be aged about forty-five. The latter, he presumed, was Mrs Andrews.

After about forty-five minutes of scrutiny, La Croix left his car and walked across the main road and up to the window of the agency. He studied the various listings in the window but at the same time observed the activities inside. Choosing a period of little public activity, he entered the agency and approached the older woman.

'Good afternoon, I am thinking of moving into the area and would like to view some of your properties for sale.'

La Croix's observant eyes quickly noticed the tray containing some business cards which, reading upside down, he could make out contained the name Sylvia Andrews.

La Croix conveniently provided Mrs Andrews with a completely fictitious identity right down to his non-existent but valid home address. After naming his preferred type and size of property, he became suitably hard to please in order to ascertain the type of personality he was dealing with. Mrs Andrews came over as quite a shy but efficient individual, obviously the product of a private education and demonstratively naive in the more ruthless side of business.

La Croix found Sylvia Andrews to be the almost perfect trophy wife. He could see why Clayton had married her and felt sure that he was the master in his own home on all matters of consequence.

After a very useful thirty-five minutes or so of purposely challenging conversation with Sylvia, La Croix decided that he knew what he needed to know about her and made his excuses about further visits to terminate the visit. He thanked Mrs Andrews for her help and felt sure that they would meet again in the very near future.

He returned to his car and considered his next course of action. Mrs Andrews had conveniently let slip, in conversation, that she was expecting her husband home around 5 pm that afternoon as they were going out to the theatre with friends. La Croix determined that his unannounced visit to the Andrews's house would take place therefore between five and six that evening. His approach would be quite straightforward and to the point. Andrews needed to get the message loud and clear that his little game of extortion and blackmail was taking him into a league far above his limited abilities and expertise. If Andrews felt that he was up to being a player, then he was just about to find out that the game he wanted to play could get very rough.

As five o'clock approached that same afternoon, La Croix was already parked further along the street. The tree-lined street afforded good cover for any casual observer particularly when the target of the observation was totally unsuspecting. He could clearly see the entrance to the Andrews's property and the slight bend in the road allowed the trees to partially screen the proximity of his position.

He sat up in his seat as a car approached towards him; it was a normally quiet street and frequented for the most part by residents. The blue BMW slowed and came to a halt outside the wrought iron gates. The gates slowly opened as if on cue and the BMW disappeared into the driveway and behind the beech hedge. La Croix was close enough to have recognised the features of Mrs Andrews at the wheel.

One bird in the nest, he thought to himself. He did not have to wait long before a black London cab approached. It pulled up outside the gates and sat with its engine running for a few moments until its occupant had paid the fare and climbed out. La Croix could clearly see that it had to be Clayton Andrews. He must have decided to take a cab back home from the office in order to arrive on schedule.

Andrews was a strange sort of man, La Croix thought. His wife must be all too oblivious to his crooked sideline. She wouldn't remain that way for much longer.

He decided to give Andrews a good fifteen minutes to enter his house, divest himself of his coat, take his mind off work and be suitably transformed back into a domesticated husband before he would pay them a visit.

This meeting was going to be as easy or as difficult as Andrews would make it, La Croix thought as he climbed out of his car and walked the short distance to the iron gates.

As he approached, his observant eyes noticed a small gap in the beech hedge which separated the Andrews's property from their neighbours. This means of entrance would allow him to reach the front door of the Andrews's residence without the need to use the intercom at the gate and the consequential loss of both surprise and control over his unannounced arrival. It also avoided the scrutiny of the CCTV cameras mounted either side of the gates.

Squeezing through the gap in the hedge on all fours only took a moment and he soon approached the very elaborate front porch and equally impressive double front doors.

His highly trained observational skills had noticed the CCTV camera mounted on the corner of the garage which covered the front aspect of the house. His coat collar conveniently shielded his face from view.

He rang the doorbell a couple of times and stood and waited for a response. The response came from Mrs Andrews who opened the door and showed some surprise at seeing a prospective client of hers facing her. He could see her mind frantically trying to comprehend why he would be paying her a visit after having only spoken with her some five hours previously.

Before Mrs Andrews could then even fathom how he had known where to come, he spoke.

'Good evening Mrs Andrews, it's your husband I need so see.'

'Hm, please come in will you,' she replied, her middle-class politeness taking over control of her voice and saying the obvious thing before her brain could question her actions.

La Croix knew that this reaction was all part of the advantage of surprise that he held.

'Darling,' she called up the stairs. 'There is someone here to see you.'

'I'll be right down,' was the muffled reply from what La Croix assumed was one of the bedrooms.

La Croix took a few moments to familiarise himself with the layout of the ground floor of the house and as he heard the sound of footsteps approaching along the galleried landing, moved ever so slightly so as to stand underneath the overhung structure and thus unseen until the person now descending the stairs was almost at ground-floor level.

'Good evening, Mr Andrews,' La Croix said in a formal voice, adding just a touch of menace for effect.

Sylvia Andrews stood and watched as her husband's face changed from peaceful contentment into shocked surprise.

'I'm sorry to have to call on you in this manner but we need to resolve an important issue without further delay.'

Andrews said nothing. La Croix could see that he was quite unable to grasp the whole purpose of this surprise visit.

'Who are you and what are you doing here?' was the first question that Andrews could come up with.

'You know me as Mr Smith.'

'Do you know this person?' his wife asked.

'Er, yes, we have had some business dealings in the past, but I don't know why you would need to see me on such an urgent basis. Could this matter not have waited until Monday morning?'

'Unfortunately not,' was the cryptic reply from La Croix.

'Our last conversation has obviously been misunderstood and I know that you will appreciate my forthright behaviour in bringing it to your attention in this manner.'

'Come into the drawing room so we can discuss your concerns,' Andrews replied. Please leave us alone for a short while, darling.'

'Oh, I think that Mrs Andrews should hear what I have to say in every detail,' La Croix added.

'Mrs Andrews, do join us in the drawing room.'

'I don't think that there is anything for my wife to listen to; I suggest that just the two of us have that chat,' Andrews interjected, trying hard to trivialise the whole situation.

'Oh, I insist that your wife join us; Mrs Andrews you will be most interested to hear what I have to say. Shall we all go through to the drawing room?'

The three of them entered the drawing room. La Croix observed the reactions of his two opponents as they nervously sat down next to each other on one of the large sofas. He remained standing, using it as a psychological advantage over his 'prey'.

'I thought that our last discussion ended with a clear understanding, Mr Andrews, of our mutual position. It has come to my notice that this is not the case.'

'What is he talking about, dear?' Sylvia asked her husband.

'It was a business matter that we were involved in some months ago,' Clayton answered, hoping that the coded conversation would continue.

La Croix thought that now was the time to end the charade and to spell out the full meaning of their previous encounter.

'Mrs Andrews, your husband has been getting involved in things that are of no concern to him.'

'My wife does not need to hear you go into all the various details. In any case, we will have to leave shortly as we are going out this evening,' Andrews said, vainly trying to deflect the sudden direct tone that La Croix had taken.

'Let's just cut out all this crap and get down to the reason for my visit,' La Croix retorted in a voice that had suddenly become a whole lot more sinister.

'Your husband, Mrs Andrews, is nothing more than a

pathetic petty criminal, not to mention, crooked solicitor. He is attempting, unsuccessfully I might add, to blackmail a close personal friend of mine. He has been asked politely to refrain from this illegal activity but has apparently chosen to ignore this request.'

'What is this man saying, Clayton?' Sylvia said, looking straight at her husband.

La Croix continued. 'Your husband has attempted to extort five million pounds from my friend, using fabricated evidence. I am here this evening to strongly advise a change in your husband's activities. I won't go into any further detail because it achieves nothing. I strongly "suggest" however, that you reconsider your current approach in this matter.' La Croix made this last euphemistic remark whilst he stared directly at Andrews.

Not waiting for an answer, La Croix continued.

'The consequences of your continued action in this matter will not be tolerated and the most extreme measures will be taken if you choose to continue.'

La Croix walked over to the grand piano and picked up one of the many family photographs that were sitting on the top.

'These must be your children. Ah, yes, I recognise them from the school they attend. It would be such a tragedy if anything was to happen to them.'

Sylvia Andrews, mouth covered in shock and terror, sat on the sofa shaking violently.

'You are dealing with people that you cannot possibly comprehend, or the lengths they will go to if this petty blackmail attempt continues. Do I now make myself clear?'

La Croix turned towards the mantelpiece and checked the time on the Victorian glass-domed skeleton clock. It was 5.40 pm.

Picking up the clock, La Croix dropped it on the marble hearth of the fireplace. The clock disintegrated with glass shattering on the hard surface and spraying fragments out into the room.

Sylvia Andrews let out a scream and grabbed hold of her husband's arm.

'This will be the last polite visit that I intend to make to see you both. I hope that you will give due consideration to my request because any further visit will prove most disturbing and extremely inconvenient for you both. I'll see myself out, don't bother to get up.'

And with that, La Croix left the shell-shocked couple alone to console each other and to allow the full meaning of his visit to sink in.

Chapter 56

August 28th, 2009. Saint-Germain-en-Laye.

Fullerton and Marguerite had decided virtually on the spur of the moment to take a further short break. Fullerton's business affairs had been consuming a lot of his time of late and the continuing pressure of their investigations seemed to have taken its toll on their physical resources. It had been a while since either of them had been back to Paris and even though there were many other places that they eventually wanted to visit, Paris was chosen.

They decided, however, to make a change in their choice of hotel. This was going to be a complete holiday with no interruptions, phone calls or meetings to deal with.

The somewhat exclusive hotel in the centre of Saint-Germain-en-Laye presented them both with the ideal choice. Marguerite had always loved the Parisian outskirts especially Versailles, and Saint-Germain-en-Laye gave them what they were looking for – a nice, reasonably quiet town, even for August, and some pleasant surroundings.

Marguerite had made their reservation and had informed the hotel that they would probably be staying for a full two weeks.

Arriving at Charles De Gaulle airport in the late afternoon, the taxi ride of about one hour gave them time to sit back and relax.

They quickly checked in to the hotel and as it was only early evening they decided to take a stroll around the town. There were a number of tourists completing their day's activities and by the time they had completed their stroll down by the river and arrived back in the centre of town, it had become a lot quieter. They walked past a quaint looking restaurant with its selection of tables under canopies, occupying the space between the ancient buildings and the narrow street, all nicely arranged with white tablecloths and floral decorations.

'Let's sit down and have a drink, Michael,' Marguerite suggested. 'It's really charming here; it reminds me of a place in Vernon not too far from where my parents live.'

The restaurant faced on to the old town square which with its cobbled streets and manicured lime trees, created a very pleasant picture.

'I think that I would like to stay here a while, Michael; we can just sit back and relax and watch the world go by,' Marguerite said as she looked up from the menu and over at Fullerton.

Fullerton had not heard a word she said because his whole attention had been taken up by the arrival of a young man in his thirties, wearing a pair of well-worn jeans and a faded green jacket over a white tea shirt.

The young man had spoken to the waiter on his way to a table in the far corner to where Fullerton and Marguerite were sitting. He was now partially concealed by one of the temporary floral arches that had been used to separate the tables into more discreet sections.

'My God!' Fullerton exclaimed as he half rose in his chair to gain a better view of this new arrival. 'Yes, yes, it's Richard!' he whispered.

Marguerite turned round in her seat. Of all places they could have chosen – they had chosen the one place in the whole country, world even, which had allowed a chance opportunity of meeting again with their son.

'Michael, has he seen us yet?' Marguerite whispered back across the table at Fullerton, not daring to move or stand up to look herself in case it drew even further attention to their own presence.

A million thoughts flashed through Fullerton's brain as he adjusted to the surprise.

'This is wonderful. Well, I'm going to go over and speak with him right now. Maybe he would like to join us.'

Marguerite stared at Fullerton for a second or two but quickly realised that this chance meeting would most definitely make up for the fact that she had hardly had time to speak to her son at the wedding.

'Just wait here while I go over,' Fullerton added.

Fullerton took a deep breath, clasped Marguerite's hand for a moment and left the table.

Richard did not notice his father's approach until he was virtually at his son's table.

'Hello, Richard,' Fullerton said with as much control in his voice as he could muster.

The young man looked up from reading the menu and stared back with some considerable surprise.

'Uncle James?' he said in a very quizzical tone. 'What a surprise!'

'I am sitting over the far side of the restaurant with Marguerite, why don't you come over and join us?' Fullerton replied, deliberately avoiding any direct greeting.

'Yes, I would like that,' Richard replied.

The two men walked back over to where Marguerite was sitting. Fullerton smiled at Marguerite as he approached to give her some comfort as to the manner of the reunion.

'Hello Marguerite,' Richard said somewhat awkwardly. 'What are you both doing here?'

Richard shook hands with Marguerite but said nothing more. He continued to look at both of them with a strange degree of intensity.

'Let's all sit down,' Fullerton said. The three of them

sat down and for a moment there was silence. A silence that spoke volumes.

Fullerton looked over at his wife who was staring intently at Richard, barely able to prevent tears welling up in her eyes. In an instant Fullerton knew what he had to do. It was one of those rare moments in life when, regardless of the consequences, a human being just knows that something important has to be said.

Fullerton reached for Marguerite's hand across the table and looked at her intently before returning his gaze to his son.

'Richard. Please listen to what I am about to say. It is extremely important and I need you to remain silent until I have finished, otherwise I might not be able to say everything that needs to be said.'

Fullerton squeezed Marguerite's hand and continued. 'It's all right, darling, I know exactly what I am doing.'

'Richard, I sense that you have probably guessed part of what I am about to say, but please just listen.'

'My name is not James Fullerton, it is Michael Fullerton . . .'

Richard had listened in silence for over an hour to his father's long and rambling disclosure about the whole series of events leading up to his father's pact with his uncle and the eventual secret exchange of identities. He heard about his uncle's political activities, the poisoning and eventual death and the magnitude of the decision that his father had had to make.

'I have one final thing to tell you, Richard. It is probably the most important.'

Fullerton then explained the events surrounding his son's birth in Paris all those years ago and why he had been sent to stay with Marguerite in France when he was young and why he had been sent to school there.

Marguerite had a handkerchief covering her face and was now sobbing uncontrollably, both hands trying unsuccessfully to conceal her intense emotional state.

'So, you see, Richard, families have their secrets and life gives us some very strange roles to play. I can only hope that you can forgive me for the actions that I have taken and try and understand the reasons behind those same actions.'

Fullerton found that he had no more to say. It was as if a huge weight had been lifted from him and he now realised just how important it was to him to be able to make a complete explanation of all the concealment, impersonation and separation. Yes, that was what had been the hardest thing to accept – the separation from his own family for the past year and the thought of the agony that he had imposed upon his own children.

Richard sat there and said nothing for what to Fullerton seemed like an age. He gave no outward sign of how he would react to the extraordinary facts his father had just placed before him.

Marguerite was still sobbing but her eyes seemed to indicate a real apprehension at the prospect of her own son's eventual response.

Finally Richard began to speak.

'Well. That was quite a presentation!'

Fullerton continued to hold Marguerite's hand as they both listened to what their son was about to say.

'Maybe it is about time that I gave you an explanation also. You are probably wondering why you have found me here in France and what I could possibly be doing in Saint-Germain-en-Laye.'

Fullerton and Marguerite looked at each other but said nothing.

'My job in London means that I have to travel away quite a bit.' Richard paused whilst he decided what he needed to say and the order in which he had to say it.

'What the hell!' Richard muttered under his voice. 'I am not in import/export. I don't have a job in London.'

Fullerton looked at his son, waiting for an explanation of what he had just heard.

Richard stared at his father.

'I know all about you and your contacts with the Intelligence Services; I know about your meetings with Benoit and Von Beck. I know about the ADF and your involvement in it.'

Turning to Marguerite, Richard continued.

'I also know that you work for the DGSE and have done for many years even when you were supposedly working at the Sorbonne.'

Fullerton and Marguerite sat back in a state of complete shock at this revelation. Before Fullerton could even summon up the thoughts to speak, Richard continued.

'I had an involvement with the Intelligence Services in France during my years with the Army. I was seconded from the SAS to work very closely with the French authorities because of my ability to speak the language. After I left the Army I was approached by the DGSE to become a covert operative. This initially was a quasi military role but "my particular talents" were found to be of more use if I was allowed to operate independently of the service. What you would probably call "deep cover".'

At that precise moment, the waiter, who had been both discreet and patient enough to leave his three customers to their obviously engrossing conversation, appeared as if out of nowhere.

Richard spoke to the waiter in French advising him that they were now ready to order some food.

'I think we should have something to eat now; I feel as if I have developed quite an appetite.'

Fullerton nodded to demonstrate that he was in total agreement. The conversation badly needed a period of relief from the profound nature of the past ninety or so minutes.

Marguerite had recovered most of her composure again and so the three of them refocused their attention on the very mundane task of ordering food.

Fullerton ordered a nice wine and the remainder of the meal was taken up in polite, if somewhat trivial, conversation about the local area and what they would all be doing over the next couple of days.

Fullerton informed his son that they were booked in to their hotel for at least a full week and Richard responded by saying that he could stay one day longer but would need to return home after that. It was decided that they would spend those two days together and each provided the other with the address of their hotel.

Fullerton noticed that Marguerite had acquired quite a sparkle in her eyes and that she spent most of the meal looking at her son and just indulging herself in being reunited.

The meal over, Fullerton summoned the waiter and settled the bill in full, not accepting any attempts on the part of his son to pay for his share.

As their hotels were reasonably close to each other, they walked back through the town together. Marguerite positioned herself in the middle, securing both of her men, one on each arm.

'Why don't you come over to our hotel for breakfast in the morning, Richard?' Marguerite suggested with a look that could only receive a positive response.

'About eight-thirty?' she added. Richard nodded and smiled.

On reaching the hotel at which Fullerton and Marguerite were staying, they shared a few brief words and then parted. The two men shook hands and Richard gave Marguerite a kiss on the cheek.

Tomorrow was going to be an exciting day, Marguerite thought to herself.

'I'm so glad about this lovely coincidence,' she said to Fullerton as they went up to their room.

'So am I,' Fullerton replied. 'He's quite a guy, your son, Mrs Fullerton!'

Marguerite just smiled and was totally content.

Chapter 57

August 29th, 2009. Saint-Germain-en-Laye.

Breakfast the next morning couldn't come fast enough for both of them. They had had time to absorb the things that Richard had said and it only served to produce a host of further questions that were also now requiring answers.

Fullerton and Marguerite arrived down for breakfast only to find that their son had beaten them to it and was already seated out on the patio when they arrived. It was the start of another fine day and everything suddenly seemed right with the world.

'Good morning Richard,' Fullerton said as they approached.

'Hi dad' Richard replied. 'Hi Maman,' Richard said as he stood to give his mother a kiss.

'Do you mind me calling you Maman?

'Absolutely not!' Marguerite replied, suddenly feeling very proud that her son should choose to be so familiar.

'That was quite the discussion yesterday evening,' Richard added as he sat down opposite his parents.

'Richard, I'm so very sorry about all the cloak and dagger activity but...' Fullerton was interrupted by his son.

'No need to apologise, dad. I know a lot about what is currently going on. More than you think in fact. Now that we've exchanged all this information, I think that we should discuss exactly what we both know because there are some very serious issues that need sorting out and we are up against some people that will stop at nothing to ensure that their various dirty little secrets are kept secret.'

'That is just fine with me,' Fullerton answered. 'I have been struggling to come to terms with all your uncle's various activities, but I still don't yet know who I can trust or, for that matter, who I am up against.'

'I'm sure that, between us, we can fill in a lot of the blanks,' Richard replied.

'Your mother knows as much as I do, Richard and she is quite as involved in all this as I am. We found that much out while we were in Avignon.'

'Yes, you said last night,' Richard said. 'I had not heard about that incident before but it all starts to fit into the same general situation.'

Looking at Marguerite, Fullerton suggested that they have a nice leisurely breakfast before discussing the intricate details.

'I will need to explain things to your sister,' Fullerton said to Richard.

'No, leave that to me,' Richard replied. 'I think that I can provide a more objective and more balanced explanation of her father's actions and why it was all so necessary.'

Fullerton nodded in agreement and acceded to his son's wishes, recognising that his son was hitherto a lot more of a person than even he had given him credit.

After breakfast, the three of them sat outside on the spacious patio and went through all the known facts surrounding James's death. This was agreed to be a good place to start as it would inevitably lead into all the other situations and no doubt involve all the various 'players'.

Fullerton, with Marguerite's help, provided a verbal outline of what they knew to be the present situation between the various entities. Richard sat back and listened as they gradually created a quite sophisticated arrangement of individuals.

'How well did you know Benoit and Von Beck?' Richard asked.

'Not that well, I only ever met Von Beck and Benoit the once. James did not trust them to be who they said they were. He always suspected that they were SIS or the equivalent.'

'Well, he was right!' Richard answered. 'Both Von Beck and Benoit were DGSE operatives and had their dirty hands in a number of illegal activities including the selling of information to whoever wanted it and would be willing to pay.'

'Anyway, you don't need to worry about Von Beck, he has been taken care of,' Richard added. 'That was one of my better moments.'

'You don't mean...' Marguerite said and stopped as she thought about what she was saying.

'That's what I do when I'm so ordered. It's a nasty world out there.'

The three of them looked at each other and for a moment lost track of their own thoughts.

'I never did like that man Von Beck,' Fullerton added as if in support of his son's actions.

'Did you ever get involved with any of these other people?' Fullerton said to Richard.

'No, none of these names ring a bell with me except for Von Beck and Benoit. I operate at a level where too much notoriety is to be implicitly avoided.'

Just then a group of businessmen and women came out onto the patio and all of a sudden, things seemed too crowded for their conversation to continue without risk.

Richard continued in a much softer voice as he leaned forward.

'What I do know, dad, is that none of these people that Uncle James was involved with are to be trusted for one moment. I think he was playing a very difficult and dangerous game and possibly even he did not know what he was up against. Incidentally, did you ever hear anything more from your lawyer friend Clayton Andrews?'

'How on earth did you come across Andrews?' Fullerton asked incredulously. 'And no, I haven't.'

'That's good,' Richard replied with a smile.

His father gave him a stern look which invited an answer.

'Trade secret I'm afraid, dad,' Richard said with a smile.

Their final hours in Saint Germain seemed to pass all too quickly, certainly for Marguerite. It was now mid afternoon and Richard had been looking at his watch for a while now.

'You leave whenever you think you should, Richard,' Fullerton said.

'Oh, you don't have to go yet,' Marguerite said as only a mother would.

'Yes, I really should be getting back,' Richard replied. 'I am away too much as it is these days and Michelle doesn't like it; in fact she is starting to hate it and is suggesting that I get another job where I can be home every night.'

The three of them stood up and wandered back through the hotel and out once more at the front where they said their goodbyes.

'Don't forget to speak to Louise, will you?' Fullerton shouted after his son.

'You can count on me,' he replied.

'Yes, I think I can,' Fullerton said under his breath as his son turned the corner and was gone.

Chapter 58

Charles Stevenson paced up and down in his sumptuous office in the Foreign Office. The news was not good, not good at all. In fact the whole situation was getting completely out of hand.

There was a knock on the door.

'Come in,' he shouted irritably.

His private secretary, a young and talented recent arrival in Westminster, came in and walked over to where her boss was standing.

'I have seen to the revisions you requested to the speech you will be making in Paris this Thursday,' she said.

'Thank you. Can you please see to it that this does not leak to the Press before I have had chance to make the announcement in Paris.'

'Of course I will,' she replied on her way out.

Stevenson picked up the phone.

'Get me the Director General of the SIS,' he barked and replaced his receiver.

This situation concerning the secret activities of the ADF that he'd authorised the SIS to 'look into', now needed his personal attention.

The phone rang. Stevenson again picked up the phone to be told that Sir Michael Donaldson was on the line.

'Michael, thank you for returning my call so promptly. I have some important matters that need urgent discussion. Can you advise when you would be available?'

'I'm available entirely at your convenience Foreign Secretary,' Donaldson replied.

'Shall we say 3.00 this afternoon in St James's Park, usual place? I don't want there to be any problems with being overheard.'

'Yes, three o'clock will be fine. See you in St James's Park at three then.'

It was a fine, sunny, autumn afternoon when the two men met. Not too many people about. The tourists, for the most part, had now left the capital and the London parks had returned to their normal relaxed state with just the occasional gardener to be seen.

'This matter involving the ADF is becoming most tiresome,' Stevenson began. 'I have given you virtually "carte blanche" to infiltrate this organisation and root out the ringleaders and all I seem to hear now is that their activities are proving more and more embarrassing to us.'

'We have had a dedicated team working on this case for about eighteen months,' Donaldson replied.

'Yes and not a lot to show for it, I understand.'

'Are you sure that you gave the job to the right man?'

'Alex Thornton is our most valuable asset for such assignments,' Donaldson replied in his own defence. Alex has just provided me with his latest report, which confirms that his group have made some real progress in identifying and neutralising most of the core members of the ADF.'

'I seem to remember that about a year ago you seemed particularly pleased with your discovery of the covert activities of James Fullerton. Christ's sake, the Prime Minister was just about to give that man a knighthood for services to industry!' Stevenson snapped. 'You told me that he had been "dealt with", but now all I hear are

305

rumours telling me that he is more active than ever. This whole business is getting too close to me for comfort.'

'Yes, we were all surprised at Mr Fullerton's resilience. We did indeed feel that we had "got the measure of him" at least,' Donaldson admitted.

'I thought your man Thornton had taken personal control of ensuring that that particular individual would not become any further nuisance to us,' said Stevenson, stating the obvious. 'Fullerton, of all people, needed to be silenced and here he is still making a real nuisance of himself. He knows where a good number of bodies are buried and I cannot afford for the kind of information that he must possess coming out into the public domain.'

'We have already come up with a plan to kill two birds with one stone,' Donaldson stated, glad of the opportunity to inform his political master of his current endeavours.

'I don't want to know what you have concocted or how you intend to carry it out. Just make sure that all this mess doesn't end up on my doorstep,' Stevenson replied tartly.

'Do I understand, Foreign Secretary that I have your complete approval for whatever needs to be done?'

'You have my complete authority to take all necessary action resulting in the elimination of the remaining ADF hierarchy, the safe return of any incriminating documents and the end to this whole sordid affair. Do I make myself clear?'

'Yes, you most certainly do, sir,' Donaldson replied. 'What's more, I expect to have this whole matter brought to a successful conclusion before the end of the year.'

'I think that that concludes our little chat, Donaldson,' Stevenson said. 'Aren't the flowers lovely at this time of year? I do so like to see our parks filled with all of this colour.'

'If that will be all, Foreign Secretary, I will take my

leave of you and return to my office. There is much to be done.'

'Yes, thank you, Donaldson. Keep me posted on your progress.'

'Goodbye, then, sir.'

Donaldson turned and walked off in the direction of Birdcage Walk. He had reached the edge of the park before searching inside his overcoat pocket and retrieving a small pocket-sized voice recorder. Switching the machine off, he smiled to himself at the thought of how handy this tape could prove to be as insurance, should the need ever arise. He decided that he didn't really trust politicians that much and Her Majesty's Secretary of State for Foreign and Commonwealth Affairs even less.

Chapter 59

September 5th, 2009. Geneva.

Richard flew into the airport in Geneva. It had been some time since he had visited Switzerland and his mind thought back to that last visit. Another covert operation involving the French Government – better forgotten.

He soon made his way through the Terminal building and easily spotted a small placard with his real name written in red marker pen on it. It was held by a young man, dressed very smartly in a dark suit and looking every bit the part of a successful chauffeur.

'*Bonjour, Monsieur,*' Richard said as he approached the young man. '*Je m'appelle Richard Fullerton.*'

'*Bonjour, Mister Fullerton,*' the young man replied smartly. '*S'il vous plaît, venez avec moi.*'

Richard followed the young man out of the Terminal building to the waiting limousine which seemed to have received some kind of preferential parking status.

The vehicle sped off and Richard sat back in the comfortable rear seat and picked up one of several local morning newspapers that had been conveniently provided.

He studied the main front page news briefly before flipping through some of the inside pages.

On one of the inside pages of that morning's edition of *Le Temps*, Richard happened to notice a small article entitled '*La Doctrine de Fournier*'.

He folded back the other pages so that he could more closely view the full article. It was a current affairs leader article written by one of France's leading investigative journalists. Richard started to read.

His father's limousine continued to speed on its way out to his father's lakeside mansion but Richard's concentration was now not on the passing scenery but on this sudden discovery.

The article had apparently been originally published in one of the French national newspapers some two months previously, a fact that had escaped Richard's notice.

The article briefly reviewed the life of a certain rurally situated Catholic priest by the name of Pierre Fournier. It provided quite an insightful look at the pressure that had been placed on Father Fournier over his publicised writings and the growing acknowledgement by a large section of French society that these writings held real meaning.

Most of the article provided Richard with no more factual evidence than he already possessed. The part that shocked him was the apparent cover-up of his seemingly untimely death at a religious care home just outside Paris. The article included the official conclusions of the sub-sequent police investigation but went on to suggest that all was not quite as normal and straightforward as it all seemed. It concluded that there were some significant differences between the witness statements and the official police evidence at the inquest.

For someone who was totally rapt up in covert activities and all too familiar with the range of methods used by governments, the assertion that this article contained about an elderly priest who simply had the courage of his convictions, came as no surprise.

Richard had to consider for a moment why this rather innocuous newspaper article should provoke such a reaction in him. He had met Father Fournier back in January and found that he somehow admired the old man. He also remembered that it was Fournier who had suggested he contact James Fullerton if he wanted more information on the activities of the ADF.

The limousine pulled in through the gates of the Fullerton estate and Richard was shaken from his thoughts for the time being. He watched as the large mansion came into view and was suitably impressed with its surroundings.

The car came to a stop just in front of the main entrance and he barely had time to collect his few belongings together before he was greeted by Marguerite.

'Hello again, Richard,' she said and gave him a kiss on both cheeks.

'It seems like ages since we met in Saint Germain,' she added.

'Yes, it does,' Richard answered, still taking in the grandeur of his father's manicured lawns and precisely landscaped vegetation.

'Come on in, Marcel will bring your bags,' Marguerite added as she took her son's arm and walked with him into the house. 'Michael is in his study just taking care of some rather urgent business matters, but he will join us very shortly.'

They went through into the main drawing room. Richard caught sight of the sun's reflection off the water at the edge of the lake. He walked over to the large windows for a better view.

'I'm sure that Michael will want to give you the grand tour when he is free,' Marguerite added. 'There are some coffee and croissants over there on the sideboard; we will have lunch out on the terrace later on.'

'How did your meetings go with your sister?' Marguerite asked.

'A lot better than I had expected,' Richard replied. 'She somehow seemed not at all surprised to hear what I had to tell her. It was as if she had already subconsciously known the truth.'

'Your father will be extremely grateful for your efforts and even more pleased with the result,' Marguerite added.

'He has been tormented by the decision that was virtually forced on him by his brother's untimely death and the sacrifice he had to make regarding you two was the most difficult decision he will ever make.'

At that moment Fullerton walked in and came over to greet his son again.

'Richard, thank you for coming here. You have no idea how nice it is to see you again now that everything is out in the open.'

'It's nice to see you again, dad,' Richard answered, not allowing himself to get all emotional. His life to date, if it had taught him anything, had taught him to keep an iron grip on his emotions. He moved over to where the coffee and croissants were and helped himself to both. This gave him a few precious moments to regain his composure and to regain his normal steely demeanour.

'When you've finished your coffee I'll show you around the place,' Fullerton said. 'We've lots of time to discuss more serious matters later.'

The three of them spent the next hour and a half wandering around both the house and grounds and generally just enjoying each other's company.

The conversation limited itself to small talk about the estate and its various components. Richard was genuinely quite interested in all that his parents had to tell him about the estate and the time passed quickly.

On returning to the main house, the three of them walked out onto the rear patio and sat down.

'We will have some lunch out here in a short while. It is such a nice day. We often sit out here; Marguerite loves the view of the lake.'

311

The three of them sat down on some comfortable patio chairs and allowed the sun to warm their faces.

Drinks had been placed on a convenient table nearby ranging from Badoit to some nice Burgundy.

'I started to read some of the newspapers that were in the car on the way over here from the airport,' Richard remarked. 'There was a very interesting article on Pierre Fournier.' He glanced at his parents.

Marguerite looked at her husband for some kind of a clue as to what she should say in reply, but receiving none decided to bring Richard completely up to date with what she now knew.

'It seems as though some of our discussions need to start before lunch,' Marguerite said, stating the obvious. 'I was involved, through the DGSE, with the French police when they were investigating his death back in March. I never believed that I had been given the full details and I now know that there was a lot more to that event than I was allowed to know at the time.'

Richard looked at his mother with some considerable surprise.

'I didn't know that you are still working for the DGSE?'

'Still am, I'm afraid,' Marguerite answered, somewhat taken aback by her son's reaction.

'Father Fournier was a very dear friend of James and he would have been terribly upset if he had been alive to learn of his murder,' Fullerton interjected.

'So, it was murder,' Richard stated.

'All the information that I either managed to obtain or was told confirmed that he had died of old age. Of course, I didn't believe what I was being told but I was never able to obtain any of the actual facts; all I received was the official story. Inspector LeBlanc told me more than he should.'

'Do they know who was involved?' Richard asked.

'I met the old man back in January myself. I was told to go and visit him and find out what he knew about the ADF.

'It's all starting to show a pattern and I don't like what I see. From what I have been able to find out and from going through James's personal files, I don't think that Father Fournier was as involved in the inner workings of the ADF as the various agencies seem to think. What I do think is that the DGSE and the SIS have a lot to hide and the only evidence of their corruption and illegal activities is held by certain ADF members.'

'Such as James?' Richard asked again.

'Yes. That is why I think he was poisoned. What the intelligence community is currently baffled about is the apparent nine lives that Mr James Fullerton seems to possess. At least two lives in any case. I agree with you Richard. It is all starting to take some consistent shape now. Even the attack on Marguerite was, in all probability meant for me. You, Marguerite, just happened to be in the wrong place at the wrong time.'

At that point, two of the servants appeared with trays containing the lunch that had been promised and the conversation fell silent.

'We'll sit down after lunch, Richard, and continue where we were up to last week,' Fullerton said as the servants came within earshot.

The lunch menu consisted of a nicely crafted seafood salad which together with a nice white wine from the Loire valley seemed most appropriate on what was turning into quite a warm autumn afternoon.

'So this is how the other half live,' Richard commented somewhat light-heartedly. 'I could get used to all this elegance of surrounding.'

Marguerite smiled at her husband but said nothing. She was still getting used to the presence of her own son and in familiarising herself with his every mannerism. It was just perfect; the two men in her life that meant the most were sitting right here opposite her. If only they could unravel the intrigue and danger that seemed at times to surround them, she would be completely content.

With lunch over and a suitable time having elapsed for the effects of the wine to have dissipated, Fullerton suggested that the three of them move back inside the house and into his office where he had all the documents that they were going to need.

It seemed a shame to miss out on the remainder of the sunshine but there were more pressing matters that needed their undivided attention.

Fullerton began the afternoon session by clarifying their position.

'We produced an excellent chart last week which, between us, shows who and what we are up against. What we have to determine is the motives of the people involved and who exactly is or are pulling the strings.'

At that precise moment, Richard's mobile phone rang. Richard stood up and moved over to the window. The number had a Paris code.

'*Oui*,' Richard answered.

'La Croix! Listen carefully,' the voice on the phone said crisply. 'Your cover has been blown and the DGSE have issued a warrant for your arrest with immediate effect. Do not contact me again on this number. You have my private coordinates.'

Richard recognised the voice on the line as that of Pascal Lefevre. He also understood that, for his boss to call him on an unsafe phone line meant that Lefevre felt that he could not wait until he was able to use the normal communication channel.

Richard also knew that his own mobile phone was now compromised and any future calls would, in all probability, be listened to.

Richard's brain started to go into overdrive as his trained senses started to play with the possible scenarios.

He looked back at his parents, who now were staring at him.

'My God, Richard, you look like you have seen a ghost,' Fullerton remarked.

'That was my boss in Paris. He has just taken a huge risk to inform me that my cover has been blown and that there is a warrant out for my arrest,' Richard said, still pre-occupied with his own thoughts.

'You know that I have told you that I work for a particular branch of the DGSE,' he went on.

'Yes, we both know that,' Marguerite replied. 'We also know that you have been involved in some matters that we haven't questioned you about. But we aren't stupid; your previous military training and selection for covert duties gives us both a fairly good idea as to some of your assignments.'

'I have been used for several situations where certain individuals have been "neutralised",' Richard continued. 'What you don't know is that I am one of just a very few individuals who are superficially a regular DGSE operative but in fact a "deep cover covert operative". That phone call was from my immediate superior, who has probably now paid with with his job and most likely, his freedom by phoning me with a warning.'

Richard paused for a moment before continuing.

'Something has happened at a very senior level and at the moment I don't know what that is.'

'Well, whatever it is,' Fullerton said, 'we are all in this thing together.'

'This phone is now compromised; I'm going to need a new phone from now on,' Richard said.

'Consider it done. I'll arrange that immediately,' Fullerton answered.

'We need to find out who is behind this latest move and what their motivation is,' Fullerton said, speaking his thoughts out loud. 'Someone or some people definitely think that you know too much and could become a potential embarrassment to them.'

Richard sat back and concentrated his mind on his present predicament.

'Only Lefevre knew exactly what my activities have been,' Richard stated, in an attempt to create a logical explanation for the recent phone call.

'Presumably Lefevre was not senior enough to make all the decisions, particularly when it came to "neutralisations". He must have received his instructions from a higher level,' Fullerton surmised.

'I never knew anyone else in the organisation, was not told about anyone else and had no reason to want to know anyone else; that was the whole "deep cover" basis of secrecy,' Richard said.

'Do you know how to get in touch with Lefevre when he is not in his office?' Fullerton asked. 'He is our only link at this present moment.'

'No, it was always "company policy" that he called me,' Richard replied. 'Lefevre was the only person that knew of my exact role or even identity. I'll bet that I'm not so invisible any more, though. All the appropriate authorities will have my complete details by now including a fairly recent photograph.'

Fullerton walked over to his private phone and put in a call.

May I speak with Sr Baldini immediately; it is most urgent. This is James Fullerton.'

'Putting you through now.'

'James, this is Francesco. What can I do for you?'

'I have an urgent matter that needs your particular talents, Francesco. I need to know the location and precise movements of a certain Pascal Lefevre in Paris and I then need one of your agents to act as a means of communication...'

Michael proceeded to give Baldini the details he would need to locate Lefevre and also the warning that Lefevre, in all likelihood, was under surveillance.

'This is extremely urgent, Francesco; I need your very best men. No expense is to be spared. I will cover all costs.'

'Consider it done, James. I will let you know as soon as my people report back to me.'

Fullerton replaced the receiver.

'You had better stay here for a while, Richard. Does anyone know that you are here in Geneva?'

'You should know me better than that,' Richard replied. 'I haven't used my real name for many years.'

Chapter 60

September 7th, 2009. Geneva.

Baldini's network of agents and contacts together with a
'small' amount of financial inducement produced the
desired results within forty-eight hours. A short phone
call to Geneva provided Fullerton with the details of how
and when he could now communicate with Lefevre.

'My good friend Francesco has arranged everything,'
Fullerton said as he joined Richard and Marguerite out
on the terrace. 'Lefevre is confined to his house in the
suburbs and is indeed being watched. It would appear
that they have set a trap for you, Richard.'

'I think that we have to assume that Lefevre has given
them, at the very least, sufficient information for them
to realise that I must now contact him,' Richard said
thoughtfully. 'They already know that he made that phone
call to me and so they already know that I will be on
my guard.'

'If Lefevre is unable to leave his house, then we must
arrange to visit him,' Fullerton replied, already thinking
about how they would accomplish this.

Richard went back into the house and returned a few
moments later with a pad of paper and a pen. He quickly
composed an itemised list of points that only Lefevre
could answer.

'How well do you trust Lefevre?' Fullerton asked.

Richard thought for a moment.

'Lefevre is your stereotypical bureaucrat and therefore

knows which side his bread is buttered, but he is a basically very sincere and honest man. Too honest in fact for the position he occupies.'

'Arrange for this list of questions to reach Lefevre,' Richard said to his father.

'Once we have the answers, we'll know who we are dealing with.'

Fullerton went into his study with the list and picked up the phone. This time he was put straight through.

'Francesco, I have some questions that we need Lefevre to answer. Can you arrange for a suitably discrete contact to be made?'

'Give me the list,' Baldini replied, ever the one to get straight to the point.

'We have been keeping a close eye on the people watching Lefevre. They have the area well covered but my men are used to dealing with this kind of a surveillance operation.'

Fullerton dictated the items that Richard had written down and again thanked his friend for his invaluable assistance.

'Francesco! It is crucial that your contact with Lefevre goes undetected. We must ensure that whoever is watching him is not aware of our contact.'

'Oh, I can tell you who is watching him,' Baldini replied. 'There are four men involved on a round the clock basis; my people have reported that they are definitely a police surveillance unit. We will have your answers in no time at all.'

As Fullerton replaced the receiver, the thought suddenly struck him. Why were the French police involved and not the DGSE?

When he returned to the terrace Marguerite said to him, 'You seem puzzled?'

'Yes, I am,' Fullerton answered. 'Baldini has just told

me that Lefevre is being watched by a police surveillance team, not the DGSE.'

'That is so very predictable,' Richard interjected. 'They invariably employ the detective branch of the police when they need to appear uninvolved.'

'We should have our answers quite quickly. Baldini tells me that he thinks it is just a routine stake-out expecting you, Richard, to make physical contact with Lefevre.'

'Bloody amateurs!' Richard said angrily. 'Do they really think that I am just going to walk up to Lefevre's front door in broad daylight!'

'I think that whilst we are waiting for my good friend Francesco to do his work, we should consider making an approach of our own,' Fullerton said, trying to refocus their attention on the main thrust of their investigation.

'I take it that nobody knows your true identity,' Fullerton remarked, looking at his son.

'Not even Lefevre,' Richard replied. 'The only person who would know about my "transfer" from the Army over to covert operations is the Minister of Defence himself.'

Fullerton said nothing, but found himself wondering about several new possibilities.

'Richard, Marguerite! Just listen to what I am about to say. After all of our scrutiny and consideration of all the facts that we have assembled between us over the past couple of weeks, we still have not arrived at the fundamental force that is driving it all. As an economist and professor, I always taught my students to recognise fact from fiction, tried and trusted theory from pure belief. Furthermore, if theory was based initially on a belief, then let it be tried and tested.'

'What are you driving at?' Marguerite interrupted, only to be silenced by Fullerton's raised hand.

'All these assassinations, including my brother, have been made to look like the work of an extremist group of as yet unknown individuals. What if the British and French governments were cultivating this generally acknowledged belief to conceal their own sordid political agenda? What if some of these murders were ordered by government and made to look like the work of political extremists?'

'I was sent to investigate some of these cases,' Richard said.

'Yes, and now you seem to be conveniently implicated in at least some of them,' Fullerton replied.

'But, why would the British and French governments want to lay the blame elsewhere?' Marguerite asked rhetorically.

Fullerton continued without providing Marguerite with an answer.

'Remember James's Top Secret file. I suggest that a certain individual was getting too close to the real truth of the matter and some high-level decisions were taken to reduce the perceived threat of exposure and its inevitable political fall-out.'

'You mean James, don't you?' Marguerite asked.

'Yes, I do. That would also explain why a second attempt was made in Avignon,' Fullerton replied.

'If you are right in what you have just said,' Richard added, 'then there are some very important people involved in this. We are talking about a joint British/French government conspiracy involving leading politicians. That's quite a theory!'

'But what I don't understand is why the various intelligence services have been so pre-occupied with discovering the identities of ADF members,' Marguerite stated, posing a valid point.

'I'm not one hundred percent sure of that, Marguerite, but I would put money on the likelihood that the powers that be do not feel comfortable with the amount of inside knowledge possessed by the ADF membership.'

'Which individuals were murdered by which faction?' Richard said, again posing a valid question.

'That is what we now need to clarify,' Fullerton replied. 'I am sure that when we hear back from Lefevre, we will have some more pieces of the puzzle.'

Chapter 61

September 10th, 2009. Geneva and London.

Richard had been back in London for three days before Fullerton could contact him and update him on the information that Baldini's agents had managed to obtain from Marcel Lefevre. Both men had agreed to adopt the most secure form of communication as they had now to assume that all 'open' forms of contact were suspect and most likely bugged. Fullerton was thankful that his phone lines in Switzerland were possibly out of the reach of the British intelligence services, but he did not intend to take even the slightest risk and therefore assumed that they had been compromised.

Fullerton used the facilities of his bank in Geneva to make any important calls. He had the increasing suspicion that his mansion on the lake was now also under surveillance. Again Baldini turned up trumps; certain individuals with a more than passing interest in the Fullerton estate were discovered and duly reported to the Swiss authorities. Needless to say, these authorities took an extremely dim view of external intelligence operatives found to be active within their national borders and took appropriate action to remove the individuals.

'Well that definitely supports our theory then,' Richard replied to what his father had to report.

'That's the conclusion I reached, Richard. I think it is time for us to stir a few things up, don't you? I have made arrangements to fly to London tomorrow morning.

I have an appointment to see my "old friend" Jason Fletcher.'

'Strangely enough I haven't yet been contacted by anyone,' Richard replied.

'I would expect that that's about to change. Be on your guard,' Fullerton said. 'I'll contact you again when I'm in London tomorrow on this same number.'

Bye, dad,' Richard said as the phone line went dead.

Richard arrived home that evening, as he normally did when he was in the country, at just before 6.00 pm. Michelle was busy preparing the evening meal and Andrew was engrossed in watching one of his favourite cartoon shows on the television.

'Hi, I'm home,' Richard called out as he closed the front door of their apartment.

'I'm in the kitchen,' Michelle replied.

'How was your day?' Richard asked as he walked into the kitchen.

'Just the usual. I took Andrew to the park this afternoon after his nap. We had a lovely time. There was a man waiting at the entrance to the apartment building when we returned who said he was looking for you.'

Richard felt some of the tension return but concealed it from his wife.

'I wonder who that could have been,' he remarked nonchalantly. 'What did he look like?'

'He was about your age, not quite so tall. Very well dressed,' Michelle told him.

'Did he say anything or leave a message?' Richard asked, trying to appear uninterested.

'He said that he had some important matters to discuss and felt sure that you would know what it was all about,' Michelle continued.

'Did he leave a business card or a phone number?'

'No he didn't. I actually found that bit strange.'

'What was strange?' Richard asked.

'He wouldn't even leave a name. Said he would try and get in touch again soon. He wanted to know if you were going to be around tomorrow morning.'

'What did you tell him?' Richard enquired, rather pointedly.

Michelle turned round to look at her husband, detecting a change in his tone of voice.

'I said that as it was Friday, you would probably be going into work a little later than normal as we had planned to meet at Andrew's school around 11.45 am.'

'Did you tell him which school?' Richard asked.

'Richard, why are you asking all these questions? Is there something wrong?'

'Did you tell him which school Andrew attends?' Richard asked again.

'No, he seemed satisfied with just knowing that you would be home tomorrow morning, that's all. He said goodbye and left after that.'

Richard left the kitchen and went and sat down next to Andrew who was still intently watching the television. Richard could almost smell the police presence. Special Branch officer was the most likely answer. Someone had been talking in order for the police to be paying him a visit. Dad was right. He didn't have to wait long. He remembered that he would be meeting with his father in the morning and also Michelle's remark about the school meeting.

'I won't be able to come to the school with you tomorrow. Dad is flying in from Geneva and he has agreed to meet at the airport.'

He added, 'I have a great idea. You haven't seen my father for ages; why don't we all go to the airport in the morning to meet him?'

325

'What about the school meeting?' Michelle replied.

'We can call the school first thing in the morning; I will make all the excuses.'

'Well, it would be nice to see your father again,' Michelle replied.

'Consider it settled,' Richard said. That arrangement should keep the police guessing for a few hours at least, he thought to himself.

Chapter 62

September 11th, 2009. London.

Richard, Michelle and Andrew all left their apartment in Muswell Hill and took the bus over to East Finchley station where they bought tickets to Heathrow. Richard had kept his eyes open for any sign of a police presence when they left their apartment but detected no one.

They passed an uneventful journey on the underground and found themselves at Heathrow about half an hour before Fullerton's flight was scheduled to land. On arriving at the terminal, Richard checked the Arrivals board and found that the only flight from Geneva that morning was due to arrive at 10.35 am.

'Let's grab a coffee while we're waiting,' Richard said. 'If we sit over there, we can see all the passengers arriving.'

They had barely had chance to drink their coffee and attend to Andrew's needs when Richard spotted his father coming though the Arrivals gate.

Richard jumped up and started walking towards his father.

'I thought we'd come and meet you here at the airport,' he said.

'Well, that saves me a phone call,' Fullerton replied.

'I've brought Michelle and Andrew with me,' Richard added. 'They're over there.'

Fullerton studied his daughter-in-law as he approached her. She seemed somehow different from how he had remembered her but he made no comments except to show how pleased he was at meeting her again.

'Michelle,' Fullerton said as he gave her a kiss on both cheeks. 'And this can't be Andrew! He is so big now.'

Fullerton hadn't seen his grandson for over two years and wouldn't have easily recognised him but for being with his parents.

'I have a car waiting for me somewhere outside. How did you all get here?'

'We came on the underground,' Michelle replied.

Whilst Michelle was collecting all of Andrew's various bits and pieces Richard pulled his father to one side and quickly filled him in on the police visit and its ramifications, which didn't need further explanation.

'I'll tell you more later, but I thought that Michelle would be safer here with us today,' he whispered.

Fullerton's driver duly appeared and the five of them went out of the terminal and across the road to the waiting limousine.

Once in the car, Richard turned to his father.

'I've told Michelle that we have a meeting to go to this morning and so she's quite happy to remain in the car while we're tied up. I also tempted her to come by saying that we would all go somewhere nice for lunch afterwards.'

'That would be wonderful. I shall enjoy that very much,' Fullerton replied, responding to Richard's cue.

Fullerton had arranged to meet with Fletcher at the Dorchester at 11.45 am which gave them just enough time to drive into central London from the airport.

On arriving in front of the hotel, Fullerton and Richard climbed out. The driver was instructed to give Michelle and Andrew a tour of some of the sights for an hour or so and then to escort them into the hotel restaurant for about 1.00 pm.

The two men entered the lobby of the Dorchester and Fullerton was soon spotted by Fletcher who had been sitting on one of the sofas by the windows.

'Mr Fullerton!'

Fullerton walked over towards Fletcher, Richard following his father's lead.

'Thank you for meeting with us at such short notice. May I introduce Simon Shaw, he works for me in Geneva. 'Let's go into the bar. I think at this hour it will be a little bit quieter.'

Once there and some drinks ordered, Fullerton set his plan into motion.

As Fullerton had instinctively guessed, it did not take long for word of Fletcher's conversation with James Fullerton to reach the ears of Fletcher's superiors in the SIS.

Alex Thornton hastily left a meeting he was chairing across town and returned to his office to learn the exact details.

'Right, let's have it!' as he entered the conference room where most of his key team members had already assembled.

For a moment that seemed like an eternity nobody spoke. All eyes were conveniently lowered in the hope that someone would say something and soon.

'Let me run through the meeting that I have just had with Fullerton in detail,' Fletcher stated forcibly. For once he was the centre of attention. He had no idea why James Fullerton had singled him out as the apparent go-between, but he was not going to spoil his moment in the sun by letting all his erstwhile colleagues know that.

'I only received a call from Fullerton yesterday,' he began.

'Why the hell wasn't I informed?' Thornton barked.

Fletcher paused for a moment, but continued with his briefing. He disliked Thornton; he did not agree with his questionable activities and certainly was not going to be intimidated by him. His trump card, for the time being,

329

was that James Fullerton wished him to act as the messenger boy, if that was the right terminology.

'Mr Fullerton called me to arrange a meeting at very short notice,' he continued. 'He has also requested that I continue to act as the intermediary in this matter.'

Thornton silently fumed but said nothing. His experience told him that he would, for the moment at least, have to eat humble pie and allow his subordinate his moment of glory.

Fletcher, seeing that he was unlikely now to be challenged, continued with his briefing.

'James Fullerton has informed me that he's in possession of certain documents that would, if made public, bring down the British government,' Fletcher said, pausing for effect. 'He will be making a similar representation to the DGSE in Paris in the course of the next day or so and expects to be taken very seriously. He has instructed me to arrange a meeting sometime in the next week with the Foreign Secretary, Mr Charles Stevenson at which time the full detail of the documents in his possession will be made known. He strongly suggests that no action is taken to recover said documents as this will only make matters considerably worse for all concerned.'

Fletcher enjoyed every moment and having completed what he had to say, sat down.

All eyes were on Thornton.

'Thank you, gentlemen and ladies, that will be all for now. Please continue with your present assignments. Fletcher, with me!' Thornton barked.

The two men walked swiftly along the carpeted corridor to the lifts and journeyed up to the fourth floor and Thornton's own office complex.

'Sit down!' Thornton ordered. 'Right, what else did Fullerton say?'

'That was all he said!' Fletcher replied. 'I was only with him for fifteen minutes or so.'

'Well he must have said more than that in fifteen minutes!'

'They did most of the talking but it didn't amount to much more than what I have already told you,' Fletcher answered.

'Who do you mean by "they"? Thornton asked.

'Fullerton had a man with him. Simon Shaw was his name I think. He works with Mr Fullerton in Geneva apparently. He, in fact, said more than Fullerton did.'

'Describe this second man to me,' Thornton pressed.

'He was much younger than Fullerton. I would guess he was about thirty-five years old, well dressed and very athletic-looking,' Fletcher replied, trying hard to visualise Fullerton's associate.

'Anything else that I should know?' Thornton said, his eyes giving Fletcher a piercing look.

'No, sir. That's everything that happened.'

'OK, Fletcher, that's all. If you think of anything else, you report it to me immediately, not the next day or the next week, immediately! You can return to your own duties.'

The casual wave of a hand from Thornton and Fletcher knew that he should make himself scarce. So much for his moment of bravado!

After Fletcher had left, Thornton considered the situation. Why would Fullerton bother to come all the way to London, at short notice and arrange to meet Fletcher of all people? Thornton knew that Fletcher had played a lead role in the past in contacting Fullerton's brother Michael, but why would James Fullerton know about Fletcher?

Thornton puzzled over this minor detail before the reality of the present took over and he placed a call to Sir Michael Donaldson. This matter was going to be hastily passed on 'upstairs'. He had been around the civil service in one form or another too long not to realise that bad news needed to be passed on while the music was still playing. He would let the Director-General decide what to do with this information.

At approximately the same time as Fullerton was baiting his trap in London, Fullerton's old friend and confidant Francesco Baldini was performing a similar duty with the French authorities.

Fullerton guessed that this dual approach would shake a few rotten apples out of the tree or, at the very least, test their fortitude.

Chapter 63

September 15th, 2009. London.

Sir Michael Donaldson entered the opulent interior of the Foreign Office and made his way to the Foreign Secretary's even more grandiose office. He was duly admitted, having arrived punctually at 10.15 am as requested.

'Good morning Michael, please come in and take a seat,' Stevenson said standing up from behind his desk and walking towards his colleague.

'Good morning, Foreign Secretary,' Donaldson replied as the two men shook hands.

'I have read your report and wondered if you had any thoughts on the matter beyond what is contained here.'

Before Donaldson could reply Stevenson continued with his monologue.

'I thought that when we met two weeks ago you understood my position and that all necessary measures would be employed to bring this matter to a quick and discrete conclusion.'

'Foreign Secretary, we did indeed put our joint plan into action. The French were amazingly cooperative and they have already instigated their part of the plan.'

'Well, that may be all very well, but I now again have Fullerton to contend with. Why do I get the feeling that we are not in control of events right now?' Stevenson added, showing his frustration with the current turn of events.

'The French authorities have launched a nationwide

police investigation into one of their covert operatives and that individual is actively being sought for questioning,' Donaldson replied.

'Does it not strike you as rather coincidental that just as we initiate our own investigation we are contacted by James Fullerton out of the blue?' Stevenson asked.

'We have already considered that possible coincidence,' Donaldson replied. 'Fullerton's associates had a meeting with our opposite numbers in Paris last Friday and have, in effect, provided them with the same ultimatum.'

'Fullerton expects to have a meeting with me this week,' Stevenson remarked. 'Needless to say, I am going to be conveniently unavailable as I will be out of the country.'

Donaldson sat back and allowed his superior to continue with his pathetic wriggling.

'I am going to need to buy some time, Michael. Do you understand?'

'Absolutely!' Donaldson replied with total conviction. He needed no detailed explanation to understand his boss's present predicament.

'I do, however, expect you to take some appropriate action,' Stevenson stated, looking intently at his intelligence chief.

'What do you suggest I do, Foreign Secretary?'

'I think that I can leave that up to you, don't you?'

Donaldson paused for a moment before replying.

'Oh, I think that a matter of this importance should be dealt with most carefully. I would of course need your specific written instructions. We don't want to create any misunderstandings or act on vague suggestions at this stage, do we?'

The last few words conveyed a sense of finality which was not lost on Stevenson.

Donaldson knew that his boss had no choice in the

matter and inwardly felt somehow pleased that this scheming politician now needed him more than ever.

Charles Stevenson nodded his assent without making any further comment.

'If that will be all, Foreign Secretary, I have a number of issues to sort out pending your written authorisation which I assume will be imminently forthcoming.'

Donaldson stood up. Not waiting to be dismissed and without shaking hands he turned and walked towards the door.

'You'll have your damned letter!' Stevenson yelled. 'There's more to this than you know.'

Donaldson was struck by this last phrase, but left the room without turning.

Chapter 64

September 18th, 2009. London and Geneva.

At precisely 5.00 am the police operation swung into action. Plain-clothes police officers from the Metropolitan Police in coordination with their counterparts from local forces, took up their positions outside of two addresses, both in north London. This was to be a discrete operation and carried out with the minimum amount of fuss and disturbance of the neighbourhoods involved.

Two suspects were duly arrested and taken into custody. Both were transported to a secure holding location in central London.

Fullerton awoke from a deep sleep to the sound of his bedside telephone. It took him a couple of seconds to comprehend the agitated voice on the other end of the line.

To his total surprise, Fullerton realised that it was his daughter-in-law on the line.

'Michelle, calm down and tell me what's the matter.'

'The police have arrested Richard,' Michelle cried. 'They just told him that he had to go with them and that he was under arrest.'

Marguerite awoke and listened. 'They just knocked on the door about half an hour ago. Richard went downstairs to see who was there and he was confronted by four police officers who asked him to go with them. He was only allowed to dress and then was driven off in a dark coloured van.'

'Do you know where they have taken him?' Fullerton asked urgently.

'They only told Richard that he was needed to assist them in their enquiries.'

'OK, now listen to me, Michelle. You have done the right thing in calling me. Try to calm down and I will take whatever action is needed. I will call you as soon as I have any news to report.'

'What is going on, Michael?' Marguerite asked.

'That was Michelle. The police have apparently arrested Richard early this morning for reasons that aren't as yet known,' Fullerton replied. 'I will damn well find out though.'

Fullerton looked at his watch; it was 7.00 am. Too early to phone anyone in the UK. He got up, showered, dressed and went downstairs. Making himself his usual strong black coffee, he went into his office and sat down at his desk.

Why had the Metropolitan Police arrested Richard? He considered the possible explanations. Nobody knew of Richard's other identity except himself and Marguerite. Not even the hierarchy of the DGSE knew that much. So what was the reason behind the arrest. It made no apparent sense at all and yet there had to be a reason.

Fullerton decided that he would place a call to his solicitors in London as soon as it was possible. They could then make the necessary phone calls and that action would provoke a more focused response.

Marguerite came down and joined her husband in his office.

'You don't think that all this has something to do with your meetings with the intelligence community, do you?' she asked.

'How on earth do you make that kind of a connection?' Fullerton responded.

'I just have a sixth sense when it comes to their mindset,' she added.

'But why Richard? Nobody knows about Richard and us and in any case, for all intents and purposes, I am just his estranged uncle.

'I will have my lawyers make them wish they had never heard the name of Fullerton,' he said through gritted teeth.

The phone rang. It was Michelle once more.

'Michael, I have just had a call from one of Louise's flat-mates; she was ever so upset. Apparently Louise has been arrested by the police this morning as well. She didn't know what to do or who to call. She phoned here looking for Richard.'

'Thanks for phoning again, Michelle. I will be contacting the police shortly myself. Call Louise's flat-mate back and tell her that it is all under control. Then do nothing and say nothing to anyone. Do you understand?'

'Yes, I understand. Is Richard in some kind of trouble?' she asked.

'No, he is not, but the people who are doing this soon will be,' Fullerton replied. 'Keep calm, I will phone you as soon as I have any news.'

'I'm beginning to think that you may well be right in your earlier assertion,' Fullerton said looking over at his wife.

At precisely 9.00 am UK time, Fullerton phoned his main solicitors in London. He was put through to Simon Craven, one of the senior partners who had been acting for Axxon since the ignominious departure of Clayton Andrews. It did not take Fullerton long to provide sufficient detail for him to act.

'I will place a call right away to the Metropolitan Police and find out the precise reason for their arrest,' Simon replied reassuringly.

'You are also instructed to contact the Foreign Secretary directly and demand their immediate and unconditional release!' Fullerton added forcefully. 'This is nothing more or less than blatant intimidation. I will be flying to London as soon as I have completed a couple of matters here in Geneva but you can reach me on my mobile phone at any time.'

'Leave this with me, James, I will call you as soon as I have made contact with the Foreign Office and the senior police officer involved.'

'I know who is behind this,' Fullerton said to Marguerite. 'When it was just Richard, there could have been another reason but now that they have arrested both of my children, it is quite obvious what their game plan is.'

'Well, you wanted to create a reaction to your ruse in the hopes that someone would expose themselves and perhaps make a mistake,' Marguerite added. 'I think that they have probably reacted about as well as can be expected, don't you?'

Fullerton thought about this and had to agree that, concern for his family aside, his meeting with Fletcher had most definitely had the desired effect.

'Quite obviously, your message has reached the ears of some very senior people in Whitehall who feel that you are getting too close for comfort,' Marguerite continued. 'In a way, it's all rather predictable, isn't it? My time with the DGSE has shown me that these people don't do subtlety. They have grown used to the fact that the law is an instrument for their sole benefit and they are not used to being on the receiving end.'

'Yes, you are probably right. I hadn't thought of it like that. My big mistake is in still assuming that most people are basically honest and forthright. Well, I had better deal with these rather pressing business matters and hope that in the meantime Simon obtains some very specific answers.'

'And I will gather up all the information that we have accumulated on these people and see if I can't find a common relationship between it all. My years at the DGSE should be able to produce some results,' Marguerite added encouragingly. 'Why do I keep feeling that this whole situation is interconnected? Once we can make that connection we will be a whole lot closer to knowing who exactly is behind this.'

Chapter 65

Driving into the centre of London that Saturday morning, Fullerton was still wondering what the intelligence community had in mind.

'I don't trust anyone any more,' Fullerton said to Marguerite as they made their way through the traffic from the City airport.

Just as they passed Canary Wharf, Michael's phone rang. It was Simon Craven.

'James, where are you? You sound as if you are in a tunnel.'

'I am in my car just passing Canary Wharf.'

'Well, I am in my office right now if you want to meet me here.'

'Perfect timing. I will see you in about ten minutes,' Fullerton said as the taxi slowed in the busy London traffic.

Arriving at Craven's office, he and Marguerite entered the building and made for the lifts. Craven was waiting for them.

'Good morning again, James,' Craven said as the lift doors opened.

'This is my wife, Marguerite,' said Fullerton as they were conducted a short way down the hallway and into Craven's plush corner office.

'What have you found out?' Fullerton said, getting straight to the point.

341

'The Foreign Secretary had been formally notified of your position and I was in contact with The Met immediately after we spoke on the phone yesterday. It took some time before I was able to ascertain exactly what had happened. The arrests of your nephew and niece were ordered by, and under the control of, Commander Foster of the Met Police's anti-terrorism group.'

'Anti-terrorism group!' Fullerton exclaimed. Marguerite gave her husband a look which suggested that he should allow Craven to finish what he had to say without interruption.

'The Met have confirmed to me that they are holding both of them in central London while they carry out routine questioning. I have already lodged an official complaint for wrongful arrest with the appropriate authorities and have arranged for you to visit them this morning.'

'What are we waiting for? Let's go!'

'Are they both being held together?' Marguerite asked.

'As far as I know, they are being held separately and in isolation,' Craven added.

'This is disgraceful!' Fullerton said. 'I know exactly what...' here he paused. There was no need for Craven to be made aware of his own detailed understanding of the present situation and the events that had obviously caused this heavy-handed reaction from the government.

Fullerton composed himself once more.

'Thank you Simon for your assistance so far. I take it you will be accompanying us to see them.'

'That will not be possible I'm afraid,' Craven replied. 'As they are being held under anti-terrorism legislation, we will not be able to make contact with them for the time being. I am doing everything that I can through legal channels to clarify the exact circumstances of this situation.'

'Can I use your phone?' Fullerton asked Craven.

'Please do.'

Fullerton dialled a certain number from memory.

'Fletcher! We need to meet and right now,' Fullerton barked down the phone. 'Usual place in thirty minutes.'

'Please continue to do whatever you can, Craven. Keep me fully informed of any developments,' Fullerton instructed his solicitor. 'I know what I shall do in the meantime.'

'Thank you for making yourself available on a Saturday morning,' Marguerite added politely.

'Not at all. I will call you with any news whatsoever and as soon as I have any.'

Thirty minutes later, Fullerton observed Fletcher as he approached.

'What can I do for you?' he enquired cautiously.

'No doubt you are aware of the situation regarding my nephew and niece,' Fullerton began.

Fletcher's genuinely puzzled look provided Fullerton with his answer.

'My nephew and niece were arrested early yesterday morning by the police. You know nothing about this?'

'Absolutely nothing at all,' Fletcher replied.

Without giving away his next thoughts, Fletcher considered quickly what must have happened since his own meeting with Thornton. Somebody, at a very senior level was starting to play rough.

'I take it that the essence of our conversation last week was duly reported to your superiors?' Fullerton enquired.

'Exactly as you would have wished; they didn't seem too happy about hearing what I had to report,' Fletcher replied.

'I take it you are referring to Thornton.'

Fletcher nodded.

'Well, I have a little proposition for you, Fletcher. By the time I have finished with the Foreign Secretary and all those people involved in the SIS, they will all be lucky if they don't go to jail, never mind lose their jobs. I need you to tell me, right here and now, everything you know about the government's Middle East policy and how it relates to the ADF.'

Fletcher continued to listen in silence.

'Your tenure in the SIS is at an end after this all comes out, which it will do. I am prepared to pay you the sum of £500,000 in exchange for all that you know or can find out.'

Fletcher had been in the employ of the SIS for a number of years, but had never found himself in quite such an 'exposed' position as now. One thing he did know was that matters were getting too critical for his liking and he did not intend to be 'piggy in the middle' any longer. He grabbed his phone and made a call. The number was busy so he left a message.

'Alex, Fletcher here. You need to call me as soon as you can. I have something very important to discuss with you concerning Mr James Fullerton.'

Fletcher looked at Fullerton to see if he approved.

Fullerton nodded and said:

'Now listen carefully to what I am about to say. There are some very powerful people involved in this on both sides. One side is starting to play hard ball. If you don't want to be a casualty, I suggest that you start answering a few questions.'

Fletcher could see the wisdom in this and nodded.

'What is Thornton's role in all this?' Fullerton continued.

'He used to head up a special investigation unit into the activities of the ADF, but I think that his role has been expanded since then,' Fletcher replied. 'I don't know anything about all this, Mr Fullerton. I just do what they tell me,' he added. 'I was brought in to make contact with your brother and to try and get him to agree to cooperate with us in infiltrating the ADF through you.'

'What else do you know about the ADF?' Fullerton asked, instinctively knowing that he had Fletcher in a particularly informative state of mind.

'The influence and activities of the ADF were threatening to expose certain illegal government programmes and Thornton was the man charged with finding out just who was involved and what exactly they knew. Your brother was supposed to be one of those information links. This goes much higher than Thornton and the French are just as much involved.'

Forty-five minutes later, Fullerton decided that Fletcher had indeed earned his inducement.

'Thank you Fletcher, you have been most cooperative. Please arrange to provide me with your bank details. I assume that it will be an overseas account.'

Chapter 66

September 22nd, 2009. London.

Fullerton was waiting on the street corner at the appointed time. A limousine pulled up in front of him. The rear window wound down and a voice said, 'Get in the front.'

Fullerton slid into the front seat and closed the door. 'I've agreed to meet you, now what's this all about?'

One of the two occupants in the rear replied.

'Just sit back and listen, Mr Fullerton. My colleague and I wish to provide you with certain discreet pieces of information. Our identities are of no significance and, given the circumstances, we feel sure that you will understand why we wish to retain our anonymity. The validity of the information which we wish you to have will, we feel, be demonstrably clear.'

Fullerton accepted the brutal logic of this last remark and made no reply. He readjusted his position in the front seat and stared straight ahead as the limousine sped through the central London streets.

The second occupant took up the conversation.

'We have taken some considerable risk in arranging this meeting with you, Mr Fullerton, but the importance of what we have to tell you has left us with no alternative option.'

Fullerton remained silent and allowed the monologue to continue uninterrupted.

'Your activities in recent weeks have caused a lot of embarrassment to some very important people on both sides of the Channel. There is a lot more to this situation than you can possibly imagine and the forces ranged against you have become significantly concerned. This whole matter is likely to escalate out of control. Whilst we have been involved in this process and are therefore fully complicit, we have reached a point beyond which even we will not go.'

Fullerton continued to stare straight ahead and still remained silent as he listened. His mind knew that he needed to remember everything that was said, but his concentration was temporarily lost as he tried to work out the identities and the motivation of his fellow occupants.

The first of the two men spoke again.

'Mr Fullerton, you are fully aware of the activities and membership of the ADF. You are also aware therefore of the untimely death of its founder, Father Pierre Fournier.'

Fullerton was expecting to hear some vital information regarding the activities of the intelligence communities but to be confronted by the mention of his old friend Pierre Fournier came as a complete surprise.

'The activities of the ADF have unwittingly coincided with some joint government covert activity. The people who are in control of this activity are now convinced that the extent of their activities has become known, at least in a significant part, to the ADF. The intelligence community operates in a very murky world Mr Fullerton, and once people start to think that their secrets are no longer secure, decisions are taken that will, and indeed have, caused a lot of unnecessary violence.'

'Who are you people?' Fullerton asked, his inquisitive nature getting the better of him.

'Things will be better served if our identities are kept secret,' the second occupant replied. 'You will be better served if you listen carefully to what we are about to tell you. We have taken some considerable risks in meeting with you and do not wish you to either misunderstand our motives, or indeed, fail to absorb the facts as they currently exist.'

'I'm sorry,' Fullerton said. 'I fully understand your predicament. I do appreciate your willingness to meet with me.'

'You are perhaps aware that some very senior intelligence officers have received tacit approval from certain equally senior politicians to "correct" the current situation. At the risk of appearing too blunt, this means that forces will be brought into play to eliminate any and all perceived threats to the continued secrecy of their covert operations.'

Fullerton at once thought about his own children and their recent arrests.

One of the two men gave their chauffeur some further instructions from which Fullerton deduced that this secretive meeting would not last for too much longer.

'What you need to understand, Mr Fullerton, is that this whole situation in which you now find yourself centres around covert government activities on both sides of the Channel involving the planned elimination of certain foreign dignitaries. You, yourself, were the target for elimination, but somehow you escaped that particular attempt.'

Michael Fullerton thought about his brother and the fact that his murder had in fact been quite successful.

'Yes, I had heard that I was on some kind of a hit list,' Fullerton commented with feigned innocence. 'I am indeed glad that, as you say, I escaped unharmed. You don't know who was behind that attempt do you?'

'All these activities are ordered and approved at very high levels but invariably they are filtered through a man by the name of Alex Thornton.'

So there we have it, Fullerton thought to himself. This now explained the connection between Jason Fletcher and Thornton.

'Needless to say,' the second man continued, 'Thornton only acted on specific instructions that he had himself received. Alex Thornton is one of those career-minded individuals who gradually lose sight of what made them join the intelligence services in the first place and slowly, but inexorably, become a mindless tool in the hands of their ever more demanding superiors.'

The two occupants took a silent look at each other unbeknown to Fullerton who still continued to stare through the windscreen of the limousine.

'Thornton gets all his instructions directly from Donaldson.'

'Do you mean Sir Michael Donaldson, Director General of the SIS?'

'The very same,' came the reply. 'Thornton was put in charge of a specially created unit to delve into the affairs of the ADF and it has provided him with a great deal of first-hand knowledge with which to achieve or further the particular ambitions of his superiors.'

'Why was Father Fournier murdered?' Fullerton asked.

The two men looked at each other before one of them made a reply.

'As far as the general public are concerned, it was just the death of an elderly, rather frail, retired priest living in retirement. In actual fact, we believe it to have been a planned "elimination" of the most influential member of the ADF and meant as a warning to others.'

This explanation seemed to fit perfectly with what Marguerite had managed to ascertain from her police contact.

The first man continued with further information.

'The government covert activities were in danger of being exposed and the powers that be needed to deflect any attention away from their involvement and onto the only organisation which could be conceivably seen as the actual perpetrators. The emphasis therefore changed towards the ADF from one of accepted annoyance at their all too effective activities into one of convenient incrimination.'

'Who else is involved in all this?' Fullerton asked as the limousine completed its circular tour of central London and came to a halt close to where the journey had begun.

'The Director General of the SIS reports to the Foreign Secretary directly. We are also quite sure that the French Minister of Defence, Mr Ives Rousseau, has a key involvement. We feel sure that you will make good use of what we have been willing to tell you, Mr Fullerton.'

Fullerton climbed out of the now stationary vehicle and stood back on the pavement as the limousine smoothly drove off and was lost in the London traffic.

He did not make any attempt to view the faces of the two occupants, a task that would have proved difficult in any case given the darkened windows. He decided to walk for a bit so that his mind could take in all that had been spoken about and discussed.

The now darkened streets and the lack of other pedestrians allowed his footsteps to ring quite noisily as they echoed back from the brick facades of the adjacent buildings.

His meeting with the Foreign Secretary was going to require some careful consideration.

Chapter 67

September 24th, 2009. London.

The revelations made by the two strangers in the car journey two days previously were of great assistance to Fullerton and Marguerite. It was now quite evident that recent events were all part of a much greater government cover-up. Fullerton had lost no time in relaying his findings to all of his close confidants and leading figures in the ADF.

That morning had also started well when Fullerton received news from Craven that the Metropolitan Police were preparing to release both his children within the hour. Could it have something to do with Fullerton's own impending meeting with Mr Charles Stevenson, Her Majesty's Secretary of State for Foreign and Commonwealth Affairs? Fullerton found that he was sufficiently cynical to believe it more than probable.

Fullerton had left Craven in charge of obtaining the release of Richard and Louise and in no doubt that he should contact him immediately if there were any problems or delays. Craven had been given the duty of collecting them both in person and escorting them back to his own office where Fullerton would meet with them after he had completed his meeting at the Foreign Office.

This was going to be a very intriguing meeting with Stevenson. Craven had further been instructed to arrange for Richard to call him as soon as he was able. Fullerton needed to find out from Richard anything of value arising from his period in police confinement. Fullerton knew that Richard would not have been overly distressed by his recent involvement with the police but he did need to know that both he and particularly Louise, were as okay as could be expected after their ordeal.

The meeting with the Foreign Secretary had been arranged for 11.00 am. It was now just a few minutes before 10.30 am and this gave Fullerton time to make one last phone call as he climbed into a taxi to take him to Whitehall.

Fullerton's ever faithful friend and confidant Francesco Baldini had continued to probe the French security community for any additional information that might either enhance or corroborate their current suspicions.

Fullerton was soon connected with his old friend and after a very brief conversation about recent events, he posed the one question that was still troubling him.

'Francesco, do you have any further information or suspicions even, about the extent to which both London and Paris have been complicit and is it, as I now suspect, all to do with the extent of the external political influence in the Middle East?'

'James, my agents have not stopped in their attempts to orchestrate some kind of a security leak. All their attempts had proved fruitless until only yesterday. It would appear that the general mood within the DGSE is one of extreme nervousness.'

At this point Baldini paused as he searched for the right turn of phrase.

'The shit is just about to hit the fan. I think this is what you English say at a time like this.'

'It is going to take quite a large fan to handle all the shit that is going to hit it if what is about to happen does in fact happen,' Fullerton replied.

Baldini continued.

'A chance meeting in the street between one of my senior and trusted colleagues and an equally senior diplomat resulted in the exchange of some crucial facts that could very well have a direct bearing on your present situation.'

Fullerton listened intently to what Baldini was saying but he was also mindful of the time.

'My old friend, I have a meeting with the British Foreign Secretary in less than twenty minutes. Please be as quick as you can with your new information.'

Baldini commenced with his report.

'It would appear that the publicly acknowledged diplomatic negotiations in the Middle East that have been going on for over four years now and which have been jointly attended by the British and French governments under the chairmanship of the Swedish government in fact broke down, "irretrievably" was the word used, some two years ago. Meetings continued to be held but this was all a complete front, purely kept up for appearances sake.

'The British government with tacit approval of their French counterparts came to the conclusion that certain political leaders in the Middle East were never going to agree to the only possible resolution of the ongoing conflict. This conclusion reached, it was only a matter of time before the "hawks" in government arrived at a more direct approach.

'Both the hard-line Israeli Prime Minister and the Leader of Hamas were deemed legitimate targets. Plans were brought forward and detailed strategies evaluated. Before any of this could be put in motion, details of these discussions were leaked to the Israelis. Retribution was quick in coming and as you know, the French Ambassador was killed during a trip to Montreal as was a prominent German politician, in Bonn.

'Following these revenge attacks, the British and French

governments apparently denied all knowledge or involvement in the matter and the situation was allowed to calm down a bit.'

'Who did you get all this information from, Francesco?' Fullerton asked incredulously.

'That I cannot divulge, my friend. I would never be able to obtain this kind of information again if I was known to provide the names of my informants. All I can say to you James is that this information carries the highest credibility and can be treated as one hundred per cent accurate.'

Fullerton paused for a minute before replying.

'Francesco, I can't thank you enough for what you have just told me. Be assured that this conversation will not be repeated to anyone by me. Now I must leave to confront a certain, very worried politician. Take good care of yourself, my old friend and we will meet again soon in Geneva.'

Fullerton ended the call and focused his mind on the matter at hand. His taxi was heading along Parliament Street as his mobile phone rang.

'Hi dad, it's Richard. We are all back safely in Craven's office. He asked me to call you. Where are you?'

'That's good to hear, Richard. I am on my way to the Foreign Office. I should see you all in about an hour's time. I have a lot to tell you. Are you sure that you're both fine?'

'Yes, Louise and I are quite OK. Still feeling a bit intimidated, but otherwise fine.'

'Did the police ask you anything that I should know about before my meeting? Fullerton asked.

'The whole charade was for your benefit, dad. They made the whole episode look as if it had terrorist connotations; I've seen it all before. They did ask me one rather strange question though.'

'What was that?' Fullerton asked as the taxi rounded the corner into King Charles Street.

'They wanted to know if you had had any recent dealings with an Italian by the name of Baldini. I said, of course, that I had absolutely no idea what they were talking about.'

'OK, Richard, thanks for that; must go, the taxi is pulling up outside the Foreign Office. Talk to you in about an hour. Say "Hi" to Louise for me. Bye.'

The taxi drew up outside the Foreign Office and he climbed out of the taxi and made his way in through the main entrance.

'My name is Fullerton, James Fullerton. I have an appointment with the Foreign Secretary at 11.00 am.'

Fullerton waited while the official made the appropriate phone call.

'Please be so good as to wait for a few moments, Mr Fullerton. Someone will be with you shortly.'

Fullerton only had a few moments to survey the opulent surroundings of the interior of this grand building before he was approached by the inevitable civil servant, perfectly dressed, as if to harmonise with the surroundings.

'Mr Fullerton?' Fullerton nodded. 'Please will you be so good as to follow me, the Foreign Secretary is expecting you.'

Fullerton didn't notice his further surroundings as he dutifully walked alongside the young man. His mind was concentrating on precisely what he needed to say and, more importantly, what he needed to hear.

The two men eventually arrived at and entered the Foreign Secretary's outer office waiting area. In no time at all, Fullerton found himself shaking hands with Charles Stevenson. Finally his quest had brought him into the presence of one of the main players in this whole sordid affair.

'Good, morning Mr Fullerton. May I call you James?'

'Good morning. You may,' Fullerton replied. He couldn't help noticing the broad smile on his adversary's face. Fullerton had learned to be suspicious of those people that seemed to smile too much.

'Please be seated and let's see if we can't sort out this whole matter,' Stevenson added.

Stevenson waited until his guest had sat down and then he took up a position opposite so that the two men were within easy conversation distance of each other.

Fullerton sensed that his adversary was searching for any little sign or clue as to the nature of this visit.

'First of all, I would like to thank you for making time to see me this morning. I am sure that you have other important matters to deal with,' Fullerton began. 'I will, however, not take any more of your time than is absolutely necessary. It is for that reason that I have prepared an extensive dossier which I will be leaving with you for your examination and detailed response. We both, I think, know why I am here. All I need to ascertain is which individuals and organisations were responsible for the series of unprovoked attacks on the ADF over the past several years.'

Fullerton had now purposely asked a question to which he already knew the answer. The purpose of this meeting was not to place the Foreign Secretary in the position of either having to accept or deny any particular point put to him, but rather to gauge the degree of his complicity in the process.

He continued without waiting for any kind of response.

'There have been attacks made on me personally and my old and cherished friend Father Fournier, who was not so lucky, has died in somewhat mysterious circumstances. My own family has just recently been arrested for reasons and on charges which seem to be fabricated at best and under legislation which was never intended for the purpose.'

Fullerton paused to see what effect his statement was having. He detected no reaction from the arch politician.

'I would therefore ask you, Foreign Secretary to give due consideration to all the points raised in this dossier.'

Fullerton placed a copy of his findings on the table situated between them.

'I have also just been advised that both my family members have now been released. I will expect there to be no repetition of this heavy-handed police involvement.'

This final remark was intended to add a sting in the tail of his otherwise diplomatic approach.

Charles Stevenson finished reading the summary pages of the dossier and considered what Fullerton had said for a moment before replying.

'Mr Fullerton, James. I would like to thank you for bringing all this information to the attention of Her Majesty's Government and assure you that it will be given the most serious and prompt attention.

'I can also assure you that your allegations will be proven to be without substance and I can assure you that Her Majesty's Government has played no part in either the ordering, sanction or the execution of these terrible activities. I will of course consider your evidence most carefully and can assure you of my complete and full cooperation in the establishment of guilt once the perpetrators are uncovered and apprehended.'

'That is most comforting to hear, Foreign Secretary,' Fullerton replied politely after hearing the well-rehearsed standard reply. 'I will await your further communication on all the matters outlined in my dossier.'

'Thank you very much, Mr Fullerton, for bringing my attention to these matters,' Stevenson replied, signalling the end of the meeting.

Fullerton shook hands with Charles Stevenson and left his office. After being escorted to the entrance of the

Foreign Office, a taxi was found waiting outside which he used to return to Craven's office.

Fullerton was shown directly into Craven's office when he arrived. Richard and Louise were waiting there patiently for him. After the usual family greetings and a brief discussion as to their welfare, Fullerton felt relieved that their ordeal in police custody had not been too traumatic, especially for Louise.

He gave Richard a knowing glance which was correctly interpreted as meaning that the serious discussions could wait until the two of them were alone.

Craven confirmed that the reasons for the arrests and the authorisation behind them were the work of the intelligence services. There was no need to guess who, in turn, was behind them.

Fullerton made light of his recent meeting with the Foreign Secretary and as far as Louise knew, the two events were completely unconnected.

'Let's go out and celebrate this evening whilst we are all together. Simon, that includes you if you can find the time,' Fullerton said instinctively.

'I see that you all have had some lunch.'

'Yes, I thought that I should at least arrange that after our return from the confines of the police station,' Simon replied.

'Thank you for arranging that, Simon,' Fullerton said warmly.

'If everyone can find something to do until around five or five-thirty, I will meet you all at that nice little restaurant just off the Kings Road.'

Richard took his cue from his father and announced that he too had something to attend to for a couple of hours and would meet up with everybody at the restaurant.

'Right, if that's settled I'll see you all later on,' Fullerton concluded.

Richard was waiting for his father downstairs in the main entrance hall of the office building when Fullerton exited the elevator.

'We have a lot to talk about, Richard,' Fullerton said. 'Let's take a taxi along to the embankment where we can talk without being overheard.'

The taxi dropped the two men off close to Westminster Bridge and they started to walk back along the Embankment in the direction of the London Eye.

'How did the meeting with Stevenson go?' Richard asked enquiringly.

'Just about how I expected it to go. He listened patiently to what I had to say, undertook to give careful consideration to all the points raised in my dossier and very convincingly stated that the British Government had no knowledge of any of these nefarious activities.'

'I never cease to be amazed at just how good these politicians are at denying the truth, even when you hit them straight in the face with it.'

Chapter 68

September 25th, 2009. London.

'Get me the Prime Minister!' Stevenson barked down the phone line. He stood up from his desk as he waited for a reply and paced a few steps back and forth whilst keeping the receiver glued to his ear.

A voice answered from 10 Downing Street.

'I don't care how busy he is! Tell him who is calling and that he will really need to hear what I have to say.'

Stevenson used language that was not normally used to summon the attention of any Prime Minister, even by a senior cabinet colleague. But crisis moments required crisis action and every political sense in Stevenson's body told him that this could very well be one of those crisis moments.

Stevenson continued to pace somewhat irritably as he continued to hold for what seemed like ages.

'Charles, what can I do for you?' came the measured opening remark from the Prime Minister as he came on the line.

'John, something rather important has just come up that will require your urgent attention.'

'Well, I am rather busy at the moment, can't it wait until later in the week?' Blakemore replied.

'No, it can't,' Stevenson stated rather emphatically.

Blakemore and Stevenson had known each other for over a quarter of a century and the one thing that Blakemore knew about his Foreign Secretary was that he did not over emphasise any situation without good cause. That was why his trusted friend had been placed at the Foreign Office in the first place and who had consistently been a safe pair of hands in some earlier difficult diplomatic situations.

There was something in the tone of Stevenson's voice that registered in Blakemore's mind and told him to give his old friend a prompt hearing.

'You didn't mention anything to me after Cabinet yesterday, Charles.'

'The situation hadn't arisen yesterday, John,' came the response.

'Trust me on this one, John. You will definitely want to hear what I have to say and it cannot be said over the phone.'

'You had better come over to Downing Street this evening. Make it about six-thirty,' Blakemore replied.

Stevenson duly walked the short distance from the Foreign Office to Downing Street, arriving in good time. He spoke to a couple of cabinet colleagues who were just leaving and then made his way to the Prime Minister's private office.

The door opened as he turned the corner and one of the Prime Minister's political aides passed him without registering any direct eye contact. He entered the Prime Minister's office without allowing the door to close.

'Charles! Come on in and sit down,' the Prime Minister said in his usual but somehow awkward manner.

'Good evening, John,' he said cautiously. He sensed an air of unusual formality in the Prime Minister's voice. This sense was considerably supported by the apparent intention of the Prime Minister to continue writing notes on various papers that were strewn in front of him. Stevenson disliked the way in which his leader seemed to enjoy working in what he would have termed a completely disorganised mess.

Stevenson sat down in one of the chairs positioned across from the Prime Minister's cluttered desk and waited.

'Right, Charles,' Blakemore said as he now looked up from his paperwork and directly at his Foreign Secretary. 'What is this important matter that you so urgently need to see me about?'

'It's Fullerton! I had a meeting with him yesterday and he handed me a dossier concerning our "treatment" of the ADF.' Stevenson paused for some kind of reaction but received none and so continued.

'The content of the dossier contains a disturbing amount of information about our intelligence services as well as considerable detail of our interaction with the French. What is perhaps more to the point is just how much factual evidence is alluded to without the provision of proof.'

John Blakemore, Her Majesty's First Lord of the Treasury looked back at his Foreign Secretary and thought for a moment.

'Who else knows about your meeting with Fullerton and this dossier?'

'Only my close office staff are aware of the meeting. Nobody knows about the dossier except Fullerton and me.'

'What do you think was his intention in meeting with you, Charles?'

'That is the strange part of all this; he provided me with this dossier, but did not provide any indication as to the intent behind it.'

'Have you discussed this with Donaldson?' the Prime Minister asked.

'I didn't want to approach anyone else until you were made aware of both the meeting with Fullerton and the existence of this dossier.'

'Leave the dossier with me until later tonight. I will need to see you again then.'

'As you wish, Prime Minister,' Stevenson replied dutifully.

'Until we meet later, do not discuss any of this with anyone, I mean anyone. Not even your close confidants at the Foreign Office.'

'As you wish,' Stevenson added, now thankful that his problem was somehow diminished by having shared it with his boss.

'Please arrange to see me at about nine pm, Charles.'

'Of course, Prime Minister,' Stevenson added subserviently as he walked back over to the door of the Prime Minister's private office and departed.

Blakemore picked up the phone and placed a call to Sir Michael Donaldson at SIS headquarters. The Prime Minister was informed that Sir Michael was not in the building at that present moment in time. They would however contact him immediately.

A few minutes later the Prime Minister received a return call from Sir Michael Donaldson who was in his car heading for Heathrow and about to depart for Washington.

'Michael! Thank you for returning my call. Something has come up which requires your particular talents.'

'I am on my way to Washington, Prime Minister! Can it wait?'

'If it could wait, I would not have called you now,' Blakemore snorted, not appreciating the dismissive tone from his intelligence chief.

'Please cancel your arrangements as far as Washington is concerned. Something far more important has arisen. It involves James Fullerton. Need I say more!'

Donaldson sat back in the rear seat of his limousine

and briefly took the phone away from his ear as he instructed his chauffeur to turn the vehicle around and head back into central London and Downing Street.

'I will be in Downing Street in about twenty-five minutes Prime Minister.'

'Good,' was the Prime Minister's sharp reply before the line went dead.

'Get me Thornton on the line!' Donaldson instructed his aide, 'and make it a priority call.'

Nine o'clock arrived and Charles Stevenson duly arrived back at 10 Downing Street as requested. He was shown directly in to where the Prime Minister was sitting.

'Hello, Charles. Take a seat. Looks like this fellow Fullerton is playing hard ball doesn't it?'

'He certainly has us by the balls, John. What are we going to do about it?' Stevenson replied.

'I have spoken to Donaldson this evening. He came up with an interesting approach. Something that should stop Fullerton in his tracks,' Blakemore continued.

'Well I hope it solves our problem, because it doesn't look good from where I'm sitting,' Stevenson replied.

Blakemore spoke.

'Go back to your office and instruct Donaldson to issue an arrest warrant for James Fullerton and all the various members of his family. Use the anti-terrorism legislation again. That should keep Fullerton locked up and out of harm's way for long enough for us to see this thing through. He is expecting your call and knows what we have been discussing.'

'As you wish Prime Minister, but I would prefer this in writing this time,' came the Foreign Secretary's response.

Blakemore stared at Stevenson for a few moments, then nodded his assent.

With that Stevenson left Downing Street and returned directly to his own office to await his written instruction.

Stevenson allowed the SIS organisation, in conjunction with the police, to swing into action but decided that some well leaked, timely information concerning the dubious activities of a certain James Fullerton could be best used by the national TV channels.

Stevenson was not disappointed when he listened to the initial 'as yet unconfirmed' reports the following morning. National newspapers were given appropriate 'informed sources' information as well, concerning the arrests.

Fullerton answered the phone back in his suite at the Dorchester.

'Mr Fullerton?' the voice said.

'Yes, this is Fullerton' Fullerton replied.

'Commander Foster of the Metropolitan Police. I have just received a formal arrest warrant for you under the Anti-Terrorism Act. It will take me about twenty minutes to arrive.'

The phone line went dead and Fullerton stood still and wondered why he was being told in advance.

'Marguerite! Grab what you need, we are leaving the hotel right this minute,' Fullerton shouted.

Fullerton explained his phone call to Marguerite as they used the lift. They grabbed an arriving taxi as soon as its occupants had vacated it and gave instructions to the driver to take them to St Pancras as fast as he could given the Friday afternoon traffic.

Fullerton used his mobile phone and called Richard.

'Richard, listen carefully. Your mother and I are taking the Eurostar right this minute. We have received a tip-off from the police that we were about to be arrested. I don't know but this could also involve you as well. I want you to see to your family and Louise as well. Take them to a safe location and I will have my people contact you with the collection arrangements. Tell Louise that she must do what I ask without delay.'

Richard needed no further instructions and immediately sprung into action.

Fullerton handsomely rewarded the taxi driver for an almost miraculous journey across town and he and Marguerite headed for the Eurostar Business Premier check-in machines.

A train to Lille was due to leave in fifteen minutes. This gave them just enough time to purchase two tickets and board the train.

At precisely 2.08 pm the train moved smoothly out the station on its way to France. Fullerton looked at his watch. It was now only thirty-five minutes since he had received the phone call. He would remember to thank Commander Foster one day for his as yet unexplained assistance.

Chapter 69

October 3rd, 2009. London.

Fullerton had half expected the reaction from the British Government authorities but had not foreseen the speed at which the recent sequence of events had taken place.

He had listened to his son's advice, had seen the wisdom and inside knowledge upon which it had been based and was now thoroughly glad that he had acted upon it.

Richard had been absolutely one hundred percent accurate with his prediction as to the Government's next move.

With a private plane discreetly notified to be on immediate standby, Fullerton had arranged a series of overnight collections that had brought all his close family members to an otherwise unimportant airport west of London. Once on board, all his family would be flown to France and then on to *Bellerive*.

Richard had been of great assistance in managing the details, not to mention the explanations. He had shown his true maturity and skill in this enterprise and Fullerton had seen a ruthless streak of efficiency and effort from his son that he had hitherto not experienced.

Richard was still one of Fullerton's trump cards and proving an invaluable asset. Fullerton was still, however, unsure as to just how involved he should allow his son to be. Greater involvement meant much greater risk.

Fullerton arranged to meet up with his son in London as soon as the family airlift had been completed. Fullerton knew that once the authorities found out about the disappearance of all his family members, 'the cat' would be really and truly 'out of the bag'.

Fullerton had chosen a rather nondescript restaurant just off Knightsbridge where he could meet up with Richard without being spotted.

It had been agreed that he would arrive at the restaurant first, thereby allowing Richard an opportunity for his skilled surveillance know-how to spot if his father had been tailed. This precaution somehow seemed a little over the top, but again he bowed to his son's much greater experience.

Neither men, it turned out had been followed and so Richard duly joined his father in the rear section of the restaurant.

'Hello, Richard,' Fullerton said quietly as his son arrived.

'Hi, Dad. No one was following either of us, but I thought it best if we played safe.

Everyone is safely out of the country. They didn't put up too much of a fuss, not after their recent holiday with the Met and Marguerite is making sure that everything is explained fully once they are safely in Switzerland.'

'That's great, Richard. Now we need to discuss what our next move should be.'

'I thought about this on the way over. I am best used if I return to Paris and find out what I can from my informants there. We know that both intelligence services are involved and it won't take Whitehall long before they pass on their suspicions and fears to the DGSE in Paris.'

'Let's just take a look at what is likely to happen next,' Fullerton said, feeling in need of a few minutes of quiet, sober consideration of both the present rapid sequence of events and those that were undoubtedly to follow.

'The British Government has swallowed our bait in one gulp. They do not have the option of hoping that we will limit our activities now to some private settling of accounts. They also do not know precisely what we know or do not know and therefore are forced into assuming that we know more than we actually do. What I do know is that the extent of their present reaction can only imply a degree of guilt and complicity that even we have not assumed possible.'

Fullerton sat back and thought about what he had just said and then looked at his son for any response.

'I know how these people act once they feel threatened and things could get really rough,' Richard added rhetorically.

'If we are to expose the full extent of the British and French governments' involvement in the series of murders and attempted murders then we will need absolute proof. The file that you found in Geneva belonging to Uncle James provided a substantial amount of vital information but we still lack the key link between the activities of the intelligence communities and the politicians themselves. We have to be able to prove that these instructions were directly authorised and sanctioned by these specific, highly placed individuals.'

'You're quite right, Richard,' Fullerton answered and the two men paused as they gave their order of food to the attending waiter.

'I have one final meeting in the morning to sort out some business negotiations and then I will be returning to Geneva.'

Richard spoke: 'As I said earlier, I can be of most use back in Paris so I think that I will travel over tomorrow morning and see just how much additional information I can collect. I still have a few people who owe me some favours, not to mention the growing number of staff members who have become increasingly alarmed over all this.'

Father and son spent the remainder of the evening enjoying each other's company. Something they had not done for a very long time.

Chapter 70

October 4th, 2009. Paris and Geneva.

Richard arrived at his small apartment in Paris by late morning. Everything seemed to be as he had left it several weeks previously. There was a new concierge residing in the small ground floor apartment provided and Richard introduced himself using his disguise and spent a few moments talking to the new occupant and ascertaining what exactly had happened to the last.

It turned out that the previous concierge, an old widow had retired and gone to join a family member in the countryside near Dijon. The new concierge was a young man in his early thirties who had taken the job in order to live in a reasonably central part of Paris.

Having established that all the activity in his building seemed quite normal and having noticed that virtually all the tenants were unchanged, Richard ventured out into the city to see who or what he could come across.

His father had arranged for one of Baldini's agents to make contact with him that evening in order to facilitate further exchanges of information with Lefevre.

Richard suspected that his former boss at the DGSE was still under surveillance but it was critically important that the exact link between the British and French authorities was discovered.

However, the time between now and this evening could be well spent by seeing which other associates within the DGSE organisation he could reach.

If Richard's long experience of intelligence operations had taught him one thing then it was that no one could necessarily be trusted. When there were internal investigations, particularly in situations as critical and as potentially damaging as those currently under way, everybody remotely involved would be into saving their own skins.

Several fruitless phone calls later, Richard began to wonder if the whole intelligence community had gone on leave. His own sphere of contacts had been, of necessity, quite limited but to be unable to reach any of his confidants was becoming quite surprising.

A two-hour surveillance of the office complex formerly occupied by his boss, however, finally yielded a minor triumph. Richard was just about to return back to his apartment when the diminutive figure of Francine Guyon appeared as she exited the building and began her daily commute back home to the suburbs. Francine had served Pascal Lefevre for many years and so could prove to be just the person to whom he needed to speak.

Mindful of the prevailing situation, Richard followed his target at a very discreet distance for some five minutes or so. He rightly assumed that Francine would probably use the 'RER' out to her home in the Paris suburbs and so closed the distance between him and his quarry as they both approached the local Metro station of Saint Fargeau. The station proved not to be too overly populated and this allowed Richard the ideal opportunity of keeping Francine under close scrutiny without the risk of being observed.

The long, cross-city journey eventually came to a halt at the Gare d'Austerlitz and the connecting RER train filled with more commuters. Richard moved a little closer to Francine through the jostling crowd, still remaining quite unobserved. Francine had managed to find a seat and had her back to Richard who remained standing further along the compartment.

The train rattled along the track on its journey to the south-eastern suburbs passing through a couple of local stations until it slowed again as it approached the town of Vitry-sur-Seine.

Francine collected her belongings together and made ready to stand up and move in the direction of the exit doors. Richard half turned his body so as to give the appearance of somebody travelling further.

Francine exited the train along with quite a considerable number of other commuters. Vitry-sur-Seine was a popular commuter town giving at least some of its inhabitants a relatively simple and quick journey to work.

Richard hastened through the crowd on the platform so as to regain a suitable but still discreet distance from Francine.

The crowd poured out onto the relatively empty streets of the town. Richard decided to wait before speaking to Francine until she had completed her journey and her fellow passengers had dispersed in the surrounding streets. He followed her along the street at a safe distance. Richard decided to continue his surveillance for a little bit longer. He could not be sure that even Pascal Lefevre's own secretary was not being monitored and his training had taught him to use all of his senses. He had been quite sure that Francine had not been followed on the train journey but as the intelligence community would undoubtedly know where she lived, they could easily pick up her movements as she neared her own apartment.

Francine made a couple of stops to buy some local produce and Richard's eyes scanned the street for any possible observers.

It did not take Francine long to purchase what she

needed and she soon carried on along the now peaceful boulevard until she reached the next street.

She rounded the corner and was lost from view for a couple of anxious moments until Richard once again rounded the same corner and luckily caught sight of her as she entered a rather smart-looking, nineteenth-century apartment building. It was a building, typical of Paris in that era, long casement windows fronting onto the street with decorative iron railings and shutters that had that look of being rarely used.

Richard gave the street a long gaze and concluded that Francine's journey home that evening had only been observed by him. As he approached the entrance to the apartment building, Richard began to focus on the names listed opposite some twenty or so intercom buttons.

Half way down the left hand column Richard spotted the name P GUYON. This must be Francine's husband's name and initial he thought.

Richard pressed the button a couple of times and waited. A man's voice answered. 'Hallo.'

'This is Francois Duval. Is that Mr Guyon?' Richard said quietly and in a measured tone to establish that he was indeed speaking to Mr Guyon.

'I am an old friend of Pascal Lefevre and need to speak with your wife urgently.'

A few seconds elapsed before Francine came on the intercom and Richard explained his connection with Lefevre. The buzzer sounded and Richard pushed open the heavy entrance door and made his way to the third floor as directed.

Francine was waiting for him at the door of her apartment and vaguely recognised Richard from his albeit infrequent visits to meet with Lefevre in his office.

'Mr Duval?' Francine said somewhat quizzically. 'Please come in.'

After the introductions had been made, the three of them sat down in the spacious living room of the apartment.

'I have worked for Pascal for many years and consider him one of my closest friends,' Richard stated.

'Yes, I think that I remember you visiting Mr Lefevre once or twice recently,' Francine added, having now made the connection.

'I have in fact followed you home from your office this afternoon but waited until now before making my presence known to you,' Richard continued. 'I couldn't be certain whether or not you were being watched. You weren't, but I had to be sure.'

'I haven't seen Mr Lefevre since the day they came and arrested him,' Francine said. 'It was all so sudden and nobody in the department knew anything about it until it happened.'

'Can you describe the people who came for Pascal?'

'There were three men; most abrupt they were too. I am sure that they were not regular policemen. It didn't feel like they were policemen somehow. They just told Mr Lefevre to go with them and that he would be informed of the reasons in due course. Mr Lefevre initially refused to leave his office without receiving an official instruction to cooperate.'

'What happened then?'

'Mr Lefevre was told to telephone his immediate superior, which he did.'

'Do you know who he called?'

'Yes, because he asked me to make the call for him and then to put it through to his office. He asked me to call Mr Ives Rousseau.'

'Thank you, Francine. That's all that I need to know. You have been most helpful.'

'Is Mr Lefevre in real trouble?' Francine asked.

'No, he isn't, but some of his superiors are going to

be by the time I have finished,' Richard answered. 'You have both been most kind. I must leave now as I have other people to see this evening. Oh, by the way. I would really appreciate it if you didn't tell anyone of my visit here today. It would only make things more difficult for you. Thanks once again.'

With that final remark Richard left the apartment and retraced his journey back into the centre of Paris. He did indeed have other things to do.

As his father had arranged for an ADF agent to make contact with him that evening, Richard pulled his mobile phone out of his pocket to ensure that he had not missed any messages whilst he was talking to Francine. There were no messages showing on his phone but the reception on the train was intermittent at best.

Richard sat back in his seat, placed his elbow on the window frame and stared out at the passing scenery. He decided that he would remain in the centre of Paris so as to be in a convenient place to meet his contact.

The train reached the centre of the city and Richard got off at the Musée D'Orsay. There were several little cafés nearby and so Richard decided to have something to eat and drink while he waited for his call.

'*Bonsoir Monsieur,*' cried one of the waiters and showed Richard to a seat by the window where he could watch the passing people and traffic.

Richard ordered a glass of wine and then stared out of the window deep in thought.

He glanced at his phone which was on the corner of the table and again checked the reception. The phone showed a full signal and so Richard sat back, picked up his glass and sipped the wine.

He had barely started to relax when his phone rang.

The restaurant was reasonably busy and so the sound was hardly heard by even those sitting closest to him.

Richard answered the call with his characteristic '*Oui, j'écoute!*' The caller quickly identified himself as one of Francisco Baldini's agents and the two men arranged to meet at 8.30 in front of the cathedral of Notre Dame.

This arrangement gave Richard plenty of time to have another drink and then walk over to the cathedral. He was glad that he had received the call, not that he doubted his father's arrangement, but he instinctively knew that this next phase of his and his father's quest for that last vital piece of information linking everything together was all that stood between them and the potential downfall of some very influential people. Not only that, it would also go a long way in addressing and making up for the death of his own uncle.

Richard ordered another drink and concentrated on the matter in hand. This evening he felt ready for anything.

Thanking the waiter and after paying for the drinks, Richard left the cosy little restaurant and started to walk back along the left bank of the river until he reached the Pont Neuf.

Part way across he left the bridge and took the steps down onto the adjacent roadway that formed the extreme end of the Ile de la Cité.

Richard walked briskly along the quay in the direction of Notre Dame and soon found himself in the square with the magnificent west face of the cathedral in full view. He glanced at his watch and saw that he had five minutes to spare.

He chose to sit down on one corner of the square so that he could more easily observe all the comings and goings, mainly consisting of tourists, even though it was nearly eight-thirty at night.

He did not have long to wait. Baldini's contact had

indicated that he would be wearing an unobtrusive, yet quite visible, white trilby hat and that he would stand more or less in the centre of the square when he arrived.

Richard soon spotted his quarry and after surveying the movements of other passers-by for a further couple of minutes, gradually approached his contact.

'*Monsieur Baldini n'est-ce pas?*' Richard said quietly mentioning Baldini's name as the agreed word of recognition.

'*Oui, c'est moi,*' the man replied as he turned round to face Richard. 'You can call me Pierre if you like,' he added.

'Let's take a stroll,' Richard suggested.

Neither of the two men were using their real names and it didn't really seem to matter. They were unlikely to meet again and true identities were superfluous. Once they had left the square and were once again relatively alone on one of the adjacent quays, Richard spoke once more.

'I need you to contact Lefevre and ask him some more questions for me.'

'I think that the situation has moved on somewhat since then,' came the reply.

'What do you mean?' Richard asked.

'Mr Baldini called me about one hour ago with some very important news. Apparently there is a DGSE plot to capture your father in Geneva and return him to France.'

'Jesus Christ!' Richard uttered under his breath. 'How did he find out about that?'

'Mr Baldini knows a lot of people and hears a lot of things, if you get my meaning.'

'I guess he does at that,' Richard replied.

No wonder that all his contacts in the intelligence community had failed to answer his calls. There seemed to be some serious developments and the whole place was in lock-down mode.

'OK!' Richard added, trying to focus his brain on what should happen next. 'How much does Baldini know about this plot?'

'I've told you all I know. I only heard this much an hour ago myself. Mr Baldini did say that he would now be contacting you again directly, once he obtains more specific details.'

Richard thought for a moment.

'I've decided not to approach Lefevre again just yet. As you say, things appear to have moved on a lot.'

'You can trust Mr Baldini. If anyone can get to the bottom of this, he can.'

What little Richard knew of Francesco Baldini told him that he had been a long-time associate of his uncle's and that his father also trusted him implicitly. He would do as 'Pierre' suggested and wait for Baldini to contact him again.

'I think we have concluded our little meeting. Thank you for what you have told me Pierre,' Richard said, as he shook hands with his contact.

'One last thing,' Pierre added. 'Do not say anything about this plot to your father. Mr Baldini was most explicit in that instruction.'

Without saying anything further, 'Pierre' just gave Richard a smile and a wink and the two men left as they had arrived; by different routes and with very different things on their minds.

Chapter 71

October 10th, 2009. Geneva.

Robert Faulkner, European Affairs Editor for *The Times* newspaper had responded to the phone call received some four hours earlier and had grabbed the first available flight from Heathrow to Geneva. He had been met on his arrival in Geneva by one of Fullerton's staff and speedily transported from the airport to *Bellerive*.

Faulkner had hardly any time in which to take in his grandiose surroundings before he was shown into one of the main living rooms of the mansion.

Fullerton was waiting for Faulkner as he entered and walked towards him and shook his hand.

'Mr Faulkner, I feel I know you from all your articles, may I call you Robert.'

'Bob will be fine, Mr Fullerton,' Faulkner replied as he observed another man who was standing over the far side of the room.

Fullerton continued.

'Thank you for attending this rather hastily arranged news briefing at short notice. I feel sure that what you are about to hear will allow you to feel that your journey was worthwhile. I would remind you that this meeting is to be held in the strictest confidence. My legal advisor is only here to ensure that everything that you are about to hear is handled in a strictly legal manner.' Fullerton gestured in the direction of his legal counsel.

He had in fact been preparing for this moment for

longer than Faulkner would ever have guessed. The reason for only announcing the date and time for the select briefing a matter of hours before it actually took place was to prevent any possible government prior knowledge of it, and the consequential interference that would undoubtedly follow.

Fullerton had purposely only invited Robert Faulkner from *The Times* because he felt that Faulkner and, more importantly, the newspaper that Faulkner represented, would provide the most appropriate vehicle to pressurise the British Government and the Foreign Secretary in particular.

'Please be seated. You can take notes if you wish but I have prepared a full written dossier which I am sure you will find to be correct in all its detail.'

Whilst Faulkner was retrieving a notebook from his attaché case Fullerton continued.

'This meeting has been arranged in order for me to provide you and your readers with a detailed account of the joint activities of the British and French Governments concerning their relationships with certain Middle East Governments and their respective leaders.'

Fullerton handed Faulkner the legally bound dossier consisting of some two hundred pages.

'This dossier contains a chronological history of the both complicated and interconnected activities of the DGSE and the SIS acting on specific instructions of their respective governments. It provides evidence, all corroborated, of the secretive, covert operations that have been sanctioned by both national governments in their attempts to change the course of political development in the Middle East.

Faulkner looked up at Fullerton in silence as the enormity of the disclosure began to sink in to his head. It only took him a few seconds to recognise what was going to become a massive headline story.

JAMES BUCKINGHAM

'All of this documentation is going to need some extremely careful scrutiny by our lawyers,' Faulkner said. 'If what you state in these pages is even half correct, this is going to be become an enormous embarrassment to the French and British governments, not to mention individuals in particular.'

At the same time as his father was briefing *The Times'* editor in Geneva, Richard was travelling into the centre of Paris again for a further rendezvous.

The arranged meeting place this time was the entrance foyer of the Louvre museum. It was usually quite busy in the middle of the day and presented a convenient place for Richard to meet his contact and receive the written details concerning the planned abduction of his father. He would also, as usual, arrive early in order to ensure that they would not be observed by any overly conscientious security operatives, should either of them have been followed.

The arranged time was 11.45 am and so Richard ensured that he was going to be there no later than 11.30 am.

The queue that had formed outside of the Louvre pyramid had fluctuated in length during the course of the morning but had now reached quite a considerable length. Richard estimated that he could not join the queue in the normal fashion and wait his turn to enter. He would have to show his security service ID if he wanted to bypass the long line of tourists that were slowly passing through the entrance doorways.

Richard observed the activity at the head of the queue from close by and decided that this choice of meeting place had not been one of his best ideas.

Just as he was thinking of approaching the entrance he felt a tap on his shoulder and turned to see an older, white-haired gentleman standing right next to him.

'I think that you are waiting for me,' the older man said. 'Let's take a walk and move away from here; it's far too crowded and we don't want to be disturbed.'

Richard looked at him and something in the manner of his speech suggested to Richard that this was someone he could trust. Anyway, who else would know where he was going to be and at what appointed time other than a further contact from Baldini.

The two men walked out of the confines of the Louvre complex and out onto the Rue de Rivoli. There the older man flagged down a taxi and invited Richard to join him inside. The taxi driver was told to drive in the direction of the Palais de Chaillot and the taxi soon gained speed as it approached the Place de la Concorde.

'My name is Francesco Baldini,' the man said. 'I decided that matters were sufficiently important for me to come and meet you myself.'

Richard looked at the man whose name he had heard so often. He knew that things must indeed be critical for his father's friend and confidant to attend in person.

'You know who I am then?' Richard asked.

'Yes, your father explained everything to me some while ago. It was just after your meeting in Saint-Germain-en-Laye in August.'

The taxi continued to weave its way through the late morning traffic.

'Things are getting really dirty now, Richard. There are some awfully powerful people who do not want their dirty little secrets to come out into the light of day and they will go to any lengths to prevent such a thing from happening. Your uncle paid the price with his life just as he was starting to get really close. When your father assumed his brother's identity there was a lot of discussion in certain circles about how your uncle had managed to avoid death. Those people responsible had absolutely guaranteed his demise and when it didn't happen, a lot of mistrust as to possible motives and hidden agendas was built up. Your father has carried on extremely courageously where his brother left off. Never quite knowing what he had become embroiled in until quite recently.'

The taxi rounded the corner and came to a halt in front of the Palais de Chaillot.

Baldini spoke to the taxi driver, paid him and the two men climbed out of the taxi and began to walk towards the immense structure of the palace.

Once there the whole of Paris seemed to be laid out before them. The Eiffel Tower directly opposite was in full view and they could see the wide sweep of the river as it continued on its way through the city.

'I have managed, with some considerable difficulty, to ascertain the essential details of the plot to capture your father in Geneva,' Baldini continued with a more intense expression on his face.

'Your father does not know anything about this and for the moment, I don't want him to know. For us to thwart this plot I need them to think that their plans have not been compromised. It will also help disguise those people who have provided such information to me in the first instance. I have built up a reputation for complete confidentiality over many years in this business and without it I would not have managed to gain such critical intelligence as this.'

Richard stood next to his father's confidant and continued to listen to the monologue.

'Word has it that a special commando-style squad has been put on alert and that an attempt will be made to "acquire" your father next Tuesday at *Bellerive*. The squad will be flown in by helicopter and land directly in the grounds. Any resistance will be met with extreme force. Once in their possession, your father will be flown directly to a holding facility in the countryside just outside Paris. Sufficient incriminating evidence will be conveniently left behind at *Bellerive* to convince all but the most conscientious investigation that the plot was the work of Middle East extremists.'

'Both British and French governments will then come up with a public display of outrage but secretly drip-feed information that will provide enough "smoke" for everybody to believe that there could not be "smoke without fire". Your father's reputation will be destroyed, his whereabouts unknown and the effectiveness of the ADF essentially eliminated.'

Baldini paused for breath and this gave Richard a chance to give his own reaction.

'What is our response going to be to all this?'

'Needless to say, we are arranging for your father to be nowhere near Geneva on Tuesday. He will be told all about this at the last minute. We hold certain suspicions about a certain member of his office staff and so cannot risk our knowledge reaching the perpetrators until it is all too late.'

'What do you want me to do in all of this?' Richard asked.

'As things are moving very rapidly, I will want you to return with me to Geneva where I have started to organise the security network around your father. Your particular skills in this kind of work will prove most useful.'

'When do we leave for Geneva?'

'First thing in the morning! I came here on a scheduled flight so as to not bring any undue attention to my movements. But I think that we will drive back to Geneva tomorrow morning. That way our movements will be even less noticeable.'

*   *   *

Robert Faulkner stood up. He had been at *Bellerive* for only a couple of hours but it seemed to him as if he had been there for much longer than that.

'I have just one further question for you Mr Fullerton before I leave.'

Fullerton also stood up and waited for Faulkner to pose his final query.

'Why have you done all this? What got you started on this whole investigation?'

'That's two questions, Mr Faulkner, but I will give you just one answer. Some very dear friends have paid with their lives in order that we could have this discussion today. I owe it to those same friends that this whole wretched business is published for the world to see.'

'Thank you Mr Fullerton for putting your trust in *The Times*. I will of course keep you fully informed of the paper's intentions regarding publication of this material once I have discussed this with my editor-in-chief.'

Faulkner placed the dossier into his briefcase and prepared to be escorted to the front door.

Fullerton spoke one final time.

'Mr Faulkner! One last point. We have as yet not fully proved just how high up, in the tiers of government, this reaches. Once this is clear, the story will be complete.'

Faulkner looked back at Fullerton and with a wry smile said: 'I think that there is enough here to be going on with for the time being.'

'Thank you again for coming at such short notice, my driver will see you delivered back to the airport,' Fullerton replied.

Chapter 72

October 13th, 2009. Milan and Besançon.

The Times had withheld any detailed publication until it had satisfied itself concerning the accuracy of the dossier and its legal impact. Fullerton picked up a copy of the Tuesday edition of the paper which had been collected specially by a member of Baldini's staff at his Milan villa.

Richard had arrived back at *Bellerive* on the Sunday afternoon with Baldini and had immediately informed his father of the planned abduction. The whole family had then been smuggled out of *Bellerive* by car that same evening and driven overnight to Milan. The Swiss authorities had, that morning, been provided with sufficient information about the planned 'visit' to *Bellerive* and had arranged a greeting party of their own.

The three days that they had been in Milan had allowed Fullerton, Marguerite and Richard to spend some quality time together, courtesy of their host. Marguerite had been out doing some shopping but with two of Baldini's men for added security.

Fullerton had arranged for his staff to keep him informed of developments in Geneva but through intermediaries. His various business interests still required his input and decision-making authority even if he was temporarily out of circulation.

The Baldini villa was fairly centrally situated in one of Milan's fashionable districts. It had been built in the early eighteenth century in a very grandiose fashion by a Roman

Catholic Cardinal but had been bought by one of Francesco
Baldini's ancestors in the early nineteenth century. The
Baldini family had lived in Milan for generations and the
family's wealth had been largely acquired through banking
and commerce.

Francesco had become the patriarch of the family and
its wide-ranging business interests on the death of his
father in 1985 and it was through some of these business
connections that he had met and become firm friends
with James Fullerton. Together they had fostered and
developed the ADF organisation into its formidable present
position.

'Good morning everybody!' came Baldini's heavy Italian-
accented greeting as he joined Fullerton, Marguerite and
Richard out on the rear terrace.

Fullerton placed the copy of *The Times* on the table in
front of him and stood up to greet his host.

'Good morning, Francesco,' Fullerton answered.

'This is the first really fine day since we arrived here,'
Marguerite added. 'The gardens and terraces are really
marvellous when the sun shines. Richard and I went for
a bit of a walk a short while ago and didn't realise just
how extensive the grounds are.'

'Yes, it is hard to believe that we are in the centre of
a large city these days, a small oasis of calm. I come back
here a lot when I need to relax and feel at home.

'I have received word from my associates in Geneva
that the Swiss authorities dealt comprehensively with the
six men who apparently approached your house in Geneva
by water. They had barely left the boat in which they
had arrived when they were all arrested and taken into
custody.'

'That should give Britain and France something more
to worry about now,' Fullerton said with a grin. 'I've been
reading yesterday's copy of *The Times* which has carried

a most comprehensive article about my dossier. No doubt Whitehall will be in some considerable panic already.'

Baldini continued.

'I have received some important communications from your office staff in Geneva via our ADF colleagues. It is in my office for you to deal with.'

'I'm inclined to leave it just where it is Francesco, I have become so relaxed these past three days,' Fullerton replied. 'I suppose however that I should deal with it right away.'

'In that case I will show you to my office. Feel free to use it for as long as you like.'

Fullerton left Marguerite and Richard on the terrace and followed Francesco back into the villa and down the long corridor leading to Francesco's office.

'Here we are, Michael. Your correspondence is in that sealed package on the desk. Please use my private line if you need to make any calls.'

'Thank you Francesco, you are most kind. Hopefully this will not take too long.'

'Take as long as you like, my friend.'

The door closed behind Baldini and Fullerton was left alone in the ornate corner office. From here he could look out onto both the rear garden with its classically laid out pathways and manicured lawns and also onto the side aspect of the villa with its view out over the rooftops of Milan.

Fullerton sat down at the huge desk and opened up his package. There was the usual daily business correspondence to deal with, although he noticed that his secretary had used his discretion and forwarded on only the most pressing and important matters for Fullerton's attention.

There was, however, a rather ordinary letter postmarked Avignon that gained his attention. It was addressed to him personally and marked expressly for his attention only.

Memories of his last visit to Avignon flooded back into his mind as he used a letter opener to slice through the well-sealed flap.

The contents consisted of a single page letter addressed to James Fullerton and signed Amand Dubois.

Michael read the letter.

Dear Mr Fullerton

We are aware of your circumstances and feel that we can be of some considerable assistance to you at this present time. A prompt meeting between us would provide you with a lot of valuable information concerning D and S.

Please arrange to contact me in the usual manner to arrange an appropriate time and place. I would stress the urgency of such a meeting.

Amand Dubois.

Fullerton had not been in contact with his ADF associates for some six months or so as a result of all the recent disturbances in his life. Dubois was known to be one of the ADF's oldest supporters but his views had always tended towards the extreme when it came to deciding upon consequential courses of action.

Fullerton looked at the date. The letter had been written on October 6th, a full week previously. It obviously required an immediate response.

The remaining correspondence yielded nothing of any greater significance and so Fullerton collected all his papers, shoved them rather unceremoniously back into the large package envelope from where they had come and walked towards the door of Baldini's office in search of his host.

Fullerton found his host in the main entrance hallway attending to some domestic matters with one of his house servants.

'Francesco! I need your kind attention once more.'

Baldini completed his instructions to the servant who then quickly disappeared and the two men walked back along the hallway until they felt that they could talk in private.

'I have just received this letter from Dubois. He wants a meeting with me. He says he can provide me with some valuable information.'

Baldini paused before answering.

'Dubois has not been one of the ADF's greatest assets of late. In fact he has acquired a reputation for being far too close to various government agencies for the liking of several of my colleagues. Some have even suggested that he is waging his own vendetta against certain politicians.'

'Well, I don't think that we can afford not to hear what he has to say,' Fullerton added.

'Yes, I agree. The form and tone of the letter do suggest something important. Do you want me to send him a coded reply regarding a place, time and date?'

'Yes, go right ahead, if you wouldn't mind. I don't have my codes with me in any case.'

Baldini turned and walked briskly down the hallway and into his office and closed the door behind him.

Fullerton stood still for a moment and then walked back through the villa and out on to the terrace once more where his wife and son were still sitting in the late morning sunshine.

They both looked up as Fullerton approached.

'You should try a glass of this wonderful local red wine, Michael,' Marguerite said, as Fullerton sat down next to them.

'No, not just now darling. I have something to tell you which may prove important. You remember Amand Dubois? He attended a meeting with me last March in Brussels. Very useful man to have working for you, but slightly too hard line for my particular taste. Well, I have just received a letter from him dated a week ago. He has suggested an urgent meeting. Baldini is sending him a suitable reply right at this moment.'

'What could he want all of a sudden?' Richard asked.

'That is what we will no doubt find out if we meet him,' Fullerton added.

'Do you trust him? Everybody is out there trying to save their own skins right now. It makes for strange bed-fellows as the saying goes.'

'Baldini is both sending him a response and no doubt employing his very efficient network of agents to check him out.'

October 14th, 2009. Besançon.

The car journey from Geneva had been quite uneventful and the four of them found themselves on the outskirts of Besançon in just over two hours.

Baldini as ever had arranged everything, even the meeting place which turned out to be a large chateau set within large, secluded grounds affording no one but those present any idea as to the nature of such a gathering. The chateau belonged to a close friend of Baldini's and as they arrived at the rather imposing entrance gateway, they were ushered through with the minimum of fuss.

The chateau came into view as the car rounded a bend in the road through a partly forested section of the large estate. Built during the reign of Louis XVI, its façade carried lots of ornate stonework and intricate architectural features.

The car pulled up outside the main entrance and they were met by two men who approached and spoke briefly to Baldini. There was already a black Peugeot parked nearby, containing two occupants.

'Please follow me,' Baldini said. 'Mr Dubois has already arrived and is waiting for us inside.'

Baldini turned and climbed the steps leading up to the main entrance and entered the chateau with the two men. The three of them followed close behind.

'The baron is away on business at the moment but he is quite happy for me to use his chateau whenever I have the express need,' Baldini said as they paused in the main entrance hallway.

'We will be meeting in here.' Baldini threw open the double doors to one of the main salons.

They all entered and found that the baron obviously enjoyed fine surroundings and even finer works of art. Dubois who was in front of the large mantelpiece examining some of the detail, turned to face them all as they entered.

Baldini made the introductions.

'Amand, you of course know James Fullerton.'

'Amand, nice to meet you again,' Fullerton responded.

'This is my wife, Marguerite and my colleague, Simon Shaw. Fullerton again used his son's alias instead of his real name.'

'A great pleasure,' Dubois replied rather formally.

Richard stared at Dubois for a moment. His face was familiar. It was something about his mannerisms too, but Richard couldn't place the connection.

Baldini suggested that they all sit down. Richard remained standing where he could more easily observe all those present.

Dubois made the first opening remarks.

'Thank you James for meeting at such short notice. I trust that you recognised the urgency of my note to you.'

'Yes, I did. That's why we're here. Please tell us what information you possess and its relevance.'

Dubois looked at Fullerton and then turned his head sideways to glance at Richard who was still standing and to his left. Richard again sensed some kind of recognition, but this time the feeling of recognition also came from Dubois.

Dubois lowered his head as he concentrated on some notes that he had pulled from his briefcase. Raising his head again, he continued to stare at Fullerton, then began to speak.

'As you know, the ADF has a long reach these days, thanks mainly to your colleague Mr Baldini who I know by reputation only. It has come to my notice that various government activities over the past months have been receiving ever closer scrutiny, particularly by yourself. Yes, Mr Michael Fullerton is becoming an increasing embarrassment to both the French and British governments.

Dubois paused, removed his glasses, wiped them with a cloth and just before replacing them said:

'Let's not keep up the pretence any longer. I believe that I am in fact addressing Mr Michael Fullerton. I realise that this isn't common knowledge, but certain people do know about this whole charade.'

Fullerton flinched inwardly but somehow managed to hide his shock.

Marguerite glanced at her husband and then at Richard.

'Yes, this last remark must come as quite a surprise to you all,' Dubois continued. 'Now, I can guess what you are all thinking now. Just how long have I known about this little deception? Possibly even, how did I come to find this out?'

Fullerton stared back at Dubois and said finally:

'You know, Dubois! My brother always held the view that your activities were just a little too convenient. You were never content to follow the prescribed ADF policy and always had to advance your own particular brand of political interference.'

'Well, now we all know about each other,' Dubois answered sharply. 'Shall I continue with what we have all come here to discuss?

'I know who is pulling the strings behind all these covert operations being run by both the DGSE in Paris and the SIS in Whitehall. No, not the people that you think are responsible. You have certainly done an excellent job, if I may say so, of tracking down those "middle men" in the intelligence services, but I mean the individuals who have created the policies that people like Thornton and Lefevre have been responsible for implementing.'

Dubois waited for some reaction from his audience, but receiving none, continued.

'Let's start with the most important question of all. Why am I choosing to tell you any of this and why now?

'Shall we just call it ... self-interest. I have seen a lot of people like you, Michael, who have wielded great influence by the use of their financial muscle. They have convinced themselves that their causes are right and that almost any means should be used to further those same causes. I do have some friends who share my views about the only way to influence the political process and it was, in the beginning, the reason why we all associated ourselves with the ADF in its formative years. Father Fournier had this ideal. Yes, "ideal" is the right word. He always believed in the process of political change and reform being achieved by a process of peaceful, yet forceful, lobbying. This policy has been seen to be demonstrably limited in its achievements. Politicians do not believe in democracy, except for themselves. They do not want to see the general public suddenly find an enquiring voice to challenge their own private ambitions...'

'OK, I think we get your message,' Fullerton said. 'What do you want for the information?'

'Mr Fullerton! That is putting the matter somewhat crudely. But since you have brought the matter up I will tell you.

'For my part, I will provide you with names and full details of all those people who have their dirty little fingers in this particular pie. I will provide you with irrefutable evidence of their direct complicity in these activities and I will want your personal undertaking that the source of this information will not be divulged to any outside entity, legal or governmental.

'For this, I will expect the sum of ten million pounds sterling to be deposited into an account of my own choosing.'

'How do we know that the information you say you have in your possession is that valuable?'

'Oh, I think that you will find that it is worth every bit of ten million. In fact I think that ten million would be worth it to me if I could find out the identity of my own brother's murderer, don't you?'

Marguerite clutched her husband's arm. Even Richard moved closer from his position by one of the long windows in his eagerness to hear every detail clearly.

Fullerton patted his wife's hand and gave Dubois a long stare before responding.

'If this is true, then it would indeed be worth a lot of money.'

At this point Baldini inserted himself into the conversation.

'Mr Dubois, you have made some very serious statements. If what you say can be completely corroborated, then of course we would be interested.'

'Let me continue, Francesco,' Fullerton interjected.

'If your information is as solid and complete as you now say it is, I will pay you your ten million.'

'If that is indeed the case, I can provide you with my banking details,' Dubois said quickly.

Reaching into his briefcase, he drew out a sheet of paper and handed it to Fullerton. It contained a list of some fifteen bank accounts spread conveniently across several national jurisdictions.

'Once I receive confirmation that the funds have been received – in total – I will provide you with all the information in my possession.'

'I will instruct my bankers in Geneva right now,' Fullerton said. He looked across at Baldini.

'Can you provide me with an office and a telephone?'

'Yes, of course,' Baldini replied. 'I suggest that, as this is going to take a couple of hours to arrange, we all agree to meet back in this room at three o'clock this afternoon. No one will however be permitted to leave the grounds until this matter has been completed to the satisfaction of both parties.'

Dubois nodded his consent and left the salon.

Richard moved over to where his father and Marguerite were standing.

'Do you trust him, dad?'

Before Fullerton could answer that question Baldini approached.

'What do you think, Francesco?'

'I think that we may not have any choice in the matter.'

'Maybe we could suggest some staged release of the money,' Richard said. 'He provides us with a piece of information and we transfer some of the money.'

Fullerton shook his head.

'No, that would take too long. It all ends here and now. If what he has proves to be vague or uncorroborated then he will suffer the consequences.'

Fullerton gave Richard a knowing look which Richard interpreted as a sign that his father was not going to be duped.

'Please show me to an office where I can use the phone, Francesco.'

Marguerite and Richard found themselves alone in the salon while all the others attended to their tasks.

Richard moved over to the window and observed the three men who were in conversation by the black Peugeot. Dubois was talking and the other two men were listening. Richard wished that he could hear what was being said. He did not recognise the other two men and then the penny dropped.

He knew where he had seen Dubois before. It was something about his voice that he remembered and the odd gesture. They had seen each other in a bar in Bonn. He was the stranger that had been talking to Von Beck. So Dubois was in this whole situation up to his neck.

Richard turned away from the window, walked past Marguerite who was sitting near to the fireplace and out into the hallway where Baldini was seeing to some other arrangements with the baron's staff.

'Francesco, I need to see both you and my father right now!'

'What has happened?' Baldini replied.

'I'll tell you in a minute, please take me to my father, it's important.'

Baldini led off down the hallway to the room which had been put at Fullerton's disposal and opened the door. They went in and Baldini closed the door behind them.

'Dad, I have met Dubois before. I had cause to be in Bonn in March to meet with a DGSE operative by the name of Von Beck. When I arrived Von Beck was talking to another man who then left before I approached them both. This stranger was Dubois. I knew I had seen him somewhere before!'

Fullerton looked at Baldini.

'What do we really know about Dubois, Francesco?'

'We know that he has had a history of being on the extremist fringe of the ADF for many years. For me, he

398

has been one of those people that you learn to work with because your aims are the same, but nevertheless do not wholly trust.'

'Your brother didn't trust him either, but he found him useful when meeting certain politicians.'

'Well, he obviously has been playing both sides off against each other if you ask me,' Richard added.

'Maybe that is why he is cashing in his chips while there is still time,' Fullerton mused. 'Anyway it's too late to change our plan, the money has been transferred.'

'If he double-crosses us, he will regret it!' Richard added.

Fullerton stared at his son realising that this remark was no idle threat.

'I think we will continue with the present agreement. Something tells me that Dubois is on the level for once.'

'Francesco, please inform Mr Dubois that the funds have been sent and that he should contact his associates this afternoon for confirmation of their receipt. Please also ask him to join us all for lunch.' He turned to Richard, 'Richard, I appreciate your concerns, but please allow me to handle these negotiations my way – at least for now.'

Richard nodded and followed his father as they all rejoined Marguerite in the salon.

Lunch was negotiated with the minimum amount of fuss. All parties engaged in polite conversation on topics suitably remote from the matters in hand. All minds however were on the afternoon session and the consequences of it.

It was shortly after three o'clock when Dubois informed Baldini that the funds had been received by his chosen banks.

Baldini, acting in a role that seemed at times to be a cross between a committee chairman and a presiding judge, arranged for all the parties to reassemble in the main salon.

When all parties were present, Baldini turned to Dubois and suggested that he now keep his part of the bargain.

Dubois spoke first.

'First of all my thanks go to you, Mr Fullerton for trusting me. I can confirm once more that your payments have all reached their various destinations and it is now up to me to provide information to you that I feel sure you will consider value for money.'

He reached down into his briefcase which had been placed on the floor by his chair by one of his associates. He withdrew a thick file, full of papers, consulted his notes once more and began to speak.

'There is a lot of information for you to review at your leisure, Mr Fullerton, and a lot of documentation in support of the statements that I am about to make. I will therefore limit my opening remarks to a list of itemised statements.

'The first matter deals with the untimely death of your brother, James Fullerton. Your brother, Michael, was one of those very rare individuals who actually believed in what he was trying to achieve. His friendship with Pierre Fournier and his belief in everything that the good old priest stood for did not leave any room for compromise. Particularly when it came to ensuring that the principles and ideals of the ADF were safeguarded.'

Everybody in the salon sat quietly and listened.

'A point was reached however when the activities of the ADF were deemed to be altogether too embarrassing for certain government agencies. These same agencies also came to understand that there were those within the membership of the ADF who had, shall I say, differing views.

'These people were approached over a period of time and "persuaded" that they would be better off if they chose some form of collaboration with the authorities.

At the beginning, the so-called "collaboration" consisted merely of providing certain discrete pieces of information about the ADF and its activities. However, the demands grew over the years until these people found themselves totally compromised and essentially under the thumb of these agencies.'

Fullerton started to speak but was immediately silenced by Dubois with a wave of his hand.

'Mr Fullerton, please allow me to finish what I have to say. There will be plenty of time for questions later.

'Unfortunately, I was one of those people whose marginal activities became compromised. We had gradually formed ourselves into a small but cohesive group that just went by the initials EG. You will remember our logo, no doubt?'

Michael said quietly:

'Breton, Levert and Deschamps!'

'That is quite correct, Michael. There were in fact five of us in this breakaway group; your brother was one of them!'

Fullerton thought back to his initial search of his brother's papers and his last meeting with Dubois in March.

'You provided me with these names when we met in March in Brussels!' he said.

'Yes, that was unfortunate, but at the time I did not know that you were not James Fullerton. That particular piece of information I found out later.'

Dubois was allowed to continue with his exposé.

'Your brother however proved difficult to deal with as he started to question our decisions and the morality of our actions. The other four of us continued with our planned activities and eventually only provided him with information after the fact and slightly inaccurate at that.

'We dealt mainly through our contacts within the DGSE

in Paris. They were the ones who passed on the information and in effect became our masters. Instead of being an aggressive wing of the ADF, we adapted to the role of informers and eventually as go-betweens in their rotten schemes to "neutralise" certain individuals who were considered an embarrassment or security risk.

'Eventually, your brother fell into that category. His investigations into these covert activities proved far too successful and the powers that be decided that things were getting too close to home. He was therefore "eliminated" by outside agents working as lone operatives.'

He paused. Then he said slowly:

'Your son should know all about this. His role in the DGSE was just the same as these operatives. La Croix is the name I believe.'

Richard felt his whole world crashing around him. No one knew about his existence, his code name or his sphere of operation except one individual and his immediate superior.

Dubois carried on:

'I think that you can now see that I have a lot of information to provide. I think that I know where most of the skeletons are buried. In this business, it pays to keep a record. Anyway, let me proceed.

'Your brother was poisoned in a London restaurant that he attended when he had as his guest a certain Alex Thornton. The operative who was responsible goes by the name of "Kessler". He is German by nationality but more than that even I do not know.

'Thornton, for his part, was blissfully unaware of the actual details that unfolded at that particular restaurant. He just provided the known time and location for James Fullerton's movements. I believe that a particularly slow-acting poison was used. It allowed the actual time of administration to be almost indeterminable.'

My God, thought Fullerton, so that was what happened!

'In my notes, you will find the names and addresses of the restaurant staff who were complicit in the food preparation. The intelligence community is very thorough in its note-taking and recording of detail.

'As for you, Richard aka "La Croix", I didn't learn of your particular association with Michael or indeed your DGSE role until much later. I think it was a certain gentleman by the name of O'Malley who was being blackmailed by your good friend Clayton Andrews. He eventually told all in order to escape certain prosecution or worse. Even then, it was only a chance coincidence that your two visual identities were matched. The Met do have their uses on occasion.

'Now let us move on to the more important part of my exposé.

'You are all I know aware that the British and French Governments have been jointly involved in some very unsavory activities, particularly in the Middle East. You are also aware that both the DGSE and the SIS are the main agencies involved. You may even be aware of which individuals are directly responsible for the implementation of certain covert activities. What you will not be aware of is just how high up this complicity extends. You are about to find out!

'I take it that you are familiar with the name of Pascal Lefevre?'

'Yes, we know who this gentlemen is,' Fullerton replied.

'As you also probably know, Pascal Lefevre is still under house arrest of sorts.'

Dubois was aware that Fullerton knew all about this; he was taking great pleasure in gradually revealing the information that he felt sure they didn't know. He went on again.

'Mr Lefevre was in charge, until recently, of a small

but effective department within the DGSE organisation but with specific assignments only. Richard, I believe that you knew Mr Lefevre quite well.'

Richard looked back at Dubois only just managing to conceal his dislike for this individual. How had he gained all this information?

'What you may not have known was that Lefevre reported directly and solely to Mr Ives Rousseau, the Minister of Defence.

'Alex Thornton, whom I know that you are very familiar with, headed up a team of SIS officials whose sole task was to gain intelligence on the ADF organisation. Michael, your involvement with Jason Fletcher was all part of this operation. The original plan was for you to speak to your brother and feed back intelligence to them. Unfortunately, certain necessities required a change in that plan.

'Thornton reported directly to Sir Michael Donaldson, the Director-General of the SIS. Again, I feel sure that you already know this. Sir Michael in turn was, through the JIC, partly responsible to your illustrious Foreign Secretary, Charles Stevenson.'

Here Fullerton interrupted him.

'Dubois, we already know all this. A lot of it is fairly common knowledge in fact. What do you have that entitles you to all the money I have just paid you?'

'Right. I am now getting to the valuable part of my report,' Dubois replied hastily, though still enjoying deliberately prolonging his revelations.

'What you didn't know is who authorised the attacks in the Middle East, not to mention the elimination of a prominent politician or two. Remember that unfortunate event in Montreal last year! Your own Prime Minister, the Right Honourable John Blakemore! And yes, before you ask, I do have the requisite proof!'

'How did you find all this out?' Fullerton demanded.

'If you can back up your last claim, you will certainly have earned the money I paid you.'

Dubois looked at each of the four people in the salon in turn – first Michael, then Richard, then Marguerite. Finally he turned his gaze on Francesco Baldini.

'Certain individuals have been most forthcoming with all this detailed evidence,' he said very deliberately. 'They also require payment, not to mention anonymity, and, before you ask, their cut will come out of what you have already paid me.'

'We will need to know which individuals have been so generous with their inside knowledge!' Fullerton responded.

'Review all this information first. I think you will be able to determine who they are.'

'I have one final question for you Dubois?' Fullerton said, looking straight at his former ADF associate. 'What do you know about the murder of Father Pierre Fournier?'

'Ah, yes,' Dubois said reflectively. 'I was wondering if you would raise that particular question. Father Fournier, as you know, had been the driving force behind the ADF in its earlier years. As he grew older you are well aware that his role in the leadership of the ADF had greatly diminished. He could not adjust to the pressures of modern day political lobbying and eventually decided to relinquish his connection with the ADF altogether.

'This did not however prevent him from establishing a similar organisation to combat what he saw as the continuing irregularities and inequalities within the Catholic Church. His followers were mainly clerical and drawn from the early ADF membership.

'Father Fournier had, however, acquired a number of political enemies over the years. He had caused some acute embarrassment for the Catholic Church in the fifties and sixties and had disobeyed his superiors on any number of occasions. I do not know who was behind his murder, but I can give you an idea as to whom to speak to about it. The whole police investigation was a cover-up, needless to say, and the official verdict of death by natural causes was a complete fabrication.'

'Who would that be then?' Fullerton asked.

'You could have tried His Eminence Maurice Cardinal Rousseau, the former Cardinal Archbishop of Paris!

'You might also take note of the fact that the good Cardinal also happened to be the older brother of the Minister of Defence, Ives Rousseau. You will now have to deal with his successor.'

With the meeting effectively at an end, Dubois stood up and walked over to the window and made a signal to one of his associates waiting again by the Peugeot.

'My associates will bring all the supporting facts and figures. There is quite a lot of paperwork for you to go through. It is yours to do with as you so wish.'

Chapter 73

October 16th, 2009. Geneva.

Fullerton had arranged to cancel all of his regular business commitments over the previous 48 hours in order to review all of Dubois's considerable documentation. Both Marguerite and Richard were on hand to assist with the analysis and by the morning of the 16th all three of them had completed an in-depth study of the subject matter.

The review process had been carried out by all three of them sitting around a large table which had been cleared for the purpose. This enabled them to discuss, review and separate out anything that they came across which could benefit the progress of their search.

'OK!' Fullerton finally announced as they all had come to the end of their examination. 'Let's gather together all these various pages that we have put onto one side over the past two days and see what we have got.'

Richard stood up and collated some hundred pages of factual detail which had been accumulating in the large in-tray in the centre of the table.

'Do you want me to collate all this and add it to our original dossier?' Marguerite asked her husband.

'Yes, that should complete the package, I think,' Fullerton replied. 'Arrange for three copies to be printed off when you have done that, Marguerite, if you would.'

That afternoon Fullerton placed a call to Charles Stevenson. Not surprisingly, Fullerton was put through almost immediately.

'Good afternoon, Foreign Secretary! I trust that you have been following the recent articles in *The Times*. It makes for very interesting reading, don't you think?'

'Mr Fullerton, I think that you will find that Her Majesty's Government completely refutes the incredible fabrications that have been reported in that particular newspaper recently and will be issuing just such a statement very shortly,' Stevenson answered in his normally measured tone.

'I will await your rebuttal with some considerable anticipation, then,' Fullerton replied.

'Mr Fullerton, your dossier, as you call it, contained a lot of fabrications and undocumented hearsay which I think most people will consider somewhat misguided, if not libellous. I am surprised that *The Times* even printed these recent articles. They usually require more substantiated evidence before they place this kind of scurrilous gossip in front of their readers.'

'Oh, I don't think that *The Times* made an ill-conceived judgement at all when they decided to run these articles,' Fullerton retorted.

'It is quite possible that certain allegations concerning this Department's involvement will prove libellous and as such will be dealt with using the full force of the law.'

'In that case, Foreign Secretary I would ask you to await the augmented version of my dossier which will be on its way to you later today. I think that you will find it very complete. I would also like to take this opportunity of thanking you for your recent kind attention. Unfortunately for you, the Swiss authorities were most pro-active in their defence of one of their most prominent residents.'

'This latest version of my dossier will be accompanied by a letter, signed by me, which will state the specific response expected from Her Majesty's Government and the time limit within which it should happen. I trust that you will convey its contents to the Prime Minister as expeditiously as possible. Time is not going to be on your side over this.'

Without waiting for a reply, Fullerton terminated the telephone call and left the Foreign Secretary to ponder its implications.

Fullerton allowed his friend Francesco Baldini to provide the French Defence Ministry with an identical copy of the augmented dossier. No doubt Mr Ives Rousseau would find it suitably stimulating.

Ives Rousseau was, in any case, going to receive some embarrassing questions from his brother's successor as Archbishop of Paris, once the situation surrounding the death of Father Fournier was made public.

Chapter 74

October 19th, 2009. Paris.

'Close the door,' came the abrupt instruction. 'Sit down and listen very carefully to what I am about to say.

'We have uncovered a double agent in our midst. The extent of the damage to both the French state and to its government is only just becoming apparent. It is because of the enormity of this discovery and its potential for causing both far greater damage and embarrassment to the French Government that I have been authorised from the highest level to take some extreme action.

'You will proceed at once to London where you will place the subject under surveillance. He is to be terminated at the earliest possible moment with the utmost secrecy being attached to your mission. The French Government will disavow any knowledge of this instruction. That is why you have been chosen for this task. Your subject is an extremely clever operative and has been used for such assignments himself in the past. You will therefore treat him with the utmost caution until such time as you have successfully executed this assignment.

'Who is the target?' came the question from the man seated opposite.

'His real name is Richard Fullerton and he lives with his wife and young son in North London.'

The first man pushed a brown folder across his desk in the direction of his guest.

'You will find all the information that you need in this

folder. Destroy this information as soon as you have memorised it.'

'Is that all?' came the terse response.

'That is all. A brief call to the following number is all that is required to confirm the successful completion of this assignment.'

The second man stood up, picked up the folder as was gone.

The first man waited for a few moments and then stood up and walked over to the long windows that looked out over the Champs Elysées. He clasped his hands behind his back and stared down at the busy evening traffic.

That should provide James Fullerton with something to remember for the rest of his life, he thought to himself. This was a rough world and there was a price to be paid for everything.

Chapter 75

October 20th, 2009. Geneva.

The letter had remained on Fullerton's desk for the past couple of days. It was very direct and to the point. A typical lawyer's letter in fact. It had been addressed to him personally, was quite non-committal but simply mentioned that the writer was in possession of some important information concerning a certain Father Pierre Fournier.

Fullerton had, of course, immediately contacted the author of the letter, a certain Victor Schellenberg in Geneva and a meeting had been arranged.

Mr Schellenberg had been invited to *Bellerive* for an eleven o'clock meeting that morning. Michael had puzzled over the connection between his brother's old friend and this high-flying Geneva lawyer since receiving the letter and had been told nothing further even when verbal arrangements were made for this meeting. No doubt he was about to find out what this all entailed over the course of the next hour or so.

Fullerton received a call from his secretary to inform him that a Mr Schellenberg had in fact now just arrived and was waiting for him in the large drawing room downstairs. Fullerton completed the item of business that he had been discussing earlier that morning with his bankers in Paris and gave Marguerite a call to join him in the drawing room.

'Good morning, Mr Schellenberg. Thank you for coming

to my home,' Fullerton said as he walked over and shook hands.

'My wife will be joining us shortly. Can I interest you in some coffee?'

'Thank you, that would be nice,' Schellenberg replied.

Fullerton's staff responded to his request for coffee and then discreetly left the two men alone.

'Your letter came somewhat as a surprise. I am intrigued to know what you have to discuss that concerns Father Fournier. As you might already know, Father Fournier was a good friend to this family.'

At that moment the door opened and Marguerite entered.

'Mr Schellenberg, please may I introduce my wife.'

'Mrs Fullerton, it is a great pleasure to meet you,' Schellenberg replied formally.

Marguerite looked at the Geneva lawyer and wondered what could have brought him all the way out to *Bellerive*.

Once seated, Schellenberg reached for his briefcase and withdrew a brown envelope that appeared to contain a number of letter-sized pages.

'We have been in possession of this package since it was lodged with us several years ago and which has now been considered available for release. It was placed in our safe keeping through an intermediary and under specific instructions as to the timing and nature of its release.'

Fullerton looked at Marguerite as if to indicate that the puzzle was still not becoming any more clear.

'Please continue, Mr Schellenberg.'

'The specific terms for the release of this document stipulated that the recipient could only be informed of its existence once a prior event had taken place. This prior event was the death of His Eminence Cardinal Maurice Rousseau. As you probably know, His Eminence died in September of last year after a short illness.'

413

'Yes, we had heard about the Cardinal's rather untimely demise,' Fullerton said.

'As there were some questions surrounding the Cardinal's death, we thought it best if we delayed the fulfilment of Father Fournier's instructions until such time as the full inquiry into the Cardinal's death had been completed.'

Schellenberg looked up at Fullerton, paused briefly and then continued with his presentation.

'As this matter has now been cleared up, we are acting in conformance now with those specific instructions. Mr James Fullerton, in the event of the death of Maurice Cardinal Rousseau, I am required to both inform you of the existence of and to present you with the sole original document placed in our possession by the said Father Fournier through intermediaries acting on his behalf.

'This package has remained under seal in this envelope from the time that it was first placed in our possession. I would ask you to confirm that this seal is still intact.'

Schellenberg slid the package over the coffee table in Michael's direction.

'It would appear that the seal is still intact,' Fullerton confirmed as requested.

'In that case I would ask you to sign this form of receipt which will then terminate our involvement in this matter.'

Fullerton rotated the form and duly added his signature where prescribed.

Schellenberg picked up the form and returned it to his briefcase. He stood up.

'This matter is now in your hands, Mr Fullerton,' he said.

The two men shook hands. Marguerite moved over in order to also shake hands and the three of them walked over to the door. Schellenberg's car was waiting outside for him and with only some final brief remarks he had climbed into the rear of the car and it sped away.

Fullerton and Marguerite walked back inside the house and back into the drawing room where the package had been left.

'That was very short and sweet!' Fullerton remarked.

'I wonder what is so important that Father Fournier thought it necessary to go to this degree of secrecy?'

'Well, you are about to find out,' Marguerite replied.

Fullerton sat down on one of the sofas again and broke the seal on the reverse of the package. He then withdrew several pages of hand-written notes. They appeared to be in Father Fournier's hand-writing although Fullerton was not able to confirm it as belonging to the old priest.

'To the only person that I feel I can trust...' the document began.

Fullerton passed each page over to Marguerite as he read it. It made easy reading because it was in the simple style of an equally simple parish priest who had nurtured an ideal from his early youth and seen it blossom into a world-wide organisation.

The pages seemed to have been written at several different times over a period of some eighteen months with the final section bearing a date that was only shortly before his own untimely murder.

Most of the dialogue was a repetition of Fournier's life. The underlying tone of the whole document, however, was its increasingly bitter attitude towards the inexorable increase in the power and control of the Catholic Church over its faithful followers but in particular the priesthood. Nowhere was this more evident than in Father Fournier's own struggle. His early life in Brittany was where his writings first came to the notice of the local church authorities and in particular his bishop, Bishop Rousseau.

Fullerton paused for a moment. He thought about the

415

name Rousseau and dwelt on the fact that this name had come up in conversation all too often recently. The late Cardinal Archbishop of Paris was named Rousseau as was the current French Defence Minister. He knew that these two were related but could there be a further family connection?

The Bishop Rousseau that Fournier mentioned was a man in his early forties in 1955. That would make him nearly 95 today if he were still living.

Fullerton turned to Marguerite and asked her a question.

'Can you call one of your many contacts in Paris and find out whether there is any connection between the late Cardinal Archbishop of Paris, Maurice Rousseau and the Rousseau that was Bishop of Laval in 1955?'

'Why on earth would you want to know that, Michael?'

'It may be just a hunch, but the name Rousseau is coming up with increasing regularity and now it appears again in Pierre's writings. See what you can find out, Marguerite, but do it as discreetly as you can.'

Fullerton continued reading the Fournier document. The text started to provide him with a sense that there was more to this antagonism between Fournier and his superiors in the church than met the eye.

Fullerton thought back to his Oxford days and even before that when he had been a young student in Paris. How simple everything seemed back then. Even the activities of his old friend Pierre Fournier, both written and verbal, seemed innocent enough. Now he was not so sure.

He continued reading the sometimes rambling text. It provided him with an insight into the world of church politics that painted a rather distasteful picture of a religious organisation normally considered to be bound up purely in the ethics and morals of Christian teaching.

Fullerton thought about what sacrifices this old priest

had purposely chosen to make; how it had affected his life within an institution that had consistently stifled any debate over social policy that contravened the official doctrine. Right from his early days as a parish priest in Saint Gregoire just outside Rennes, Pierre Fournier had found not the slightest acceptance for his radical brand of social enlightenment.

As Fullerton continued to read the hand-written text, it became clearer to him that Pierre must have decided to create a record of his endeavours as he moved into old age, a record that could in some way provide the reader with an insight into his private, personal world and in so doing leave an unchallenged version of his ideals for posterity.

Turning the page, Fullerton began to read what had been written about Fournier's life as a rural parish priest in the Laval diocese and his constant battles with Bishop Rousseau.

France in the 1950s was still recovering from the tremendous upheaval created by the Second World War. A whole generation had fought and struggled and the immediate post-war period had given rise to some radical social ideas. The Catholic Church, institutionally unable to react to any kind of rapid social and political change, considered all current thinking to be verging on heresy.

To many within the Catholic Church at that time, Father Fournier epitomised that heretical tendency. Bishop Rousseau had been supported in his authoritarian position regarding Father Fournier by his own Archbishop, but Fournier's writings strongly hinted at a more personal vendetta between the two men.

Fullerton stopped reading as Marguerite reappeared.

'I managed to contact just the right person regarding your request for more information about the Rousseau family and whether or not there was any connection with

413

a Bishop Rousseau in Brittany in the nineteen fifties,' she announced.

'What did you discover?' Fullerton asked with interest.

'You're not going to believe this,' Marguerite said. 'The Rousseau family originate from a small town in the Loire valley where they had lived for some generations. Charles Rousseau married a local girl by the name of Marie in Blois in 1914. She was only sixteen when they married and local gossip held that she might well have been pregnant. They went on to produce a large family over the following number of years; ten children in fact. Three of the children died in infancy but the other seven, three boys and four girls all survived. The eldest child, born in early 1915, was a boy who was christened Charles after his father. There then followed nine more children over a period of nearly thirty years. Of the boys, Maurice was born in 1935 and Ives, the last and final child was born in early 1944.

'Maurice grew up and entered the Catholic Church as a priest in 1956. His career was most illustrious, culminating in his appointment as Archbishop of Paris in 1990.

'Ives, the youngest, who was born towards the end of the war was also academically bright and chose a career as a lawyer. He practised his profession in Paris before entering politics. You know him currently as the present Minister of the Interior.

'As for Charles, the eldest son, he had also entered the church and rose to become Bishop of Laval.'

'My God!' Fullerton said, astonished. 'So they were all brothers! There is more to this whole story than we ever thought probable or even possible.'

'Nobody suspected your reason for asking about the Rousseau family did they?'

'No, not at all. My choice of contact will not have had any idea as to my motive. She does a lot of research work during the course of her professional duties and so would not have considered my questions at all strange.'

'We know about Ives and Maurice but what happened to Charles?' Fullerton pondered.

'I can answer that,' Marguerite added. 'I thought you might ask that question. Charles Rousseau, as I have just said was consecrated Bishop of Laval at the early age of thirty-eight and great things were expected of him. He remained in that position for some seven years during which time he was continually plagued by the political activities of a certain parish priest within his diocese.'

'Pierre Fournier!' Fullerton added triumphantly.

'The resulting embarrassment for the local church as a result of the continued activities of Father Fournier, even following the most severe reprimands, ultimately appears to have required a scapegoat.

'Bishop Rousseau seems to have been chosen as that scapegoat. A lot of this, initially local concern about the effect that the writings of Fournier was having, eventually grew out of control and more powerful clerics reached the conclusion that something had to be done.

'Much was written in the newspapers at the time about Fournier's activities and many of his papers made it into print. Fournier himself was eventually moved into effective isolation at a monastery in central France. His writings however continued to be circulated. Bishop Rousseau was deemed to have acted with too little authority in the matter and was also discreetly moved into obscurity. This premature termination of an otherwise extremely promising church career was not forgotten by some, the most notable being his younger brothers.'

'Poor old Pierre must have acquired some powerful enemies. With the formation of the ADF and its gradual rise to prominence, these clerics must have come to despise him,' Fullerton mused.

'It would appear so,' Marguerite agreed.

'Pierre Fournier never left the Church and never forgave the Church, but the Church never ever forgave him for his views on social equality and freedom of speech,' Fullerton remarked.

'No, it is more than that' he added. 'The Catholic Church would have been quite content for Father Fournier to hold his views as long as they were not seen or heard to conflict with the official position. Poor old Pierre would not compromise himself in this way and continued to antagonise the Church. So he was pushed into obscurity, but the damage had been done.'

Chapter 76

'He is going to regret the day that our paths crossed,' Fullerton murmured as he concluded his preparations for getting back at the Rousseau family and Ives Rousseau in particular.

Dubois had been as good as his word and had provided Fullerton with the direct connection between the apparent natural death of Pierre Fournier and Ives Rousseau himself. He had not only managed to authenticate the connection between Ives Rousseau and the murder of Pierre Fournier, he had even located the agents involved in the planned event itself. A considerable amount of money must have changed hands, Fullerton thought, for this kind of information to reach the light of day.

Nothing as yet had been heard from the French Defence Ministry following the delivery by Baldini of the augmented version of the dossier.

Fullerton did not consider this too surprising: it was all too typical of government. At first ignore, then discount, then discredit, and then and only then take action. He reckoned that the dossier was somewhere between the first and second stages of this all too familiar process. He decided that he would now provide the Minister with the *coup de grâce* by presenting the truth behind the Fournier murder cover-up. He also recognised that many people had made sacrifices for what they believed in. He thought of his brother and of his old friend Pierre Fournier

421

and just wanted some justice for them if for any reason at all.

Fullerton collected all the relevant material concerning the death of Father Fournier and arranged for it to be hand-delivered to the French Defence Ministry and to Ives Rousseau in particular.

Chapter 77

October 25th, 2009. London.

It was a wet, rather cold Sunday morning in Muswell Hill as the apartment building where Richard Fullerton lived came into view. Kessler had stolen a nondescript vehicle the night before and visited the target address for a final time before implementing his plan.

Studying the apartment building from a safe distance he observed some comings and goings of other tenants. The apartment block consisted of three storeys with one main entrance leading out onto the street and therefore allowed for easy surveillance.

His initial decision had been to wait for somebody to exit the building and gain entrance whilst the door was temporarily unlocked; walk right up to the door of the apartment on the first floor and shoot his quarry on sight. This rather direct approach had been replaced by the more careful and circumspect alternative of waiting patiently for his target to leave the building.

It was around 9.30 am and he settled down for what could prove to be a long wait. Sunday morning had been chosen for several reasons. Not many people about and the likelihood of his target making some trivial journeys to the local shops or indeed a visit to the local park with his son.

He had brought a newspaper with him so as to give the appearance of someone waiting for a reason. He fancied a drink but knew better than to visit the local corner shop and provide any interaction between himself and a possible witness or CCTV system.

An hour passed before some noisy children walked past his half-open passenger side window. They were on their way to the neighbourhood park which began some hundred yards or so ahead of them. He watched them as they continued along the footpath and eventually disappeared from his view as they entered the park entrance.

His gaze turned to two figures approaching him on the other side of the street. An adult male pushing a stroller containing a young boy aged about four. He thought that they too must be returning from the park but he hadn't noticed them cross over the road.

As they approached, he realised that the man pushing the stroller matched his target description. His senses immediately came to full alert as he focused all his attention on the approaching individual.

In no time at all, they were only some fifty metres or so away from him and he was sure, from the photograph in his possession, that this was in fact Richard Fullerton. His height, weight, age, hair colour, general physical appearance all matched.

Sliding over to the passenger side of the vehicle, he quietly opened the door and climbed out. He checked his revolver and loaded a round into the firing chamber. Concealing his weapon once more he moved away from his vehicle and walked diagonally across the street without appearing to be heading directly for his target.

When they were only five metres apart he drew his weapon and fired virtually at point blank range at Richard's chest. The single shot sent his target reeling backwards and onto the asphalt surface. Stooping by his inert target, he reached inside his jacket for any confirmation of ID. His target possessed no wallet but his left hand jacket pocket contained an empty envelope with the name of

Mr R Fullerton typed on the address label. After a second shot to the head, he turned and walked quickly but without rushing back towards his waiting vehicle. Ninety seconds later he was driving past the still body of his target and back towards the centre of town. One last glance in his mirror confirmed that nobody had as yet reacted to the sound of the two gunshots or even appeared to render any assistance.

Dumping the vehicle in some side street, he entered the local underground station and headed for King's Cross and a train to the Continent.

As arranged, he called the given phone number and confirmed the successful completion of the assignment.

Chapter 78

October 27th, 2009. London.

The shock of the news of his son's murder had a most profound effect on Fullerton. It had been twenty-four hours since the tragic news had reached him and all he could think about was reaching London as fast as he could. His private plane had brought him to London late that previous evening and he and Marguerite had spent most of the night at the police station. They had reluctantly left in the early hours of the morning and returned to the Dorchester Hotel to grab what little sleep they could.

Fullerton had only agreed to leave the police to do their job when he had received the personal assurance of the Deputy Commissioner that he would be contacted as soon as any developments occurred.

Michelle and her son had been driven by the police to her parents' home in Surrey. She was completely distraught and was very concerned about the traumatic effect this terrible act would have on her small son.

Both Fullerton and Marguerite were up early. Three to four hours sleep seemed to have achieved its objective at least for now.

They ordered breakfast in their room and a selection of newspapers. Breakfast was, however, barely touched except for the coffee.

Monday's newspapers had carried very little about the murder due to the short period that had elapsed between the time of the murder, the subsequent release of any official information and print deadlines. The current morning's editions were carrying front-page coverage of the story but with only outline details.

'MILLIONAIRE BUSINESSMAN'S NEPHEW SLAIN', was the headline in the *Daily Mail*.

Fullerton glanced at the array of stories being carried to a greater or lesser extent by the British press. He did not read them in any detail. It seemed somehow to be a superfluous exercise. He knew what must have happened and even had a very clear idea as to who was involved.

Marguerite was quite overcome. She stared at her husband that morning in the hotel room and knew what must be going through his mind too. She knew all too well that they had been in a high-stakes game for some months now and her intelligence agency background told her that some people played a very rough game when deemed necessary. What she found surprising were her own thoughts that Tuesday morning. They had effectively issued an ultimatum to both the French and British establishments. What did they think would be the reaction!

The silence was deafening from government sources on both sides of the Channel. Neither politicians nor any government agencies had issued any kind of a statement at all.

'How are you feeling, darling?' she found herself saying to her husband and then inwardly scolded herself for making such a useless and meaningless remark. She was just about to say something else to cover the last remark when Fullerton looked up and spoke.

'It's all right. I know what you meant. I just feel a kind of numbness at the moment. I'm almost hoping that it is a kind of dream and I will wake up to find that it never happened.'

Marguerite stood up, walked round behind where her husband was sitting and put her arms round his shoulders.

427

'We should have seen this coming,' she said. 'It was my fault. We were trained to recognise the likely consequences of any action and to plan accordingly. When it came to my own family, I did nothing.'

Fullerton said:

'What I can't believe is that they would actually do such a thing. Have they lost all feeling, all sense of humanity?'

The telephone rang and Fullerton grabbed the receiver.

'Mr Fullerton? This is the Metropolitan Police, I have the Deputy Commissioner on the line for you, please hold.'

'Mr Fullerton, this is Brian Mardell. We spoke briefly yesterday. We unfortunately have some difficult questions for you and will of course need you to formally identify the body. I wonder if you could make yourself available later this morning.'

'Yes, of course, Commissioner. Where would you like us to come?'

'We will send a car for you at ten-thirty this morning if that will be convenient.'

'That will be fine, Commissioner.'

'I will see you when you arrive and we can discuss things then.'

'What about my daughter?' Fullerton added.

'She is under police guard and has been moved to a different address. Please be assured that the police are treating this whole matter with the utmost seriousness,' Mardell continued.

Fullerton replaced the receiver. 'The police will send a car for us at ten-thirty,' he said to Marguerite.

'This is pay-back!' Fullerton murmured. 'If they think that this is going to somehow stop me from exposing their dirty little secrets then they have chosen to pick a fight with the wrong man!'

The telephone rang again.

'Hello, hello?'

Fullerton recognised the familiar voice of Francesco Baldini.

'Francesco! I wasn't expecting a call from you.'

'Michael, I'm so very sorry to hear about Richard. It's terrible news. Please convey my sympathies to Marguerite. However, at the risk of appearing totally unsympathetic, I have some extremely important information for you.'

'That's OK, Francesco, I understand. Please continue.'

'The information that you need to hear came partly from my own sources but it has been backed up by the call that I have just had from Dubois. That man is really earning his money!'

'You know that we have put our friend, the Minister of the Interior between the proverbial rock and a hard place. Well, my sources tell me that the order for Richard's elimination came directly from him.'

'How on earth has that bit of information come to be known so quickly?' Fullerton replied incredulously.

'Quite simple apparently,' Baldini continued. 'The hit man who was sent to London only knew his target as Richard Fullerton. It was purely by chance that he subsequently learned that Richard Fullerton was aka La Croix. As La Croix, the two men had worked together in covert operations as members of the same team. Why he didn't recognise Richard at the time is anybody's guess but these operations happen so quickly; they are matters of split seconds sometimes.

'Once he learned that his target had been La Croix, he didn't take long to expose the source of his orders to the right people. One of those people happened to work for me in Paris. Dubois also apparently got wind of it too and chose to call me as well. I'm sorry to bring you this news right now, Michael, but these people will stop at nothing to protect themselves.'

429

'Francesco, dear friend, thank you for telling me all this. Strangely enough, I find that I can accept what has happened a bit better now. We will speak again soon.'

Chapter 79

October 30th, 2009. London.

Fullerton and Marguerite had decided to remain in London for the foreseeable future, or at least until after Richard's funeral. No date had as yet been set because of the nature of his death and the resulting police investigation.

The past few days had been quite hectic; a strange combination of both public and private duties. Carefully structured press and TV interviews had been arranged. Fullerton had left all the details to one of his media PR firms but had been quite specific as to the nature of the interviews and the subject matter that could be discussed.

He had not given the police all the facts provided to him by Baldini. This was now a private matter between himself and Ives Rousseau. He had directed Baldini to present the French Minister of the Interior with the latest damning evidence and await his formal response. So, it came as no real surprise when he heard the previous evening's TV news broadcast, live from Paris which covered the shock suicide of one of France's most promising politicians.

Ives Rousseau, the French Minister of Defence had been found shot dead in his Paris home late the previous evening. The French authorities had already determined that it was suicide and that the Minister had taken his own life due to the pressure he was under, having been recently diagnosed with a terminal form of cancer.

Fullerton listened to the coverage with some considerable cynicism.

'Cancer indeed!' he mumbled. 'Terminal cancer of his morality, more like!'

Fullerton placed a call to Milan and Francesco Baldini.

'Francesco! Michael here. No doubt you have heard the news about Rousseau?'

'Indeed I have, Michael. There is some considerable anxiety in French Government circles as to whether this is just the tip of the iceberg or not. The French press smell a huge scandal and are like a pack of wild dogs at the moment.'

'Well, I will be giving the British press something to shout about soon. They are all going to regret their complicity.

'Let me know if you hear anything further out of all of this, won't you Francesco?'

'You can count on me for that.'

Fullerton stared out of the hotel room window. It was a rather dull, overcast kind of day. It seemed almost as if the weather had tried to match his present state of mind. It was nearly ten o'clock and he had a meeting to go to with the Metropolitan Police later that morning. The official post-mortem results were now complete and both Fullerton and Marguerite were to be formally notified of the results before they were made public.

Marguerite had used her mobile phone to contact her sister and arranged for her to come down to the hotel that afternoon and then stay for dinner. Fullerton was worried that Marguerite was taking Richard's murder very badly, but she continued to reassure him on that point.

The telephone rang again. It was Fullerton's team in the hotel, two floors below. Fullerton had arranged for some of his key staff to fly to London from Zurich and to set up a kind of mini operations room. They had managed to group several rooms together to provide sufficient space for the staff as well as a headquarters for business use.

'Michael, it's Patrick again,' came the voice of his Communications Director. 'I have Downing Street on the phone. They want to arrange a meeting between you and John Blakemore.'

Fullerton thought for a moment before providing an answer.

'Patrick, tell them that you will call them back shortly.'

Fullerton replaced the receiver and walked over to where Marguerite was sitting. She was studying the latest newspaper coverage that they were getting.

'The Prime Minister wants to arrange a meeting,' he said.

'What does that man want?' Marguerite replied, somewhat irate.

'Oh, I think that I can guess exactly what that man wants. Charles Stevenson has no doubt informed his boss that he is not going to be the only fall guy for the misguided policy of the British Government. He has had the augmented dossier for two weeks now and has therefore also had time to consider its veracity.'

'But why would the Prime Minister expect you to agree to such a meeting?' Marguerite added.

'Oh, I think that I can guess the answer to that as well. He knows that the game is up and that the British Government's covert policy in the Middle East is about to become public knowledge. Remember how they think, Marguerite! Ignore, Discount, Discredit and finally Take Action.'

Fullerton paused and looked down. Their actions so far had now cost them their son.

'I will agree to a meeting...' he said finally.

Marguerite looked at him.

'...but it will be a meeting on my terms and I will decide the outcome. I want both those men in the same room at the same time when I speak. I want the meeting in front of the appropriate judicial authorities and I will want their resignations.'

'Do you think that they will agree to all that?'

'They don't have any choice and what's more they know that they have no choice. Besides, they will undoubtedly have heard what has happened in Paris.'

'Do you think that the Prime Minister knew about Richard's murder before it took place?'

Fullerton sat down beside his wife and held her hand.

'Baldini has strongly intimated that his sources do not think that there is any connection between Rousseau's actions and anyone else. In fact, he has assured me that the information that he received from Dubois is positive proof of Rousseau acting alone. I will have my way in this matter, Marguerite. Both James and now Richard have paid too high a price.'

Fullerton stood up, went over to the phone and called Patrick O'Neil.

'Patrick come up to my room and before you do that arrange for Simon Craven to be available first thing in the morning here at the hotel.'

Ten minutes later, there was a knock on the door and Fullerton went over to let Patrick into the room.

'Patrick, come in.'

O'Neil closed the door behind him and followed Michael back over to where Marguerite was still sitting. O'Neil nodded at Marguerite, smiled and sat down.

'Right, to business,' Fullerton began. 'Patrick, you can call Downing Street back and arrange a meeting but I have decided that it will only take place on the following terms or not at all. Patrick, I want you to be completely clear on this point. A meeting on my terms or not at all.

Those attending the meeting will be as follows: John Blakemore, Charles Stevenson, myself, Marguerite and my own legal representative. That is where Simon will come in. I personally would invite Sir Jeremy Roberts, QC but I will leave that side of things up to Simon.'

'I have placed a call to Simon Craven, Michael,' Patrick said. 'He is presently in court, but has been asked to call me back as soon as he returns to his office.'

'Good. Explain the situation to him when he calls and ask him to see if Sir Jeremy is available.'

'Michael, I was wondering about protocol here. They will strongly resent a member of their own judiciary being invited to attend a meeting with or without any prior notification of the matters to be discussed,' Patrick added respectfully.

Fullerton stood up.

'No doubt they will use every rule and regulation they can think of to cloud and thwart the whole purpose of this meeting. They either agree to my wishes or they don't. If they don't, and you have my permission to tell them this, they can all just read about it in the morning editions. Do I make myself clear?'

'Perfectly clear, Michael. This is going to be one hell of a meeting!' O'Neil replied.

'I certainly hope so!'

'What do you want me to say to the press about Richard? They are still pushing for any further bits of information.'

'I will leave that entirely in your hands, Patrick, but don't tell them too much,' Fullerton said as he showed O'Neil over to the door.

'Let me know as soon as you have spoken with Craven.'

'Will do.'

Chapter 80

November 6th, 2009. London.

The meeting at 10 Downing Street had been arranged to take place at 11.00 am. All parties had agreed the purpose and format for the meeting. Fullerton had been surprised by the ease in which everything had been arranged. The presence of Sir Jeremy Roberts QC raised a little resistance but eventually Downing Street had acceded to this inclusion.

Michael and Marguerite decided to be driven over even though the distance was within easy walking distance. It was a precaution that had been recommended by the police in view of the recent situation.

Arriving just before 11.00 am, the car was directed through the wrought-iron gates at the entrance to Downing Street and they pulled up outside the shiny black door of the Prime Minister's official residence. Walking in through the entrance they were met by some Downing Street officials and Sir Jeremy Roberts who himself had only just arrived.

'Hello, Jeremy. Thank you for coming. I believe that things are still as we discussed the other day.'

'That's fine, Michael,' Sir Jeremy replied. 'This is your meeting. I will leave you to ask for my opinions as you see fit.'

'Gentlemen, will you please follow me,' came the instruction from some official.

They were shown into the Cabinet Room where the three of them were greeted by the Foreign Secretary, Charles Stevenson.

'Mr Fullerton, Mrs Fullerton, nice to meet you again,' came the smooth voice of the consummate politician. 'The Prime Minister will be with us presently I am told,' he continued. 'Will you all please be seated. I suggest that we use this end of the table.'

They all sat down and spent the next few minutes in a fairly strained silence. It seemed an age before the door finally opened again and the Prime Minister entered.

Marguerite had not met John Blakemore before. He seemed shorter than he had looked when she saw him on the TV.

Fullerton shook hands with the Prime Minister and, as some official closed the door to the Cabinet Room, the atmosphere suddenly changed. The tone of the meeting became that of a very serious discussion.

John Blakemore was the first to speak.

'Mr Fullerton, first of all let me offer my sincere condolences for the loss of your nephew, Richard. It was a tragic event and one that must not go unpunished. Rest assured that Her Majesty's Government will assist in any way possible to bring the murderer to justice.'

Ignoring the obviously false platitudes, Fullerton at once decided to bring the meeting into focus.

'Prime Minister, you have no doubt seen the dossier of evidence that has been compiled against this administration, yourself and the Foreign Secretary in particular. I agreed to your request for a meeting, possibly against my better judgement, in order to provide you with one opportunity to retrieve what vestige of morality and common decency you might still retain.'

John Blakemore smiled back at Fullerton. Charles Stevenson looked at both of them as if he knew that this had to be his boss's last roll of the dice.

The Prime Minister now put his thoughts into words.

'I telephoned you, Mr Fullerton, to arrange this meeting

in order that we could discuss matters like two grown-up individuals who have experienced the ways of the world in its every form and who can appreciate that sometimes a worthy compromise is better than a hollow victory.'

Fullerton remained silent whilst his host summoned all his political skills to the fore in an attempt to regain the initiative.

'I have been acquainted with the salient points in your very complete dossier. My right honourable friend, the Foreign Secretary has seen to that.

'However, I would respectfully suggest that your conclusions are somewhat misplaced. Your assertion for instance that the British government was directly employing foreign-born assassins to eliminate certain Middle Eastern politicians is, I might say so, just one step too far. Your dossier does place this government in a position of some considerable embarrassment should it ever become public knowledge. We both know that the testimony of most of your so-called witnesses would also be called into question if not totally discredited in a court of law.'

Fullerton listened to the Prime Minister patiently as the monologue continued for a further twenty or so minutes. How these people could talk without actually saying anything. Perhaps that was what was wrong with modern politics, he thought to himself.

Finally the Prime Minister appeared to have completed his dissertation with a remark that sent a shock right through Fullerton.

'You know, Mr Fullerton. You have caused both this government and that of our French neighbours quite enough trouble over the past couple of years. I just don't understand why you people think that your effort is worthwhile.'

As Fullerton thought of his brother's sacrifice and that of his son, he gave a slight smile as he remembered the good times with them. Reaching down into his briefcase, he pulled out a green file folder and, without uttering a word, slid it across the table towards the Prime Minister.

Looking quite unconcerned, the Prime Minister turned the folder around so that he could open it. He began to read.

Marguerite, who had been a silent witness to the whole discussion, stared at John Blakemore as he read the enclosed documents. She saw the blood drain visibly from the Prime Minister's face as the full impact of the contents of the documents became clear to him. Finally he looked up again, ashen-faced and obviously in shock.

It was now Fullerton's turn to speak.

'Sir Jeremy. I would ask you to record everything that will be said from now on. The Prime Minister and the Foreign Secretary will be tendering their resignations with immediate effect. If they do not comply with this requirement, full particulars of their actions and complicity in the deaths of Father Pierre Fournier and James Fullerton will be made public.

'I have asked Sir Jeremy to draft the appropriate letters of resignation for you both to sign. Failure to comply with this requirement will result in full public disclosure and inevitable imprisonment.'

Chapter 81

November 11th, 2009. Kimpton.

The funeral service for Richard had been arranged for Wednesday, November 11th at Kimpton Parish church. His sister had thought about a service in the cathedral but Fullerton decided that a simple service in Kimpton with burial next to his uncle was more appropriate. The family had finally agreed that there would be no fuss, particularly in view of the prevailing circumstances and so it was without any publicity that the immediate family members made their way out of London that particular morning.

The Metropolitan Police had considered their own presence to be mandatory for obvious reasons; an escort had been made available for family members. The involvement of the Hertfordshire Police in and around Kimpton had been coordinated to control the inevitable, though unsought, press coverage.

Sure enough as the cars arrived in convoy from London, photographers and TV film crews leapt out of waiting vehicles to gain an advantage over their rivals.

The local Hertfordshire Police had conveniently cordoned off the whole section of street outside the church and so the convoy was able, with minimal delay, to proceed up to the church gate. Fullerton and Marguerite walked ahead towards the church with Michelle, Andrew and her parents and finally Louise following in close contact behind.

Other than the immediate and close family members,

the only other people present for the short service in the church was Francesco Baldini, Robert Faulkner from *The Times* and a few of Richard and Michelle's close friends from Muswell Hill.

Marguerite and especially Michelle were glad to reach the church entrance and enter inside out of the glare of the ever eager cameramen.

They all stood as the six pallbearers, led by the funeral director, walked slowly down the aisle.

The coffin was placed on a trestle in the centre of the aisle and the seven men slowly and quietly withdrew.

Fullerton's mind wandered a bit as the Rector commenced the short Anglican burial service. He found himself thinking about his son's wasted life and whether or not it had all been worth the sacrifice. He felt somehow responsible for the loss and powerless to provide any worthwhile comfort for the rest of his family. The service seemed over in no time at all as the Rector gave his blessing.

Something extra needed to be said and Fullerton knew that he had to be the one to say it and it had to be right then.

Fullerton stood up and moved forward and spoke quietly to the Rector. The Rector then invited those present to be seated. Fullerton turned and faced those few who were in the church that morning.

Robert Faulkner, whose presence there was due entirely to Francesco's insistence that some actual, but reliable coverage of the service should be recorded for later broadcast, grabbed his pocket tape recorder and pressed the 'Record' button.

Fullerton stared at those sitting in the pews for what seemed like an eternity before speaking.

'I had not planned to say anything at this service, but something inside of me has other ideas.'

Fullerton looked at Marguerite who was covering her

mouth with her hand and gripping Michelle's hand with the other.

Fullerton also glanced at Faulkner who was sitting at a distance from the family grouping. Faulkner knew what that glance meant. This was going to make headlines!

'Richard has suffered a tragic death and had left behind his wife Michelle and son Andrew. He has also left behind a sister. What the world doesn't know is that he left behind a mother and father too. I am *Michael* Fullerton and Richard was my son. My wife Marguerite was his mother.'

Faulkner couldn't believe what he was hearing. He checked to make sure that his tape recorder was still running.

Fullerton laid bare all his emotions, all his regrets and especially all his recent actions which had only been possible as a result of the sacrifices made by his family and close friends.

Faulkner sat and listened to this impromptu monologue and sensed the depth of feeling that only a recently bereaved father had for his son.

Michael Fullerton sensed that he had said enough and looked at each of his family members in turn before walking back to where Marguerite was sitting and sat back down beside her.

The vicar signalled to the undertakers that they could walk forward to the coffin. They carried Richard's coffin slowly back down the aisle and out into the weak November sunlight. Michelle followed behind as did the others.

A short interment service took place at the graveside which was right next to where the body of Richard's uncle lay. The family then returned to their cars oblivious of the flashing of cameras in the distance.

Fullerton spoke briefly to Faulkner as they walked back through the churchyard.

'Please come and see me tomorrow, there will be a lot more for you to hear then.'

The journey back into London seemed to pass unnoticed as all of them were deep in their own thoughts and wondering what the future held for them as a family.

Chapter 82

November 12th, 2009. London.

All the political journalists and TV reporters had filed into 10 Downing Street in response to the surprising news from the Downing Street press office that the Prime Minister planned to make an important announcement at 11.30 am that morning. The usual banter between both press colleagues and rivals had failed to come up with any convincing reason for this press conference. The usual pre-conference leaks had been completely absent and the rumour mill had been working overtime to create something for discussion by the voracious news media in the intervening hours.

The room was jammed to capacity as 11.30 approached. Martin Grimshaw, the Downing Street, Chief of Staff was already in the room and had provided no indication at all as to the Prime Minister's intentions.

At a little after 11.30 am the doors opened and the Prime Minister, John Blakemore entered. He was clutching a couple of sheets of paper containing a hand-written text which he now placed on the lectern.

The final few people quickly took their seats and the conversation in the room died as the Prime Minister prepared to speak.

Blakemore eyed his invited audience.

'I have called this press conference in order to make an important announcement. Following the conclusion of this statement, there will be no questions.'

444

The experienced commentators glanced at each other sensing something important was about to happen.

The Prime Minister began with the usual introduction.

The record of this government over the past eight years has been one of considerable achievement and progress. We have made significant progress in many areas including health, education, welfare reform and overseas relations. In this task I have been ably assisted by my Cabinet colleagues who have led their various departments with distinction. There are various problems that we have still to overcome but I feel sure that this government will retain the confidence of the people of this country as it overcomes these difficulties.

The Prime Minister paused as the murmurs rose all along the front couple of rows. Again, Blakemore waited for silence to return.

I have this morning had a meeting with Her Majesty the Queen and can now inform you all that I have tendered my resignation to Her Majesty who has been graciously pleased to accept. This resignation will be of immediate effect and until such time as the party elect a new leader, the role of Prime Minister will be carried out by the Deputy Prime Minister.

Some reporters at the rear of the room didn't wait for the remainder of Blakemore's speech and scrambled to leave. Then the Prime Minister added:

I do not intend to provide any specific reasons for the action that I have taken except to say that this government will be better served by a new leader who can continue the good work that has already been achieved and build on the work that has already been started. That is all.

The room was stunned into silence. Everybody was looking at each other for some kind of reaction but no one had expected or anticipated this bombshell.

Reality quickly returned and everybody now also scrambled to leave the room and relay the staggering news back to their respective news hubs. TV channels that were covering the press conference live immediately switched back to shocked news anchors in the studios who were almost unable to comprehend what had just happened and put any kind of a storyline together.

The *BBC 24 Hour* news channel seemed to sum it up. 'Shock decision by the Prime Minister to quit.'

Behind the scenes, newspaper editors and TV producers alike put their respective teams into high gear to obtain the most pertinent comments from among the most illustrious of senior politicians and commentators alike.

The Leader of the Opposition, who had been watching the TV live broadcast from Conservative Central Office wasted no time in assuming an attitude of complete surprise at hearing the Prime Minister's announcement. In that he did not have to put any spin on his particular remarks. It was one of those moments in time when you remembered exactly where you were and what you were doing.

At four o'clock that same afternoon, the already stunned news media were sent into an almost frenzied state when the Foreign Secretary, Charles Stevenson also announced his intention to stand down as an MP with immediate effect. He, however, unconvincingly cited his recent period of ill health and his advancing years as the official reason.

Michael Fullerton received word of the announcements

at the Dorchester Hotel where he, Marguerite and the rest of his family were still staying following Richard's funeral.

'Is this going to be an end to the whole wretched business, Michael?' Marguerite asked, looking at her husband.

'I left them with a way out and they have obviously chosen to take it,' Fullerton replied.

'You didn't answer my question!' Marguerite added.

Fullerton turned round in his seat on the sofa and looked over at his wife.

'Do you really want to know the answer to that question?'

Marguerite thought for a moment and then was silent. She chose not to say anything further for the moment. Now, maybe, was not quite the time for this discussion. They both needed some time to come to terms with their loss and time was on their side.

Faulkner was as good as his word and *The Times* carried the most lurid details of two governments' complicity in some very embarrassing dealings regarding foreign heads of state and the lengths to which their own intelligence services had been involved.

Several other resignations followed during the course of the next week; notably amongst them the head of the SIS, Sir Michael Donaldson.

The fall-out was indeed spectacular and did nothing at all to convince the general public at large that their elected politicians had learned any lessons at all about dignity, honesty and above all, morality.

Chapter 83

November 24th, 2009. London.

Their stay in London had far outstripped their original intentions but there were some things that needed completing. Fullerton had never liked leaving any loose ends, even during his time at Oxford, and he wasn't going to allow any now.

The shock resignations of both the Prime Minister and the Foreign Secretary nearly two weeks previously had barely left the front pages and endless commentary had ensued on virtually all the news channels and current affairs programmes.

All the great and the good had offered their own insights into the possible and probable reasons behind these announcements, but the two principals involved had resolutely refrained from making any further public comment and in fact had not even been seen.

Michael and Marguerite had somehow, over the previous twelve days, avoided the inevitable by not raising publicly the subject of further legal action against both the British and French Governments. This had not prevented the press from reaching a similar conclusion on their behalf.

Some days earlier, however, Sir Jeremy had managed to obtain from Fullerton his instruction to proceed with a review of the evidence and to present his findings as soon as possible. It was at the personal instigation of Sir Jeremy Roberts that Fullerton agreed now to have a formal discussion on the matter and to listen to the legal advice that would be proffered

Sir Jeremy was due at the Dorchester Hotel at eleven o'clock and Fullerton was somehow dreading the fact that someone, presumably himself, was going to have to make a decision.

'Good morning Jeremy, do come in,' Fullerton said as his legal advisor arrived at his suite.

Fullerton had arranged for his old friend Francesco Baldini to be present for this meeting. Baldini's greater political sense would undoubtedly assist them in reaching a decision.

The Queen's Counsel came swiftly to the point.

'Having reviewed all the information myself and having taken the advice of some distinguished and learned colleagues, I can advise you that both governments have some extremely difficult questions of legality to answer. The evidence that you have compiled is remarkably detailed and provides a damning indictment against the policies and specific individuals of both the British and French Governments. In short, my team has concluded that we would be willing to recommend and prosecute direct legal action against the individuals involved.'

'By that, I assume you mean the Prime Minister and the Foreign Secretary?' Fullerton responded.

'Possibly a considerable number of people in the intelligence communities as well,' Sir Jeremy said.

'What is the likelihood of a successful prosecution and what would be the fallout?' Fullerton asked, already fully aware of the answer to his own question.

'Well!' Sir Jeremy began. 'There is absolutely no doubt that the integrity of the whole British Government would be called into question. Whether or not there would ultimately be a successful prosecution is more clouded. The government could simply state that the policy of a sovereign nation, whilst possibly misguided and probably illegal, was unlikely to be found guilty by its own legal system.'

'Would the public interest be best served by the publication of any or all of this dossier, Jeremy?' Fullerton questioned.

'I'm sure that there would be a lot of people that would love to obtain a copy of your dossier for their own political benefit,' Marguerite volunteered.

'That could give rise to a potentially dangerous development, Michael,' Sir Jeremy said. 'Once everything is in the public domain, if it was ever allowed to be released, there would be no control over who used what parts of the dossier for what purpose.'

'What would James, Pierre and Richard have wanted us to do if they were here now?' Marguerite asked, beginning to think that Fullerton was in danger of starting a vendetta. As always, she had shown her invaluable knack of going straight to the heart of things. Fullerton thought of all the sacrifice, but found himself thinking about something that his old, dear friend Pierre Fournier had said when they last met.

'Eventually people will see the truth for themselves.'

Fullerton looked at his wife and then at his legal counsel.

'People will inevitably see the truth for themselves,' he said firmly. 'This matter ends here and now.'

Chapter 84

December 10th, 2009. Saint Gregoire.

Fullerton and Marguerite had done what they had earlier decided to do and that was to visit the little town of Saint Gregoire just outside Rennes in the pretty Breton countryside.

They flew into the airport at Rennes and drove themselves the few miles to Saint Gregoire.

The present parish priest was a young man in his late twenties who had some considerable knowledge of his illustrious predecessor, particularly his writings.

They found the church unlocked when they arrived. The daily service had just ended and they were pleased to find Father Colbert in the church busily dealing with some local parishioners and their important local issues.

Marguerite greeted Father Colbert and introduced herself and her husband to him.

'Thank you Father, for allowing us to visit your church and to share a few moments with Father Fournier.'

'We have seen a number of people who have visited this church to learn more about Father Pierre. Nearly all of them only know of him from his writings, but I believe that you both knew him directly.'

'Yes, he was a very dear friend of ours for many years,' Fullerton replied. 'I first met him in Paris when I was a student there.'

'Let me show you where his grave is,' Father Colbert continued.

The three of them walked out of the church and over to a quiet corner of the churchyard facing the town hall.

'You can see his grave over there. It was chosen specially by the townspeople. There are still a few who can remember his time here as a priest.'

Fullerton and Marguerite walked along the final few metres of the dusty path until they were stood in front of a simple white marble headstone.

FR PIERRE MARTIN FOURNIER

NÉ AVRIL 13, 1926

DEC FEVRIER 1, 2009

A COEUR VAILLANT

RIEN IMPOSSIBLE

Marguerite was struck by the appropriateness of the inscription.

The sun was shining and the surrounding trees were swaying gently in the breeze.

'My old friend,' Fullerton said softly. 'I hope that you will be at rest now. A lot has happened and much has been sacrificed. Be assured that you will be remembered and what you strived for all your life will not be lost to future generations. I will see to that.

'Marguerite, what do you think Pierre would have most wanted had he been given that opportunity?' he asked.

'I remember his love of teaching and how he enjoyed seeing young minds wrestle with sometimes difficult issues,' Marguerite replied. 'Why do you ask, Michael?'

'Darling, as usual, you go straight to the heart of the matter. I will set up an endowment at the Sorbonne. It will be known as the Pierre Fournier Endowment in Political Science. We can also arrange for a library of all his literary publications to be housed in one place in Paris. A new building, if need be.'

'I think that Pierre would be very grateful,' Marguerite replied.

Walking back towards the church, Fullerton was struck by the simple beauty of the surroundings in Saint Gregoire.

'You know Marguerite. Pierre had a very simple doctrine really. Give young minds the energy and freedom to think for themselves and you have already created the future.'

'Let's get back to our future!'

The journey back to Geneva from Saint Gregoire that December day seemed to complete a chapter in their lives and Marguerite knew that all would be well.